To special people,
for a special time,
with special love:

Susan Alan
Beatrice Baer
Melba Beals
Frances Brauer
Lillian Oksman
Consuelo Smith
Patricia Tuttle

To Claude-Eric
for giving me so much,
especially writing.

To Dan for lessons learned
and shared.
For everything!

And to Beatrix
for being wonderful
and always loving.

D.S.

Danielle Steel is a descendant of the Löwenbräu beer barons. Her mother is Portuguese and her father is German. Their common language is French, although they all speak eight languages. Danielle's father's family, the prominent banking and brewing clan, has always lived in Munich and the family seat was a moated castle in Bavaria, Kaltenberg. Her mother's family were diplomats and her maternal grandfather was a Portuguese diplomat assigned to the United States for a number of years.

American-born, Danielle lived in Paris for most of her childhood. At the age of 20 she went to New York and started working for 'Supergirls', a before-its-time public relations firm run by women who organised parties for Wall Street brokerage houses and designed PR campaigns for major firms. When the recession hit, the firm went out of business and Danielle 'retired' to write her first book, *Going Home*.

Danielle has established herself as a writer of extraordinary scope. She has set her various novels all over the world, from China to New York to San Francisco, in time-frames spanning 1860 to the present. She has received critical acclaim for her elaborate plots and meticulous research, and has brought vividly to life a broad range of very different characters.

Also by Danielle Steel

THE PROMISE
(Based on a screenplay by
Garry Michael White)
GOLDEN MOMENTS
SEASON OF PASSION
GOING HOME
SUMMER'S END
TO LOVE AGAIN
LOVING
THE RING
PALOMINO
ONCE IN A LIFETIME
REMEMBRANCE
THURSTON HOUSE
LOVE POEMS
A PERFECT STRANGER
CROSSINGS
CHANGES
FULL CIRCLE
FAMILY ALBUM
FINE THINGS
KALEIDOSCOPE
SECRETS
WANDERLUST
ZOYA
STAR

DANIELLE STEEL

Now and Forever

WARNER BOOKS

A *Warner* Book

First published in Great Britain by Sphere Books Ltd 1979
Published by arrangement with Dell Publishing Co. Inc.
Reprinted 1980 (four times), 1981 (twice), 1982, 1983 (three times),
1984, 1985 (twice), 1986, 1987 (twice), 1988, 1989, 1990, 1991, 1992
Reprinted by Warner Books 1994
Reprinted 1994, 1995, 1996 (twice), 1999

Printed in England by Clays Ltd, St Ives plc

ISBN 0 7515 0550 1

Warner Books
A Division of
Little, Brown and Company (UK)
Brettenham House
Lancaster Place
London WC2E 7EN

'There are three kinds of souls,
three kinds of prayers.
One: I am a bow in your hands, Lord.
Draw me lest I rot.
Two: Do not overdraw me, Lord.
I shall break.
Three: Overdraw me, and who cares
if I break!

Choose!'

From 'Report to Greco'
by Nicos Kazantzakis

CHAPTER I

The weather was magnificent. A clear blue sunny day, with sharply etched white clouds in the sky. The perfect Indian summer. And so hot. The heat made everything slow and sensual. And it was so totally unlike San Francisco. That was the best part. Ian sat at a small pink marble table, his usual seat, in a patch of sunlight at Enrico's restaurant on Broadway. The traffic whizzed by while lunch-hour couples strolled. The heat felt delicious.

Under the table, Ian swung one long leg easily over the other. Three daisies bobbed in a glass, and the bread was fresh and soft to the touch. The almost too thin, graceful fingers tore one slice of bread carefully away from the others. Two young girls watched him and giggled. He wasn't 'cute', he was sexy. Even they knew it. And beautiful. Handsome. Elegant. He had class. Tall, thin, blond, blue-eyed, with high cheek-bones and endless legs, hands that one noticed, a face one hated to stop looking at . . . a body one watched. Ian Clarke was a beautiful man. And he knew it, in an offhand sort of way. He knew it. His wife knew it. So what? She was beautiful too. It wasn't something they really cared about. But other people did. Other people loved to watch them, in that hungry way one stares at exceptionally good-looking people, wanting to know what they're saying, where they're going, who they know, what they eat . . . as though some of it might rub off. It never does. One has to be born with it. Or spend a great deal of money to fake it. Ian didn't fake it. He had it.

The woman in the large natural straw hat and pink dress had noticed it too. She stared at him through the mesh of the straw. She watched his hands with the bread, his mouth as he drank. She could even see the blond hair on his arms as he rolled up his sleeves in the sun. She was several tables away, but she saw. Just as she had seen him there before. But he never saw her. Why would he? She saw everything, and then she stopped watching. Ian didn't know she was alive. He was busy with the rest of the view.

Life was incredibly good. Ripe and golden and easy. His for the plucking. He had worked on the third chapter of his novel all morning, and now the characters were coming to life, just like the people wandering along Broadway . . . strolling, laughing, playing games. His characters were already that real to him. He knew them intimately. He was their father, their creator, their friend. And they were his friends. It was such a good feeling, starting a book. It populated his life. All those new faces, new heads. He could feel them in his hands as he rat-tat-tapped on the typewriter keys. Even the keyboard felt good to his touch.

He had it all, a city he loved, a new novel at last, and a wife he still laughed and played with and loved making love to. Seven years and everything about her still felt good to him: her laughter, her smile, the look in her eyes, the way she sat naked in his studio, perched in the old wicker rocking chair, drinking root beer and reading his work. Everything felt good, and better now, with the novel beginning to blossom. It was a magical day. And Jessie was coming home. It had been a productive three weeks, but he was suddenly lonely and horny as hell . . . Jessie.

Ian closed his eyes and blotted out the sounds of traffic drifting by . . . Jessie . . . of the graceful legs, the blonde hair like fine satin, the green eyes with gold specks . . . eating peanut butter and apricot jam on raisin bread at two in the morning, asking him what he thought of the spring line for her shop . . . 'I mean honestly, Ian, tell me the truth, do you hate the spring things, or are they okay? From a man's point of view . . . be honest . . .' As though it really mattered, from a man's point of view. Those big green eyes searching his face as though asking him if she were okay, if he loved her, if . . . he did.

Sipping his gin and tonic, he thought of her, and felt indebted to her again. It gave him a tiny pinched feeling somewhere in the pit of his stomach. But that was part of it: he did owe her a lot. She had weathered a lot. Teaching jobs that had paid him a pittance, substitute teaching that had paid less, a job in a bookstore, which she had hated because she felt it demeaned him. So he had quit. He had even had a brief fling with journalism, after his first novel had bombed. And then her inheritance had solved so many of their problems. Theirs, but not necessarily his.

'You know, Mrs. Clarke, one of these days you're going to get sick and tired of being married to a starving writer.' He had watched her face intently as she'd shaken her head and smiled in the sunlight of a summer day three years before . . .

'You don't look like you're starving to me.' She patted his stomach, and then kissed him gently on the lips. 'I love you, Ian.'

'You must be crazy. But I love you too.' It had been a rough summer for him. He hadn't made a dime in eight months. But Jessie had her money, of course. Dammit.

'Why am I crazy? Because I respect your work? Because I think you're a good husband, even if you're not working on Madison Avenue anymore? So what, Ian? Who gives a damn about Madison Avenue? Do you? Do you miss it so much, or are you just going to use it to torment yourself for the rest of your life?' There was a faint tinge of bitterness in her voice, mixed with anger. 'Why can't you just enjoy what you are?'

'And what's that?'

'A writer. And a good one.'

'Who says?'

'The critics "says," that's who says.'

'My royalties don't says.'

'Fuck your royalties.' She looked so serious that he had to laugh.

'I'd have a tough time trying—they're not big enough to tickle, let alone fuck.'

'Oh, shut up . . . creep . . . sometimes you make me so mad.' A smile began to warm her face again and he leaned over and kissed her. She ran a finger slowly up the inside of his thigh, watching him with that quiet smile of hers, and he tingled all over . . .

He still remembered it. Perfectly.

'Evil woman, I adore you. Come on, let's go home.' They had left the beach hand in hand, like two kids, sharing their own private smile. They hadn't even waited until they'd gotten home. A few miles later, Ian had spotted a narrow creek a little distance from the road, and they had parked there and made love under the trees, near the creek, with the summer sounds all around them. He still remembered lying on the soft earth with her afterward, wearing only their shirts and letting their toes play with the pebbles and grass. He still remembered thinking that he would never quite understand what bound her to him . . . why? And what bound him to her? The questions one never asks of marriage . . . why, for your money, darling, why else? No one in his right mind ever asked those questions. But sometimes he was so tempted to. He sometimes feared that what bound him to her was her faith in his writing. He didn't want to think it was that, but that was certainly part of it.

All those nights of argument and coffee and wine in his studio. She was always so goddam sure. When he needed her to be. That was the best part.

'I know you'll make it, Ian. That's all. I just know you will.' So goddam sure. That's why she had made him quit his job on Madison Avenue, because she was so sure. Or was it because she'd wanted to make him dependent on her? Sometimes he wondered about that too.

'But *how* do you know, dammit? How can you possibly know I'll make it? It's a dream, Jessie. A fantasy. The great American novel. Do you know how many absolute zeroes are out there writing crap, thinking "this is it"?'

'Who gives a damn? That's not you.'

'Maybe it is.' She had thrown a glass of wine at him once when he'd said that, and it made him laugh. They had wound up making love on the thick fur rug while he dripped wine from his chin to her breasts and they laughed together.

It was all part of why he had to write a good one now. Had to. For her. For himself. He had to this time. Six years of writing had produced one disastrous novel and one beautiful book of fables that the critics had hailed as a classic. It had sold less than seven hundred copies. The novel hadn't even done *that* 'well'. But this one was going to be different. He knew it. It was his brainchild against hers, Lady J.

Lady J was Jessie's boutique. And Jessie had made it a smash. The right touches, the right flair, the right line at the right time. She was one of those people who casts a spell on whatever they touch. A candle, a scarf, a jewel, a flash of colour, a hint of a smile, a glow of warmth, a dash of pizzazz, a dollop of style. A barrel of style. Jessie had been born with it. She oozed it. Stark naked and with her eyes closed, she had style.

Like the way she flew into his studio at lunchtime, her blonde mane flying, a smile in her eyes, a kiss on his neck, and suddenly one fabulous salmon rose dropped across his papers. One perfect rose, or one brilliant yellow tulip in a crystal vase next to his coffee cup, a few slices of prosciutto, some cantaloupe, a thin sliver of Brie . . . *The New York Times* . . . or *Le Figaro*. She just had it. A gift for transforming everything she touched into something more, something better.

Thinking of her made Ian smile again as he watched the people at the other tables. If Jessie had been there she would have worn something faintly outrageous, a sundress that exposed her back but covered her arms, or something totally covered up but with a slit that gave passersby just the quickest flash of leg, or an unbearably beautiful hat that would only allow them to catch a glimpse of one striking green eye, while the other flirted, then hid. Thinking of her like that drew his attention to the woman in the straw hat a few tables away. He hadn't seen her before. And he thought she was definitely worth seeing. On a hot, sunny afternoon, with two gin and tonics under his belt. He could barely see her face. Only the point of her chin.

She had slender arms and pretty hands with no rings. He watched her sip something frothy through a straw. He felt a familiar stirring as he thought of his wife and watched the girl in the hat. It was a damn shame Jessie wasn't home. It was a day to go to the beach, and swim, and sweat, and get covered with sand, and rub your hands all over each other, oozing suntan oil. The way the woman in the straw hat moved her mouth on the straw in her drink bothered him. It made him want Jessie. Now.

His cannelloni arrived, but it had been a poor choice. Too creamy, too hot, and too much. He should have ordered a salad. And he was loath to order coffee after his few bites of lunch. It was too easy a day to be hard on yourself. It was so much easier just to let yourself go, or your mind, at least. That was harmless. He was having a good time. He always did at Enrico's. He could relax there, watch strangers, meet writers he knew, and admire the women.

For no reason in particular, he let the waiter bring him a third drink. He rarely drank anything other than white wine, but the gin was cool and pleasant. And a third drink wouldn't kill him. There was something about hot days in a usually cool climate . . . you went a bit mad.

The crowd at Enrico's ebbed and flowed, crowding the sidewalk for tables, shunning the red booths indoors. Businessmen freed their necks of ties, models preened, artists scribbled, street musicians played, poets joked. Even the traffic noises were dimmed by the music and the voices. It reminded him of the last day of school. And the topless bars were silent on either side of the restaurant, their neon doused until nightfall. This was much better than neon. It was real. It was young and alive and had the spice of a game.

The girl in the hat never revealed her face as Ian left, but she watched him, and then silently shrugged, and signalled for the check. She could always come back, or maybe . . . what the hell . . .

Ian was thinking of her on his way to the car, slightly tipsy but not so much that it showed. He was dreaming up verses to 'Ode to a Faceless Beauty'. He laughed to himself as he slid behind the wheel of Jessie's car, wishing he were sliding into Jessie. He was unbearably horny.

He was driving Jessie's little red Morgan. And thoroughly enjoying it. It had been a damn handsome gift, he reflected, as he pulled out the choke. A damn handsome gift. For a damn handsome woman. He had bought it for her with his advance for the fables. The whole cheque for the car. Madness. But she had adored it. And he adored her.

He swung back onto Broadway and stopped at a light, passing Enrico's again on his way home, just as a whisper of pink brushed past his right eye. The hat swirled on one finger now as her face looked up toward the sky, her behind undulating freely as she walked in high-heeled white sandals. The pink dress tugged at her hips, but not blatantly, and her red hair framed her face in loose curls. She looked pretty in pink, and so goddam sexy. So round and so ripe and so young . . . twenty-two? . . . twenty-three? He felt the same hunger again in his loins as he watched her. Her copper hair reflected the sun. He wanted to touch it. To tear the hat from her hand and run away, to see if she'd follow him. He wanted to play, and he had no one to play with.

He drove slowly past her, and she looked up, and then her face flushed and she looked away, as though she hadn't expected to see him again and now it changed everything. She turned her head and looked at him again, the surprise replaced by a slow smile and a barely visible shrug. Destiny. Today had been the day after all. She had dressed for it. And now she was glad. She seemed unwilling to go, under the heat of his gaze. He hadn't driven on. He simply sat there, while she stood at the corner and watched him. She was not as young as he'd thought. Twenty-six . . . twenty-seven? But still fresh. Fresh enough, after three gin and tonics and not a great deal of food.

Her eyes searched his face, clawing a little, but carefully, and then, as he watched, she approached, showing the full bosom in sharp contrast to the girlish shape of her arms.

'Do I know you?' She stood holding her hat, one ankle suddenly crossing the other; it made her hipbones jut forward, and Ian's trousers were instantly too tight.

'No. I don't think so.'

'You've been staring.'

'Yes . . . I'm sorry. I . . . I liked your hat. I noticed it at lunch.' Her face eased and he returned her smile, disappointed, though. She was older than Jessie, perhaps even a year or two older than he. Made up to look exquisite at a thirty-foot distance, at twenty feet the illusion was shattered. And the red hair showed a thin line of black roots. But he *had* been staring, she was right.

'I'm really awfully sorry. Do you need a lift?' Why not? She couldn't be headed far off his path; probably to an office a few blocks away.

'Yeah, sure. Thanks. It's too hot to walk.' She smiled again, and struggled with the handle on the door. Ian released it for her from within, and she pounced onto the seat, displaying a comforting amount of cleavage. That much was real.

'Where can I take you?'

She paused for a moment and then smiled. 'Market and Tenth. Is that out of your way?'

'No, that's fine. I'm not in a hurry.' But he was surprised at the address. It was an odd place to work, a bad place to live.

'Did you take the day off?' She was looking at him questioningly.

'Sort of. I work at home.' He wasn't usually that expansive, but she made him uncomfortable, made him feel as though he should talk. She wore a heavy perfume, and her skirt had slipped well up her thighs. Ian was hungry. But for Jessie. And she was still ten hours away.

'What do you do?' For an odd moment he wanted to say he was a gigolo, kept by his wife. He argued the point in his head as he frowned.

'I'm a writer.' The answer was curt.

'Don't you like it?'

'I love it. What made you ask that?' This time he was surprised.

'The way you started to frown. You're a nice-looking guy when you smile.'

'Thank you.'

'*De nada*. You also drive a nice-looking car.' Her eyes had sized up the scene. The well-cut St. Tropez shirt, the

Gucci shoes with no socks. She didn't know they were Gucci, but she knew they were expensive. 'What is this? An MG?'

'No. A Morgan.' *And it's my wife's . . .* the words stuck in his throat. 'What do you do?' Tit for tat.

'Right now I wait table at the Condor, but I wanted to see what the neighbourhood looks like in the daylight. That's why I came down here for lunch. It's a whole different crowd. And at this time of day they're a lot more sober than they are when we get them later.'

The Condor was not known for its decorous clientele. It was the home of the 'Original Topless', and Ian assumed that the woman waited on tables half nude. She shrugged and then let her face grow soft in a smile. She looked almost pretty again, but there was a sadness somewhere in her eyes. A kind of regret, haunting and distant. She glanced at him oddly once or twice. And again Ian found that she had made him uncomfortable.

'You live at Market and Tenth?' It was something to say.

'Yeah. In a hotel. You?' That one was a bitch to answer. What could he say? But she filled the pause for him. 'Let me guess. Pacific Heights?' The brightness in her eyes was gone now, and the question sounded brittle and accusing.

'What makes you say that?' He tried to sound amused and look mock-hurt, but it didn't come off. He looked at her as they stopped in a snarl of Montgomery Street traffic. She could have been someone's secretary, or a girl doing a bit part in a movie. She didn't look cheap. She looked tired. And sad.

'Sweetheart, you smell of Pacific Heights. It's all over you.'

'Don't let fragrances fool you. As in "all that glitters" . . .' They laughed lightly together and he played with the choke as the traffic jam eased. He turned the car onto Market.

'Married?'

He nodded.

'Too bad. The good ones always are.'

'Is that a deterrent?' It was an insane thing to have said, but he was more curious than serious, and the gin and tonics had taken their toll.

'Sometimes I go for married guys, sometimes I don't. Depends on the guy. In your case . . . who knows? I like you.'

'I'm flattered. You're a nice-looking woman, as you put it. What's your name?'

'Margaret. Maggie.'

'That's a nice name.' She smiled at him again. 'Is this it, Maggie?' It was the only hotel on the block, and it was no beauty.

'Yeah, this is it. Home sweet home. Beautiful, ain't it?' She tried to cover her embarrassment with flippancy, and he found himself feeling sorry for her. The hotel looked bleak and depressing.

'Want to come up for a drink?'

He knew from the look in her eyes that she'd be hurt if he didn't. And, hell, he was in no shape to go home and work. And he still had nine and a half hours to kill before driving out to the airport. But he also knew what might happen if he accepted Maggie's invitation. And letting that happen seemed like a rotten thing to do to Jessie the day she was coming home. He had held out for three weeks. Why not one more afternoon? . . .

But this girl looked so lonely, so unloved, and the gin and the sun were spinning in his brain. He knew he didn't want to go back to the house. Nothing in it was his, not really his, except five file drawers of his writing and the new Olivetti typewriter Jessie had given him. The gigolo king. Jessie's consort.

'Sure. I've got time for a drink. As long as you make it coffee. What'll I do with the car?'

'I think you can park it in front of the door. It's a white zone, they won't tow you away.'

He parked the car in front of the hotel, and Maggie carefully watched the back of the car as he pulled in to the kerb. It was an easy plate to remember. It spelled what she thought was his name. Jessie.

CHAPTER II

Jessica heard the landing gear grind out of the plane's belly and smiled. Her seat belt was in place, her overhead light was out, and she felt her heart begin to beat faster as the plane circled the runway for the last time. She had a clear view of the lights below.

She looked at her watch. She knew him so well. Right now he would be frantically looking for a parking space in the airport garage, terrified that he was late and might miss her at the gate. He'd find a space then, and run like hell for the terminal, and would be panting and smiling, nerves jangled, when he reached her. But he'd get there in time. He always did. It made coming home something special.

She felt as though she had been away for a year, but she'd bought such good things. The spring line would be lovely. Soft pastels, gentle wools cut on the bias, creamy plaids, silk shirts with full sleeves, and some marvellous suedes. She could never resist the suedes. It would be a great spring at the boutique. The goodies she had ordered wouldn't begin to arrive for another three or four months, but she was already excited thinking about them. She had them all memorized. The spring line was set. She liked to plan ahead like that. Liked knowing what was coming. Liked knowing that she had her life, and her work, all mapped out. Some people might find that boring, but it never bothered Jessie.

She and Ian were planning a trip to Carmel in October. Thanksgiving would be spent with friends. Maybe Christmas skiing at Lake Tahoe, and then a quick hop to Mexico for some sun after the New Year. And then the spring line would start to come in. It was all perfectly planned. Like her trips, like her meals, like her wardrobe. She had what it took to make plans—a business that worked, a husband she loved and could always count on, and reliable people around her. Very little was variable, and she liked it that way. She wondered if that was why she had never wanted a baby: it would be a variable. Something she couldn't totally plan. She didn't know how it would look or act, or exactly when it might be born, or what she would do with it once she had it. The idea of a baby unnerved her. And life was so much simpler like this. Just Jessie and Ian. Alone. And that way there were no rivals for Ian's affection. Jessie didn't like to compete, not for Ian. He was all she had now.

The wheels touched the runway, and she closed her eyes . . . Ian . . . she had longed for him over the past weeks. The days had been full and the nights busy, yet she had usually called him when she'd reached the hotel in the evening. But she hadn't been able to reach out and touch him, or be held. She hadn't been able to laugh into his eyes, or tickle his feet, or stand next to him under the shower, chasing drops of water past the freckles on his back with her tongue. She stretched her long legs ahead of her as she waited for the plane to come to a halt.

It was hard to be patient. She wanted the trip to be over. She wanted to run out and see him. Right now. There had never been other men. It was hard to believe, but there hadn't. She had given it some thought, once or twice, but it had never seemed worth it. Ian was so much better than anyone else, in her eyes. Sexier and smarter and kinder and more loving. Ian understood so well what she needed, and fulfilled so many needs. In the seven years they'd been married, she had lost track of most of her close women friends in New York, and hadn't replaced them with others in San Francisco. She didn't need women friends, a confidante, a 'best' friend. She had Ian. He was her best friend, her lover, even her brother, now that Jake was dead. And so what if now and then Ian had a 'fling'? It didn't happen often, and he was discreet. It didn't bother her. Men did those things when they had to, when their wives were away. He didn't use it, or flaunt it, or grind it into her heart. She just suspected that he did it. That was all. She understood. As long as she didn't have to know. She assumed, which was different from knowing.

Her parents had had a marriage like that, and they had been happy for years. Watching them, Jessie had understood about the things you didn't talk about, didn't hurt each other with, didn't use. A good marriage relied on consideration, and sometimes keeping your mouth shut and just letting the other guy be was consideration . . . love. Her parents were dead now; they hadn't been young when she'd been born. Her mother had been in her late thirties, her father just past forty-five. And Jessie had been four when Jake was born. But marrying late, they had respected each other more than most couples did. They were not inclined to make changes in each other. It had taught Jessie a lot.

But they were all gone now. It had already been three years. Almost exactly. Her parents had died within months of each other. Jake had died a year before that, in Vietnam, at the crest of his twenties. Gone. Jessica was the only one left. But she had Ian. Thank God there was Ian. It sent little tremors up her spine when she thought of it that way . . . what would she do without Ian? Die . . . the way her father had done without her mother . . . die . . . she couldn't live without Ian. He was her all now. He held her late at night when she was afraid. He made her laugh when something touched too deep and made her sad. He remembered the moments that mattered, knew the things that she loved, understood her private language, laughed at all her worst jokes. He knew. She was his woman, and his little girl. That was what she needed. Ian. So what did it matter if there were occasional indiscretions she didn't really know about? As long as he was there when it counted. And he always was.

She heard the doors slide open; the people began to press into the aisles. The five-hour flight was over. It was time to go home. Jessie brushed the creases from her slacks with one hand and reached for her coat with the other. It was a bright orange suede that she wore over beige suede pants and a print silk shirt in shades of caramel. Her green eyes glowed in her suntanned face, and her blonde hair swung thick and free past her shoulders. Ian loved her in orange, and she had bought the coat in New

York. She smiled to herself, thinking how he'd love it—almost as much as the Pierre Cardin blazer she'd brought him. It was fun to spoil Ian.

Three businessmen and a gaggle of women pressed out before her, but she was tall enough to see over the chattering women's heads. He was there at the gate, and she waved as he grinned broadly, waving back, and then he moved swiftly toward her, gently weaving his way through the people ahead of her. Then he had reached her and was taking her in his arms.

'It's about time you came home . . . and looking like that, you'll be lucky if I don't rape you right here.' He looked so pleased. And then he kissed her. She was home.

'Go ahead. Rape me. I dare you.' But they stood where they were, drinking each other in, saying it all with their eyes. Jessie couldn't keep a smile from her lips, or her hands from his face. 'You feel so good.' She loved the softness and spiced lemon smell of his skin.

'Jessie, if you knew how I missed you . . .' She nodded, knowing. She had missed him at least as much.

'How's the book?'

'Nice.' They spoke in the brief banalities of those who know each other better than well. They didn't need many words. 'Really nice.' He picked up her large brown leather tote from the floor where she'd dropped it to kiss him. 'Come on, sexy lady, let's go home.' She looped her arm into his, and together they walked in long even strides, her hair brushing his shoulder, her every move a complement to his.

'I brought you a present.'

He smiled. She always did.

'Bought yourself one too, I see. That's some coat.'

'Do you like it? Or is it awful? I was afraid it was a little too loud.' It was a burnt caramel bordering on flame.

'On you it looks good. Everything does.'

'Jesus, you're being nice to me! What did you do? Smash up the car?'

'Now, is that a nice thing to say? I ask you. Is that nice?'

'Did you?' But she was laughing and so was he.

'No, I traded it for a Honda motorcycle. I thought you might like that better.'

'What a nice thought! Gee, darling, I'm just thrilled. Now come on, tell the truth. How bad is the car?'

'Bad? I'll have you know that it happens to be not only in impeccable condition, but clean, a condition it was *not* in when you left. That poor little car was filthy!'

'Yeah, I know.' She hung her head and he grinned.

'You're a disgrace, Mrs. Clarke, but I love you.' He kissed the tip of her nose and she slid her arms around his neck.

'Guess what?'

'How many guesses do I get?'

'One.'

'You love me?'

'You guessed it!' She giggled and kissed his neck.

'What do I get as a prize for guessing?'

'Me.'

'Terrific. I'll take it.'

'Boy, I'm glad to be home.' She heaved a small sigh and stood in the circle of his arms as they waited for her bags to appear on the turntable. He could see the relief in her eyes. She hated going away, hated flying, was afraid to die, was afraid he'd die in a car wreck while she was gone. Ever since her parents and her brother . . . so many terrors. It wasn't as if they had died violently. Her mother had just been old. Old enough. Sixty-eight. And her father in his seventies. He had died of grief less than a year later. But Jessie hadn't been ready for the double loss and it was incredible to see what it had done to her. She had never fully recovered from her brother's death, but after her parents . . . At times Ian wondered if she'd make it. The terrors, the hysteria, the nightmares. She felt so alone and so frightened. At times she wasn't even someone he knew. She was suddenly so dependent on him, so unlike the old Jessie. And it seemed as though she wanted to be sure he was equally dependent on her . . . That was when he had let her talk him into quitting his job and writing full-time. She could afford it. But in some ways he wasn't sure *he* could. It suited both of them though, most of the time. And supporting him made Jessie feel more secure. He really *was* all she had now.

She looked up at him again and smiled.

'Just wait till I get you home, Mrs. Clarke.'

'Lech.'

'Yep. And you love it.'

'Yes. I do.'

People were watching them, but they didn't notice. They gave people something pretty to look at, something to smile at, to feel good about, to wish for. And something to enjoy as well. They were two beautiful people who had it all. That usually aroused an interesting medley of emotions in those who watched them.

They walked to the garage to reclaim the Morgan and Jessie grinned with pride when she saw it.

'Christ, it looks good. What did you do to it?'

'Have it washed. You should try it sometime. You'll love the effect.'

'Oh, shut up.' She swung at him playfully, and he ducked, catching her arm as she laughed.

'Before you beat me up, Amazon, get in the car.' He slapped her on the behind and unlocked the door.

'Don't call me an Amazon, you miserable creep! Masher!'

'Masher? Did I hear you call me a masher?' He looked shocked and walked back to where she stood. 'Lady, how dare you call me a name like that?' And with that he swung her off her feet and slid her onto the seat of the car. 'There. And let me tell you, with a broad your size, that's no mean feat!'

'Ian, you're a shit.' But he knew she wasn't sensitive about her height. They both liked it. 'Besides, I think I'm shrinking.'

'Oh? Down to six-one now, are you?' He chuckled as he finished strapping her bag to the luggage rack in the back. He still had the top down on the car, and she was watching him with a smile.

'Go to hell. You know perfectly well I'm only five-eleven, but I measured myself the other day and I was only five-ten-and-a-half.'

'You must have been sitting down.'

He slid in beside her and turned to look into her eyes. 'Hello, Mrs. Clarke. Welcome home.'

'Hello, my love. It's so good to be back.' They shared a long smile as he started the car, and she shrugged out of the new coat and rolled up the sleeves of her blouse. 'Was it hot here today? It still feels warm now.'

'It was boiling and gorgeous and sunny. And if it's anything like that tomorrow, you can call the boutique and tell them you're snowed in in Chicago. We're going to the beach.'

'Snowed in, in September? You're crazy. And, darling, I really can't.' But she liked the idea and he knew it,

'Oh, yes you can. I'll kidnap you if I have to.'

'Maybe I could go in late.'

'Now you've got the idea.' He smiled victoriously as he pulled the choke.

'Was it really that nice today?'

'Nicer. And it would have been better yet if you had been home. I got crocked at lunch at Enrico's, and I didn't know what to do with myself all day.'

'I'm sure you found something.' But there was no malice in her tone, and no expression on his face.

'Nah. Nothing much.'

CHAPTER III

'Jessie, you are without a doubt the most beautiful woman I know.'

'It's entirely mutual.' She lay on her stomach, smiling up at him, the scent of their bodies heavy in the air, their hair tousled. They had not been awake very long. Only long enough to make love.

'It can't be mutual, silly. I'm not a beautiful woman.'

'No, but you're a magnificent man.'

'And you are adorably corny. You must live with a writer.' She smiled again and he ran a finger gently up her spine.

'You're going to get into trouble again, darling, if you do that.' She accepted a puff on the cigarette they shared, and exhaled over his head before sitting up to kiss him again.

'What time are we going to the beach, Jessie, my love?'

'Who said we were going to the beach? Jesus, darling, I have to get to the shop. I've been gone for three weeks.'

'So be gone for another day. You said you were going to the beach with me today.' He looked faintly like a pouting boy.

'I did not.'

'You most certainly did. Well, almost. I told you I'd kidnap you, and you seemed to like the idea.' She laughed, running a hand through his hair. He was impossible. A great big boy. But such a beautiful boy. She could never resist him.

'You know something?'

'What?' He looked pleased as he gazed down into her face. She was beautiful in the morning.

'You're a pain in the ass, that's what. I have to work. How can I go to the beach?'

'Easy. You call the girls, tell them you can't come in till tomorrow, and off we go. Simple. How can you waste a day like this, for Chrissake?'

'By making a living.'

Those were the comments he didn't like. They implied that he didn't make a living.

'How about if I go in this morning and cut the day short?'

'Yeah. And leave the boutique just as the fog comes in. Jessica, you're a party pooper. Yep. Party pooper. A-1.' But she was already on her way to make coffee, and answered him over her shoulder as she walked naked into the kitchen.

'I promise I'll leave the shop by one. How's that?'

'Better than nothing. Christ, I love your ass. And you lost weight.' She smiled and blew him a kiss.

'One o'clock, I promise. And we can have lunch here.'

'Does that mean what I think it does?' He was smiling again and she nodded. 'Then I'll pick you up at twelve-thirty.'

'That's a deal.'

Lady J nestled on the ground floor of a well-tended Victorian house just off Union Street. The house was painted yellow with white trim, and a small brass plaque on the door was engraved with LADY J. Jessie had had a broad picture window put in, and she did the window display herself twice a month. It was simple and effective, and as she pulled the Morgan into the driveway she looked up to see what they'd done with the display while she was gone. A brown tweed skirt, a camel-coloured stock shirt, amber beads, a trim knit hat, and a little fox jacket draped over a green velvet chair. It looked pretty damn good, and it was the right look for fall . . . though not for Indian summer. But that didn't matter. No one bought for Indian summer. They bought for fall.

The things she had ordered in New York flashed through her mind as she pulled her briefcase out of the car and ran up the few steps to their door. It was open; the girls had known she'd be in early.

'Well, look who's home! Zina! Jessie's back!' A tiny, fine-featured Oriental girl clapped her hands and jumped to her feet, running toward Jessie with a look of delight. 'You look fantastic!' The two were a striking pair. Jessie's fair, lanky beauty was in sharp contrast to the Japanese girl's delicate grace. Her hair was shiny and black and hung in a well-shaped slant from the nape of her neck towards the point of her chin.

'Kat! You cut your hair!' Jessie was momentarily taken aback. Only a month before the girl's hair had hung to her waist—when she hadn't worn it in a tight knot high on her head. Her name was Katsuko, which meant peace.

'I got sick of wearing it up. How do you like it?' She pirouetted swiftly on one foot and let her hair swing around her head as she smiled. She was dressed in black, as she often was, and it accented her litheness. It was her catlike grace that had given her the nickname Jessie used.

'I love it. Very chic.' They smiled at each other and were rapidly interrupted by a war cry of glee.

'Hallelujah! You're home!' It was Zina. Auburn-haired, brown-eyed, sensual, and Southern. She was buxom where the other two were elegantly small-breasted, and she had a mouth that said she loved laughter and men. Her hair danced close to her head in a small halo of curls, and she had great, sexy legs. Men dissolved when she moved, and she loved to tease. 'Did you see what Kat did to her hair?' She said 'hair' as though it would go on forever. 'I'd have cried for a year.' She smiled, letting her mouth slide over the words. She made each one a caress. 'How was New York?'

'Beautiful, wonderful, terrible, ugly, and hot. I had a ball. And wait till you see what I bought!'

'What kind of colours?' For a girl who almost always wore white or black, Kat had a flair for hot colours. She knew how to buy them, mix them, contrast them, blend them. Everything except wear them.

'It's all pastel, and it's so beautiful, you'll die.' Jessica strutted the thick beige carpeting of Lady J. It felt good to be back in her domain. 'Who did the window? It looks great.'

'Zina.' Kat was quick to single out her friend for praise. 'Isn't that a nice touch with the green chair for contrast?'

'It's terrific. And I see nothing's changed around here. You two are still as tight as Siamese twins. Did we make any money while I was gone?' She sat in her favourite beige leather chair, a deep one that allowed her plenty of room for her legs. It was the chair men usually sat in while they waited.

'We made lots of money. For the first two weeks anyway. This week's been slow; the weather's been too good.' Kat was quick with the report, and the last of it reminded Jessie that she had only four hours in which to work before Ian would come to spirit her away to the beach.

Zina handed her a cup of black coffee as she looked around. What she saw was the fall line she had bought, mostly in Europe, five months before, and against the beige and brown wools and leathers of the shop's subtle decor it showed up well. Two walls were mirrored and there was a jungle of plants in each corner. More greenery dripped from the ceiling, highlighted by subtle lighting.

'How's that Danish line doing?' The Danes had gone heavy on red—skirts, sweaters, three different styles of blazers, and a marvellous wrap-around coat in a deep cherry red that, in its own way, made a woman feel as exotic and sexy as fur would have. It was a great coat. Jessie had ordered one for herself.

'The Danish stuff is doing fine,' Zina intervened with her New Orleans drawl. 'How's Ian? We haven't seen him in weeks.' He had turned up once to cash a cheque, the day after Jessie had left.

'He's working on the new book.' Zina smiled warmly and nodded. She liked him. Kat was never as sure. She helped with the account books, so she knew how much of Jessica's profits he spent. But Zina had been in the shop much longer, and she had come to know Ian and appreciate him. Kat was newer, and still wore the brittle mantle of New York over her heart. She had been a sportswear buyer there until she'd tired of the pressure and decided to move to San Francisco. She had landed the job at Lady J within a week of her arrival, and she felt as lucky to be there as Jessie did having her in the shop. She knew the business. Totally.

The three women spent a half hour chatting over coffee while Katsuko showed Jessie some clippings of articles mentioning the boutique that had appeared in the papers. They had two new customers who had practically bought out the shop. And they talked easily of what Jessie had lined up for the fall. She wanted to set up a fashion show before she left for Carmel in October. Kat could get started on ideas for that.

The shop was alive with her presence, and together they made a powerful threesome. All three had something to offer. It showed in the fact that the boutique hadn't suffered while she'd been gone. She couldn't afford to have it do that, and she wouldn't have tolerated it, either. Both of the girls knew that, and they cherished their jobs. She paid well, they got marvellous clothes at a discount, and she was a reasonable woman to work for, which was rare. Kat had worked for three bitches in a row in New York, and Zina had escaped a long line of horny men who wanted her to type, take shorthand, and screw, not necessarily in that order. Jessica expected long hours and hard work, but she put in the same herself, and often more. She had made Lady J a success, and she expected them to help her maintain it. It wasn't a difficult task. She infused fresh life into it every season, and her clientele loved it. Lady J was as solid as a rock. Just like Jessica herself, and everything around her.

'And now, you two, I'd better dig through my mail. How bad is it?'

'Not too bad. Zina answered the dingy stuff. The letters from Texas from women who were here in March and wonder if the little yellow turtleneck is still on sale. That kind of stuff . . . she answered them all.'

'Zina, I love you.'

'At your service.' She swept a deep curtsy and the bright green halter she wore over white trousers bobbed with the weight of her breasts. But the other two had stopped teasing her long ago. Each was content with herself, and all three had good reason to be.

Jessie wandered into her small office three steps up in the back and looked around, pleased. Her plants were thriving, her mail was neatly divided and stacked, her bills had been paid. She saw at a glance that all was in order. Now all she had to do was sift through it. She was halfway through reading her mail when Zina appeared in the doorway, looking puzzled.

'There's a man here to see you, Jessie. He says it's urgent.' She looked almost worried. He was not one of their usual customers, and he hadn't come there to buy.

'To see me? What about?'

'He didn't say. But he asked me to give you his card.'

Zina extended the small rectangle of stiff white paper, and Jessie looked into her eyes.

'Something wrong?' Zina shrugged ignorance and Jessie read the name: 'William Houghton. Inspector. San Francisco Police.' She didn't understand and looked back at Zina for clues. 'Did anything happen while I was gone? Did we get robbed?' And Christ, wouldn't it be like them not to worry her at first, but wait and tell her an hour or two later!

'No, Jessie. Honest. Nothing happened. I don't have any idea what this is about.' The drawl sounded childish when Zina was worried.

'Neither do I. Why don't you bring him in here? I'd better talk to him.'

William Houghton appeared, following Zina with some interest. The fit of her white slacks over her trim hips was in sharp contrast to the fullness in her halter. The inspector looked hungry.

'Inspector Houghton?' Jessie stood to her full height, and Houghton seemed impressed. The three were an interesting group; Katsuko had not missed his thorough gaze either. 'I'm Jessica Clarke.'

'I'd like to speak to you alone for a minute, if that'll be all right.'

'That's fine. May I offer you a cup of coffee?' The door closed behind Zina, and he shook his head as Jessie indicated a chair near her desk and then sat back down in her own. She swivelled to face him. 'What can I do for you, Inspector? Miss Nelson said it was urgent.'

'Yes. It is. Is that your Morgan outside?' Jessie nodded, feeling queasy under the sharp look in his eyes. She was wondering if Ian had forgotten to pay his tickets again. She had had to fish him out of jail once before, for a neat little fine of two hundred dollars. In San Francisco, they didn't fool around. You paid your tickets or they took you to jail. Do not pass Go, and do not collect two hundred dollars.

'Yes, that's my car. My name's on the plates.' She smiled pleasantly and hoped that her hand didn't shake while she lit another cigarette. It was absurd. She hadn't done anything wrong, but there was something about the man, about the word 'Police', that produced instant guilt. Panic. Terror.

'Were you driving it yesterday?'

'No, I was in New York on business. I flew back last night.' As though she had to prove that she was out of town, and for a legitimate reason. This was crazy. If only Ian were here. He handled things so much better than she did.

'Who else drives your car!' Not 'does anyone else?', but 'who else?'

'My husband does.' Something sank in the pit of her stomach when she mentioned Ian.

'Did he drive it yesterday?' Inspector Houghton lit a cigarette of his own and looked her over, as if assessing her.

'I don't know for certain. He has his own car, but he was driving mine when he picked me up at the airport. I could call him and ask.' Houghton nodded and Jessica waited.

'Who else drives the car? A brother? A friend? Boyfriend?' His eyes dug into hers on the last word, and at last she felt anger.

'I'm a married woman, Inspector. And no one else drives the car. Just my husband and I.' She had gotten the point across, but something in Houghton's face told her it was not a victory.

'The car is registered to your business? You have commercial plates, and the address on the registration is this store.' Store! Boutique, you asshole, boutique! 'I assume you own this place?'

'That's correct. Inspector, what is this about?' She exhaled lengthily and watched the smoke as she felt her hand shake slightly. Something was wrong.

'I'd like to speak to your husband. Would you give me the address of his office, please?' He instantly took out a pen and waited, holding it poised over the back of one of his cards.

'Is this about parking tickets? I know my husband . . .

well, he's forgetful.' She smiled for Houghton's benefit, but it didn't take.

'No, this is not about parking tickets. Your husband's business address?' The eyes were like ice.

'He works at our home. It's only six blocks from here. On Vallejo.' She wanted to offer to go with him, but she didn't dare. She scribbled the address on one of her own cards and handed it to him.

'Thank you. I'll be in touch.' But what the fuck about, dammit? She wanted to know. But he stood up and reached for the door.

'Inspector, I'd appreciate it very much if you'd tell me what this is about. I—' He looked at her oddly again, with that searching look of his that asked questions but did not answer them.

'Mrs. Clarke, I'm not entirely sure myself. When I am, I'll let you know.'

'Thank you.' Thank you? Thank you for what? Shit.

But he was already gone, and as she walked back into the main room of the boutique, she saw him get into an olive green sedan and drive off. There was another man at the wheel. They travelled in pairs. The antenna on the back of the car swung crazily as they drove toward Vallejo.

'What was that all about?' Katsuko's face was serious, and Zina looked upset.

'I wish to hell I knew. He just asked me who drives the car and then said he wanted to talk to Ian. Goddammit, I'll bet he hasn't been paying his parking tickets again.' But it didn't feel like that, and Houghton had said it wasn't that—or was it? Jesus. Some welcome home.

She went back to her office and dialled their home number. It was busy. And then Trish Barclay walked into the shop and Jessie got tied up with nonsense like the fur jacket in the window, which Trish bought. She was one of their better customers, and Jessie had to keep up the façade, at least for a while. It was twenty-five minutes later when she got back to the phone to call Ian. This time there was no answer.

It was ridiculous! He had to be there. He had been

there when she'd left for the boutique. And the line had been busy when she'd called . . . the police had been on their way over. Christ, maybe it was serious. Maybe he had had an accident with the car and hadn't told her. Maybe someone had been hurt. But he'd have said something. Ian wouldn't just let something like that happen and not tell her. The phone rang endlessly, and no one answered. Maybe he was on his way over. It was a little after eleven.

But Nick Morris needed something 'fabulous' for his wife's birthday; he'd forgotten, and he had to have at least four hundred dollars' worth of goodies for her by noon. She was a raving bitch and she wasn't worth it, but Jessie gave him a hand. She liked Nick, and before he left the store weighted down with their shiny brown and yellow boxes, Barbara Fuller had walked in, and Holly Jenkins, and then Joan Wilcox, and . . . it was noon. And she hadn't heard from Ian. She tried the phone again and began to panic. No answer. Maybe this time he *was* on his way over. He had said he'd pick her up at twelve-thirty.

At one o'clock he hadn't shown up and she was near tears. It had been a horrible morning. People, pressures, deliveries, problems. Welcome home. And no Ian. And that asshole Houghton making her nervous with his mysterious inquiries about the car. She took refuge in her office as Zina went out to lunch. She needed to be alone for a minute. To think. To catch her breath. To get up the courage to do what she didn't want to do. But she had to know. It would be an easy way of finding out, after all. Hell, all she had to do was call down there, ask if they had an Ian Powers Clarke, and heave a sigh of relief when they said no. Or grab her chequebook and run down there and get him out if he was in the can for parking violations again. No big deal. But it took another swallow of coffee, and yet another cigarette, before she could bring her hand to the phone.

Information gave her the number. Hall of Justice. City Prison. This was ridiculous. She felt foolish, and grinned thinking of what Ian would say if she were calling the jail when he walked in. He'd make fun of her for a week.

A voice barked into her ear at the other end. 'City Prison. Palmer here.' Jesus. Now what? Okay, you called, so ask the man, dummy.

"I . . . I was wondering if you have a . . . a Mr. Ian Clarke, Ian Powers Clarke, down there, Sergeant. On parking violations.'

'What's the spelling?' The desk sergeant was not amused. Parking violations were serious business.

'Clarke. With an 'E' at the end. Ian. I-A-N C-L-A-R-K-E.' She took another drag on her cigarette while she waited, and Katsuko stuck her head in the door with an inquiry about lunch. Jessica shook her head vehemently and motioned to close the door. Her nerves had begun to fray hours ago, with the arrival of Inspector Houghton.

The voice came back on the phone after an interminable pause.

'Clarke. Yeah. We got him.' Well, bully for you. Jessica heaved a small sigh of relief. It was disagreeable, but not the end of the world. And at least now she knew, and she could have him out in half an hour. She wondered how many tickets he hadn't paid this time. But this time she was going to let him have a piece of her mind. He had scared the shit out of her. And that was probably what Houghton had wanted to do. He had, too, by not admitting that the problem was parking violations. Bastard.

'We booked him an hour ago. They're talking to him now.'

'About parking tickets?' How ridiculous. Enough was enough. And Jessica had had more than enough already.

'No, lady. Not about parking tickets. About three counts of rape and a charge of assault.' Jessie thought she could feel the ceiling pressing down on her head as the walls rushed in to squeeze the breath out of her lungs.

'What?'

'Three counts of rape. And a charge of assault.'

'My God. Can I talk to him?' Her hands shook so hard it took both of them to hold the phone, and she felt her breakfast rise in her throat.

'No. He can talk to his lawyer, and you can see him

tomorrow. Between eleven and two. Bail hasn't been set. The arraignment's on Thursday.' The desk sergeant hung up on her then, and she was holding the dead receiver in her hand, with a blank look in her eyes and tears beginning to stream down her face, when Katsuko opened the door and held out a sandwich. It took her a moment to absorb what she saw.

'My God. What happened?' She stopped in her tracks and stared into the bedlam of Jessica's eyes. Jessica never came apart, never cried, never wavered, never . . . At least they never saw that side of her at the shop.

'I don't know what happened. But there's been this incredible, horrible, most ridiculous fucking mistake!' She was shouting and she picked up the sandwich Kat had brought in and threw it across the room. Three counts of rape. And one count of assault. What in hell was going on?

CHAPTER IV

'Jessie? Where are you going?'

She brushed past Zina, returning from lunch, as she rushed out the door.

'Just make believe I never got back from New York. I'm going home. But don't call me.' She yanked open the door of her car and got in.

'Are you sick?' Zina was calling from the top of the steps, but Jessica just shook her head, pulled the choke, turned on the ignition, and roared into reverse.

Zina walked into the boutique bewildered, but Katsuko could tell her nothing more than what she had seen. Jessie was upset, but Kat didn't know why. It had something to do with the policeman's visit that morning. The two girls were worried, but she had told them not to call her at home, and the afternoon at the boutique was too busy for them to have time to speculate. Katsuko figured it had something to do with Ian, but she didn't know what. Zina was left in the dark.

When she got home, Jessica grabbed for the phone with one hand and her address book with the other. A cup half filled with coffee sat on the kitchen table. Ian had been in the middle of his breakfast when they'd taken him away, and something in Jessie's heart told her that Houghton had been the one who had taken Ian away. She wondered if the neighbours had seen it.

A stack of pages from the new book lay near the coffee. Nothing else. No note or message to her. He must have been shocked. And obviously it was an insane accusation. They had the wrong man. In a few hours the nightmare would be over, and he would be home. Her sanity had returned. Now all they needed was an attorney. She simply wouldn't allow herself to panic.

Her address book yielded the name she wanted, and she was in luck; he was free when she called, and not out to lunch as she'd feared he would be. He was a man she and Ian respected, an attorney with a good reputation, senior partner of his firm. Philip Wald.

'But Jessica, I don't do criminal work.'

'What difference does that make?'

'Quite a lot, I'm afraid. What you want is a good criminal defence attorney.'

'But he didn't do it, for Chrissake. We just need someone to straighten things out and get him out of this mess.'

'Have you spoken to him?'

'No, they wouldn't let me. Look, Philip, please. Just go down there and talk to them. Talk to Ian. This whole thing is absurd.' At the other end of the phone, there was silence.

'I can do that. But I can't take the case. It wouldn't be fair to either of you.'

'What case? This is just a matter of misidentification.'

'Do you know what it's based on?'

'Something to do with my car.'

'Did they have your licence plate?'

'Yes.'

'Well, yes, then they might have transposed the numbers or letters.' She didn't say anything, but it was hard to transpose the spelling of 'Jessie' and come up with the wrong name. That was the only thing that bothered her. The tie-in with her car. 'I'll tell you what. I'll go down and see him, find out what's going on, and I'll give you some names of defence attorneys. Get in touch with them, and whoever you settle on, tell him I'll give him a call later and fill him in on what I know. And tell them I told you to call.'

She sighed deeply. 'Thank you, Philip. That helps.'

He gave her the names and promised to come by the house as soon as he'd seen Ian. And she settled down with Ian's cold coffee to phone Philip's friends. Criminal defence attorneys all. The calls were not cheering.

The first one was out of town. The second one was in court for at least the next week and could not be disturbed with a new case. The third was too tied up to talk to her. The fourth was out. But the fifth spent some time with her on the phone. Jessie hated his voice.

'Does he have a previous record?'

'No. Of course not. Only parking violations.'

'Drugs? Any problems with drugs?'

'None.'

'Is he a drinker?'

'No, only wine at social occasions.' Christ, the man already thought Ian had done it. That much was clear.

'Did he know this woman before . . . ah . . . was he previously acquainted with her?'

'I don't know anything about the woman. And I assume that this is all a mistake.'

'What makes you think so?'

Bastard. Jessie already hated him.

'I know my husband.'

'Did she identify him?'

'I don't know. Mr. Wald can tell you all that when he comes back from seeing Ian.' At the jail . . . oh Jesus . . . Ian was in jail and it was for real, and this goddam lawyer was asking her stupid questions about whether or not Ian knew the woman who was accusing him of rape. Who cared? She just wanted him home, dammit. Now. Didn't anyone understand that? Her chest got tight and it was hard to breathe as she attempted to keep her voice calm to hide the rising panic pumping at her insides.

'Well, young lady, I'll tell you. You and your husband have a pile of trouble on your hands. But it's an interesting case.' Oh, for Chrissake. 'I'd be willing to handle the matter for you. But there is the question of my fee. Payable in advance.'

'In advance?' She was shocked.

'Yes. You'll find that most of my colleagues, if not all, handle matters the same way. I really have to collect before I get into a case, because once I appear in Superior Court for your husband, I then become the attorney of record, and legally I'm locked into the case, whether you pay the fee or not. And if your husband goes to prison, you just may not pay up. Do you have any assets?'

Ian go to prison? Fuck you, mister.

'Yes, we have assets.' She could hardly unclench her teeth.

'What kind of assets?'

'I can assure you that I could manage your fee.'

'Well, I like to be sure. My fee for this would be fifteen thousand dollars.'

'What? In advance?'

'I'd want half of that before the arraignment. I believe you said that's on Thursday. And half immediately after.'

'But there's no way I could possibly turn my assets into cash in two days.'

'Then I'm afraid there's no way I could possibly handle the case.'

'Thank you.' She wanted to tell him to get fucked. But by then she was beginning to panic again. Who in God's name would help her?

The sixth person whose name Philip had given her turned out to be human. His name was Martin Schwartz.

'Sounds like you've got yourself one hell of a problem, or at least your husband does. Do you think he did it?' It was an interesting question, and she liked him for even assuming there was some doubt. She hesitated for only a moment. The man deserved a thoughtful answer.

'No, I don't. And not just because I'm his wife. I don't believe he could do something like that. It isn't in him, and he doesn't need to.'

'All right, I'll accept that. But people do strange things, Mrs. Clarke. For your own sake, be prepared to accept that. Your husband may have a side to him you don't even know.'

It was possible. Anything was possible. But she didn't believe it. She couldn't.

'I'd like to talk to Philip Wald after he sees him,' Schwartz went on.

'I'd appreciate it if you would. There's something called an arraignment scheduled for Thursday. We're going to need legal counsel by then, and Philip doesn't feel he's qualified to take the case.' The case . . . the case . . . the case . . . she already hated the word.

'Philip's a good man.'

'I know. Mr. Schwartz . . . I hate to bring this up, but . . .'

'My fee?'

'Your fee.' She heaved a deep sigh and felt a knot tighten in her stomach.

'We can discuss that. I'll try to be reasonable.'

'I'll tell you frankly, the man I spoke to before you asked for fifteen thousand dollars by Thursday. I couldn't even begin to swing that.'

'Do you have any assets?' Oh Christ, not that again.

'Yes, I have assets.' Her tone was suddenly disagreeable. 'I have a business, a house, and a car. And my husband also has a car. But we can't just sell the house, or my business, in two days.'

It interested him the way she said 'my business', not 'our'. He wondered what 'his' business was, if any.

'I wasn't expecting you to liquidate your assets on the spot, Mrs. Clarke.' His tone was calm but firm. Something about him soothed her. 'But I was thinking that you may need some collateral for the bail—if they make the charges stick, which remains to be seen. Bail can run pretty high. We'll worry about that later. As for my fee, I think two thousand dollars up to trial would be reasonable. And if it goes to trial, an additional five thousand dollars. But that won't be for a couple of months, and if you're a friend of Philip's, I won't worry.' It struck her then that people who weren't 'friends of Philip's' were in a world of trouble. She felt suddenly grateful. 'How does that sound to you?'

She nodded silently to herself, aghast but relieved. It was certainly better than the fee she had heard a few moments before. It would clean out her savings account, but at least she could manage the two thousand. They could worry about the other five later, if it came to that. She'd sell the Morgan if she had to, and without thinking twice. Ian's ass was on the line, and she needed him one hell of a lot more than she needed the Morgan. And there was always her mother's jewellery. But that was sacred. Even for Ian.

'We can manage.'

'Fine. When can I see you?'

'Anytime you like.'

'Then I'd like to see you tomorrow in my office. I'll talk to Wald this afternoon, and get up to see Mr. Clarke in the morning. Can you be in my office at ten-thirty?'

'Yes.'

'Good. I'll get the police reports and see what the score is there. All right?'

'Wonderful. I suddenly feel as though a thousand-pound weight is off my back. I'll tell you, I've been totally frantic. I'm way out of my league. Police, bail, counts of this and counts of that, arraignments . . . I don't know what the hell is going on. I don't even know what the hell happened.'

'Well, we're going to find out. So you just relax.'

'Thank you, Mr. Schwartz. Thank you very much.'

'See you in the morning.'

They hung up and Jessica was suddenly in tears again. He had been nice to her. Finally someone had been decent to her in all this. From police inspectors who would tell her nothing, to desk sergeants who announced the charges and hung up in her ear, to attorneys who wanted fifteen thousand dollars in cash on their desks in forty-eight hours, to . . . Martin Schwartz, a human being. And according to Philip Wald, Schwartz was a competent lawyer. It had been an incredible day. And oh God, where was Ian? The tears burned a hot damp path down her face again. It felt as though they had been coming all day. And she had to pull herself together. Wald would be there soon.

Philip Wald arrived at five-thirty. His face wore an expression of grave concern and his eyes were tired.

'Did you see him?' Jessie could feel her eyes burn again and had to fight back the tears.

'I did.'

'How is he?'

'He's all right. Shaken, but all right. He was very concerned about how you are.'

'Did you tell him I'm fine?' Her hands were shaking violently again and the coffee she'd been drinking all day had only made matters worse. She looked a far cry from 'fine'.

'I told him you were very upset, which is certainly natural, under the circumstances. Jessica, let's sit down.' She didn't like the way he said it, but maybe he was just tired. They'd all had a long day. An endless day.

'I spoke to Martin Schwartz,' she said. 'I think he'll take the case. And he said he'd call you this afternoon.'

'Good. I think you'll both like him. He's a very fine attorney, and also a very nice man.'

Jessica led Philip into the living room, where he took a seat on the long white couch facing the view. Jessica chose a soft beige suede chair next to an old brass table she and Ian had found in Italy on their honeymoon. She took a deep breath, sighed, and let her feet slide into the rug. It was a warm, pleasant room that always gave her solace. A place she could come home to and unwind in . . . except now. Now she felt as though nothing would ever be all right again, and as though it had been years since she had known the comfort of Ian's arms, or seen the light in his eyes.

Almost instinctively, her eyes went to a small portrait of him that she had done years before. It hung over the fireplace and smiled at her gently. It was agonizing. Where was he? She was suddenly and painfully reminded of the feeling she had had looking at Jake's high-school pictures when she'd gone through his things after they'd gotten the telegram from the Navy. That smile after it's all over.

'Jessica?' She glanced up with a shocked expression, and Philip looked pained. She seemed distraught, confused, as though her mind were wandering. He had seen her staring at the small oil portrait, and for a moment she had worn the bereft expression of a grieving widow . . . the face that simply does not understand, the eyes that are drowning in pain. What a ghastly business. He looked at the view for a moment, and then back at her, hoping she might have composed herself. But there was nothing to compose. Her manner was in total control; it was the expression in her eyes that told the rest of the story. He wasn't at all sure how much she was ready to hear now, but he had to tell her. All of it.

'Jessica, you've got trouble.' She smiled tiredly and brushed a stray tear away from her cheek.

'That sounds like the understatement of the year. What else is new?' Philip ignored the feeble attempt at humour and went on. He wanted to get it over with.

'I really don't think he did it. But he admits to having slept with the woman yesterday afternoon. That is to say, he . . . he had intercourse with her.' He concentrated on his right knee, trying to run the distasteful words into one long unintelligible syllable.

'I see.' But she didn't really see. What was there to see? Ian had made love to someone. And the someone was accusing him of rape. Why couldn't she feel something? There was this incredible numbness that just sat on her like a giant hat. No anger, no anything, just numb. And maybe pity for Ian. But why was she numb? Maybe because she had to hear it from Philip, a relative stranger. Her cigarette burned through the filter and went dead in her hand, and still she waited for him to go on.

'He says that he had too much to drink yesterday at lunch, and you were due home last night. Something about your being away for several weeks, and his being a man—I'll spare you that. He noticed this girl in the restaurant, and after a few drinks she didn't look bad.'

'He picked her up?' She felt as though someone else were speaking her words for her. She could hear them, but she couldn't feel her mouth move. Nothing seemed to be functioning. Not her mind, not her heart, not her mouth. She almost laughed hysterically, wondering what would happen if she had to go to the bathroom; surely she would pee all over the suede chair and not even know she was doing it. She felt as if she had overdosed on Novocain.

'No, he didn't pick her up. He left the restaurant to go home and work on his book, but he drove past Enrico's again on his way, and she just happened to be standing at the corner when he stopped for a light. And just for the hell of it, he offered her a lift. She didn't look like much when she got in, she was quite a bit older than he had thought. She claims thirty on the police report, but he says she's at least thirty-seven or -eight. She gave him the address of a hotel on Market where she claimed she lived, and Ian says he felt sorry for her when she invited him up for a drink. So he went up with her, had a drink —there was half a bottle of bourbon in her room—and he says it went to his head, and he . . . they had intercourse.' Wald cleared his throat, looked away, and went on. Jessica's face showed no expression; the cigarette filter was still in her hand. 'And he says that was it. To put it bluntly, he put on his pants and went home. He had a shower, took a nap, made a sandwich, and came out to meet your plane, That's the whole story. Ian's story.' But she could hear in his voice that there was more.

'It sounds fairly tawdry, Philip. But it does not sound like rape. What are they basing the charges on?'

'Her story. And you've got to remember, Jessica, how

sensitive an issue rape is these days. For years women cried rape, and men made damaging statements about those women in court. Private investigators uncovered the supposedly startling fact that the plaintiff was not a virgin, and instantly the men were exonerated, the cases dismissed, and the women disgraced. For many reasons, it doesn't work like that anymore. No matter what really happened. Now the police and the courts are more cautious, more inclined to believe the women, and give the victim a much fairer deal. It's a damn good thing too, and about time . . . except once in a while, some woman comes along with an axe to grind, tells a lie, and some decent guy takes a bad fall. Just like some decent women used to get hurt the way things were before, now some decent guys get it in the . . . ahem . . . where it hurts.'

Jessica couldn't suppress a smile. Philip was so utterly, totally proper. She was sure he made love to his wife with his Brooks Brothers boxer shorts on.

'Frankly, Jessica, I think that what happened here is that Ian fell into the hands of a sick, unhappy woman. She slept with him, and then called it rape. Ian says she was seductive in her manner and claimed to be a waitress in a topless bar, which is not the case. But she could have been playing a very sick psychological game with him. And God knows how often she's done this before, in subtle ways, with threats, accusations. Apparently, though, she's never gone to the police before. I think you're going to have a hell of a time proving she's lying. Certainly not without a trial. Rape is hard to prove, but it's also hard to prove that it wasn't rape. If she's insisting it was, then the district attorney has to prosecute. And apparently the inspector on the case believes this woman's story. So we're stuck. If they've decided they want Ian's head, for whatever reasons, it'll have to go to a jury.'

They were both silent for a long time, and then Philip sighed and spoke again.

'I read the police reports, and the woman claims that he picked her up and she asked him to take her back to her office. She's a secretary at a hotel on Van Ness. Instead, he took her to this hotel on Market where they . . .

where they had that last drink. Given that part of the story, he's damn lucky they didn't hit him with a charge of kidnap as well. In any case, he allegedly forced her into both normal intercourse, and . . . unnatural acts. That's where the second and third counts of rape come in, and the one charge of assault. Though I assume they'll drop the assault—there's no medical proof of it.' Somehow Philip sounded horrifyingly matter-of-fact about the details, and Jessica was beginning to feel sick. She felt as though she were swimming in molasses, as though everything around her was slow and thick and unreal. She wanted to scrape the words off her skin with a knife. 'Unnatural acts.' What unnatural acts?

'For Chrissake, Philip, what do you mean by 'unnatural'? Ian is perfectly normal in bed.' Philip blushed. Jessie didn't. This was no time to be prim.

'Oral copulation, and sodomy. They are felonies, you know.' Jessica pursed her lips and looked fierce. Oral copulation hardly seemed unnatural.

'There was no clear evidence of the sodomy, but I don't think they'll drop it. Again, it's her word against his, and they're listening, and unfortunately, before I got down there, Ian admitted to the inspector on the case that he had had intercourse with the woman. He didn't confess to the oral copulation or the sodomy, but he shouldn't have admitted to intercourse at all. Damn shame that he did.'

'Will it hurt the case?'

'Probably not. We can have the tape withheld in court on the grounds that he was distraught at the time. Martin will take care of it.'

Jessica sat with her eyes closed for a moment, not believing the weight of it all.

'Why is she doing this to us, Philip? What can she possibly want from him? Money? Hell, if that's what she wants, I'll give it to her, what*ever* she wants. I just can't believe this is really happening.' She opened her eyes and looked at him again, feeling the now familiar wave of confusion and unreality sweep over her again.

'I know this is very hard on you, Jessica. But you have an excellent attorney now. Put your faith in him; he'll do a good job for you. One thing you absolutely must not do though, under any circumstances, is offer this woman money. The police won't drop the case now, even if she does, and you'll be compounding a felony and God knows what else if you try to bribe her. And I'm serious—the police seem to be taking a special interest in this. It isn't often that they get their hands on a Pacific Heights rape case, and I get the feeling that some of them think it's about time the upper class got theirs. Sergeant Houghton, the inspector on this case, made some very nasty cracks about "certain kinds of people who think they can get away with anything they want at the expense of certain other people of lesser means." It isn't a pretty inference, but if that's how he's thinking, he ought to be treated with kid gloves. I got the feeling that he doesn't like how Ian looks, or what he saw of you. I almost wonder if he doesn't think you're a couple of sickoes doing whatever amuses you for kicks. Who knows what he thinks—I'm just giving you my impression—but I want you to be very careful, Jessica. And whatever you do, don't pay this woman off. You'll be hurting Ian, and yourself, if you try to do that. If she wants money, if she calls you . . . let her talk. You can testify to it later. But don't give her a dime!' He was emphatic on the last point, and then ran a hand through his hair.

'I hate to have to tell you all this, Jessica. Ian was sick about it. But obviously you have to know what went on. It isn't very pretty, though, and I must say you're taking it remarkably well.'

But the tears welled up again at that, and she wanted to beg him not to be nice to her, not to congratulate her on how well she was taking it. She could handle the rough stuff, but she knew that if anyone put his arms around her, sympathized, cared . . . or if Ian should walk in the door just then . . . she would sob until she died.

'Thank you, Philip.' He thought her voice sounded oddly cold, as though she were warding him off. 'At least it's obviously not rape, and that's bound to be made clear in court. If Martin Schwartz is any good.'

'Yes, but . . . Jessie, it's going to be ugly. You have

to be prepared for that.' His eyes sought hers and she nodded.

'I understand that.' But she didn't. Not really. It hadn't even begun to sink in yet. How could it? Nothing had sunk in since eleven o'clock that morning. She was in shock. She only knew two things, and she didn't even understand those two things: that Ian was gone, that she couldn't see him, feel him, hear him, touch him; that he had slept with another woman. She had to face that now too. Publicly. The rest would sink in later.

There wasn't much more Philip could do, and he didn't know Jessica well enough to offer her any comfort. Only Ian knew Jessica that well. And Jessie made Philip nervous. She remained so calm. He was grateful that she was subdued, but it made him feel cold toward her, and confused. He found himself wondering what she was really thinking. He thought of his own wife and how she might react to something like this, or his sister, any of the women he knew. Jessie was a different breed of cat entirely. Too poised for his taste—and yet there was something shattering about her eyes. Like two broken windows. They were the only hint that all was not well within.

'Is there any chance he can call me? I thought you had a right to make one phone call from jail.' He had before, when they had busted him for his tickets.

'Yes. But I gather that he didn't want to call you, Jessica.'

'He didn't?' She seemed to recede still further into her own reserve.

'No. He said he wasn't sure how you'd feel. Said something about maybe this would be the last straw.'

'Asshole.' Philip looked away, and in a few moments took his leave. It had been an excessively unpleasant day. He found himself feeling grateful that he didn't practise criminal law. He couldn't stomach it. He didn't envy Martin Schwartz this case, however much money he made on it.

Jessie sat in the living room long after Philip had left. She was waiting for the sound of the phone . . . or of

Ian's key in the door. This couldn't be happening. Not really. He would come home. He always did. She tried to pretend that the house wasn't quiet. She sang little songs and talked to herself. He couldn't leave her alone . . . no! . . . she sometimes heard her mother's voice late in the night . . . and Jake's . . . and Daddy's . . . but never Ian's . . . never Ian . . . never . . . He would call, he had to. He couldn't leave her alone, scared like that, he wouldn't do that to her, he had promised he never would, and Ian never broke his promises . . . but he had. He had broken a promise now. She remembered it as she sat on the floor in the hall, in the dark, late into the night. That way she would hear his key sooner when he came home. He would come home, but he had broken a promise. He had slept with another woman, and now he was making her face it. She couldn't ignore it anymore. She hated her . . . hated her . . . hated . . . her, but not him. Oh God . . . maybe Ian didn't love her anymore . . . maybe he was in love with the other woman . . . maybe . . . why didn't he call, dammit? Why didn't he . . . why had he . . . the tears ran down her face like hot summer rain as she lay on the smooth wood floor in the hall and waited for Ian. She lay on the floor until morning. The phone never rang.

CHAPTER V

The offices of Schwartz, Drewes, and Jonas were located in the Bank of America Building on California Street, an excellent address. Jessica rode to the forty-fourth floor looking prim, sleek, and tired. She wore a large pair of dark glasses and a sombre navy blue suit. It was an outfit reserved for business meetings and funerals. This was a little bit of both. It was ten-twenty-five. She was five minutes early, but Martin Schwartz was waiting.

A secretary led her down a long carpeted corridor with a sweeping view of the bay. His offices took up one corner on the north side of the building. It was evidently a large, prosperous firm.

Martin Schwartz's office boasted two walls of glass, but the decor was Spartan and chill. He rose from behind his desk, a man of medium height with a full head of grey hair. He wore glasses, and he was frowning.

'Mrs. Clarke?' The secretary had announced her, but he would have known her anyway. She looked the way he had expected her to—wealthy, elegant. But she was younger than he had expected, and more composed than he had dared to hope.

'Yes. How do you do?' She held out a hand, and he took in her full height. She was a striking young woman. He mentally made a pair of her and the unshaven, tired, but still handsome young man he had seen in the city prison that morning. They must look quite something together. They would also look good in court. Maybe too good—too beautiful, too young. He didn't like the looks of this case.

'Won't you sit down?' She nodded, slid into a chair across from his desk, and declined his offer of coffee.

'You've seen Ian?'

'I have. And Sergeant Houghton. And the assistant district attorney assigned to the case. And I spoke to Philip Wald for over an hour last night. Now I want to talk to you, and then we'll see what kind of a case we really have here.' He attempted a smile and shuffled some papers on his desk. 'Mrs. Clarke, have you ever been into drugs?'

'No. And neither has Ian. Nothing more than a few joints once in a while. But I don't think we've smoked any grass in over a year. Neither of us ever liked it much. And we don't drink anything more exotic than wine.'

'Let's not jump ahead of ourselves. I want to get back to drugs. Are any of your friends in that scene?'

'Not that I know of.'

'Would anything of that nature be likely to turn up in an investigation of you or Mr. Clarke?'

'No, I'm sure that nothing would.'

'Good.' He looked only slightly relieved.

'What makes you ask?'

'Oh, some of the angles that I sense Houghton might be working on. He made some disagreeable remarks about your shop. Some girl in there who looks like a belly dancer, apparently, and an 'exotic' Oriental he mentioned. Also the fact that your husband is a writer, and you know the kind of fantasies people have about that. Houghton is a man with a vivid imagination, a typical lower-middle-class mind, and a strong dislike for anything that comes from your part of town.'

'I suspected as much. He came to talk to me at the shop before he arrested Ian. And the 'bellydancer' he's having fantasies about is a young lady who has the misfortune to wear a size 38 bra with a D cup. She happens to go to church twice a week.' Jessica was not smiling. But Martin Schwartz was.

'She sounds delightful.' He forced a smile out of her, with some effort.

'And if Sergeant Houghton thinks we look like we have too much money, he happens to be mistaken about that too. But what he does see can be explained by the fact that my parents and my brother died several years ago. I inherited what they had. My brother had no wife and children to leave anything to, and there were no other brothers or sisters.'

'I see.' And then after a brief pause he looked up at her again. 'It must be lonely with no family.' She nodded silently and kept her eyes on the view.

'I have Ian.'

'Any children?' She shook her head, and he began to understand something. The reason she was not angry, why she so desperately wanted her husband home, without a single word of criticism about the charges. The reason for the almost frightening urgency he had sensed in her voice on the phone, and again now in his office. The 'I have Ian' said it all. He suddenly knew that as far as Jessica Clarke was concerned, that was *all* she had.

'I take it there's no chance they might drop the charges?'

'None. Politically, they can't. The victim in this case is making such a stink. She wants his ass, if you'll pardon the expression. And I think it's reasonable to expect that they'll be prying fairly heavily into your lives. Can you weather it?' She nodded, and he didn't tell her that Ian was afraid she couldn't stand the pressure. 'Is there anything I should know? Any indiscretions on your part? Problems with the marriage? Sexual . . . well, "exoticisms," shall we say, orgies you may have gone to, whatever?'

She shook her head again, looking annoyed.

'I'm sorry I have to ask, but it'll all come out anyway. It's best to be candid now. And of course we'll want our own investigation of the girl. I have a very good man. Mrs. Clarke, we're going to do our damnedest for Ian.'

He smiled at her again, and for a moment she felt as though she were living a dream. This man was not real, he wasn't asking her if she'd ever gone to orgies, or been into drugs . . . Ian wasn't really in jail . . . this man was a friend of her father's and it was all a big game. She felt him staring at her then, and she had to return to the pretence that this was reality. Worse yet, to the reality that Ian was in jail.

'Can we get Ian out of jail before the trial?'

'I hope so. But that will most likely depend on you. If the charges were a little less severe, we might have been able to get him released on his own recognizance—in other words, with no bail to pay. But on charges of this nature, I'm almost certain the judge will insist on bail being posted, despite the fact that Ian has no previous record. And his getting out will depend on whether or not you can put up the bail. They're talking about setting it at twenty-five thousand dollars. That's pretty steep, and it means you'd either have to put twenty-five thousand dollars in cash in the keeping of the court until the trial is over, or pay twenty-five hundred to a bailbondsman and give him collateral to cover his bond. Either way, it's a stiff fee. But we'll see about getting it down to something more reasonable.'

Jessica heaved a deep sigh and absentmindedly took off

her dark glasses. What he saw then shocked him. Two deep purple trenches lay beneath her eyes, which were bloodshot and swollen and filled with terror. He was looking at a woman with the eyes of a child. The poise was all a front. He had been so sure she was the balls in the outfit, but maybe not, maybe not. Maybe she was only the bucks, and Ian was her lifeline. It made him feel better, somehow, about Ian. He was in better shape than she was, that was for sure.

Schwartz forced his mind back to the question of bail as Jessica's eyes continued to watch him. She seemed unaware of how much she had just shown him.

'Do you think you'll be able to meet the bail, Mrs. Clarke?' She looked tiredly into his eyes and shrugged slightly.

'I suppose I can put up my business.' But she knew that she couldn't pay the bailbondsman's fee if she handed Schwartz the two-thousand-dollar cheque in her bag. And she had no choice. They needed a lawyer before they could even begin to worry about a bailbondsman. She'd have to get a loan on the car. Or on . . . something. What the hell. It didn't matter now. Nothing did. She'd even put up the house if she had to. But what if . . . she had to know. 'What if we can't quite meet the bail right away?'

'There's no credit there, Mrs. Clarke. You pay the full bailbondsman's fee and put up satisfactory collateral or they simply don't let Ian out of jail.'

'Until when?'

'After the trial.'

'God. Then I don't have much choice, do I?'

'In what sense?'

'We'll just put up whatever we have to.'

He nodded, sorry for her. It was rare that he felt anything stir in his heart for a client, and had she ranted and whined and cried, she would have annoyed him. Instead she had won his respect—and his pity. Neither of them deserved this kind of trouble. It made him wonder again what the real story was with the rape charges. He felt in his gut that it had not been a rape. But the question was, could that be proven?

He spent another ten minutes explaining the arraignment procedures: a simple appearance in court to put the charges on record, establish the bail, and set a date for Ian's next appearance in court, at a preliminary hearing. The victim would not be at the arraignment. Jessica was relieved.

'Is there a number, Mrs. Clarke, where I can reach you today if I need you?' She nodded and scribbled the number of the boutique. It was the first time she'd thought of going in.

'I'll be there after I see Ian. I'm going over to see him now. And Mr. Schwartz, please call me Jessica, or Jessie. It sounds like we're going to be seeing a lot of each other.'

'Yes, we will. And I want you back in my office on Friday. Both of you, if you've managed to get Ian out on bail.' The 'if' sent a shiver down her spine. 'No, actually, make it Monday. In case you do get him out, you two will deserve a little time off. And then we'll get down to work in earnest. We don't have much time.'

'How much time?' It was like asking a doctor how long you had to live.

'We'll have a better idea of that after the arraignment. But the trial will probably come up in about two months.'

'Before Christmas?' She reminded him again of an overgrown child as she asked.

'Before Christmas. Unless we get a continuance for some reason. But your husband told me this morning that he wants to get this over with as quickly as possible, so you could put it behind you and forget it.'

Forget it? she thought. Who would ever forget it?

He stood up and held out a hand, removing his glasses for a moment. 'Jessica, try to relax. Leave the worrying to me for a while.'

'I'll do my best.' She stood up too, shook his hand, and he was once again taken aback by her height. 'Thank you, Martin, for everything. Any message for Ian?' She paused in the doorway.

'Tell him I said he's a lucky man.' His eyes warmed her and she smiled at the compliment and slipped out the door.

Martin Schwartz sat down, swivelled his chair to face the view, chewed on his glasses, and shook his head. This was going to be a bitch of a case. He was sure Ian hadn't done it, but they both would be a real problem in court. Young, happy, beautiful, and rich. The jury would resent his screwing around on a woman like Jessie; the women in court would hate Jessie; the men in court would dislike Ian because they wouldn't believe that writing was work. And they looked as if they had too much money, no matter how sensible the explanation of Jessie's inheritance was. He just didn't like the looks of this case. And the victim was obviously a strange woman, maybe a sick one. His only hope was that they'd find out enough on her to destroy her. It was an ugly game to play, but it was Ian's only chance.

CHAPTER VI

Jessica stopped in the lobby to call the boutique. Zina's voice was concerned when she heard her.

'Jessie, are you all right?' They had finally tried her at home at ten-thirty that morning, but she had already gone out.

'I'm fine.' But Zina didn't like the sound of her voice. 'Everything okay at your end?'

'Sure, we're okay. Are you coming in?'

'After lunch. See ya later.' She hung up before Zina could ask more questions and went to reclaim the Morgan from the garage. She was off to the Hall of Justice to see Ian.

She was two thousand dollars poorer, but now she felt better. She had left the cheque in a blue envelope with the secretary at the front desk. The first part of Martin

Schwartz's fee. She had been as good as her word. Now there were a hundred and eighty-one dollars left in their joint savings account, but Ian had an attorney. What a price they were going to pay for one piece of ass!

She tried not to let herself think as she drove across town. She wasn't so much angry as confused. What had happened? Who was this woman? Why was she doing this to them? What did she have against Ian? After speaking to Martin, Jessie was more certain than ever that Ian had done nothing wrong—except pick the wrong woman for an afternoon of delight. Oh Jesus, had he picked the wrong woman!

She found a parking space on Bryant Street, across from a long strip of neon-lit bailbondsmen's offices. She found herself wondering which one she'd be haggling with by the next afternoon. They all looked so sleazy; she wouldn't have wanted to enter any of those places to get in out of the cold, let alone to do business. She walked quickly into the Hall of Justice, where a metal detector checked her out while a guard rifled through her handbag. She had to stop for a pass for the jail, show her driver's licence, and identify herself as Ian's wife. There was a crowd of people standing in line, but the line moved forward quickly.

It was a shaggy, dishevelled-looking lot of humanity, and she was strikingly out of place. Her height set her apart from the rest of the women and most of the men, and the navy blue suit looked absurd. There were white women in imitation leather pants wearing fake leopard jackets, beehive hairstyles, and floppy white sandals. Black men in puce satin, and black girls in what looked like cheap satin nightgowns or pyjamas. It was an interesting crowd, but for a movie, not for a life. She couldn't help wondering if the woman Ian had slept with looked like one of these. She hoped not—not that it mattered at this point. Her knees were already quaking, and she didn't know what she'd say to him. What could she say?

Her hand trembled as she pressed the elevator button for the sixth floor. There was an alternating sensation of sinking and rising in her stomach as she wondered what the jail would be like. She had seen it briefly the one time she had bailed him out, but there had never been time for a visit, thank God. She'd just gone down and gotten him. This time it was all so different.

The elevator let her out on the sixth floor, and all she knew was that she wanted to see Ian. Suddenly she knew she could crawl through any amount of fear and anger, over a thousand puce satin pimps, just to get to Ian.

The visitors waited in single file outside an iron door and a guard let them into the room beyond in groups of five or six. They made their exit through another door at the far side of the room. But it seemed to Jessie that they were being swallowed up, never to be seen again.

A moment later, Jessica was inside. The room was hot and stuffy, windowless and fluorescent-lit. There were long glass panes in the interior walls with little shelves on either side holding telephones. She realised then that she would see him through a window. She hadn't thought about that. What could you say on a phone?

His face appeared in a far window as she wondered which one to go to, and he stood there, watching her as she felt tears burn her eyes. She couldn't let herself cry . . . couldn't . . . couldn't . . . couldn't! She walked slowly toward the phone, feeling a vice tighten around her heart and her legs turn to straw, but she was walking, one foot after the other, and he couldn't see her hands tremble as she waved hesitantly. And then suddenly she was facing him, and she had the phone in her hand. They watched each other briefly in silence. And then he spoke first.

'Are you okay?'

'I'm fine. How are you?'

He was silent again for a moment and then nodded with a small, crooked smile.

'Terrific.' But the smile faded quickly. 'Oh baby, I'm so sorry to put you through this. It's all so crazy and so goddam . . . I think all I want to tell you, Jess, is that I love you, and I don't know how this whole fucking mess happened. I wasn't sure how you'd take it.'

'What did you think? That I'd run away? Have I ever done that?' She looked so hurt he wanted to turn away. It was hard to look at her. Very hard.

'No, but this isn't exactly your run-of-the-mill problem, like a thirty-dollar overdraft at the bank. I mean this is . . . Jesus, what can I say, Jessie?' She gave him a tiny smile in answer.

'You already said it. And I love you too. That's all that matters. We'll get this thing straightened out.'

'Yeah . . . but . . . Jess, it doesn't sound like it's going to be easy. That woman is sticking to the accusations, and this cop, Houghton, he acts like he thinks he's got the local hotshot rapist on his hands.'

'Adorable, isn't he?'

'He talked to you?' Ian looked surprised.

'Just before he went to the house to see you.' Ian looked pale.

'Did he tell you what it was about?' She shook her head and looked away. 'Oh, Jess . . . what an incredible horror show to put you through. I just can't believe it.'

'Neither can I. But we'll survive it.' She gave him her best brave girl smile. 'What do you think of Martin?'

'Schwartz? I like him. But that's going to cost you a pretty penny, isn't it?' Jessie tried to look noncommittal and started to say something, but he cut her off. 'How much?' There was a look of bitterness in his eyes for a moment.

'That's not important.'

'Maybe not to you, Jessie, but it is to me. How much?'

'Two thousand now, and another five if it goes to trial.' There was no avoiding that look in his eyes. She had had to tell him.

'Are you kidding?'

Jessie shook her head in reply.

'The man I spoke to before him wanted fifteen thousand, in cash, and by the end of this week.'

'Jesus Christ, Jessica . . . that's insanity. But I'll pay you back for Schwartz.'

'You're boring me, sweetheart.'

'I love you, Jess.' They exchanged a long tender look and Jessica felt the hot coals behind her eyes again.

'How come you didn't call me last night?' She didn't tell him that she had lain on the floor all night, waiting, frightened, almost hysterical, but too tired to move. She had felt as though her body were paralysed while her mind was racing.

'How could I call you, Jess? What could I say?' That you love me . . . 'I think I was in shock. I just kept sitting here, stunned. I couldn't understand it.'

Then why did you screw her, damn you? But the flash of anger left her eyes again as soon as she looked up at him. He was as unhappy as she was. More so.

'Why do you suppose she accused you of . . . of . . .'

'Rape?' He said it as if it were a death sentence. 'I don't know. Maybe she's sick or crazy, or pissed off at someone, or maybe she wanted money. What the hell do I know? I was a fool to do that anyway. Jessie, I—' He looked away and then back into her eyes with tears hovering in the corners of his own. 'How are we going to live with this? How are you going to live with it, Jessie? Without hating me? And . . . I just don't see . . .'

'Stop it!' She spat the words into the phone in a whisper. 'Stop it right now! We'll see this thing through and it'll be over and straightened out and we'll never have to think about it again.'

'But won't you? I mean honestly, Jessie, won't you? Every time you look at me, won't you hate me a little bit for her, and for the money this'll cost you, and . . . fuck.' He ran a hand through his hair and reached into his pocket for a cigarette. Jessie watched him and then suddenly noticed his pants. He was wearing white cotton hospital pyjama bottoms.

'Good God, what happened to your pants? Didn't they give you time to get dressed?' Her eyes grew wide as she envisioned Sergeant Houghton dragging him out of the house bare-assed and in handcuffs.

'Adorable, aren't they? They took my pants down to the lab to test them for sperm.' It was all so goddam tawdry, so ugly, so . . . 'I'm going to need some pants for court tomorrow morning, by the way.' And then he grew pensive for a moment and took a long drag on his cigarette. 'I just don't understand it. You know, if she wanted money, all she had to do was call and blackmail me. I told her I was married.' How nice . . . and then for no reason she could fathom, she looked at Ian, at his wrinkled white cotton pyjamas, at the boyish face and rumpled blond hair, at the madhouse of people around her, and she started to laugh.

'Are you okay?' He looked suddenly frightened. What if she got hysterical? But she didn't look hysterical, she looked genuinely amused.

'You know something nutty? I'm fine. And I love you, and this is ridiculous, dammit, so will you please come home—and you know what else? You look cute in pyjamas.' It was the same laughter he had heard a million times at two in the morning when she'd teased him about walking around the house reading his work, stark naked, and with a pencil behind each ear. It was the laughter of splashing water at each other in the shower, of tickling him when he got into bed. It was Jessie, and it suddenly made him smile, as he hadn't smiled since this whole nightmare had begun.

'Lady, you are absolutely screwy, but I adore you. Will you please get me out of this shithouse so I can come home and—' He stopped on the word and looked suddenly pale.

'Rape me? Why not?' And then they grinned again, but quietly. She was okay now. She had Ian right in front of her, she knew she was loved and safe and protected. With Ian suddenly gone and that incredible silence, it had been as though he were dead. But he wasn't dead. He was alive. He would always be alive, and he was all hers. Suddenly she wanted to dance, standing there in the jail in the midst of pimps and thieves, she wanted to dance. She had Ian back.

'Mr. Clarke, how come I love you so much?'

'Because you happen to be mentally retarded, but I love you that way. Hey, lady, could you be serious for a moment?' His face showed that he meant it, but Jessie still had laughter in her tired, bloodshot eyes.

'What?'

'I meant what I said about paying you back. I will.'

'Don't worry about it.'

'But I will. I think it's time I went back to some kind of job anyway. It doesn't work like this, Jess, and you know it too.'

'Yes, it does. What do you mean, "it doesn't work"?' She looked frightened again.

'I mean I don't like being kept, even if it is for the supposed benefit of my writing career. It's lousy for my ego, and worse for our marriage.'

'Bullshit.'

'No bullshit. I'm serious. But this isn't the time or the place to talk about it. I just want you to know, though, that whatever money you put out on this, you're getting back. Is that clear?' She looked evasive, and Ian's voice got louder in her ear. 'I mean it, Jessie. Don't fuck around with me on this. You're not paying for it.'

'Okay.' She looked at him pointedly, and at the same moment a guard tapped her on the shoulder. The visit was over. And they had so much left to say.

'Take it easy, sweetheart. I'll see you in court tomorrow.' He had seen the stricken look on her face.

'Can you call me tonight?'

He shook his head. 'No, they won't let me now.'

'Oh.' But I need to hear you . . . I need you, Ian . . . I . . .

'Get yourself a good night's sleep before the court thing tomorrow. Promise?' She nodded, looking like a child, and he smiled at her. 'I love you so much, Jess. Will you please take care, for me?'

She nodded again. 'And you too? Ian . . . I . . . I'd die without you.'

'Don't think like that. Now go on, I'll see you tomorrow. And Jess . . . thank you. For everything.'

'I love you.'

'I love you too.'

On the last words, the phones suddenly went dead in their hands, and she waved at him as she followed the flock of visitors into the elevator. She was alone with them again now. Ian was gone. But it was different this time.

She felt full of the way he looked and sounded, of the colour of his hair, and even the smell of his skin. He was vivid again now. He was still with her.

CHAPTER VII

Zina and Katsuko were both busy with customers when Jessica walked in, and she had a moment to compose herself in her office before joining them. It was crazy, really. Guess where I've been? To visit Ian in jail. From city prison to Lady J in one swift leap. Madness.

The girls were helping a couple of women who wanted dresses for Palm Springs. They were overweight, overdressed, overbearing, and not overly friendly. And Jessica found it nearly impossible to work. She kept thinking of Ian, of the jail, of Martin Schwartz, of Inspector Houghton. The inspector's eyes seem to haunt her.

'And what does your husband do?' One of the women asked her, while looking over a rack of their new velvet skirts. They were a rich Bordeaux colour with black satin trim. Copies of St. Laurent.

'My husband? He rapes . . . I mean, writes!' The women found it hilarious, and even Zina and Kat had to laugh. Jessica laughed through tears in her eyes.

'My husband used to be that way too—before he took up golf.' The second woman found the interlude delightful and settled on two skirts and a blouse while the first woman went back to the slacks.

It was a long day, but it saved her from talking to Zina and Kat. It was almost five before they sat down for a round of hot coffee.

'Jess, is everything okay now?'

'Much better. We had a few problems, but everything will be worked out by tomorrow.' At least then he'd be home, and they could work it out together. Just so he came home!

'We were worried as hell about you. I'm glad everything's fine.' Zina seemed satisfied, but Katsuko continued to search Jessie's eyes. Something didn't sit right.

'You look like shit, Jessica Clarke.'

'Flattery, flattery. It's just this grim suit.' She looked around, wondering if she should change into something from the shop's fall line just to pick up her sagging spirits. But it was late, and she was tired, and she didn't have the energy to get into or out of anything. It would only be another ten or fifteen minutes before Zina locked the doors for the night.

Jessica stood up, stretched, and was aware of the ache in her back and neck from the long crazy night she'd spent on the floor. Not to mention the tension of the day. She was arching her back gingerly, trying to ease out the kinks, when a woman walked into the boutique. Jessie, Kat, and Zina quickly glanced at each other, deciding who would stand up and be helpful, but it was Jessie who turned toward the woman with a smile. The woman looked pleasant, and it did Jessie good to deal with the clients. It kept her mind off herself.

'May I help you?'

'Do you mind if I browse? I heard about the boutique from a friend, and you have some lovely things in the window.'

'Thank you. Let me know if you need any help.'

Jessica and the woman exchanged an easy smile, and the customer began to look through the sportswear. She was elegant, somewhere in her mid- to late thirties, maybe even forty, but it was hard to tell. She wore a trim, simple black pantsuit, a cream linen blouse, a small bright scarf at her neck, and a healthy amount of obviously expensive gold jewellery—a handsome bracelet, a nice chain, several very solid looking rings—and a striking pair of onyx-diamond earrings that had caught Jessie's attention when she'd walked into the shop. The woman spelled money. But her face showed warmth, and something else—as though she enjoyed the pretty things she was wearing, but understood that there were other things in her life that mattered more.

Jessie watched her as she moved from rack to rack. She looked content, happy. And she had a kind of grace that made her easy to watch. The face was young, the hair ash blonde streaked with grey. In an odd way she reminded Jessie of a Siamese cat, particularly the pale china blue of her eyes. Something about her made you want to know more.

'Did you have anything special in mind? We have some new things in the back.' The woman smiled at Jessie and shrugged.

'I should be shot for this, but what about that suede coat over there? Have you got it in an eight?' She looked guilty, like a small child buying more bubble gum than she was supposed to, but she also looked as though she were having a good time. And as though she could afford one hell of a lot of bubble gum, or anything else.

'I'll take a look.' Jessica disappeared into the stockroom, wondering if they did have the coat in a smaller size.

They didn't. But they had a similar one that sold for forty dollars more. Jessica removed the price tag and took the coat out to the woman. It was a warm cinnamon colour with a soft clinging shape. It was actually a better-looking coat than the first one, and the woman noticed that instantly.

'Damn. I was hoping I'd hate it.'

'It's a hard coat to hate. And it looks well on you.'

They watched the woman swirling gracefully in the brown suede coat. It suited her marvellously, and she knew it. It was a pleasure to see clothes on someone like that. But then, she could have worn the rug and looked fabulous.

'How much is it?'

'Three hundred and ten.' Zina and Kat exchanged a quizzical glance, but they knew enough not to question the price aloud. Jessie always had a method to her madness, and she was usually right. Maybe this was someone special Jessie had been hoping to lure into the shop. She certainly looked like someone one ought to recognize. And the woman did not look overwhelmed by the price of the coat.

'Does it have matching pants?'

'It did, but they're gone.'

'That's too bad.' But she managed to casually collect three sweaters, a blouse, and a suede skirt to go with the coat before she decided that she'd done enough damage for one day. It was a beautiful sale for the shop, and an easy one. She pulled out her chequebook, encased in emerald green suede, and looked up at Jessie with a smile. 'And if you see me back here in less than a week, throw me out the door.'

'Do I have to?' Jessie looked mock-regretful.

'That's an order, not a request!'

'What a pity.' The two women laughed and the shopper filled out her cheque. It was for well over five hundred dollars. But she hardly looked worried. Her name was Astrid Bonner, and her address was on Vallejo, only a block from Jessie's home.

'We're almost neighbours, Mrs. Bonner.' Jessie told her her address, and Astrid Bonner looked up with a smile.

'I know that house! It's the little blue and white one, I'll bet, with all those fabulous bright flowers out front!'

'You can see us for miles!'

'Don't apologise; you do wonders for the area! And you have a little red sports car?' Jessie pointed out the window.

'That's me.' They laughed together and Zina quietly locked the doors. It was a quarter to six. 'Would you like a drink?' They kept a bottle of Johnnie Walker in the back. Some of their customers stayed late to chat. It was another nice touch.

'I'd love to, but I won't. You probably want to get home.' Jessie smiled and Katsuko put Mrs. Bonner's purchases in two large shiny brown boxes filled with yellow and orange tissue paper and tied them with plaid ribbons.

'Do you own the shop?'

Jessie nodded.

'You have some beautiful things. And I needed that coat like another hole in my head. But . . . no will power. It's my worst problem.'

'Sometimes a splurge is good for the soul.'

Astrid Bonner nodded quietly at the remark and the two women exchanged a long glance. Jessie felt very comfortable with her. She was sorry Astrid Bonner wouldn't stay for the drink; Jessie had nothing to rush home for, and she would have liked to talk to her. She wondered which of the houses on the next block was hers. And then she had an idea.

'Can I give you a lift home, by the way? I'm leaving now.' It would also spare her the questions that Zina and Kat might have saved to hurl at her after hours. She couldn't face that yet. And Astrid Bonner would give her safe passage. She still hadn't told them she wouldn't be in the following morning, while she went to the arraignment.

'A lift would be terrific. Thank you. I usually walk when I'm this close to home, but with these two boxes . . . delightful.' She smiled and looked even younger. Jessie wondered how old she really was.

Jessica picked up her coat, grabbed her bag, and waved at the other two. 'Good night, ladies. See you sometime tomorrow. I won't be in in the morning.' The four smiled at one another, Jessie unlocked the door for Astrid, Zina locked it again behind them, and they were on their way. No questions, no answers, no lies. Jessie was enormously relieved. She hadn't realized how she had been dreading that all afternoon.

She unlocked the car and Astrid slid in, the boxes tall on her lap, and they headed for home.

'The shop must keep you busy.'

'It does, but I love it. And I'm Jessica Clarke, by the way. I just realized that I haven't introduced myself. I'm sorry.' They exchanged another smile, and the evening breeze rustled through Astrid Bonner's freshly done hair. 'Would you like me to put the top up?'

'Of course not.' She laughed suddenly and looked at Jessie. 'I'm not that old and stuffy, for God's sake. And I must say, I envy you that shop. I used to work on a magazine in New York. That was ten years ago, and I still miss fashion in any form.'

'We came out from New York too. Six years ago. What brought you here?'

'My husband. Well, no actually it was a business trip. Then I met my husband out here—and never went back.' She looked pleased at the memory.

'Never? Are they still expecting you back?' The two women laughed in the soft twilight.

'No, I returned for all of three weeks. Gave them notice and that was that. I was the career-woman sort, never going to marry, all of that . . . and then I met Tom. And bingo, end of the career.'

'Did you ever regret it?' It was an outrageously personal thing to ask, but she seemed to invite one to feel at ease with her. And Jessie did.

'No. Never. Tom changed everything.' Jessica found herself wanting to say 'how awful' and then wondering why. After all, Ian had changed things for her too, but not like that; he hadn't cost her a career, hadn't forced her to leave New York. She had wanted to move to San Francisco, but she couldn't conceive of giving up Lady J.

'No, I never regretted it for a moment. Tom was a remarkable man. He died last year.'

'Oh. I'm sorry. Do you have children?'

Astrid laughed and shook her head. 'No, Tom was fifty-eight when I married him. We had a splendid ten years—alone. It was like a honeymoon.' Jessie was reminded of her life with Ian, and smiled.

'We feel sort of the same way. Children might interfere with so much.'

'Not if that's what you want. But we both thought we were too old. I was thirty-two when I married him, and I just wasn't the motherly type. We never regretted it. Except that life is awfully quiet now.'

So Astrid was forty-two. Jessie was surprised.

'Why don't you take a job?' she said.

'What could I possibly get a job doing? I worked for *Vogue*, but there's nothing like that out here. And even *Vogue* wouldn't want me anymore, not after ten years. You get rusty, and I've gotten about as rusty as you can get. And besides, I have no intention of moving back to New York. Ever.'

'Get something in a field related to fashion.'

'Like what?'

'A boutique.'

'Which brings us back to where we started, my dear. I'm green with envy over yours.'

'Don't be too envious. It has its problems.'

'And its rewards, I'll bet. Do you go back to New York often?'

'I came back two days ago.' And yesterday my husband got arrested for rape. It was on the tip of her tongue to say it, but Astrid would have been horrified. Anyone would have been. She sighed deeply, forgetting for a moment that she was not alone.

'Was the trip as bad as all that?' Astrid asked, smiling.

'What trip?'

'The trip to New York. You said you just got back from New York two days ago, and then you sighed as though your best friend had died.'

'I'm sorry. It's been a long day.' She tried to smile, but suddenly everything felt heavy again; the nightmare had rushed back to overwhelm her. There was a moment's pause, and then Astrid looked at her over the brown boxes on her lap.

'Is anything wrong?' It was a deep, searching look, and hard to meet it with a lie.

'Nothing that won't be smoothed out soon.'

'Anything I can do to help?' What a nice woman, they were total strangers and she was asking Jessie about her problems. Jessie smiled and slowed at the corner.

'No, everything's okay really. And you already did help. You finished my day with a nice dollop of sunshine. Now, which house is it?'

Astrid smiled and pointed. 'That one. And you were an angel to drive me home.'

It was a sombre brick mansion with black shutters and white trim and politely carved hedges around it. Jessie wanted to whistle. She and Ian had noticed the house often and had wondered who lived there. They had suspected the owners travelled a lot, because the house often looked closed.

'Mrs. Bonner, I'd like to return the compliment on the house. We've envied you this one for years.'

'I'm flattered. And call me Astrid. But your house looks like so much more fun, Jessica. This one is awfully . . . well . . .' She giggled. 'Grown-up, I suppose is the right word. Tom already had it when we married, and he had some beautiful things. You'll have to come over for coffee sometime. Or a drink.'

'I'd love it.'

'Then how about right now?'

'I . . . I'd love to, but to tell you the truth, I'm just beat. It's been a very hectic couple of days since I got back, and I ran myself ragged for three weeks in New York. Would a rain check be possible?'

'With pleasure. Thanks again for the ride.' She let herself out of the car, and waved as she climbed the steps to her house. Jessie waved back. That was some house! And she was pleased with having met Astrid Bonner. A delightful woman.

Jessica drove into her own driveway, thinking of Astrid and what she had said. It sounded as though she had given up a lot for her husband. And she looked happy about it.

Jessie walked into the dark house, kicked off her shoes, and sat down on the couch without turning on the lights. She was reviewing the day. It had been unbelievable. Everything from the meeting with Martin Schwartz, to emptying her savings into his pockets, to seeing Ian in jail, to the civilised exchanges with Astrid Bonner . . . when would life become real again?

She thought about making herself a drink, but she couldn't get up the energy to move. Her mind raced, but her body had turned to stone. The machinery just wouldn't move anymore. But her mind . . . her mind . . . she kept thinking about the visit to Ian. She was home again now. Alone, where he had always waited for her at night. The house was so unbearably quiet . . . the way Jake's apartment had been when she'd gone back to it . . . after he died . . . why did she keep thinking of Jake now? Why did she keep comparing him to Ian? Ian wasn't dead. And he would be home tomorrow—wouldn't he? He would. But what if . . . she just couldn't stop. The doorbell rang and she didn't even hear it until finally the insistent buzzer yanked her attention off the merry-go-round of her thoughts. It required her last ounce of energy to get up and answer the door.

She stood in her stocking feet in the darkness of the front hall and spoke through the door. She was too tired even to try to guess who it was.

'Who is it?' Her voice barely penetrated through to the opposite side. But he heard her. He looked over his shoulder at his companion and nodded. The second man walked slowly back toward the green car.

'Police.'

Jessie's heart flew into trip-hammer action at the sound of the word, and she leaned trembling against the wall. Now what?

'Yes?'

'It's Inspector Houghton. I want to speak to Mrs. Clarke.' But he already knew it was she. And on the other side of the door, Jessica was tempted to tell him that Mrs. Clarke was not at home. But her car was plainly visible out front, and he'd just hang around waiting. There was no escaping them anymore. They owned her life, and Ian's.

Jessie slowly unlocked the door and stood silently in the dark hall. Even without shoes, she stood about an inch taller than the inspector. Their eyes held for a long moment. All the hatred she could not feel for Ian's betrayal she lavished on Inspector Houghton. He was easy to hate.

'Good evening. May I come in?' Jessie stood to one side, flicked on the lights, and then preceded him into the living room. She stood in the centre of the room, facing him, and did not invite him to sit down.

'Well, Inspector? What now?' Her tone hid nothing.

'I thought we could have a little chat.'

'Oh? Is that usual?' she was frightened, but she was even more afraid to show it. What if he wanted to rape her? A real rape this time. What if . . . oh God . . . where was Ian?

'This is perfectly usual, Mrs. Clarke.'

They seemed to circle each other with their eyes, enemies from birth. A python and his prey. She didn't like her role. She feared him, but would not show it. He found her beautiful, but he didn't let that show either. He hated Ian for a number of reasons. That showed.

'Mind if I sit down?' Yes. Very much.

'Not at all.' She waved him to the couch and sat down in her usual chair.

'Lovely house you have, Mrs. Clarke. Have you lived here long?' He glanced around, seeming to take in all the details, while she fantasized about telling him to go fuck himself and scratching his eyes out. But now she knew that wasn't real. You might hate cops, but you didn't let your hostilities show. She was innocent, Ian was innocent, but she was terrified.

'Inspector, is this a formal interrogation or a social call? Our attorney told me today that I don't have to speak to anyone unless he's present.' She was watching the brown double-knit leg and the maroon sock, wondering if he was going to try to rape her. He was wearing a shiny mustard-coloured tie. She was beginning to feel nauseated, and suddenly panicked, wondering if she had taken the pill that morning. And then suddenly she looked at him and knew she'd kill him if he tried. She'd have to.

'No, you don't have to speak to anyone unless your attorney is presnt, Mrs. Clarke, but I have a few questions, and I thought it would be more pleasant for you to answer them here.' Big favour.

'I think I'd rather answer them in court.' But they both knew she didn't have to answer anything in court. She was the defendant's wife. Legally, she didn't have to testify.

'Suit yourself.' He stood up to leave and then stopped at the bar. 'You a drinker, too?' The question infuriated her.

'No, and neither is my husband.'

'Yeah, that's what I thought. He claims he was ripped

when he took the victim to the hotel. I figured he was lying, though. He doesn't look like a drinker.' Jessie's heart sank and her eyes filled with hatred. This sonofabitch was trying to trap her.

'Inspector, I'm asking you to leave. Now.'

Houghton turned to her then and searched her eyes with a look of feigned kindness. But his own eyes returned the anger of Jessie's. His voice was barely audible as he stood a foot away from her.

'What are you doing with a weak-kneed punk like him?'

'Get out of my house!' Her voice was as low as his and her whole body was trembling.

'What'll you do when he goes to the joint? Find another gigolo sweetheart like him? Believe me, sister, don't sweat it. They're a dime a dozen.'

'*Get out*!' The words were like two fists in his face, and he turned on his heel and walked to the door. He paused for a moment and looked back at her.

'See ya.'

The door closed behind him, and for the first time in her life Jessica wanted to kill.

He was back at ten that night, with two plainclothesmen and a search warrant, to look for weapons and drugs.

This time Houghton was straight-faced and businesslike, and he avoided her eyes for the entire hour they were there, digging into closets and drawers, unfolding her underwear, dumping her handbags on the bed, pouring out soap flakes, and spreading Ian's clothes and papers all over the living room.

They found nothing, and Jessie said nothing about it to Ian. Ever. It took her four and a half hours to get everything put away, and another two hours to stop sobbing. Her fears had been justified. They had raped her. Not in the way she had feared, but in another way. Photographs of her mother lay strewn all over her desk, her birth-control pills lay dumped out in the kitchen, half of them gone, to be tested at the lab. Her whole life was spread all over the house. It was her war now too. And she was ready to fight. That night had changed everything. Now they were *her* enemy too, not just Ian's.

And for the first time in seven years, Ian was not there to defend her. Not only that, but it was he who had put her face to face with this enemy. He had brought this down around her ears as well as his own. And she was helpless. It was Ian's fault. Now he was the enemy too.

CHAPTER VIII

Jessica waited with Martin Schwartz in the back rows of the courtroom until after ten. The docket was heavily overscheduled, and the court was running late. The procedures Jessie watched looked very dull. Most of the charges were rattled off by number, bails were arbitrarily set, and new faces were brought in. Ian finally arrived through a door leading in from the jail, accompanied by a guard on each side.

Martin walked to the front of the room, and the charges were, mercifully, read off by number, not description. Ian was asked if he understood what he was accused of, and he answered, gravely, in the affirmative.

The bail was set at twenty-five thousand dollars. Martin asked to have it reduced and the judge pondered the question while a female assistant D.A. jumped to her feet and objected. She felt that the matter before the court warranted a heavier bail. But the judge didn't agree. He lowered it to fifteen thousand, smacked his gavel, and had another man brought in. The preliminary hearing had been set for two weeks hence.

'Now what do we do?' Jessica whispered to Martin as he came back to her seat. Ian had already left the court and was back in the jail.

'Now you scare up fifteen hundred bucks to pay to a bailbondsman, and give him something worth fifteen thousand in collateral.'

'How do I do that?'

'Come on. I'll take you over myself.'

But Jesus . . . fifteen thousand? Now it suddenly hit her. Fifteen thousand. It was enormous. Could anything be worth that much money? Yes. Ian.

They went down to the lobby and across the street to one of a long row of neon-lit bail offices. They didn't look like nice places, and the one they walked into was no better than the rest. It reeked of cigar smoke, the ash-trays were full to overflowing, and two men were asleep on a couch, apparently waiting. A woman with teased yellow hair asked them their business and Martin explained. She called the jail and made a note of the charges while looking lengthily at Jessie. Jessie tried not to flinch.

'You'll have to put up the collateral. Do you own your own home?'

Jessie nodded, and explained the mortgage. 'And I own my own business as well.' She gave the woman the name and address of the boutique, the address of the house, and the name of the bank where they had their mortgage.

'What do you think your business is worth? What is it, anyway? A dress shop?' Jessie nodded, feeling degraded somehow, though she was not quite sure why. Maybe it was because the woman now knew what the charges were.

'Yes, it's a dress shop. And we have a fairly large inventory.' Why did she want to impress this idiot woman? But then she knew that it was because the woman held the key to Ian's bail. Martin Schwartz was standing to one side, watching the proceedings.

'We'll have to call your bank. Come back at four o'clock.'

'And then can you bail him?' Oh God, please, can you bail him? The panic was coming back in her throat again, thick and sweet and bitter, like bile.

'We'll bail him depending on what your bank says about the house and the shop,' she said flatly. 'Do you use the same bank for both?' Jessie nodded, looking grey. 'Good. That'll save time. Bring the fifteen hundred with you when you come back. In cash.'

'In cash?'

'Cash or a bank cheque. No personal cheques.'

'Thank you.'

They went back to the street and Jessie took a long breath of fresh air. It felt like years since she'd had any. She breathed again and looked at Martin.

'What happens to people who don't have the money?'

'They don't bail.'

'And then what?'

'They stay in custody till after the verdict.'

'Even if they're innocent? They stay in jail all that time?'

'You don't know if they're innocent until after the trial.'

'What the hell ever happened to "innocent until proven guilty"?'

He shrugged and looked away, remaining silent. It had depressed him to be in the bail office. He rarely went to bailbondsmen with clients. But Ian had asked him to and he had promised. It seemed odd to treat such a tall, independent-looking woman as though she were frail and helpless. But he suspected that Ian was right: beneath the coat of armour, she hid a terrifying vulnerability. He wondered if that armour would crack before this was over. That was all they needed.

'What do poor people do about lawyers?' Jesus. He had enough headaches without playing social worker.

'They get public defenders, Jessica. And we have plenty to think about ourselves right now, without worrying about poor people, don't you think? Why don't you just get yourself to the bank and get this over with?'

'Okay. I'm sorry.'

'Don't be. The system is lousy, and I know it. But it's not set up for the comfort of the poor. Just be grateful that you're not one of them right now, and let it go at that.'

'That's hard to do, Martin.'

He shook his head and gave her a small smile. 'Are you going to the bank?'

'Yes, sir.'

'Good. Do you want me to come with you?'

'Of course not. Is baby-sitting service always part of the deal, or did Ian strong-arm you into that?'

'I . . . no . . . oh, for Chrissake. Just go to the bank. And let me know when you get him out. Or before that, if there's anything I can do.'

How about lending us fifteen thousand bucks, baby? She smiled, said good-bye, and walked slowly to her car. She still didn't have any idea of how she'd come up with the money. And what the hell would she tell the bank? The truth. And she'd beg them if she had to. Fifteen thousand . . . it looked like the top of Mount Everest.

After six cigarettes and half an hour of agonizing conversation with the bank manager, Jessica took out a personal loan for fifteen hundred dollars against the car. And they assured her that all would be in order when the bail office called. There was a look of astonishment on the bank manager's face throughout the conversation, and he tried desperately to conceal it. Unsuccessfully. And Jessica had not even told him what the charges were, only that Ian was in jail. She prayed that the bail office wouldn't tell them the charges either, and that if they did he would keep his mouth shut. He had already sworn to her that he would see that everything remained confidential. And at least she had the fifteen hundred dollars . . . she had it . . . she had it! And her house and the business were worth ten times the collateral that she needed. But somehow she still didn't feel that it was enough. What if they still wouldn't let Ian out? And then she thought of it. The safe-deposit box.

'Mrs. Clarke?'

She didn't answer. She just sat there.

'Mrs. Clarke? Was there something else?'

'Sorry. Oh . . . I . . . was just thinking of something. Yes, I . . . I think I'd like to get into my vault today.'

'Do you have the key with you?'

She nodded. She kept it on her key chain. She reached into her bag and handed it to him.

'I'll have Miss Lopez open the box for you.'

Jessie followed him pensively, and then found herself following Miss Lopez, whom she did not know. And then she was standing in front of her safe-deposit box and Miss

Lopez was looking at her, holding the box. It was a large one.

'Would you like to go into a room with this?'

'I . . . I . . . yes. Thank you.' She shouldn't have done it. She didn't need it. It was a mistake . . . no . . . but what if the house and Lady J weren't enough? She knew she wasn't making sense now. She was panicking. But it was better to be sure . . . to be . . . for Ian. But it was all so painful. And now she had to face it alone.

Miss Lopez left her in a small, sterile room with a brown Formica desk and a black vinyl chair. On the wall hung an ugly print of Venice that looked as though it had been cut from the top of a candy box. And she was alone with the box. Jessie opened it carefully and took out three large brown leather boxes and two faded red suede jewellery cases. There was another, smaller box at the bottom, in faded blue. The blue box was filled with Jake's few treasures. The studs Father had given him on his twenty-first birthday, his school ring, his Navy ring. Junk, mostly, but very Jake.

The brown leather boxes contained the real treasures. Letters her parents had written to each other over the years. Letters they had exchanged while her father was in the service during the war. Poems her mother had written to her father. Photographs. Locks of her hair and Jake's. Treasures. All the things that had mattered. Now, all the things that hurt most.

She opened the blue box first and smiled through a veil of tears as she saw Jake's trinkets lying helter-skelter on the beige chamois. It still held the faintest hint of Jake's smell. She remembered teasing him about the high-school ring. She had told him it was hideous, and he had been so damn proud of it. And now there it was. She slipped it on her finger. It was much too big for her. It would have been too big for Ian too. Jake had been almost six foot five.

She turned to the brown boxes then. She knew their touch so well. They were engraved with her parents' initials, tiny gold letters in the lower right-hand corners. Each box identical. They were a family tradition. In the first box she found a picture of the four of them taken one Easter. She had been eleven or twelve; Jake had been seven. It was really more than she could face. She closed the box quietly and turned to what she had come for.

The red suede jewellery cases. It was incredible, really. She was actually going to take her mother's jewellery with her. It was so precious to her, so sacred, so much still her mother's that Jessie had worn none of it in all these years. And now she was willing to leave it in the hands of strangers. For Ian.

She carefully unfolded the cases and looked at the long row of rings. A ruby in an old setting that had been her grandmother's. Two handsome jade rings her father had brought back from the Far East. The emerald ring her mother had wanted so much and had gotten for her fiftieth birthday. The diamond engagement ring . . . and her wedding ring, her 'real' one, the worn, thin gold band she had always worn, always preferred to the emerald-and-diamond one Jessie's father had bought to match the emerald ring. There were two simple gold chain bracelets. A gold watch with tiny diamonds carefully set around the face. And a large handsome sapphire brooch with diamonds set around it that had also been Jessie's grandmother's.

The second case held three strands of perfectly matched pearls, pearl earrings, and a small pair of diamond earrings that she and Jake had bought her together the year before she'd died. It was all there. Jessie's stomach turned over as she looked at it. She knew she wouldn't really be able to leave it with the bailbondsman, but at least she had it if she needed it. Two days before she wouldn't have considered such a thing, but now . . .

She put the rest of the boxes back into the metal vault and left the room almost two hours after she had entered it. The bank was almost ready to close.

When she went back to Bryant Street the woman was eating a dripping cheeseburger over the afternoon paper. 'Got the money?' She looked up and spoke to Jessica with her mouth full.

Jessica nodded. 'Did you talk to the bank about the collateral?' She had had enough, and wading through the private agony that safe-deposit box represented had topped it off. She wanted the nightmare to end. Now.

'What bank?' The woman's face wore an unexpectedly blank expression, and Jessie clenched her hands to keep from screaming.

'The California Union Trust Bank. I wanted to bail my husband out tonight.'

'What were the charges?' For Chrissake, what was this woman trying to *do* to her? She remembered that Jessica was due back with some money—how could she have forgotten the rest? Or was she playing a game? Well, if she was, fuck her.

'The charges were rape and assault.' She almost shouted the words.

'Did you own any property?' Oh, shit.

'For God's sake, we went through all that this morning, and you were going to call my bank about my business and our mortgage. I was here with our attorney, filled out papers, and . . .'

'Okay. What's your name?'

'Clarke. With an "E." '

'Yeah. Here it is.' She pulled out the form with two greasy fingers. 'Can't bail him now, though.'

'Why not?' Jessie's stomach turned over again.

'Too late to call the bank.'

'Shit. Now what?'

'Come back in the morning.' Sure, while Ian sat in jail for another night. Wonderful. Tears of frustration choked her throat, but there was nothing she could do except go home and come back in the morning.

'You want to talk to the boss?'

Jessie's face lit up.

'Now?'

'Yeah. He's here. In the back.'

'Fabulous. Tell him I'm here.' Oh God, please . . . please let him be human . . . please . . .

The man emerged from the back room picking his teeth with a dirty finger that boasted a small gold ring with a large pink diamond. He had a beer can in his other hand. He was wearing jeans and a T-shirt, and had a lot of curly black hair on his arms and at the neck of the shirt; his hair was almost an Afro. And he wasn't much older than Jessie. He grinned when he saw her, gave a last stab at his teeth, then removed his hand from his mouth and extended it for her to shake. She shook it, but with difficulty.

'How do you do. I'm Jessica Clarke.'

'Barry York. What can I do you for?'

'I'm trying to bail my husband.'

'From what? What are the charges? Hey . . . wait a minute. Let's go in my office. You want a beer?' Actually, she did. But not with him. She was hot and tired and thirsty and fed up and scared, but she didn't want to drink anything with Barry York, not even water.

'No thanks.'

'Coffee?'

'No, really. I'm fine, but thanks.' He was trying to be decent. One had to give him credit for that. He led her into a small, dingy office with pictures of nude women on the walls, sat down in a swivel chair, put a green eye-shade on his head, switched on a stereo, and grinned at her.

'We don't see many people like you, Mrs. Clarke.'

'I . . . no . . . thank you.'

'So what's with the old man? What's the beef? Drunk driving?'

'No, rape.' Barry whistled lengthily while Jessie stared at his stomach. At least he was honest about what he thought. 'That's a bitch. What's the bail?'

'Fifteen thousand.'

'Bad news.'

'Well, that's why I'm here.' Good news for you, Barry, baby; maybe you can even buy yourself a gold toothpick after this, with a diamond tip. 'I spoke to the young lady out there earlier today, and she was to call my bank, and . . .'

'And?' His face hardened slightly.

'She forgot.'

Barry shook his head. 'She didn't forget. We don't do bonds that high.'

'You don't?'

He shook his head again. 'Not usually.' Jessica thought she was going to cry. 'I guess she just didn't want to tell you.'

'So I lost a day, and my husband is still in jail, and my bank is expecting to hear from you, and . . . now what, Mr. York? What the hell do I do now?'

'How about some dinner?' He turned the stereo down and patted her hand. His breath smelled like pastrami and garlic. He stank.

Jessica simply looked at him and stood up. 'You know, my attorney must be all wrong about this place, Mr. York. And I have every intention of telling him just that.'

'Who's your attorney?'

'Martin Schwartz. He was here with me this morning.'

'Look, Mrs. . . . what's your name again?'

'Clarke.'

'Mrs. Clarke. Why don't you sit down and we'll talk a little business.'

'Now or after dinner? Or after we listen to a few more records?'

He smiled. 'You like the records? I thought that was a nice touch.'

He turned the stereo up again and Jessie didn't know whether to laugh, cry, or scream. It was obvious that she'd never get Ian out of jail. Not at this rate. 'You want to have dinner?'

'Yes, Mr. York. With my husband. What are the chances of your getting my husband out of jail so I can have dinner with him?'

'Tonight? No way. I've got to talk to your bank first.'

'That's exactly where I left it at twelve-thirty this afternoon.'

'Yeah, well, I'm sorry. And I'll take care of it myself in the morning, but I can't do anything after banking hours, not on a bond the size of the one you're talking about. What are you putting up as collateral?'

'My business and/or my house. That's up to you. I'm willing to put up either one or both. Or I was. But I have another idea.' It was crazy, it was stupid, it was immoral, it was wrong, but she was so goddam fed up, she had to. She reached into her bag and pulled out the two cases with her mother's jewellery in them. 'What about these?'

Barry York sat down very quietly and didn't say a word for almost ten minutes.

'Nice.'

'Better than that. The emerald and the diamond rings are very fine stones. And the sapphire brooch is worth a great deal of money. So are the pearls.'

'Yeah. Probably so. But the problem is I don't know nothing until I take them to a jeweller. I still can't get the old man out tonight.' The old man . . . asshole. 'Very nice jewellery, though. Where'd you get it?'

We stole it. 'It's my mother's.'

'She know the old man's in the can?'

'Hardly, Mr. York. She's dead.'

'Oh, I'm sorry. Listen, I'll take this to the appraiser first thing tomorrow morning. I'll call your bank. We'll get the old man out by noon. Swear, if the stuff is good. I can't do anything before that. But by noon, if everything is in order. Do you have my fee?'

Yes, darling, in pennies. 'Yes.'

'Okay, then we're all set.'

'Mr. York, why can't you just take all the jewellery tonight and let him come home? He won't go anywhere, and we'll get all this financial nonsense straightened out tomorrow. If your assistant had called the bank when she said she would . . .'

He was shaking his head, picking his teeth again and holding up his other hand. 'I'd like to. But I can't. That's all. I can't. My business is at stake. I'll take care of it first thing in the morning. I swear. Be here at ten-thirty and we'll get everything done.'

'Fine.' She rose to her feet, feeling as though the weight of the world were resting on her shoulders. She folded up the two suede cases and put them back in her bag.

'You're not leaving me those?'

'Nope. That was just if I could get him out tonight. I thought you'd recognize their value. Otherwise, I'd much rather put up my house and the business.'

'Okay. Yeah.' But he didn't look pleased. 'That's a hell of a big bond, you know.' She nodded tiredly.

'Don't worry. It's a nice house and a good business, and he's a decent man. He won't run away on you. You won't lose a dime.'

'You'd be surprised who runs away.'

'I'll see you at ten-thirty, Mr. York.' She held out a hand and he shook it, smiling again.

'You sure about dinner? You look tired. Maybe some food would do you good. A little wine, a little dancing . . . hell, enjoy yourself a little before the old man gets home. And look at it this way, if he got busted for rape, you gotta know he wasn't just out with the boys.'

'Good night, Mr. York.'

She walked quietly out of the door, out to her car, and drove home.

She was asleep on the couch half an hour later, and she didn't wake up until nine the next morning. When she did, she felt as though she had died the night before. And she had a terrifying case of the shakes.

It was all beginning to take its toll. The ever deepening circles under her eyes now looked irreparable, the eyes themselves seemed to be shrinking, and she noticed that she was beginning to lose weight. She smoked six cigarettes, drank two cups of coffee, played with a piece of toast, and called the boutique and told them to forget about her again today. She arrived back at Yorktowne Bonding at ten-thirty. On the dot.

There were two new people at the desk—a girl with dyed black hair the colour of military boots who was snapping bubble gum, and a bearded young man with a Mexican accent. This time Jessie asked for Mr. York right away.

'He's expecting me.' The two clerks looked up as though they had never heard the words before.

He appeared two minutes later in dirty white shorts and

a navy blue T-shirt, carrying a copy of *Playboy* and a tennis racket.

'You play?' Oh, Jesus.

'Sometimes. Did you talk to the bank?'

He smiled, looking pleased. 'Come into my office. Coffee?'

'No, thanks.' She was beginning to feel as though the nightmare would never end. She would simply spend the rest of her life ricocheting among the Inspector Houghtons and Barry Yorks, the courtroom and jails, the banks and . . . it was endless. Just when it seemed about to end, there would be another false door. There was no way out. She was almost sure of it now. And Ian was only a myth anyway. Someone she had made up and never known. The keeper of the Holy Grail.

'You know, you look tired. Do you eat right?'

'I eat splendidly. But my husband is in jail, Mr. York, and I would very much like to get him out. What are the chances of that, in the immediate future?'

'Excellent.' He beamed. 'I talked to the bank and everything's in order. You put up the house and agree to a lien on your earnings at the boutique if he defaults. And we keep the emerald ring and sapphire brooch for you.'

'What?' He had made it sound as if he were ordering lunch for her, but he had caught her attention with the mention of her mother's jewellery. 'I don't think you understood, Mr. York. The house and the business are all I'm putting up. I told you last night that I was only offering my mother's jewellery if I could get him out then, without your calling the bank and all. Sort of a guarantee.'

'Yeah. Well, I'd feel better with that same guarantee now.'

'Well, I wouldn't.'

'How would your husband feel staying in jail?'

'Mr. York, isn't there a law against bailbondsmen taking too much as collateral?' Martin had told her about it.

'Are you accusing me of being dishonest?' Oh, God, she was going to blow it . . . oh no . . .

'No. Look, please . . .'

'Look, baby, I'm not gonna do business with some broad

who calls me dishonest. I do you a favour and stick my ass out on a limb for your old man on a fifteen-thousand-dollar bond, and you call me a thief. I mean, look, I don't gotta take that shit from no one.'

'I'm sorry.' The tears were burning her eyes again. She was beginning to wonder if she'd live through this. And then he looked over at her and shrugged.

'All right. I'll tell you what. We'll just keep the ring. You can take the brooch. Does that sound any better?'

'Fine.' It sounded stinking, but she didn't care anymore. It didn't matter. It didn't even matter if Ian ran away and they took the house and the business and the car and the emerald ring. Nothing mattered.

York managed to make the forms take twice as long as necessary, and to slide a hand across her breast as he reached for another pen. She looked up into his face and he smiled and told her she'd be beautiful if she ate right, and how he'd had a tall girlfriend in high school. A girl named Mona. Jessica just nodded and went on signing her name. Finally all the paperwork was done. He bit the end off a long thin cigar and picked up the phone to notify the jail.

'I'll have Bernice take you across the street, Jessica.' He had decided to call her by her first name. 'And listen, if you ever need any help, just call. I'll keep in touch.' She prayed that he wouldn't, and shook his hand before leaving his office. She felt as though she would stumble on the way out. She had reached her limit. Days ago.

By the time Barry York had delegated the gum-chewing clerk to take Jessie across the street to bail Ian, it was almost noon. To Jessie it felt like the middle of the night. She was confused and exhausted and everything was beginning to blur. She was living in an unreal world filled with evil, leering people.

The woman he'd called Bernice took charge of the papers, shuffled them for a moment, and then walked across the street with Jessie and into the Hall of Justice. She slipped the sheaf of papers Jessie and Barry York had signed into a slot in a window on the second floor, and then turned to look at Jessica for a moment.

'You going to stick by your old man?'

'I beg your pardon?'

'You going to stay with your husband?'

'Yes . . . of course . . . why?' She was feeling confused again. And why was this woman asking her that?

'That's a hell of a beef, sister. And what's a good-looking chick like you want with a loser like him? He's going to cost you a bundle on this one.' She shook her head and snapped her gum twice.

'He's worth it.'

The girl shrugged and waved at the bank of elevators. 'You can go up to the jail now. We're all through.' No, lady, *I'm* all through. That's different. The clerk departed with a last snap of her gum and headed down a stairway.

Jessica reached the jail a few moments later and had to ring a small buzzer to bring a guard to the door.

'Yeah? It's not visiting time yet.'

'I'm here to bail out my husband.'

'What's his name?'

'Ian Clarke.' You know, the famous rapist. 'Yorktowne Bonding just called about it.'

'I'll check.' Check? Check what? With the house, the business, and Mom's emerald ring on the line, you're going to check, mister? Well, screw you. And Yorktowne Bonding . . . and Inspector Houghton . . . and . . . Ian too? She wasn't really sure anymore. She didn't know what she felt. She was angry at him, but not for what he had done, only for not being there when she needed him so badly.

She waited at the door for almost half an hour, stupefied, dazed, leaning against the wall and hardly knowing why. What if she never saw him again? But suddenly the door opened and he stood there facing her. He was unshaven, bedraggled, filthy, and exhausted. But he was free. Everything she owned was riding on him now. And he was free. She sank slowly towards him with an unfamiliar whimpering sound, and he led her gently into the elevator.

"It's all right, baby . . . it's all right. Everything's going to be all right, Jess . . . sshhh . . .' It was Ian. Actually, really, honestly Ian. And he held her so gently and almost carried her down to the car. She couldn't take any more and he knew it. He didn't know all the details of what had been happening, but when he saw the bail papers and noticed the mention of her mother's emerald ring, he understood much more than she could tell him.

'It's okay, baby . . . everything's going to be fine.'

She clutched him blindly as they stood beside the car, the tears streaming down her cheeks, her face in a rictus of shock and despair, the same little squeaking noises escaping from her between sobs.

'Jessie . . . baby . . . I love you.' He held her tightly, and then quietly drove her home.

CHAPTER IX

'What are you doing today, darling?'

Jessie poured Ian a second cup of coffee at breakfast and glanced at the clock. It was almost nine and she hadn't been to the boutique for two days. She felt as though she had been gone for a month, existing in a kind of twilight zone all her own. A never-ending nightmare, but it was over now. Ian was home. She had spent most of the day before asleep in his arms. And he looked like Ian again. Clean, shaven, a little more rested. He was wearing grey slacks and a wine-coloured turtleneck. Every time she looked at him she wanted to touch him to make sure he was real.

'Are you going to write today?'

'I don't know yet. I think I might just spend the day feeling good.' But he didn't ask her to play hookey with him. He knew she had to work. She had done enough for him in the past few days. He couldn't ask for more.

'I wish I could stay home with you.' She looked at him wistfully over her coffee and he patted her hand.

'I'll pick you up for lunch.'

'I have an idea. Why don't you hang around the boutique today?'

He watched her eyes and knew what she was thinking.

She had been like that for months after Jake had died. That terror that if he left her sight, he'd vanish.

'You wouldn't get any work done, my love. But I'll be around. I'll be right here most of the time.' But what about the rest of the time? She reached over and held his hand. Nothing was said. There was nothing to say. 'I thought maybe I'd talk to a couple of people about work.'

'No!' She pulled back her hand and her eyes darted fire. 'No, Ian! Please.'

'Jessica, be reasonable. Have you thought of what this disaster is costing us? Costing *you*, to be more exact? And this is as good a time as any to get a job. Nothing exotic, just something to bring a little money in.'

'And what happens when you have to start making court appearances? And during the trial? Just how much good do you think you'll be to anyone then?' She held tightly to his hand again and he saw the pain in her eyes. It was going to take months for the desperation to pass.

'Well, what exactly do you expect me to do, Jess?'

'Finish the book.'

'And let you pick up the tab for this mess?'

She nodded. 'We can straighten it out later, if you want to. But I don't really give a damn, Ian. What does it matter who signs the cheques?'

'It matters to me.' It always has mattered, always will matter. But he knew, too, that he'd never be able to concentrate on anything while this was hanging over his head. The trial . . . the trial . . . it was all he could think of. While she had slept all those hours the previous afternoon, it had kept running through his mind . . . the trial. He was in no frame of mind to get a job. 'We'll see.'

'I love you.' There were tears in her eyes again, and he tweaked the end of her nose.

'If you get dewy-eyed on me once more, Mrs. Clarke, I'm going to drag you back to bed and really give you something to cry about.' She laughed in response and poured some more coffee.

'I just can't believe you're home. It was so incredibly awful while you were gone . . . it was . . . it was like . . .' The words caught in her throat.

'It was probably like peace and quiet for a change, and you were too silly to enjoy it. Hell, you didn't think I'd stay down there forever, did you? I mean, even for a writer that kind of living research gets stale after a while.'

'Jerk.' But she was smiling now; she had nothing to fear.

'Want me to drive you to work?'

'As a matter of fact, I'd love it.' She beamed as she put the cups in the sink and grabbed her orange suede coat off the back of a chair. She was wearing it over well-tailored jeans and a beige cashmere sweater. She looked like Jessie again—everywhere except around the eyes. She slid the dark glasses into place and smiled at him. 'I think I'd better hang on to these for a couple of days. I still look like I've been on a two-week drunk.'

'You look beautiful and I love you.' He pinched her behind as they headed out the front door, and she leaned backward to kiss him haphazardly over one shoulder. 'You even smell nice.'

'Nothing but the best. Eau de Mille Pieds.' She said it with a broad grin and he groaned.

'Oh, for Chrissake.' It was one of their oldest jokes. Water of a thousand feet.

She pointed out Astrid's house to him on their way to the boutique, and told him about her visit to the shop.

'She seems like a nice woman. Very quiet and pleasant.'

'Hell, I'd be quiet and pleasant too, with that kind of money.'

'Ian!' But she grinned at him and ran a hand through his hair. It felt so good to be sitting next to him again, to be looking at his profile as he drove, to feel the skin on his neck with her mouth as she kissed him. She had awakened a dozen times during the night to make sure he was still there.

'I'll come by for you around twelve. Okay?'

She looked at him for a moment before nodding. 'You'll be here? For sure?'

'Oh, baby . . . I'll be here. Promise.' He took her in his arms and she held him so tightly that it hurt. He knew she was thinking of the day he'd been arrested and hadn't shown up for lunch. 'Be a big girl.' She grinned and hopped out of the car and blew him a last kiss before running up the steps of the shop.

Ian lit a cigarette as he drove away, and glanced over to look at the ships on the bay. It was a beautiful day. Indian summer was passing, and it was not as warm as it had been a few days before, but the sky was a bright blue and there was a gentle breeze. It made him think back to that day five days before. It felt like five years before. He still couldn't understand it.

He paused at a stop sign, and another thought came to mind. The emerald ring Jessie had put up as bail. It still astounded him. He knew how she felt about her mother's things. She wouldn't even wear them. They were sacred, the last relics of a long-demolished shrine. And that ring meant more to her than any of the other pieces. He had watched her slip it on her finger once while her hand trembled out of control. She had put the ring back in the case, and never gone to the vault again. And now she had turned it over to a bailbondsman, for him. It told him something that nothing else ever had. It was crazy, but he felt as though he loved her more than he had before all this had begun, and maybe Jessie had learned something too. Maybe they knew what they had now. Maybe they'd take better care of it. He knew one thing. His days of discreet interludes were over. Forever. All of a sudden he had a wife. More of a wife than he had ever known he had. What more could he want? A child, perhaps, but he had resigned himself to the absence of children. He was happy enough with just Jessie.

'Morning, ladies.' Jessie strolled into the store with a quiet smile on her face. And Katsuko looked up from the desk.

'Well, look who's here. And on a Saturday, yet. We were beginning to think you'd found a better job.'

'No such luck.'

'Is everything okay?'

'Yes. Everything's okay.' Jessica nodded slowly and Katsuko knew that it was. Jessie was herself again.

'I'm glad.' Katsuko handed her a cup of coffee and Jessie perched on the corner of the chrome-and-glass desk.

'Where's Zina?'

'In the back, checking the stock. Mrs. Bonner came back looking for you yesterday. She bought one of the new wine velvet skirts.'

'It must have looked great on her. Did she try it with the cream satin shirt?'

'Yup. Bought them both, and the new green velvet pant-suit. That lady must have money burning holes in her pockets.' Yeah. And loneliness burning holes in her heart. Jessie had had a taste of it now. She knew.

'She'll be back,' Katsuko added.

'I hope so. Even if she doesn't buy. I like her. Anything taking shape for the fashion show?'

'I had a few ideas yesterday, Jessie, I made some notes and left them on your desk.'

'I'll go take a look.' She stretched lazily and wandered towards her office, carrying her coffee. It was a slow morning, and she felt as if she had come back after a very long absence, a long illness maybe. She felt slow and careful and frail. And everything looked suddenly different. The shop looked so sweet, the two girls so pretty . . . Ian so beautiful . . . the sky so blue . . . everything seemed better and more. She read her mail, paid some bills, changed the window, and discussed the fashion show with Katsuko while Zina waited on customers. The morning sped by, and Ian was there five minutes before noon. With an armload of roses. The delicate salmon ones Jessie loved best.

'Ian! They're fabulous!' There were about three dozen, and she could see an awkward square lump in his jacket pocket. He was spoiling her and she loved it. He smiled at her and headed toward her office.

'Can I see you for a minute, Mrs. Clarke?'

'Yes, sir. For three dozen roses you can see me for several weeks!' The two girls laughed and Jessie followed Ian into her office. He closed the door gently and grinned at her.

'Have a nice morning?'

'You brought me back to this secluded spot to ask me if

I had a nice morning?' He was grinning and she was starting to giggle. 'Come on, tell the truth. Is it bigger than a breadbox?'

'What?'

'The surprise you bought me, of course.'

'What surprise? I buy you roses and you want more! You greedy spoiled miserable . . .' But he was looking too pleased with himself to convince even Jessie. 'Oh . . . here.' He pulled the box out of his pocket and grinned from ear to ear. It was a solid chunk of gold bracelet; inside it was engraved ALL MY LOVE, IAN. He had literally stood over the jewellers all morning while they did the engraving. It was no time to spend money, but he'd known that she needed something like that, and it had suddenly come to him as he'd sat down to work. It was a beautiful bracelet, and the proportions were just right for her hand. It had cost him the last of his private savings.

'Oh, darling . . . it's beautiful.' She slipped it onto her wrist and it held there. 'Wow. It's just perfect! Oh Ian . . . you're crazy!'

'I happen to be madly in love with you.'

'I'm beginning to think you struck oil, too. You spent a fortune this morning.' But there was no edge to her voice, only pleasure, and Ian shrugged. 'Wait till I show the girls!' She planted a kiss on the corner of his mouth, opened the door, and bumped into Zina, who was walking past to the stockroom. 'Look at my bracelet!'

'My, my! Does that mean you're engaged to the handsome man with the roses?' She giggled and winked at Ian.

'Oh, shut up. Isn't it super?'

'It's gorgeous. And all I want to know is where you find another one like him.'

'Try Central Casting.' Ian looked over Jessie's shoulder with a grin.

'I might just do that.' Zina disappeared into the stockroom, and, with a look of victory, Jessie showed her new bracelet to Katsuko. A few minutes later, she and Ian were on their way out the door to lunch.

'Boy, I love my bracelet!' She was like a child with a new toy, and held up her arm to look at it in the sunlight.

'Darling, it's just gorgeous! And how did you get them to engrave it so fast?'

'At gunpoint, of course. How else?'

'Oh, for Chrissake . . . you know, you really have a lot of class.'

'For a rapist.' But he was smiling when he said it.

'Ian!'

'Yes, my love?' He kissed her and she laughed as she got into the car. He had more style than any man she knew.

They went to the movies that night, and slept late on Sunday morning. It was another warm blue day, with puffy, pasted-on-looking clouds that rolled along high in the sky, looking like painted scenery.

'Want to go to the beach, Mrs. Clarke?' He stretched lazily on his side of the bed and then reached over and kissed her. She liked the feel of his beard stubble against her cheek. It was rough but it didn't quite hurt.

'I'd love to. What time is it?'

'Almost noon.'

'You're lying. It must be nine.'

'I am not. Open your eyes and take a look.'

'I can't. I'm still asleep.'

But he nibbled her neck and made her laugh and her eyes flew open.

'Stop that!'

'I will not. Get up and make me breakfast.'

'Slave driver. Haven't you ever heard of women's lib?' She lay on her back sleepily and yawned.

'What's that?'

'Women's lib. It says husbands have to cook breakfast on Sunday . . . but . . . on the other hand.' She looked at her bracelet again with a broad smile. 'It doesn't say you have to give your wife such gorgeous jewellery. So maybe I'll make you breakfast.'

'Beulah Big Heart, don't knock yourself out.'

'I won't. Fried eggs okay?' She lit a cigarette and sat up.

'I have a better idea.'

'The Fairmont for brunch?' She grinned at him and flashed the bracelet again.

'No. I'll help. You're too busy waving your bracelet at me to make us a decent breakfast anyway. How about a smoked-oyster-and-cheese omelette?' He looked enchanted with the combination and Jessie made a terrible face.

'Yerchk! Can we skip the smoked oysters?'

'Why not skip the cheese?'

'How about skipping the omelette?'

'The Fairmont for breakfast, then?'

'Ian, you're crazy . . . but I love you.' She nibbled at his thigh and he ran a hand down the smoothness of her spine.

It was another hour before they got out of bed. Even their lovemaking was different now. There was an odd combination of desperation and gratitude, of 'Oh God, I love you' mixed with 'Let's pretend everything's better than normal'. It wasn't, but the pretence helped. A little. Their motors were still racing a little too fast.

'Are we or are we not going to the beach today?' He sat up in bed, his blond hair tousled like a boy's.

'Sounds fine to me, but I still haven't been fed yet.'

'Aww . . . poor baby. You didn't want my smoked-oyster omelette.'

She tugged at a lock of his hair. 'I prefer what I got instead.'

'Shame on you.'

She stuck out her tongue at him, got out of bed, and headed for the kitchen.

'Where are you going bare-assed like that?'

'To the kitchen, to make breakfast. Any objection?'

'Nope. Need a voyeur on hand?'

A minute later she heard the garden door slam and then saw him reappear in the kitchen, wearing a blanket around his waist and carrying a mixed bouquet of her petunias.

'For the lady of the house.'

'Sorry, she's out. Can I have them instead?' She kissed him gently and took the flowers from his hand and set them down on the drainboard as he took her into his arms and let the blanket fall to the floor.

'Darling, I happen to love you madly, but if you don't

stop, the bacon will burn and we'll never get to the beach.'

'Do you care?' They were both smiling and the bacon was splattering furiously while the eggs began to bubble.

'No. But we might as well eat while it's ready. Damn.' He patted her behind and she turned off the flame and served scrambled eggs, bacon, toast, orange juice and coffee. Still naked, they sat down to breakfast.

They didn't get to the beach until almost three, but it was still a beautiful day and the sun stayed warm until six. They had a fish dinner in Sausalito on the way home, and he bought her a silly little dog made out of seashells.

'I love it. Now I feel like a tourist.'

'I thought you should have something really expensive to remember this evening with.' They were in high spirits as they crossed the bridge going home, but his words struck her oddly. Suddenly they were buying souvenirs and clutching at memories.

'Hey, sweetheart, how's the book coming?'

'Better than I want to admit. Don't ask me yet.'

'For real?'

'For real.'

She looked at him, pleased. He looked almost proud of himself and a little bit afraid to be.

'Have you sent any of it to your agent yet?'

'No, I want to wait till I finish a few more chapters before I do that. But I think this one is good. Maybe even very good.' He said it with a solemnity that touched her. He hadn't sounded like that about his work in years. Not since the fables, and they had been very good. Not very profitable, but definitely good. The critics had certainly agreed, even if the public hadn't.

On the way home, they stopped outside the yacht club near the bridge and turned off the lights and the motor. It was nice to sit and watch the water lap at a small lip of beach while the foghorns bleated softly in the distance. They were both oddly tired, as though each day were an endless journey. Their few days of trauma had taken a heavy toll. She noticed it in the heavy way he slept now, and she herself felt tired all the time, no matter how happy she was again. There was a new passion, too. A new need, a new hunger for each other, as though they must stock up for a long empty winter. They had rough times ahead. This was just the beginning.

'Want to go out for an ice cream cone?' There was a restless look around his eyes.

'Honestly? No. I'm bushed.'

'Yeah. Me too. And I want to do some reading tonight. The chapter I just finished.'

'Can I read some too?'

'Sure.' He looked pleased as he started the car and headed for home. It was funny how neither of them wanted to go home. The stop near the yacht club, the offer of an ice cream cone—what was the lurking demon they feared at home? Jessica wondered; but she knew who her private demon was. Inspector Houghton. She constantly expected him to jump out at her and take Ian back into custody. She had thought about it all day at the beach, wondering if he would spring from behind a dune and try to spirit Ian away. She hadn't said anything to Ian. Neither of them ever spoke of his arrest now. It was all either of them could think of, and the only thing they wouldn't talk about.

He was stretched out in front of the fire reading his manuscript when she decided that she had to remind him. She hated to bring it up, but somebody had to.

'Don't forget about tomorrow, love.' She said it softly, regretfully.

'Huh?' He had been deep into his work.

'I said don't forget about tomorrow.'

'What's tomorrow?' He looked blank.

'We have a ten o'clock appointment with Martin Schwartz.' She tried to make it sound like a double appointment with the hairdresser, but it didn't come off like that. Ian looked up at her and didn't say a word. His eyes said it all.

CHAPTER X

The meeting with Martin Schwartz was sobering. Sitting there with him, having to discuss the charges, they couldn't hide from it anymore. Jessica felt sick as she sat and listened. It was real now. She even felt sick thinking of the security she had put up. It came home to her now. She had put everything on the line. The house. The shop's profits. Even the emerald ring. Everything . . . Jesus . . . and what if Ian panicked and ran? What if . . . my God . . . she'd lose it all. She looked at him, feeling a lump rise in her throat, and tried to concentrate on what was being said. She almost couldn't hear. She just kept thinking of the fact that she needed one man so desperately that she had given all for him. And now what would happen?

Martin explained the preliminary hearing to them, and they agreed to hire an investigator to see what could be learned of the 'victim'. Plenty, they hoped, and all of it unsavoury. They were not going to be kind to Miss Margaret Burton. Destroying her was Ian's only way out.

'There's got to be a reason for it though, Ian. Think about it. Carefully. Did you rough her up in some way? Sexually? Verbally? Humiliate her? Hurt her?' Martin looked at Ian pointedly, and Jessie looked away. She hated the uncomfortable look on Ian's face. 'Ian?' And then Martin looked at her. 'Jessie, maybe you ought to let us have this out alone for a few moments.'

'Sure.' It was a relief to leave the room. Ian didn't look up as she left. They were down to the nitty-gritty now. Of who had done what to whom, where, how, for how long, and how often. He died thinking of what Jessie would hear in court at the trial.

She wandered the carpeted halls, looking at prints on the wall, smoking, alone with her own thoughts, until she found a small love seat placed near a window with the same splendid view as the one from Martin's office. She had a lot to think about.

A secretary came to get her half an hour later and escorted her back to Martin's office. Ian looked harassed and Martin was scowling. Jessie tried to make light of it.

'Did I miss all the good parts?' But her smile was forced and they didn't try to return it.

'According to Ian, there were no "good" parts. It must have something to do with a personal grudge.'

'Against Ian? Why? Did you know her?' She turned to her husband with a look of surprise. She had understood that the woman was a stranger to him.

'No. I didn't know her. But Martin means that she was out to hurt someone, anyone, maybe just a man, and I came along at the wrong time.'

'You can say that again.'

'I just hope we can prove it, Ian. Green ought to come up with something on her.'

'He'd better, at twenty bucks an hour.' Ian frowned again and looked at Jessie, as she nodded almost imperceptibly. This was no time to get tight with money. They'd find it wherever they had to, but they couldn't skimp on this.

Martin explained the preliminary to them once more to make sure it was clear. It was a sort of mini-trial at which the plaintiff/victim and the defendant would state their sides of the story, and the judge would decide if the matter should be dropped, or go on to a higher court for an ultimate decision—in this case, to trial. Martin held out no hope that the matter would be dropped. The opposing stories were equally vehement, the circumstances cloudy. No judge would take it upon himself to decide a case like that at the preliminary state. It didn't help that the woman had maintained the same job for years and was respected where she worked. And there were certain psychological aspects of the case that made Martin Schwartz exceedingly uncomfortable: the fact that Ian was being virtually supported by his wife and hadn't had a successful book in a number of years, though he'd been writing for almost six, could have produced a certain resentment against women; at least, a good prosecutor could make it look that way. The investigator would be out to talk to Ian that afternoon or the following morning.

Jessie and Ian rode down in the elevator in silence, and Jessie finally spoke as they reached the street.

'Well, babe, what do you think?'

'Nothing good. Sounds like if we don't dig up some dirt on her, she's got me by the balls. And according to Schwartz, the courts frown on that kind of character assassination these days. But in this case, it's our only hope. It's her version against mine, and of course the medical testimony too, but that sounds pretty weak. They can tell that there was intercourse, but no one can tell if it was rape. The assault charge has already been dropped. Now we're just down to the nitty-gritty and my "sexual aberrations". ' Jessica nodded and said nothing.

It was a quiet drive to the boutique. She was thinking about the hearing with dread. She didn't want to see that woman, but there was no way to escape it. She had to see her, had to listen, had to hold up her end, if only for Ian's sake, no matter how ugly the whole thing got.

'Want me to leave you the car, love? I can walk home.' Ian prepared to get out after he drove her to the shop.

'No, darling, I . . . actually, come to think of it, I'm going to need it today. Does that louse you up?' She was trying to sound pleasant, but she had just had a thought. She needed the car today, and there were no maybe's about it, whether it loused him up or not.

'No sweat. I've got the Swedish sex bomb if I need it.' He was referring to his Volvo, and she grinned.

'Want to come in for a cup of coffee?' But neither of them felt talkative. The morning's interview had left them feeling pensive and distant from each other.

'No, I'll let you get to work. I want to spend a little time by myself.' It was pointless to ask him if he was upset. They both were.

'Okay, love. I'll see you later.' At the door to the boutique they parted with a quick kiss.

She rapidly took refuge in her office and made an appointment for one-thirty. It was the only thing she could think of. Ian would be crushed, but what choice did she have? And he was in no position to object.

'Well, what do you think?' She hated the man's looks and resented him already. He was fat and oily and sly.

'Not bad. Pretty slinky little number. How's it look under the hood?'

'Impeccable.' He was examining the little red Morgan as if it were a piece of meat in a supermarket or a hooker in a bordello. Jessie's skin crawled; this felt like selling their child into white slavery. To this fat nauseating man.

'You in a hurry to sell her?'

'No. Just curious about the price I might get for it.'

'Why do you want to sell her? Need the bread?' He looked Jessie over carefully.

'No. I need a larger car.' But it was all very painful. She still remembered her astonishment and delight the day Ian had driven up in the Morgan and handed her the keys, with a broad grin on his face. Victory. And now it would be like selling her heart. Or his.

'Tell you what, I'll make you an offer.'

'How much?'

'Four thousand . . . nah . . . maybe, as a favour to you, forty-five hundred.' The dealer looked her over and waited.

'That's ridiculous. My husband paid seven for it, and it's in better condition now than when he bought it.'

'Best I can do. And I think it's the best you'll get on short notice. It needs a little work.' It didn't, and they both knew it, but he was right about the short notice. A Morgan was a beautiful car, but very few people wanted to own one, or could afford to.

'I'll let you know. Thank you for your time.' Without further comment she got back in the car and drove off. Damn. What a miserable thing to even consider. But she had the rest of Schwartz's fee to pay, and now the investigator, the business and the house were already tied up by Yorktowne Bonding, and she already had a loan out on the car. She'd be lucky if the bank would even let her sell it. But they knew her well enough. They just might let her. And despite Ian's flourish about going out and getting a job, he had done nothing. He was knee deep in the book and going nowhere except to his studio with a pencil stuck behind his ear. Artistic, but hardly lucrative at this point. And even if he did get a job, how much money could he make in the month or two before the trial, waiting on tables or tending bar while he wrote at night? Maybe the book would sell. There was always that to hope for. But Jessie knew from experience that that took time, and too often they had teased themselves with that slim hope. She knew better now. It would have to be the Morgan. Sooner or later.

She kept to herself for the rest of the day, and it was a pleasant surprise when Astrid Bonner walked into the shop shortly before five. She might bring relief from the day's tensions.

'Well, Jessica, you certainly are hard to get hold of!' But she was in high spirits. She had just bought a new topaz ring, a handsome piece of work, thirty-two carats' worth encased in a small fortune in gold, and she 'hadn't been able to resist it'. On anyone else it would have been vulgar; on Astrid it had style. But it made Jessie's heart ache again over the Morgan. The topaz with the narrow diamond baguettes had probably cost Astrid twice the amount she needed so badly.

'Life has been pretty crazy ever since I got back from New York. And that's some ring, Astrid!'

'If I get tired of it, I can always use it as a doorknob. I can't quite decide if it's gorgeous or ghastly, and I know no one will ever tell me the truth.'

'It's gorgeous.'

'Truth?' She looked at Jessie teasingly.

'So much so I've been green with envy since you walked in.'

'Goody! It really was a shockingly self-indulgent thing to do. Amazing what a little ennui will do to a girl.' She laughed coquettishly and Jessie smiled. Such simple problems. Ennui.

'Want a lift home, or did you come to do some shopping?'

'No shopping, and I have the car, thanks. I came by on my way home to invite you and your husband to dinner.' The girls had told her that Jessie was married.

'What a sweet thought. We'd love it. When do you want us?'

'How about tomorrow?'

'You're on.' They exchanged a smile of pleasure and Astrid walked comfortably around Jessie's small, cheerful office.

'You know, Jessica, I'm falling in love with this place. I might have to con you out of it one of these days.' She laughed mischievously and watched Jessica's eyes.

'Don't waste your energies conning me. I might just give it to you. Right about now, I might even gift wrap it!'

'You're making me drool.'

'Spare your saliva. Can I talk you into a drink? I don't know about you, but I could use a stiff one.'

'Still those problems you mentioned the other day?'

'More or less.'

'Which means mind my own business. Fair enough.' She smiled easily; she didn't know that Jessica had spent the day trying to forget that Barry York had a lien on her business. It made Jessica sick to think about it, and all the while Ian was out of touch with the world, working on that bloody book night and day. Jesus. She needed someone to talk to. And why did he have to start tuning out right now? He always got that way when he was into a book. But now?

'I have an idea, Jessica.'

Jessie looked up, startled. For a moment she had totally forgotten Astrid.

'How about having that drink at my place?'

'You know what? I'd love that. You're sure it's not too much trouble?'

'It's no trouble; it would be fun. Come on, let's get going.'

Jessie bid a rapid good night to the girls and found herself relieved to leave the boutique. It hadn't used to be like that. She used to feel good just walking in the door in the morning, and pleased with herself and her life as she walked out at night. Now she hated to think of the place. It was shocking how things could change in so little time.

Jessie followed Astrid home in her car. The older woman was driving a two-year-old black Jaguar sedan. It was perfect for her, as sleek and elegant as she was. This woman was surrounded by beautiful things. Including her home.

It was a breathtaking mixture of delicate French and English antiques, Louis XV, Louis XVI, Hepplewhite, Sheraton. But none of it was overwhelming. There was an airy quality to the house. Lots of yellow and white, delicate organdy curtains, eggshell silks, and, upstairs, bright flowered prints and a magnificent collection of paintings. Two Chagalls, a Picasso, a Renoir, and a Monet that lent a summer night's mood to the dining room.

'Astrid, this is fabulous!'

'I must admit, I love it. Tom had such marvellous things. And they're happy things to live with. We bought a few pieces together, but most of it was already his. I picked out the Monet, though.'

'It's a beauty.' Astrid looked proud. She had every right to.

Even the glasses she poured the Scotch into were lovely —paper-thin crystal, with a rainbow hue to them as they were held up to the late afternoon light. And there was an overpowering view of the Golden Gate Bridge and the bay from the library upstairs, where they settled down with their drinks.

'God, what a magnificent house. I don't know what to say.' It was splendid. The library was wood-panelled and lined with old books. There was a portrait of a serious-looking man on one wall, and a Cezanne over the small brown marble fireplace. The portrait was of Tom. Jessie could easily see them together, despite the broad difference in age. There was a warm light in his eyes; one sensed approaching laughter. As she looked at the portrait, Jessie suddenly realized how lonely Astrid must be now.

'He was a fine-looking man.'

'Yes, and we suited each other so well. Losing him has been an awful blow. But we were lucky. Ten years is a lot, when they're ten years like the ones we had.' But Jessie could tell that Astrid still hadn't decided what to do with her life. She was floating—into dress shops and jewellers, into furriers, off on trips. She had nothing to anchor her. She had the house, the money, the paintings, the clothes . . . but no longer the man. And he was the key. Without Tom none of it really meant anything. Jessie could imagine what that might be like. It gave her chills thinking of it.

'What's your husband like, Jessica?'

Jessie smiled. 'Terrific. He's a writer. And he . . . well, he's my best friend. I think he's crazy and wonderful and brilliant and handsome. He's the only person I can really talk to. He's someone very special.'

'That says it all, doesn't it?' There was a gentle light in Astrid's eyes as she spoke, and Jessie suddenly felt guilty. How could she so blatantly rave about Ian to this woman who had lost the man who meant every bit as much to her as Ian meant to Jessie?

'No, don't look like that, Jessica. I know what you're thinking, and you're wrong. You should feel that way. You should say it with just exactly that wonderful victorious look on your face. That's how I felt about Tom. Cherish it, flaunt it, enjoy it, don't ever apologise for it, and certainly not to me.'

Jessica nodded pensively over her drink, and then looked up at Astrid.

'We're having some nasty problems right now.'

'With each other?' Astrid was surprised. It didn't show in Jessica's face. Something did, but not trouble with her husband—she had looked too happy when she described him. Maybe money problems. Young people had those. There was something, though. It surfaced at unexpected moments. A whisper of fear, almost terror. Sickness, perhaps? The loss of a breast? Astrid wondered, but didn't want to pry.

'I guess you might call this a crisis. Maybe even a

big one. But the problem isn't with each other, not in that sense.' She looked out at the bay and fell silent.

'I'm sure you'll work it out.' Astrid knew Jessie didn't want to talk about it.

'I hope so.'

Their talk turned unexpectedly to business then, to how the shop was run and what sort of clients Jessie had. Astrid made her laugh telling her some of the stories from her days at *Vogue* in New York. It was almost seven before Jessie got up to go home. And she hated to leave.

'See you tomorrow. At seven-thirty?'

'We'll be here with bells on. I can't wait to show Ian the house.' And then she had a thought. 'Astrid, do you like the ballet?'

'I adore it.'

'Want to come see the Joffrey with us next week?'

'No . . . I . . .' There was a moment of sadness in her eyes.

'Come on, don't be a drag. Ian would love to take us both. God, what that would do to his ego!' She laughed, and Astrid seemed to hesitate. Then she nodded with a small girl's grin.

'I can't resist. I hate to be the fifth wheel—I went through that after Tom died, and it's the loneliest thing in the world. It's actually much easier to be alone. But I'd love to go with you, if Ian won't mind.'

They left each other like two new school friends who have the good fortune to find that they live across the street from each other. And Jessie ran home to tell Ian about the house.

He was going to love it, and Astrid. She reminded Jessie of herself, as she would have liked to be. All the poise in the world, and so gentle, so open and sunny. She might be uncertain about the course her life would take, but she had long since come to terms with herself, and it showed. She radiated loving and peace, no longer grabbing at life like Jessie. But Jessie didn't really envy her. She still had Ian, and Astrid no longer had Tom. And, as she drove home, Jessica found herself speeding the car into the driveway, anxious to see Ian, not just his portrait.

As she approached their front door she saw a man walking away from the house toward an unfamiliar car parked in the driveway. He gave her a long examining glance and then nodded. And Jessie felt terror wash over her. Police . . . the police were back . . . what were they doing now? The terror reached her eyes as she stood there, rooted to the spot. The nightmare was back again. At least he wasn't Inspector Houghton. And where was Ian? She wanted to scream, but she couldn't. The neighbours might hear.

'I'm Harvey Green. Mrs. Clarke?' She nodded and stood there, still eyeing him with horror. 'I'm the investigator Martin Schwartz referred to your case.'

'Oh. I see. Have you spoken to my husband?' She suddenly felt the cool breeze on her face, but it would take a while for her heart to stop pounding.

'Yes, I've spoken to him.'

'Is there anything you want me to add?' Other than money . . .

'No. We have everything under control. I'll be in touch.' He made a gesture of mock salute toward his colourless hair and walked on toward his car. It was beige or pale blue, Jessie wasn't even sure in the twilight. Maybe it was white. Or light green. Like him, it was totally nondescript. He had unpleasant eyes and a forgettable face. He would blend well in a crowd. He looked ageless, and his clothes would have been out of style in any decade. He was perfect for his role.

'Darling, I'm home!' But her voice had a nervous lilt to it now, as his did when he spoke. 'Darling? . . . We've been invited to dinner tomorrow.' Not that either of them cared. Suddenly Harvey Green seemed much more of the present than Astrid.

'Invited? By whom?' Ian was pouring himself a drink in the kitchen. And not the usual white wine either. It was bourbon or Scotch, which he rarely drank, except when they had guests from back east.

'That new customer I met at the shop. Astrid Bonner. She's lovely; I think you'll like her.'

'Who?'

'You know. I told you. The widow who lives in the brick palazzo on the corner.'

'All right.' He tried to muster a smile, but it was rough going. 'Did you see Green on your way in?'

She nodded. 'I thought he was a cop. I jumped about four feet in the air.'

'So did I. Fun, isn't it, living like this?'

She tried to pass over the remark and sat down in her usual chair.

'Could you make me one too?'

'Scotch and water?'

'Why not?' It would be her third.

'Okay. That must be some place the widow's got herself.' But he didn't sound as though he really cared. He dropped ice cubes in another glass.

'You'll see it tomorrow. And Ian . . . I invited her to join us at the ballet. Do you mind?' It was a moment and two sips before he looked into her eyes and answered, and when he did, she didn't like what she saw.

'Baby, at this point, I really don't give a damn.'

They tried to make love that night after dinner, and for the first time since they'd met, Ian couldn't. He didn't give a damn about that either. It felt like the beginning of the end.

CHAPTER XI

'Are you dressed yet?' Jessica could hear Ian rattling around in the room where he worked, and she had just finished brushing her hair. She was wearing white silk slacks and a turquoise crocheted sweater, and she still wasn't sure if she looked right. Astrid was liable to be wearing something fabulous, and it sounded as though Ian had stayed submerged in the studio. 'Ian! Are you ready?' The rattling stopped and she heard footsteps.

'More or less.' He smiled at her from the bedroom

doorway, and she looked into his eyes as she walked towards him.

'Mr. Clarke, you look absolutely beautiful.'

'So do you.' He was wearing the new dark blue Cardin blazer she'd brought him from New York, a cream-coloured shirt, and a wine-coloured paisley tie with beige gabardine slacks she had found in France. They sculpted his long graceful legs.

'You look terribly proper and terribly handsome, and I think I'm terribly in love with you, darling.'

He swept her a neat bow and put his arms around her as she reached him.

'In that case, how about if we stay home instead?' He had a mischievous gleam in his eyes.

'Ian, don't you touch me! Astrid would be so disappointed if we didn't make it. And you'll love her.'

'Promises, promises.' But he offered her his arm as she picked up the white silk jacket she'd left on the chair in the hall. He was going to the dinner to humour her. He had other things on his mind.

They walked the half block to the brick house on the corner, and it was the first night there had been a chill in the air. Autumn was coming, in its own gentle fashion. San Francisco in the fall was nothing like that season in New York. It was part of the reason they'd both fallen in love with San Francisco in the first place. They loved the easy, temperate weather.

Jessica rang the bell, and they waited. For a moment there was no answer.

'Maybe she's decided she doesn't want us.'

'Oh, shut up. You just want to go home and work on your book.' But she smiled at him and then they heard footsteps.

The door opened a second later and there was Astrid, resplendent in a floor-length black knit dress and a long rope of pearls. Her hair was loosely swept up in the back and her eyes sparkled as she led them inside. She looked even more beautiful than Jessica had found her before. And Ian was obviously stunned. He had been expecting a middle-aged widow, and had agreed to the evening mostly as a concession to Jessie. He had had no hint of this vision in black with the Dresden-doll waist and long, elegantly arched neck—and that face. He liked the face. And the look in her eyes. This was no dowager. This was a woman.

The two women embraced, and Ian stood back for a moment, watching them, intrigued by the older woman he did not yet know, and by the formidable home he was beginning to glimpse over her shoulder. It was impossible not to stare, whether he looked at her or at the house.

'And this is Ian.' He obeyed the summons, feeling like a small boy being introduced by his mother—'Say good evening to the nice lady, darling'—and held out his hand.

'How do you do.' He was suddenly glad he had worn the new Cardin jacket and tie. This was not going to be just any old dinner. And she was probably a roaring snob. She had to be, in a setup like that. And widowed, yet. Nouveau riche as all hell . . . but somehow a murmuring suspicion told him that that wasn't the case either. She didn't have the dead-fish eyes of a snob, or the overworked eyebrows. She had nice eyes, in a nice face. She looked like a person.

Astrid laughed gaily as she led them upstairs to the library, and Ian and Jessica exchanged glances as they passed delicate sketches and etching on the stairs . . . Picasso . . . Renoir . . . Renoir again . . . Manet . . . Klimt . . . Goya . . . Cassatt . . . He wanted to whistle, and Jessie grinned at him like a conspirator who had assisted in getting him into the neighbourhood haunted house. He raised both eyebrows and she stuck out her tongue. Astrid was ahead of them and already down the hall. He wanted to whisper, and Jessie wanted to giggle, but they couldn't. Not till they got home. But she was thoroughly enjoying the look on his face; it made her feel suddenly mischievous. She pinched him delicately on the behind as she passed in front of him to enter the library.

Astrid had a plate of hors d'oeuvres waiting for them and a handsome pâté. A fire roared in the grate. Ian accepted a slice of pâté on a slim piece of toast and then laughed into Astrid's eyes.

'Mrs. Bonner, I don't know how to say this, and I feel about fourteen years old, but I am overwhelmed by your home.' And my hostess. He smiled the ingenuous smile that Jessie loved, and Astrid laughed with him.

'I'm delighted, that's a lovely compliment, but calling me "Mrs. Bonner" isn't. You may feel fourteen, but you make me feel about four hundred. Try "Astrid" '—she threw up both hands impishly—'or I may have to kick you out. And not "Aunt Astrid" either, God forbid.' All three of them laughed, and she slid out of her shoes and tucked her legs under her in a large comfortable chair. 'But I really am glad you like the house. It's embarrassing sometimes, now that Tom isn't here anymore. I love it so much, but I occasionally feel that I never quite grew into it all. I mean, it's so . . . so . . . well, as though it should be my mother's and I'm just house-sitting. I mean, really, me? In all this? How ridiculous!' Except that it wasn't ridiculous at all. It suited her perfectly. Ian wondered if she knew how perfectly, or if she meant what she had just said. He imagined Tom had built the place around her, right down to the paintings and the view.

'It suits you very well, you know.' Ian was watching her eyes, and Jessie was watching the exchange.

'Yes, it does, in some ways, and not in others. It frightens people away sometimes. The lifestyle does. The opulence. The . . . I guess you could call it an aura. A lot of it is Tom, and some of it is just . . . oh . . . things.' She waved vaguely around the room, encompassing rapidly a fortune in art objects. Things. 'And some of it is me.' Ian liked the fact that she conceded the point. 'People expect you to be a lot when you live like this. Sometimes they expect me to be something I'm not, or they don't stick around long enough to see what I am. I told you, Jessie, I'd trade you for your jewel of a house any day. But . . .' She grinned like a cat stretching lazily in the sun. '. . . This isn't a bad place to live, either.'

'Looks like a damn nice place to live, if you ask me, Mrs. . . . Astrid.' They exchanged a quick burst of laughter over the slip. 'But I doubt if you'd trade us for our "jewel", once you plugged in the hair dryer and the washing machine blew, or when the plumbing fell through to the basement. Our place has a few kinks.'

'That does sound like fun.' It was clear that nothing like that happened here, and Jessie was grinning broadly, remembering the last time all the fuses had blown, and Ian had refused to deal with it; they had spent the rest of the evening by candlelight—until he wanted to work, and needed the electric typewriter. He looked up sheepishly, knowing what she was thinking.

'Well, children? Do you want a tour of the place?' Astrid interrupted their thoughts. Jessie hadn't seen the whole thing, and Ian nodded quickly.

She tiptoed barefoot along the carpeted hall, flipping switches under brass sconces, opening doors, turning on more lights. There were three bedrooms upstairs. Hers in bright, flowery yellow prints with a large four-poster bed and the same splendid view of the bay. She had a small mirrored boudoir and a white marble bath, which was repeated in pale green across the hall, to go with a quietly elegant bedroom full of small French Provincial antiques.

'My mother sleeps here when she comes to the city, and this suits her perfectly. You'll know what I mean when you see her. She's very lively and little and funny, and she likes lots of flowers everywhere.'

'Does she live in the East?' Ian was curious, and remembered only that Jessie had told him Astrid had originally come from New York.

'No, Mother lives on a ranch out here, of all things. She bought it a few years ago, and she's having a great time with it. Much to our astonishment, it actually agrees with her. We thought she'd be bored in six months, but she's not. She's very independent, and she rides a lot and loves to play cowboy. At seventy-two, if you please. She reminds one a bit of Colette.'

It made Jessie smile to think of a tiny white-haired woman in cowboy gear ensconced in the delicately appointed room. But if she was anything like Astrid, she could pull it off. With cowboy boots custom-made by Gucci and a hat by Adolfo.

The bedroom next to Astrid's was more sombre, and

had apparently belonged to her husband. Jessie and Ian exchanged a rapid, casual glance . . . they had had separate bedrooms? But Jessie remembered the difference in age. There was a small, elegant study next to his room, rich in red leathers, with a handsome old desk covered with pictures of Astrid.

Astrid passed quickly through the room and went back out to the hall, closing the door of the green guest room as Jessie and Ian followed.

'It's a magnificent house.' Jessie sighed. It was the sort of place that made you want to appear for the next dinner invitation with everything you owned in your arms. You wanted to stay there forever. Now they both understood why she didn't close the house and find something smaller. It told a tale of people who cared—about beauty, about each other, and about living well.

'And you saw the downstairs. It's not very exciting, but it's pretty.' Jessie wondered why there was no trace of servants. One expected at least a white-aproned maid, or a butler, but she seemed to live alone.

'Do you both like crab? I really should have called to ask, but I forgot.' She looked faintly embarrassed.

'We love crab!' Jessie answered for them both.

'Oh, good! Seems that every time I order it for friends, and forget to ask beforehand, it turns out that someone is allergic to it or something. I love it.'

It was an unusual feast. Astrid piled a mountain of dismembered cracked crabs on a vast plate in the centre of the dining-room table, set out a huge carafe of white wine, added a salad and hot rolls, and invited her guests to dig in. She rolled up the sleeves of her black knit dress, invited Ian to take off his jacket, and sat there like a child, vying for the claws with whoever saw them first.

'Ian, you're a fiend. I saw that one first, and you know it!' She rapped him gently on the knuckles with the claw as she removed it, giggling and sipping her wine. She was right—she did look like a young girl whose mother was out for the evening and had let her have her friends over for dinner 'as long as you're all good.' She was delightful, and both Jessie and Ian fell in love with her.

It was an easy-going evening; they looked like three people with no problems at all—just expensive taste, and a liking for pleasure. It was after midnight when Ian stood up and held out a hand to Jessie.

'Astrid, I could stay here till four in the morning, but I have to get up tomorrow and work on the book, and if Jessie doesn't get enough sleep, she turns into a monster.' But it was obvious that they all shared regret that the evening was over. 'You'll come to the ballet with us next week?'

'With pleasure. And I'll have you know that Jessie said I would love you, and she was obviously one-hundred-percent right. I can't think of two peoplie I'd rather be a fifth wheel with.'

'Good. Because you're not. Fifth wheel, my ass.' They all laughed, and Astrid hugged them both as they left, as though she had known them for years. They felt as though she had, as Astrid stood barefoot in the doorway, waving before closing the shiny black door with its brass lion-head knocker.

'Christ, Jess, what a nice evening. And what a marvellous woman. She's amazing.'

'Isn't she? But she must be lonely as hell. There's something about the way she invites people into her life, as though she has a lot of leftover loving and no one to give it to most of the time.' Jessie yawned on the last words and Ian nodded. Talking over the evening was always the best part. She could no longer remember when Ian hadn't been around to share secrets, and opinions, and questions. He had been with her forever.

'What do you suppose her husband was like, Jess? I suspect he wasn't as much fun as she is.'

'What makes you say that?' His comment surprised her; there was nothing to suggest that Tom Bonner had been less amusing than his wife. And then Jessica laughed as she guessed what Ian meant. 'The separate bedrooms?' He grinned sheepishly and she pinched him. 'You're a creep.'

'I am not. And let me tell you, madam, I don't care if I live to be ninety, you'll never get me out of our bedroom . . . or our bed!' He looked adamant and very pleased with himself as he held her closer on the short walk home.

'Is that a promise, Mr. Clarke?'

'In writing, if you'd like, Mrs. Clarke.'

'I may just hold you to that.' They paused for a moment and kissed before walking the last few steps toward their home. 'I'm glad you liked Astrid, love. I really enjoy her. I'd like to get to know her better. She's a good person to talk to. You know, I . . . well, I almost wanted to tell her what's happening to us. We started to talk the other day, and . . .' Jessie shrugged; it was hard to put into words, and Ian was beginning to scowl. 'She just kind of makes me want to tell her the truth.' Ian stopped walking and looked at her.

'Did you?'

'No.'

'Good. Because I think you're kidding yourself, Jess. She's a nice woman, but no one is going to understand what's happening to us right now. No one. How do you tell someone you have a trial pending on charges of rape? Do us both a big favour, babe, and don't talk about it. We've got to hope this whole mess will blow over and we can forget it. If we tell people, it could haunt us for years.'

'That's what I decided. And, hey, come on . . . trust me a little, will you please? I'm not stupid. I know it would be hard for most people to handle.'

'So don't ask them to.'

Jessica didn't answer, and Ian walked ahead of her to open the door to the house. For the first time Jessie could remember, their chosen separateness from the rest of the world, almost like a secret society, now felt like lonely isolation. She couldn't talk to anyone but Ian. He had forbidden it. In the past it had always been a matter of choice.

Jessie followed him inside and left her jacket in the front hall.

'Want a cup of tea before bed, love?' She put a kettle of water on and heard him go into his studio.

'No, thanks.'

She stood in the doorway of his studio for a moment and smiled at him as he sat at his desk. He had a snifter of cognac beside him and a small stack of papers on the desk in front of him. He loosened his tie and sat back and looked at his wife.

'Hello, beautiful lady.'

'Hi.' They exchanged the subtlest of smiles for a moment and Jessie cocked her head to one side. 'You planning to work?'

'Just for a little while.'

She nodded and went to take the kettle off the stove; it was whistling fiercely. She made a cup of tea, turned off the rest of the lights, and walked quietly into the bedroom. She knew that Ian wouldn't come to bed for hours. He couldn't. He couldn't try to make love to her tonight. Not after last night. The sour taste of failure had stayed with them. Like the rest of what was happening to them, it was new, and painful, and raw.

Their evening at the ballet with Astrid was as great a success as the dinner at her home. They picked her up just in time to make the curtain, and Jessie had prepared a late supper that was waiting for them at home. Steak tartare, cold asparagus, a variety of cheeses and French bread, and a home-made fudge cake. Off to the side, was a large bowl of fresh strawberries and whipped cream, a huge crystal bowl filled with Viennese style *Schlag*, for the berries or the cake. It was a feast, and her audience approved.

'Dear girl, is there anything you can't do?'

'Plenty.' But Jessie was pleased at the compliment.

'Don't believe her. She can do anything.' Ian seconded the compliment with a kiss as he poured a round of Bordeaux. Chateau Margaux '55. It felt like an occasion, and he had brought out one of his favourite wines.

By now the three were a trio, telling jokes, sharing

stories, and feeling at ease. They were well into their second bottle of wine when Astrid stood up and glanced at the clock.

'Good God, children, it's two o'clock. Not that I have anything to do tomorrow, but you do. I feel very guilty keeping you up.' Ian and Jessica exchanged a sharp glance: they did have to be up early the next morning. But Astrid did not see the look. She was hunting for her bag.

'Don't be silly. Evenings like this are a gift for us.' Jessie smiled at her friend.

'They couldn't be as much so as they are for me. You have no idea how I've loved this. And what are you up to tomorrow, Jessica? Can I tempt you with lunch at the Villa Taverna?'

'I . . . I'm sorry, Astrid, but I can't make lunch tomorrow.' Another look flashed its way to Ian. 'We have to go to a business meeting in the morning and I don't know what time we'll be through.'

'Then why don't all three of us go to lunch?' She had found her handbag and was ready to leave. 'You can call me when you're through with your meeting.'

'Astrid, we'd better make it another day, much as I hate to.' Ian was regretful but firm.

'I think you're both mean.' But now she sensed something between them, a tension that hadn't been there before. Something was just a wee bit off balance, but she couldn't tell what, and she found herself remembering the problem Jessica had hinted at when they had first met. There had never been any mention of it again, and Astrid had gone on assuming that Jessie meant a money problem. It was hard to believe, but it obviously couldn't be anything else. Not health, not problems with the marriage certainly—there was too much hugging, touching, kissing, quick pats on the back, rapid squeezes as they stood side by side—there was much too much of that for anyone to believe the marriage was in trouble.

'Maybe we can all go to a movie this weekend.' Ian looked at the two women and tried to make light of the too-quiet moment. 'Not as classy as the ballet, but there's a new French thriller on Union. Anyone interested?'

'Oh, let's!' Jessie clapped her hands and looked at Astrid, who grinned and put on a cautious look.

'Only if you absolutely swear to buy me a gallon of popcorn.'

'I swear.' Ian solemnly held up a hand in a formal oath.

'Cross your heart?'

'Cross my heart.' He did, and the three of them started to laugh. 'You sure drive a hard bargain.'

'I have to. I'm addicted to popcorn. With butter!' She looked at him sternly and he gave her a brotherly hug. Astrid returned the hug and leaned over to give Jessie a kiss on the cheek. 'And now I shall bid you both good night. And let you get some sleep. I'm really sorry it got so late.'

'Don't be. We aren't.'

Jessica followed her to the door, and Astrid left with a curious feeling. Almost an eerie sensation. There was nothing she could see or touch or be absolutely sure of, but something seemed to hang in the air, just over their heads—like a hunk of concrete.

The preliminary hearing was scheduled for the next morning.

CHAPTER XII

Jessica walked into the miniature courtroom with Ian's hand held tightly in hers. She wore the navy blue suit and dark glasses again, and Ian looked tired and pale. He hadn't gotten much sleep, and he had a headache from his share of the wine the night before. The three of them had knocked off both bottles of Margaux.

Martin Schwartz was waiting for them in the courtroom. He was going through a file on a small desk at the side of the room, and he motioned to them to join him outside.

'I'm going to ask for a closed hearing. I thought you

should know, so you wouldn't be surprised.' He looked terribly professional, and they both felt confused. Ian spoke up first, with a worried frown.

'What's a closed hearing?'

'I think the victim may speak more openly if there are no observers in court. Just you, her, the assistant D.A., the judge, and myself. It's a sensible precaution. If she brings friends, she'll want them to think she's as pure as the proverbial driven snow. And she may react badly to having Jessica there.' For no reason she could understand, Jessica flinched involuntarily at the sound of her own name.

'Look, if I can take it, so can she.' Jessie was unbearably nervous, and she dreaded seeing the woman. She wanted to be anywhere but there. Every fibre of her being shrieked at the prospect of what lay ahead. The enemy. So much to face in one human being. Ian's infidelity, her own inadequacy, the threat to their future, the memory of the almost unscalable mountain of trying to bail him. All of it wrapped up in that one woman.

Martin could see how tense they both were. He pitied them, and he accurately suspected what was at the root of Jessie's nerves: Margaret Burton.

'Just trust me, Jessie. I think a closed hearing will be best for all concerned. We should be getting under way in a few minutes. Why don't you two go for a walk down the hall? Just stay close enough, and I'll come out and signal when the judge is ready to start.' Ian nodded tersely and Martin strode back inside. Ian's arm felt as if it had a lead weight hanging from it. Jessie.

They had nothing to say as they paced the length of the hall, turned at the far end, and came back again. Jessica found her mind drifting to memories of other marble halls . . . City Hall, where she and Ian had gotten their marriage licence . . . waiting outside the principal's office in high school . . . the funeral parlour in Boston when Jake had died . . . and then, one by one, her parents.

'Jessie?'

'Huh?' She was frowning oddly as she looked at him, as though she had difficulty coming back to the present.

'Are you okay?' He looked worried; she had been squeezing his arm too tightly and walking faster and faster as they paced the hall. He had had to shake her arm to catch her attention.

'Yeah. I'm okay. Just thinking.'

'Well, stop thinking. Everything's going to be fine. Relax.' She started to say something, and he could tell from the look in her eyes that it wasn't going to be pleasant. She was much too nervous to be cautious or kind.

'I'm . . . I'm sorry . . . this is just such a weird day. Doesn't it seem weird to you? Or is it just me?' She began to wonder if she were going crazy.

'No, it doesn't seem weird. Shitty, yes, but not weird.' He tried to smile, but she wasn't looking at him. She was looking off into the distance, dreamy-eyed again. She was beginning to frighten him. 'Look, dammit, if you don't pull yourself together right now, I'm going to send you home.'

'Why? So I don't see her?'

'Is that what you're worried about, for Chrissake? Seeing her? Is that all? Jesus. My ass is on the line, and you're worried about seeing her. Who gives a shit about her? What if they revoke my bail?'

'They won't.'

'How the hell do you know?'

'I . . . I . . . oh, Ian, I don't know. They just can't, that's all. Why would they?' She hadn't even thought of that. Now it was one more thing to worry about.

'Why *wouldn't* they?'

'Well, maybe if I'd seduced Inspector Houghton, or Barry York, our beloved bailbondsman, maybe they wouldn't. But since I didn't, maybe they will.' Her tone was bitter and scared.

'Go home, Jessica.'

'Go to hell.'

And then Ian stopped talking and looked past her. Time seemed to stop as Jessica too turned to look. It was Margaret Burton.

She was wearing the same hat. But with a polite little beige suit. She was even wearing white gloves. The clothes were cheap, but they were tidy-looking, and very proper. She looked very dull. Like the stereotype of a school-teacher or a librarian, somebody terribly serious and asexual. Her hair was pulled back in a tight knot at her neck, scarcely visible under the hat. The black roots were nowhere to be seen. She was wearing no makeup and her shoes were low-heeled and dowdy. It was obvious that a woman like this could only be made love to at gunpoint.

Ian said nothing, but looked for a long moment, then turned away. Jessica was staring, with a look of hatred on her face that Ian had never seen. She was rooted to the spot.

'Jess . . . come on, baby. Please.' He took her elbow and tried to propel her back down the hall, but she wouldn't move. Margaret Burton disappeared into the courtroom without ever having shown a sign of having seen them. And Jessica still wouldn't move. Inspector Houghton followed quickly on Miss Burton's heels, and Martin Schwartz came out and beckoned to Ian, while Jessie simply stood and stared.

'Look, Jessie, just sit down on that bench for a few minutes. I'll be back as soon as I can.' She was in terrible shape, and he had enough to worry about.

'Ian?' She turned and looked at him with a stricken expression in her eyes, and he felt his guts turn to sand. 'I just don't understand anything anymore.' There weren't even tears in her eyes. Only pain.

'Neither do I. But I've got to go inside now. Will you be okay out here, or do you want to go home?' He wasn't sure he trusted her alone. The look in her eyes was getting to be all too familiar.

'I'll be here.'

That wasn't what he had asked her, but he didn't have time to argue. He disappeared inside the courtroom, and Jessie sat alone on the cold marble bench. She watched people come and go. Ordinary-looking people. Men with attaché cases. Women with tissues clutched in their hands. Small bedraggled children in shoes that were worn through at the heel and pants that were too short for their skinny legs. Bailiffs, lawyers, judges, victims, defendants, witnesses . . . people. They came and went while Jessie sat and thought of Margaret Burton. Who was she? Why had she done it? Why Ian? She had looked so goddamned proud, so self-righteous as she had walked into the courtroom. The courtroom . . .

Suddenly her eyes were rivetted to the door. It was of dark, highly polished wood with brass knobs and two tiny glass windows, like eyes, looking out . . . looking out . . . looking in . . . inside . . . she had to be there . . . inside . . . to see her . . . to listen . . . to find out why . . . she had to.

A small sign hung crookedly from one of the doorknobs—CLOSED—and a grey-uniformed bailiff stood slightly off to one side, looking uninterestedly at passersby. Jessica stood to her full height, smoothed her skirt, and suddenly felt very calm. She fixed a small smile in place. There was the tiniest of tremors in the corner of her right eye, the convulsions of a butterfly, but who would notice? She looked very much in command, and smiled curtly at the bailiff as she strode to the door and put a hand on the knob.

'Sorry, ma'am. Courtroom's closed.'

'Yes. I know.' She looked almost pleased at his news, as though she were responsible and was comforted to learn that her orders had been carried out. 'I'm sitting in on the case.'

'An attorney?' He started to step aside. The tremor in her eye now felt as though it would tear off the lid.

She nodded quietly. 'Yes.' Oh, Jesus. No. What if he asked for credentials? Or went inside to talk to the judge? Instead he held open the door for her with a smile, and Jessie walked sedately into the room. The whole scene had been typically Jessica. No one ever questioned her. But what now? What if the judge stopped the proceedings? What if he threw her out? What if . . .

The judge was small and undistinguished, with glasses and blond-grey hair. He looked up momentarily, unimpressed by the new arrival, and directed a raised eyebrow at Martin Schwartz. After a sharp glance at Jessica,

Schwartz nodded reluctantly, then threw a rapid look at the assistant district attorney, who shrugged. She was in.

Inspector Houghton was seated near the bench, making some sort of statement. The room was wood-panelled, with leather-covered seats in the front row, and straight-backed chairs behind them. It was hardly larger than Martin Schwartz's office, but there was an aura of tremendous tension in the air. Ian and Martin sat together at a desk, slightly to the left. And only a few feet away sat Miss Burton and the assistant district attorney, who, much to Jessie's chagrin, was a woman. Young, tough-looking, with oversprayed hair and an abundance of powder on too fleshy cheeks. She wore a matronly green dress and a sedate string of pearls, and at the corners of her mouth the hard edges of anger had formed. She exuded righteous indignation for her client.

The young attorney turned to look at Jessica, and Jessie figured her to be about her own age, somewhere in her early thirties. The two women exchanged a look of ice. But Jessica saw contempt in the other woman's face as well, and then she understood what this was going to be. A class war. Big, nasty, college grad, preppie Pacific Heights Ian had raped poor little lower-class, abused, misunderstood secretary, who was going to be defended by clean, tough, pure, devoted middle-class young attorney. Jesus. That was all they needed. Jessica suddenly wondered if she had worn the wrong thing. But even in slacks and a shirt, Jessica had the kind of style those women would hate. How insane even to have to consider what she was wearing.

Miss Burton hadn't seen Jessica come in, or had shown no sign of it, at any rate. Nor had Ian. She slipped quietly into a straight-backed chair behind him, and then suddenly, as though he had been slapped, he raised his head and spun around in his seat, a look of shock on his face when he saw her there behind him. He started to shake his head, and then leaned toward her as though to say something, but Jessica's eyes were steely. She squeezed his shoulder briefly, and he averted his gaze: it was pointless to argue. But as he turned away, his broad shoulders seemed to sag.

Inspector Houghton rose from the seat from which he'd been addressing the judge, thanked the court, and returned to a chair on the other side of Margaret Burton. Now what? Jessica's heart pounded. Suddenly she wasn't so sure she wanted to be there. What would she hear? Could she take it? What if she fell apart? Went crazy . . . screamed . . .

'Miss Burton, take the stand, please.'

As Margaret Burton slowly left her seat Jessica's heart seemed hell-bent on freeing itself from her body. A pulse thundered at her temple and she wondered if she'd faint as she stared down at her trembling hands. The oath was administered to Miss Burton, and Jessica looked up, her whole body trembling now. *Why her*? She was so plain, so ugly, so . . . cheap. But no, she wasn't really ugly. There was something about her, a grace to the hands folded over her knees, the vestige of prettiness in a face now grown too hard to be arresting. Something . . . maybe. Jessie wondered how Ian felt, sitting just in front of her. He seemed a thousand miles away. Margaret Burton seemed much, much closer. Jessica felt as though she could see every pore, every hair, the slightly flared nostrils, the weave of the dreary beige suit. She had a wild urge to run up and touch her, slap her maybe, shake her into telling the truth. Tell them what happened, damn you! The truth! Jessica's breath caught and she coughed, trying to clear her head.

'Miss Burton, would you please explain what happened on the day in question, from the moment you first saw Mr. Clarke. Tell us simply, in your own words. This is not a trial. This is merely a preliminary hearing, to determine if this matter deserves further attention from the court.'

The judge spoke as though he were reading an orange-juice label—words he had spoken a thousand times before and no longer heard. But it was all the invitation Margaret Burton needed. She cleared her throat with a small look of importance and the tiniest of smiles. Inspector

Houghton frowned as he watched her, and the prosecuting attorney seemed to be keeping an eye on the judge.

'Miss Burton?' The judge looked off into space as he spoke, and everyone waited.

'Yes, sir. Your honour.' Jessica felt that the 'victim' didn't look sufficiently distraught. Victorious, maybe, but not distraught. Not violated. Pleased? That was crazy. Why should she be pleased? But Jessie could not put aside that impression as she stared at the woman who claimed her husband had raped her. And then the recital began.

'I had lunch at Enrico's, and afterward I started walking up Broadway.' She had a flat, unpleasant voice. A little too high. A little too loud. She would have nagged well. And she sounded too loud to be hurt. Hurt inside. Jessica wondered if the judge was listening to more than just the words. He didn't look it.

'I was walking up Broadway,' she went on, 'and he offered me a ride.'

'Did he threaten you, or just offer a ride?'

She shook her head, almost regretfully. 'No, he didn't threaten. Not really.'

'What do you mean, "not really"?'

'Well, I think he might have gotten mad if I'd turned down the ride, but it was kind of a hot day, and I couldn't see a bus for blocks, and I was late getting back to the office, and . . .' She looked up at the judge and his face was blank. 'Anyway, I told him where I worked.' She stopped for a moment, looked down at her hands, and sighed. Jessie wanted to wring her neck. That pathetic little sigh. She dug her hand into Ian's shoulder without thinking, and he jumped, and turned to look at her with a worried face. She forced a tiny smile and he patted her hand before looking back at Margaret Burton.

'Go on.' The judge was prodding her. She seemed to have lost the thread of her tale.

'I'm sorry, your honour. He . . . he didn't take me back to my office, and . . . well, I know I was crazy to accept the ride. It was just such a pretty day, and he looked like a nice man. I thought . . . I never realised . . .' Unexpectedly, a small tear glided from one eye and then the other; Jessie's grip on Ian's shoulder became almost unbearable. He reached for her hand and gently held it until she nervously pulled it away.

'Please go on, Miss . . . Miss Burton.' He checked the name on the papers on his desk, took a swallow of water, and looked up. Jessie was reminded that this hearing was no more than daily routine to him; he seemed totally separate from the drama that absorbed the rest of them.

'I . . . he took me . . . to a hotel.'

'You went with him?' But there was no judgment in the voice; it was only a question.

'I thought he was taking me back to my office.' She sounded strident and angry suddenly. The tears were gone.

'And when you saw that he hadn't taken you back to your office, why didn't you leave then?'

'I . . . I don't know. I just thought it would . . . he only wanted to have a drink, he said, and he wasn't unpleasant, just silly. I thought he was harmless and it would be easier to go along with it—with the drink, I mean—and then . . .'

'Was there a bar in the hotel when you went inside?' She shook her head. 'A desk clerk? Did anyone see you go in? Could you have called for help? I don't believe Mr. Clarke held a gun on you, or anything of the sort, did he?'

She flushed and shook her head reluctantly.

'Well, did anyone see you?'

'No.' The word was barely audible. 'There was no one there. It looked like . . . like sort of an apartment hotel.'

'Do you remember where it was?'

She shook her head again, and Jessica felt Ian stir restlessly in front of her, and when she looked there was anger on his face. At last. He looked alive again, instead of buried under grief and disbelief.

'Could you tell us the location of the hotel, Miss Burton?'

Again, the negative shake of the head. 'No. I . . . I

was so upset I . . . I just didn't look. But he . . . he . . .' Suddenly her face was transformed again. The eyes lit up and almost glowed with such hatred and fury that for an instant Jessie almost believed her, and she saw Ian go suddenly very still. 'He took my life and threw it away! He ruined it! He . . .' She sobbed for a moment, and then took a deep breath as the glitter left her eyes. 'As we went inside, he just grabbed me, and dragged me into an elevator and up to a room, and . . .' Her silence said it all, as she hung her head in defeat.

'Do you remember what room?'

'No.' She didn't look up.

'Would you recognise the room again?'

'No. I don't think so.' No? Why not? Jessie couldn't imagine not remembering a room you'd been raped in. It would be engraved on your mind forever.

'Would you recognise the hotel?'

'I'm not sure. I don't think so, though.' She still had not looked up, and Jessie doubted her story still further—and then realised what had been happening: if she was doubting the story, then at some point she must have believed it might be true. In that one burst of tears and fury, the woman had convinced them all. Or come damn close to it. Even Jessica. Almost. She turned to look at Ian and saw him watching her, his eyes bright with tears. He knew what was happening too. Jessica reached for his hand again, this time quietly and with strength. She wanted to kiss him, hold him, tell him it would be all right, but now she wasn't so sure. She was sure of only one thing—of how much she hated Margaret Burton.

Martin Schwartz was looking none too happy either. If the Burton woman claimed not to remember where the hotel was, they had lost the last shred of hope of finding a witness who had seen them there. Ian couldn't place the hotel either. He had been just drunk enough that his memory was blurred, and the address he thought he remembered had turned out to be wrong. It was a warehouse. There were plenty of small sleazy residential hotels in the area, and Martin had sent Ian into dozens of lobbies before the preliminary hearing: Nothing looked familiar. So it was going to remain a case of his word against hers, with no one to corroborate either side. Schwartz was liking the looks of the case less and less. She was a damn unpleasant witness. Erratic, emotional, one moment hard as a rock, the next heart-wringing and tearful. The judge would ship them off to trial for sure, if for no other reason than to avoid dealing with the issue himself.

'All right, Miss Burton,' the judge said, fingering a pencil and gazing at the opposite wall, 'what happened in that room you don't remember?' His tone was dry and uninterested.

'What happened?'

'What did Mr. Clarke do after he dragged you into that room? You did say he dragged you?'

She nodded.

'And he wasn't using a weapon?' She shook her head, and finally looked up at her audience.

'No. Only . . . only his hand. He slapped me several times and told me he'd kill me if I didn't do what he wanted.'

'And what was that?'

'I . . . he . . . he forced me to . . . to have . . . oral copulation with him . . . to do . . . to, well . . . to do it to him.' My, how painful you make it sound . . . Jessica wanted to slap her again.

'And you did?'

'I did.'

'And then? Did he . . . did Mr. Clarke have an orgasm?'

She nodded.

'Please answer the question.'

'Yes.'

'And then?'

'Then he sodomised me.' She said it in a dull, flat voice, and Jessie could feel Ian flinch. She herself felt increasingly uncomfortable. She had anticipated drama, not this slow, drawn-out recital. Christ, how humiliating it all was. How dry and ugly and awful. The words, the acts, the thoughts, all so old and dreary.

'Did he climax again?'

'I . . . I don't know.' She had the grace to blush.

'Did you?' Her eyes flew open then and Houghton and the young district attorney watched tensely.

'I? But how could I? He . . . I . . . he raped me.'

'Some women enjoy that, Miss Burton, in spite of themselves. Did you?'

'Of course not!'

'You did not climax, then?' Jessica was beginning to enjoy the other woman's discomfiture.

'No, of course not! No!' She almost shouted it, looking hot and angry and nervous.

'All right. And then what?' The judge looked terribly bored and unimpressed by Miss Burton's indignation.

'Then he raped me again.'

'How?'

'He . . . he just raped me. You know . . . the usual way this time.' Jessica almost wanted to laugh. A 'usual rape'!

'Did he hurt you?'

'Yes, of course he did.'

'Very much?'

But she was looking down again, distant and pensive and sad. It was at those moments that one should feel sorry for her. And for a tiny flash of a second, Jessica wondered about her own reactions. At any other time, the story she was hearing would have touched her. Maybe even very much. But now . . . how could she let it touch her? She didn't believe the woman. But what did the judge think? There had been no answer to his last question.

'Miss Burton, I asked if Mr. Clarke hurt you very much.'

'Yes. Very much. I . . . he . . . he didn't care about me. He just . . . he just . . .' The tears flowed slowly down her face and it was as though she were talking about someone else, not Ian, not a total stranger who had raped her. Why would he care about her if he were raping her? 'He didn't care if I got pregnant, or . . . or anything. He just . . . just left.' And now the tears turned to anger again. 'I know this type, they play with poor girls like me! Girls with no money, no fancy family, and then they . . . they do what he did . . . they leave . . .' Her voice sank back to a whisper then as she looked blindly into her lap. 'He left, and went back to her.'

'Who?' The judge looked confused, and Miss Burton looked up again, with a slightly dazed look on her face. 'Who did he go back to?'

'His wife.' She said it very plainly, but without looking at Jessica.

'Miss Burton, did you know Mr. Clarke from somewhere, from before this? Had you ever been romantically involved with him before?' So the judge had also picked up on that—a faint suggestion that Ian was not a stranger after all.

'No. Never.'

'Then how did you know about his wife?'

'He looked married. And anyway, he told me.'

'I see. And he just left you at the hotel afterward?' She nodded again. 'What did you do then? Call the police? Go to a doctor? Call a cab?'

'No. I walked for a while. I felt confused. And then I went home and washed up. I felt awful.' Now she was believable again.

'Did you see a doctor?'

'After I called the police.'

'And when did you do that? It wasn't immediately, was it?'

'No.'

'Why not?'

'I was scared. I had to think about it.'

'And you're sure of your story, now, Miss Burton? This is the whole truth? The story you originally told the police was a little different from this, wasn't it?'

'I don't know what I told them then. I was confused. But this is the truth now.'

'You're under oath now, Miss Burton, so I hope this is the truth.'

'It is.' She nodded expressionlessly, her eyes dead.

'There's nothing you want to change?'

'No.'

'And you're certain that this was not a misunderstanding, an afternoon fling that went sour?' And then suddenly the hatred blazed up in her eyes again, and she squeezed them tightly shut.

'He ruined my life.' She hissed the words into the silent room.

'All right, Miss Burton. Thank you. Mr. Schwartz, any questions?'

'Only a few, Your Honour. And I'll be quick. Miss Burton, has anything similar ever happened to you before?'

'What do you mean?'

'I mean, have you ever been raped, even in fun, as a sort of game, by a lover, a boyfriend, a husband?'

'Of course not.' She looked incensed.

'Have you ever been married?'

'No.'

'Engaged?'

'No.' Again there was no hesitation.

'No broken engagements?'

'No.'

'Any serious, broken-off loves?'

'None.'

'A boyfriend now?'

'No.'

'Thank you, Miss Burton. What about romantic interludes? Have you ever picked up a stranger before?'

'No.'

'Then you agree that you picked up Mr. Clarke?'

'No! I . . . he offered me a ride, and . . .'

'And you accepted, even though you didn't know him. Does that seem wise to you, in a city like San Francisco?' His tone was politely concerned, and Margaret Burton looked angry and confused.

'No, I . . . it . . . no, I've never picked anyone up before. And I just thought that . . . he looked like he was okay.'

'What do you mean by okay, Miss Burton? He was drunk, wasn't he?'

'A little tiddly maybe, but not bombed. And he looked, well . . . like a nice guy.'

'You mean rich? Or fancy? Or what? Like a Harvard grad?'

'I don't know. He just looked clean-cut.'

'And handsome? Do you think he's handsome?'

'I don't know.' She was looking at her lap.

'Did you think he'd get involved with you, maybe? Fall in love? That's a fair assumption. You're a nice-looking woman, why not? A hot summer day, a good-looking guy, a lonely woman . . . how old are you, Miss Burton?'

'Thirty-one.' But she'd fumbled.

'You told the police thirty. Isn't it more like thirty-eight? Isn't it just possible that—'

'Objection!' The district attorney was on her feet, her face furious, and the judge nodded.

'Sustained. Mr. Schwartz, this is not a trial, and you might as well save the pressure tactics for later. Miss Burton, you don't have to answer that. Are you almost through, Mr. Schwartz?'

'Almost, Your Honour. Miss Burton, what were you wearing on the day of your encounter with Mr. Clarke?'

'What was I wearing?' She looked nervous and confused. He had been pelting her with difficult questions. 'I . . . I don't know . . . I . . .'

'Was it something like what you have on now? A suit? Or something lighter, more revealing? Something sexy, maybe?' The prosecuting attorney was frowning fiercely again, and Jessica was beginning to enjoy the situation. She liked Martin's style. Even Ian looked intrigued, almost pleased.

'I . . . I don't know. I guess I must have worn a summer dress.'

'Like what? Something low-cut?'

'No. I don't wear things like that.'

'Are you sure, Miss Burton? Mr. Clarke says you were wearing a very short, low-cut pink dress, with a hat—were you wearing that same hat? It's a very nice hat.'

Suddenly she was torn between the compliment and the implication.

'I don't wear pink.'

'But the hat is pink, isn't it?'

'It's more a kind of neutral colour, more like beige.' But there was a pinkish cast to it. That was obvious to all.

'I see. And what about the dress? Did that have a kind of beige cast to it too?'

'I don't know.'

'All right. Do you go to Enrico's often?'

'No, I've been just a couple of times. But I've walked by it.'

'Had you seen Mr. Clarke there before?'

'No. I don't remember seeing him.' She was regaining her composure. These questions were easy.

'Why did you tell him you were a topless waitress on Broadway?'

'I never told him that.' Now she was angry again, and Martin nodded, looking almost preoccupied.

'All right, thank you, Miss Burton. Thank you, Your Honour.'

The judge looked questioningly at the assistant district attorney, who shook her head. She had nothing to add. He indicated that Margaret Burton could step down, then spoke the words Jessica had dreaded. 'Mr. Clarke, please take the stand.'

Ian and Margaret Burton passed inches from each other, their faces without expression. Only moments before, she had said that he had ruined her life, yet now she looked right through him. Jessica felt more confused than ever by the woman.

The oath was administered, and the judge looked over his glasses at Ian.

'Mr. Clarke, would you please give us your account of what happened?' The judge looked excessively bored as Ian launched into his version of that day's events. The lunch, the drinks, picking her up, the seductive way she was dressed, her story about being a topless waitress, the drive to Market Street to an address she had given him but which he could no longer remember. And finally her invitation to her room, where they had had a drink and made love.

'Whose room was it?'

'I don't know. I assumed it was hers. But it was kind of empty. I don't know. I'd had a lot to drink at lunch. and I wasn't thinking very clearly.'

'But clearly enough to go upstairs with Miss Burton?'

Ian flushed. He felt like an errant schoolboy called to the principal's office . . . *Ian, did you look up Maggie's dress? Tsk, tsk, tsk!* But it wasn't like that at all. The stakes were too high for this to be child's play.

'My wife was away, and had been for three weeks.' Jessie's heart was pounding again. Was it supposed to be her fault, then? Was that the implication? Was that what he thought, what he wanted her to feel? She was responsible for his feelings of inadequacy?

'And what happened after it was all over?'

'I left.'

'Just like that? Did you intend to see Miss Burton again?' Ian shook his head.

'No. I didn't intend to see her again. I felt guilty as hell for what had already happened.' Martin was frowning at his answer and Jessie cringed. The judge had picked up on it too.

'Guilty?'

'I mean, because of my wife. I don't usually do that sort of thing.'

'What sort of thing, Mr. Clarke? Rape?'

'No, for God's sake, I didn't rape her!' He had bellowed his denial and small beads of sweat were glistening on his forehead. 'I mean, I felt guilty for cheating on my wife.'

'But you did force Miss Burton upstairs at the hotel?'

'I did not. She took me upstairs. It was her room, not mine. She invited me up.'

'What for?'

'A drink. And probably for exactly what she got.'

'Then why do you suppose she claims you raped her?'

'I don't know.' Ian looked blank and exhausted, and the judge shook his head and looked around the room.

'Ladies and gentlemen, neither do I. The purpose of this hearing is to determine if there was a misunderstanding afoot, if the problem is one that can be simply resolved here and now, to determine in effect if a rape did take place, and if the case merits further judicial attention. It is my job to decide to dismiss the action or send it on to a higher court to be tried. In order for me to make the decision to dismiss the action, I have to feel quite certain that this was clearly not a rape.

'In the event that I am unable to decide, that the matter is not clear, then I have no choice but to send it on to a higher court, and possibly to a jury, to decide. And it would appear that this is no simple matter before us now. The stories of the two parties are widely divergent. Miss Burton says rape, Mr. Clarke says not. There is no evidence in either direction. So I am afraid this matter will have to be handled by a higher court, and presumably given a jury trial. We cannot simply dismiss the matter. Serious allegations have been made. I move that the matter be referred to Superior Court, and that Mr. Clarke be arraigned in Superior Court two weeks from today, in the court of Judge Simon Warberg. Court is dismissed.' And without further ado, he got up and walked out of the room. Jessica and Ian rose and looked at each other in confusion as Martin shuffled papers for a moment. Margaret Burton was whisked away by Inspector Houghton.

'Now what?' Jessica spoke to Ian in a whisper.

'You heard the man, Jess—we go to trial.'

'Yeah.' She looked for a last moment at the retreating back of the Burton woman, fresh hatred filling her soul for this woman who was inexplicably destroying their lives. She knew no more now than she had three hours ago. Why?

'Well, Martin?' Jessica turned to Martin now. He looked very serious. 'What do you think?'

'We'll discuss it in my office, but I smell one thing I don't like. I can't be sure, but I had a case like this once years ago. Crazy case with a crazy plaintiff. It had to do with vengeance. Not against the guy she said had raped her, but against someone who actually had raped her in her late teens. She had waited twenty-two years to get revenge against an innocent man. I can't tell you why, it's just a gut feeling, but this reminds me of that case.' He had spoken in a barely audible whisper. Jessica leaned toward him to hear, and was intrigued by his idea. She had had a strange feeling about the Burton woman too. Ian still looked too shaken to react to much of anything. He looked at Jessie then with irritation in his eyes.

'I told you to wait outside.'

'I couldn't.'

'Yeah. I had a feeling you'd wind up in here. Fun, wasn't it?' He sounded bitter and tired. They were the only people left in the courtroom, and he looked around as though he'd just waked up from a bad dream. It had been a gruelling session, and even Jessica felt as though she had aged five years in the course of the morning.

'When will the trial be?' she asked Martin. She didn't quite know what to say to Ian: there was so much to say; too much.

'In six weeks. You heard the judge say that the Superior Court arraignment is in two. The trial will be four weeks after that. And we're going to have to do some very fast work.' Martin was wearing a look of intense sobriety, and Jessica found herself aching to ask how that other client had come out, the one who had been accused of rape by the woman seeking revenge, but she was afraid to know. Ian hadn't asked the question either, and Martin hadn't volunteered the information. 'I want Green on the case night and day, and I want you both available for meetings whenever I call you.' His voice was stern.

'We'll be available.' Jessie spoke first, trying to keep the tears out of her voice. 'We'll win, won't we, Martin?' She was still whispering, but she wasn't sure why. It was no longer necessary.

'I think it'll be a tight one. It's her word against yours, Ian. But yes, we ought to win.' He didn't sound sure enough for Jessie, though, and the full weight of the situation settled on her heart again. How had it all happened? Where had it all started? Was it really just a matter of her having been in New York for too long? Had he just been horny? Was it bad luck? Was the Burton woman some kind of lunatic who'd been gunning for anyone, or had Ian been singled out? Whose fault was it? And when would it all go away?

'Will they revoke Ian's bail?' That had been her constant terror. And Ian's.

'They can, but they won't. There's no reason to, as long as he keeps making his court appearances, and the judge didn't mention it. Just don't either of you go off on any trips, just now. No business trips, no disappearing acts, no visits back east to your family. Stick around; I'll be needing you. All right?'

They nodded solemnly and he walked them slowly from the courtroom as Jessie thought of what he'd said. Family? What family? As old and frail as Ian's parents were, they would be the last people to turn to. She and Ian had already agreed on that. His parents were so proper and so gentle, and much too old to understand any of this. He was their only child, and truly it would have killed them. Besides, why tell them? It would all work out. It had to.

Ian and Jessie shook hands with Martin and he left them outside the courtroom. It had been an endless morning.

'Do we have a minute to stop at the john?' Jessica looked at Ian nervously. She felt strange and uncomfortable with him, as though someone had just told them he had cancer. She wasn't sure whether to cry or to offer encouragement, or just to run away and hide. She wasn't even sure what she felt yet.

'Sure. I think it's down the hall. I have to go too.' Conversation was awkward between them. It was going to be hard to find the way back. But as they walked along the hall, he stopped her suddenly and turned to face her, holding her arm. 'Jessie, I don't know what to say. I didn't do it, but I'm almost beginning to wonder if that even matters. I can't stand seeing what this is doing to you. I was a total ass for a couple of hours, and you're the one who's paying the price.'

She smiled tiredly in answer. 'And what about you? You're enjoying this maybe? Baby, we're in it now, and we just have to keep on walking till we're through it. That's all. And for Chrissake, don't give up now.' She was looking at him with a gentleness he hadn't seen all day. She slid her arms around him as they stood in the long marble hall, and he folded her into his arms without saying a word. He needed her desperately, and she knew it.

'Come on, hot stuff, I have to pee.' Her voice was gruff and sexy, and he smiled at her as they walked on down the hall, hand in hand. There was something very special between them. Always had been, always would be—if they could just survive what was happening to them now.

'I'll be back in a second.' She pecked a gentle kiss at his neck, squeezed his hand, and disappeared into the ladies' room.

Inside, she let herself into one of the booths and bolted the door. There were women on either side of her. A pair of red platform shoes and navy slacks on her left, slim ankles and simple black pumps on her right. Jessica straightened her stockings, smoothed down her skirt, and unbolted the door at the same moment that the black pumps emerged to her right. She cast a casual glance in that direction as she headed toward the sink, only to find herself rooted to the floor, staring into Margaret Burton's face—staring down at it, actually, with the difference in their height—the pale pink hat only slightly obscuring her view of the enemy's face.

Margaret Burton stood very still and stared back at her, as Jessica felt her insides turn cold. She was right there in front of her . . . within reach . . . grab her . . . hit her . . . kill her . . . but she couldn't move. There was only the sound of a sharp intake of breath as the Burton woman came to her senses and ran toward the door, the hat flying gently to Jessica's feet. It had taken only a few seconds, but it seemed hours, days, years . . .

and she was gone, as Jessie stood there helpless, tears starting down her face. She stooped down very slowly and picked up the hat before walking slowly toward the door. She could hear someone knocking nervously, frantically. It was Ian. He had seen Margaret Burton fly through the door as he'd come out of the men's room across the hall. And suddenly he was terrified. What had happened? What had Jessica done?

She emerged silently, the hat in her hand, tears on her face.

'What happened?'

Jessica only shook her head, clutching the hat.

'Did she do anything?'

She shook her head again.

'Did you?'

And again, a silent no.

'Oh, babe.' He pulled her into his arms, and took the hat from her hand, tossing it onto a nearby bench. 'Let's get the hell out of here and go home.' In fact, he was going to get her out of town. To hell with what Martin said, they needed to get away. Carmel, maybe. Anywhere. He wondered how long Jessica could take the pressure. How long he could. The hat seemed to look at him accusingly from the bench as he held his wife in his arms, and he shuddered. It was the hat she had worn that day at Enrico's. That day . . . the day he'd be paying for for years, one way or another. He kept an arm around Jessica's shoulders and walked her slowly toward the elevator. He wanted to pour his soul into hers, but he wasn't even sure he had enough for himself anymore, let alone for anyone else. He wanted the horror to be over, and it was only beginning.

When the elevator came she walked silently into it. Her eyes were soldered to the doors, and he wanted to shake her. He was watching her slip away again: he had seen this mask before.

The elevator spat them out into the chaos of the lobby. It was filled with police and inspectors, private lawyers and assistant district attorneys, and people waiting in line to get passes to the jail. Ian and Jessica melted into the sea of swarming people. And here and there was an ordinary, untroubled face, someone in the building to pay a parking ticket, or fill out a car-registration form. But they were so few that they blended in with the rest, which was why neither Jessica nor Ian saw Astrid, on her way to get a new sticker for the one that had fallen off her plates at the car wash. They were only a few feet away and never saw her. But she saw them, and was stricken by the expression on their faces. They passed six feet away, and she let them go. It was the same look she had worn when the doctors had told her just how sick Tom really was.

CHAPTER XIII

The following morning, Ian made up his mind. Jessica had to get away. They both did. And when she was making breakfast, he even went to the trouble of clearing it with Martin over the phone. Martin agreed, and Ian announced it to Jessie as a *fait accompli.*

'We're doing what?' She looked at him incredulously as she stood barefoot in her robe in the kitchen.

'We're leaving for Carmel in half an hour.' This time he smiled when he said it. 'Pack your gear, my love.'

'You're crazy. Martin said—'

'—to send him a postcard.' Ian smiled victoriously as Jessica chuckled.

'And just when did he say that?'

'Just now.'

'You called him?' She still looked dubious, but amused.

'I just hung up. So, my beloved—' he approached her slowly, with a wisp of a smile—'get your beautiful ass moving before we waste the day.'

'You're a nut.' He kissed her and she smiled up at him with her eyes closed. 'But such a nice nut.'

They reached Carmel in two hours with Ian at the wheel of the Morgan. The air was cooler than it had been for weeks, and it was brilliantly sunny all the way down. They put the top down on the Morgan and arrived wind-blown and happier. It was almost as though the constant sweep of wind on the highway had cleared the worry from their minds. The trip hadn't been such a bad idea after all, and after the first fifty miles, Jessie had stopped imagining that Inspector Houghton was following them. She was constantly haunted by him, but maybe now it would stop. It was just that he seemed omnipotent. He would go away and then could come back again, with a search warrant, a gun, a friend, a look in his eye . . . a twist of his mouth . . . he terrified her, and she didn't dare tell Ian how much. She never mentioned him. She had also been worried about the expense of the trip, but Ian had insisted that he had enough left in his account to cover it. She had been ordered to mind her own business and warned that they were going economy all the way, no deluxe accommodations this time. She felt guilty, doubting his assurances, but she was obsessed with their finances now, and the upcoming staggering expense of the trial. And Ian was so strange about money, maybe because he had never had any. He had a way of buying her fabulous presents and creating magnificent moments when they were plainly out of funds. He would take the last of what he had and throw it out the window in style. In the past, this trait had amused her. Right now it did not.

But she was grateful for the trip to Carmel. She knew how much she needed it. Her nerves had been on the raw edge of disaster. And she knew that Ian's had been too, no matter how hard he'd tried to cover up.

Astrid had told them about a little hotel where she had stayed the previous spring that she'd insisted was a bargain. So they forfeited the deluxe delights of the familiar Del Monte for the cosy plaid and pine atmosphere of L'Auberge. It was run by a middle-aged French couple, and among its other pleasures, it boasted 'Café Complet' in bed in the morning. The Café Complet consisted of home-made croissants and brioches, with bowls of steaming *café au lait.*

They walked to the beach and canvassed the shops, and on Saturday took a picnic out to the edge of a cliff overlooking the sea.

'More wine, love?'

Ian nodded and pushed a long strand of blonde hair from her eyes. They were lying side by side, and she was looking up at the sky while he rested on one elbow and looked down at her. He smoothed her face with his hand and kissed her gently on the lips, the eyes, the tip of the nose.

'If you do that, I'll never sit up to get you your wine, my love.' He smiled again and she blew him a kiss.

'You know something, Ian?'

'What?'

'You make me very happy.' His face clouded as she said it, and she caught his chin in her hand and forced him to look at her. 'I mean it. You do.'

'How can you say that now?'

'Because now is no different from any other time, Ian. You do beautiful things to me. You give me what I need, and I need a lot. Sometimes you pay a price for that. And okay, so it's hard now, but this'll be over soon. It won't go on forever. All in all I think we're damn lucky.' She sat up and faced him, and finally he looked away.

'Lucky, eh? I guess that's one way to look at it.' He sounded bitter, and she reached for his hand.

'You don't feel lucky anymore?'

'I do. But do you, Jessie, really? Be honest.' He looked back at her with an unfamiliar look in his eyes, a kind of openness that frightened her: as though he were questioning everything. Her. Himself. Them. Life. Everything.

'Yes, I feel lucky.' Her voice was a whisper in the brisk wind of the sunny October day.

'Jessica, my love, I was unfaithful to you. I made love to another woman. A neurotic tramp, but still another woman. You've been supporting me for almost six years. I am not a successful writer. And I'm about to go on trial for rape, I may go to prison, and even if I don't, this is going to be the ugliest thing we've ever lived through.

And you feel lucky? How do you manage that little feat?'

She looked down at her hands for a long time, and then back up into his face. 'Ian, I don't care if you made love to another woman. I don't like it, but it doesn't matter. It doesn't change anything. Not for me. Don't *you* let it change anything. I don't suppose it was the first time, but I don't want to know. That's not the point. The point is, so what? So you made love to someone, so what? So you jacked off, so what? *I don't care*. Does that make any sense to you? I don't care. I care about you, about us, about our marriage, about your career. And I don't "support" you. Lady J supports us both. We're lucky to have it, and one of these days you're going to sell a book and a movie and another book and a pile of brilliant work, and make a fortune. So what's the problem?'

'Jessica, you're crazy.' He was smiling at her, but his eyes still looked serious.

'No, I'm not. And I mean it. You make me happy. You make me glow, you make me care, you make me know I'm loved, you're always there for me. You know who I am and what I am and why I am better than I do even. Ian, that's so rare. I look at other people and they never seem to have what we have.' Her eyes were fiery now, and the colour of jade.

'I don't know what to say, Jessie . . . I love you. And I need you too. Not just to support me while I write. I need . . . oh, hell—' he smiled, more to himself than to her— 'I need you sitting bare-assed and solemn-faced at two in the morning, telling me why my fourth chapter isn't working. I need the way you fly in the door at night with that look of "Oh, wow!" on your face . . . the way you know, the way you . . . respect me, even when I don't respect myself.'

'Oh, Ian.' She slid into his arms again and closed her eyes as he held her.

'I need you a lot, babe. But . . . something's going to have to change.'

Her eyes opened slowly. He had just said something important. She knew it from the change in the way he held her more than from the words.

'What do you mean?'

'I don't know yet. But something's got to change, after we survive this holocaust we're going to walk through in the next couple of months.'

'Like what, dammit? Change what?' Her voice was unexpectedly shrill, and she sat back from him a little so she could read his eyes.

'Take it easy, Jessie. I just think it's about time for an overhaul. I don't know, maybe it's time I shelved my fancy ideas about a writing career. Something. We can't go on exactly like this, though. In some ways it doesn't work.'

'Why not?'

'Because I feel kept. You pay the bills, or most of them, and I can't live with that anymore. Do you know what it feels like to have no income? To feel guilty every time you dig into the kitty, the "joint account", so-called, to buy a couple of T-shirts? Do you have any idea how it feels to have you footing the bill for this disaster now? To have you pick up the tab on my alleged "rape"? Jesus, Jessie, it chokes me. It's killing me. Why the hell do you think I've been impotent lately? Because I'm so thrilled with myself for how I'm running my life?'

'You can't really take that seriously. You're under an incredible amount of strain right now.' She wanted to brush it aside, but he wasn't going to let her.

'That's right. I am under a lot of strain. But part of that strain is because we haven't got things set up the way they should be. Did you ever wonder what would happen if you didn't have Lady J, or if your parents hadn't left you some money?'

'I'd be working for someone else, and you'd be working in advertising and hating it. Doesn't that sound like fun?'

'No. But what if you weren't working at all, and I were working at something else?'

'Like what?' Her face seemed to freeze on the words.

'I don't know like what. I haven't figured that out yet.'

'Ian, you're out of your mind. I've never seen you work as hard on a book as you are on this one now, I've never heard you sound so sure about anything you've written. And now you want to quit?'

'I didn't say that. Not yet. But maybe. What I'm saying is: What would happen to you, to us, to our marriage, if you didn't support us, Jessie, if *I* did? What if we just kept your money as a nest egg, as an investment?'

'And what would I do all day? Needlepoint? Play bridge?'

'No. I was thinking of something else. Maybe for later.' There was something soft and distant in his eyes as he spoke.

'What's the something else?'

'Like . . . well . . . like what if we finally had children —after this whole mess is over, I mean. We haven't talked about that for a long time. Not since before . . .' She knew what he meant by 'before'. Before things had changed. Before her parents had died. Before she'd inherited their money . . . before. That one word said it all. They both knew. 'Jessie . . . baby, I want to take care of you. Besides, you've earned it.'

'Why?'

'What do you mean, "why"?' He looked momentarily confused.

'I mean why should we scramble everything up now? Why should you suddenly take on the whole burden? I love working; it's not a burden for me. It's fun.'

'Can't kids be fun too?'

'I didn't say they weren't.' Her face was as tight as a drum.

'But?'

'Oh, for Chrissake, Ian, why do we have to get into that now?' That one hadn't come up in years.

'I didn't say now. We're just talking what if's.'

'That's ridiculous. It's like playing games.' She turned away and suddenly felt Ian's hand on her arm. Hard.

'It's not like playing games. I'm serious, Jessie. I've turned myself into a fucking gigolo in the last six years. I'm a failure as a writer, and I just balled some two-bit tramp and got falsely accused of rape. I'm trying to figure out what means something in my life and what doesn't, and what needs changing. And maybe part of what needs changing is us. Not even maybe. I know it does. Now are you going to listen, and talk to me, or aren't you?'

She sat silent, looking at him. But she knew she had no choice. He let go of her arm and poured two more glasses of wine. 'I'm sorry. But this is important to me, Jess.'

'Okay. I'll try.' She took the glass of wine and sighed deeply as she looked up at the sky. 'All this because I told you that you make me happy? *Oy vey* . . . I should have kept my mouth shut!' She smiled back at him, and he kissed her again.

'I know. I'm a bastard. But Jessie . . . I want to make it work with us. I want to make it better. I don't want to go screwing other women, or hating myself or . . . it matters. It really matters. And I'm glad I make you happy, and you make me happy too. Very happy. But we can do better, I know we can. I've got to feel like your husband, like a man, like I carry the weight, or most of it at least, even if it means selling the house and living someplace where I can pay our rent. But I *need* to do things like that for you. I'm tired of having you "take care" of me. And I don't mean to sound ungrateful, Jess, but . . . I just need to, dammit.'

'Okay. But why? Why now? Because of that idiot woman? Margaret Burton? Because of her, you have to give up writing and move us into some shack in the Mission where you can pay the rent?' She was getting bitchy now and he didn't like it. The comment hadn't missed its mark.

'No, sweetheart. Margaret Burton is just a symptom, just like the hundred or two hundred pieces of ass before her. Is that how you want to play this, Jessie? Shitty, or straight? Take your pick. I'm willing to play either way.'

She polished off the rest of her wine at a gulp and shrugged. 'I just don't get the point.'

'Maybe that is the point. Just like when I talk about having a child. You don't get the point of that either, do you? Doesn't that mean anything to you at all, Jessie?'

She shook her head solemnly, looking down, avoiding his eyes.

'I just don't understand that. Why? Look at me, dammit. This is important to me. To both of us.' But when she looked up, he was surprised.

'It scares me.'

'A baby?' She had never admitted that to him before. Usually she'd gotten nasty about it and closed the subject rapidly. It made him feel tender toward her to hear that. Scared?

'It scares you physically?' He reached for her hand gently and held it.

'No. It . . . I'd have to share you, Ian, and I . . . I can't.' Tears swam in her eyes and her chin trembled as she looked at him. 'I really can't share you, Ian. I can't, not ever. You're all I have. You're . . .'

'Oh, baby . . .' He took her in his arms and rocked her gently, tears stinging his own eyes. 'What a crazy thing to think. A baby's not like that. It would never be. We're special. A baby would be something more, not less.'

'Yes, but it would be yours. Real family.' And then he understood. He had his parents, of course, but they were so remote and so old. He hardly ever saw them. But a baby would be so present, so real.

'You're my real family, silly. You'll always be my real family.' How often had he told her that, after her parents had died? A thousand times? Ten thousand? It was strange to think back to those days. She had been so fiercely independent and sure of herself when he'd married her. But she had loved both her parents and adored her brother; just hearing her speak of them was like hearing reminiscences of very dear friends who had had a marvellous time together. And spending time with them was an extraordinary experience—four exceedingly handsome people, with lightning minds and quick laughter and immeasurable style. They'd been quite something. And when they were gone, part of her went too. Not an obvious part. She still had as much spirit, as much life, as much style, but suddenly in her soul she was an orphan.

She had loved Ian before, but she hadn't needed him in the same way. Then she'd become like a frightened child lost in a war zone, stricken, scared, wandering from the burnt shell of one memory to another. Lost and alone. The attempted suicide had come after Jake. And it had left her different. Dependent. It was Ian who had led her to safety again after that. That was when she had started calling him 'real family'. Where before their closeness had been a loosely woven, sparkling mesh, suddenly there was nothing loose about it, and over the years it had all gotten too goddam tight. And now there wasn't even room in her heart for a child. He had known that for a long time, but he had thought that eventually the panic would ebb. It hadn't, now he was sure of it. Her own needs were still too intense, and probably always would be. It was a bitter thing for him to accept.

'Oh, God, Ian, I love you so much and I'm so scared . . . I'm so fucking scared.' He felt her in his arms again, his mind pulled back to her, away from his own thoughts. She took a deep breath and held tightly to him as he slowly stroked her hair, thinking of what he now understood and had to accept. Had to. Nothing was ever going to change. Oh, some things would, and he was going to see about making those changes, but she was never going to stand on her own two feet again, not entirely, not enough for them both to reach out to a child.

'I'm scared too, Jess. But it's going to be okay.'

'How can it be okay if you're going to change everything after we get through this? You want me to sell the shop, have a baby, and you're going to stop writing and get a job and make us move and . . . oh, Ian! It sounds horrible!' She sobbed in his arms again and he laughed softly as he held her. Maybe she was all he needed. Maybe it wasn't even normal for a man to want a child as much as he did. Maybe it was just an ego trip. He brushed the thoughts from his mind.

'Jesus, did I say I was going to change all that? It does sound pretty heavy. Maybe we should just pick a couple of things, like I'll have a baby, and you get a job, and . . . I'm sorry, babe, I didn't mean to hit you with ten thousand things at once. I just know that something needs fixing.'

'But all that?'

'No, probably not all that. And not unless you agree with me. It wouldn't work otherwise. We've both got to want it.'

'But you make it sound like our life will never be the same again.'

'Maybe it won't, Jessie. Maybe it shouldn't be. Did you ever think of that?'

'No.'

'And you're not going to, either, huh? Look at you, hunched over like an Indian squaw, trying not to hear anything I'm telling you, with an ant crawling up your arm . . .' He waited. It took half a second. She leapt to her feet with a scream.

'A what?'

'Oh . . . tsk . . . how could I forget? That's right, you're afraid of ants.' He brushed her sleeve lightly as he stood up next to her and she punched him in the chest.

'Goddam you, Ian Clarke! We're having a serious talk and how can you do that to me! There was no ant on me, was there? *Was there*?"

'Would I lie to you?'

'I hate you!' She was still trembling with a jumble of emotions, terror and fury and fear because of the ant, and the much more real emotions of moments before. He'd invented the ant to lighten the mood.

It was a reprieve. Ian was good at them.

'What do you mean, you hate me? You said I made you happy.' He looked all innocence as he put his arms around her.

'Don't touch me!' But she was limp in his arms and trying hard to conceal a smile. 'You know—' her voice was soft again now—'sometimes I wonder if you really love me.'

'Sometimes everyone wonders stuff like that, Jess. You can't have the kind of ironclad guarantees you want, sweetheart. I love you just as much as your mother and father did, just as much as Jake did, just as much as . . .

anyone. But I'm not them. I'm me, your husband, a man, just like you're my wife, not my mother. And maybe one day you'll get sick of me and walk off into the sunset with someone else. Mothers aren't supposed to do that to their kids, but wives do that sometimes. I have to accept that.'

'Are you trying to tell me something?' She was suddenly stiff in his arms.

'No, silly, only that I love you. And that I can only be and do so much. I think I'm trying to tell you not to be so insecure and not to worry so much. Sometimes I think that's why you put up with so much shit from me, and pay the bills and all the rest, because that way you know you've got me. But I'll tell you a secret—that way you don't got me. As it so happens you've got me, but for all the other reasons.'

'Like what?' She was smiling again.

'Oh . . . like the beautiful way you sew.'

'Sew? I can't sew.' She looked at him strangely and then started to laugh.

'You can't?'

'Nope.'

'I'll teach you.'

'You're adorable.'

'Come to think of it, lady, so are you. Which reminds me. Reach into my pocket.' Her eyebrows lifted with interest and she grinned mischievously at him.

'A surprise for me?'

'No, my laundry bill.'

'Creep.' But she slipped her hand carefully into his jacket pocket as they talked, her eyes sparkling with excitement. It was easy to find the little square box. She pulled it out with a grin and held it clutched in her hand.

'Aren't you going to open it?'

'This is the best part.' She giggled again and he grinned at her.

'It's not the Hope diamond, I promise.'

'It's not?'

'Oh, for Chrissake . . .' And then she suddenly snapped open the box. And he watched.

'Oh . . . it's . . . oh, Ian! You nut!' She gave a whoop

of laughter and looked at it again. 'How in God's name did you get it?'

'I saw it, and I knew you had to have it.'

She laughed again and started to put it on. It was a thin gold chain with a gold pendant shaped like a lima bean. The thing she had hated most in the world as a child.

'Good God, I never thought I'd see the day when I'd wear one of the bloody things. And in gold, yet.' She laughed again, kissed him, and tucked in her chin to look down at the small gold nugget on its chain.

'Actually, it looks very elegant. If you didn't know what it was, you'd never guess. I had a choice between a kidney bean, a lima bean, and some other kind of bean. They're done by the same very fancy designer, I'll have you know.'

'And you just saw it in a window?'

'Yep. And I figured that if you have faith as a mustard seed, you can move mountains and all that stuff. So hell, if you have faith like a lima bean, you can probably move half the world.'

'Which half?'

'Any half, sexy lady. Come on, let's go back to the hotel.'

'Lima beans . . . sweetheart, you're crazy. May I ask how large a portion of your fortune this sensational lima bean cost you?' She had noticed that it was eighteen-carat gold and that the box was from a very extravagant store.

'You most certainly may not. How can you ask such a thing?'

'Curiosity.'

'Well, don't be so curious. And do me a favour. Don't eat it.' She laughed again and bit his neck as she reached over for the rest of the wine.

'Sweetheart, there is one thing you can bet on. I ain't never gonna eat lima beans. Not even a gold one.' And then they both burst into laughter, because that was exactly what she had told him the first time he had cooked dinner for her at his place eight years before.

He had fixed roast pork, mashed potatoes, and lima

beans. She had devoured the meat and potatoes, but he had found her rapidly shovelling lima beans into her handbag when he'd come back from the kitchen with the glass of water she'd requested, and she had looked at him, thrown up her hands, burst into laughter and said, 'Ian, I ain't never gonna eat lima beans. Not even if they're solid gold.' And this one was indeed solid gold. For the tiniest of moments, her stomach felt queasy at the thought of the expense. But that was Ian. They were going down the tubes in style. With picnics and passion and gold.

The mood for the rest of the weekend was sheer holiday spirit. Jessica flashed her gold lima bean at every possible opportunity, and they teased and hugged and kissed. L'Auberge restored their love life to what it had always been. They had dinner by candlelight in their room—a feast of fried chicken from a nearby take-out place, devoured with a small bottle of champagne they had bought on the way back to the hotel. They giggled like children and played like honeymooners, and the threats of the morning were forgotten. Everything was forgotten except Ian and Jessie. They were the only people who mattered.

The only sorrow, and it was a hidden one, was Ian's hope of a child, now put away. Insanely, desperately, he had wanted to father a child, now, before the trial, before . . . what if . . . who knew what was coming? A year from then he could be in prison or dead. It wasn't a cheerful way to look at things, but the realities were beginning to frighten him. And the possibilities were even more terrifying when he let himself think of them. A baby would be a fresh blade of grass springing from ashes. But now that he understood how panicked Jessie still was, the subject was closed. His books were his children. He would simply work that much harder on the new book.

On Sunday, Jessie bought Ian a Sherlock Holmes hat and a corncob pipe. They shared a banana split for lunch, then rented a tandem bike and rode around near the hotel, laughing at their lack of precision. Jessica collapsed when faced with a hill.

'What do you mean, "no"? Come on, Jessie, *push!*"

'The hell I will. You push. I'll walk.'

'Stinkpot.'

'Look at that hill. Who do you think I am? Tarzan?'

'Well, look at your legs, for Chrissake. They're long enough to run up that hill carrying me, let alone bicycling.'

'You, sir, are a creep.'

'Hey . . . look at the spider on your leg.'

'I . . . what? . . . Aaaahh . . . Ian! Where?' But he was laughing at her, and when she looked up she knew. 'Ian Clarke, if you do that to me one more time, I'll . . .' She was spluttering and he was laughing harder than ever. 'I'll . . .' She hit him a walloping blow on the shoulder, knocking him off the bicycle and into the tall grass next to the path. But he reached out and grabbed her as she stood laughing at him, and pulled her down beside him. 'Ian, not here! There are probably snakes in here! Ian! Dammit! Stop that!'

'No snakes. I swear.' He was reaching into her blouse with a leer that made her giggle.

'Ian . . . I mean it—no! Ian . . .' She forgot about the snakes almost immediately.

CHAPTER XIV

'Well, how did you like my favourite hideaway in Carmel?' With a smile, Astrid poked her head in the door of Jessica's office.

'We adored it. Come on in. How about some coffee?'

Jessie's smile said it all. The two days in Carmel had been a peaceful island in a troubled sea.

'I'll skip the coffee, thanks. I'm on my way downtown to talk to Tom's attorneys. Maybe I'll stop by again on my way home.' Jessica showed her the gold lima bean, gave her a brief, expurgated account of the weekend, and blew Astrid a kiss as she left. For the rest of the day, Lady J was a madhouse.

There were deliveries, new clients, old customers who wanted something new but needed it altered 'right now', invoices that got misplaced, and two shipments that Jessie needed desperately never showed up at all. And Katsuko couldn't help, because she was swamped with details for the fashion show. So Zina juggled the customers while Jessie tried to untangle the problems. And the bills. The next two weeks were more of the same.

Harvey Green appeared twice at the boutique to discuss minor things with Jessie, things about Ian's habits and her own, but she had little to tell him. Neither did Ian. They led a simple life and had nothing to hide. The two girls in the boutique still didn't know what was happening, and the weeks since Jessie's frantic and erratic disappearances from the shop had been too hectic for questions. They assumed that the problem, whatever it was, had blown over. And Astrid was careful not to pry.

Ian was lost in his new book, and the two subsequent court appearances went smoothly. As Martin had predicted the bail was not revoked: there was never even a suggestion of it. Jessica joined Ian both times in court, but there was nothing to see. He would walk to the front of the courtroom with Martin, they would mumble for a few moments in front of the judge, and then they could all leave. By now it seemed like an ordinary part of their everyday lives; they had other things to think about. Jessie was worried about part of the fall line that hadn't moved, another shipment that had never shown up, and the money that was draining from her bank account. Ian was troubled by chapter nine, and incoherent about anything else. That was what their real life was about, not mechanical appearances before a bored judge.

It was a month later when Harvey Green came up with the first part of his bill. Eighteen hundred dollars. The statement arrived at the boutique, as she had requested, and Jessica gasped when she opened it. She felt almost sick. Eighteen hundred dollars. For nothing. He hadn't unearthed a damn thing, except the name of a man Margaret Burton had gone to dinner with twice and never slept with. Peggy Burton appeared to be clean. Her co-workers thought her a decent woman, not very sociable, but reliable and pleasant to work with. Several mentioned that she was occasionally distant and moody. She had no torrid love affairs in her past, no drug problems, no drinking habits to speak of. She had never returned to any hotel on Market Street in all the time Green had been tailing her, nor had she had any men into her apartment at any time since the surveillance had begun. She went home alone every night after work; had gone to three movies in a month, again alone; and an attempt to pick her up on the bus had totally failed. An assistant of Green's had made eyes at her for several blocks, got an encouraging look in response, he said, and had then received a firm 'No, thanks, buster' when he'd invited her out for a drink. He had said she'd even looked pissed at him for asking. At worst, she was confused. At best . . . she was the second best thing to the Virgin Mary, and Ian's case would look very flimsy in court. They had to find something. But they hadn't. And now Harvey Green wanted eighteen hundred dollars. And they couldn't even let him go. Martin had said the Burton woman would have to be watched right up until the trial, possibly even during the trial, although both he and Green admitted that the police had probably told her to behave herself. The prosecution didn't want their case shot down by a random piece of ass Miss Margaret Burton might indulge herself with a few weeks before the trial.

Green hadn't even been able to come up with any dirt on her past. She had been married once, at the age of eighteen, and the marriage had been annulled a few months later. But he didn't know why, or who she had married. Nothing. And there was no record of it, which was probably why she hadn't admitted to it at the preliminary hearing. (What he knew he had learned from a woman Margaret Burton worked with.) What Jessie was paying for was a clean bill of health on the woman.

Jessie sat at her desk, staring at Green's bill, and opened

the rest of her mail. A statement from Martin for the five thousand they still owed, and nine statements from New York for her purchases for the spring line. Ian's bill for his physical two months before, still due, for two hundred and forty-two dollars, and her own chest X ray for forty, as well as a seventy-four-dollar bill from a record store where she'd splurged before she'd gone to New York. As she sat there, she wondered what had ever made her think that seventy-four dollars for records wasn't so awful. She could still remember saying that to Ian at the time. Yeah . . . not so awful if you haven't found yourself with ten thousand dollars in legal bills in the meantime . . . and the florist . . . and the cleaner's . . . and the drugstore . . . she could feel her stomach constrict as she tried not to add up the amounts. She reached for the phone, looked at the card in her address book, and called.

She phoned the bank before going to the appointment, and she was lucky, more or less. Based on the previous performance of her account, the bank was willing to leave her loan uncovered by collateral. She could sell it. She had been secretly hoping that they wouldn't let her. But now she had no choice.

She sold the Morgan at two in the afternoon. For fifty-two hundred dollars. The guy gave her 'a deal'. She deposited the cheque in the bank before closing, and sent a cheque of her own to Martin Schwartz for five thousand dollars. He was paid. It was taken care of. She could breathe now. For weeks she had had nightmares about something happening to her and nobody being able to help Ian with the bills . . . horrible fantasies of Ian begging Katsuko for the money, and being refused because she wanted the money to buy kimonos for the shop, while Barry York threatened to drag Ian back to jail. Now they were saved. The legal fees were paid. If something happened to her, Ian had his attorney.

She then borrowed eighteen hundred dollars from Lady J's business account to pay Green his fee. She was back at her desk at three-thirty—with a splitting headache. Astrid showed up at four-thirty.

'You're not looking too happy, Lady J. Anything wrong?'

Astrid was the only one who called her that, and it made her smile tiredly.

'Would you believe *everything's* wrong?'

'No, I wouldn't. But—anything special you want to tell me?' Astrid sipped the coffee Zina had poured for her and Jessie sighed and shook her head.

'Nothing much to tell. Not unless you have about six hundred spare hours to listen, and I don't have that much spare time to tell you anyway. How was your day?'

'Better than yours. But I didn't take any chances. I got up at eleven and spent the afternoon having my hair done.' Jesus. How could she tell her? How could Astrid possibly understand?

'Maybe that's where I went wrong. I washed my hair myself last night.' She grinned lopsidedly at her friend, but Astrid didn't smile. She was worried. Jessie had been looking tired and troubled for weeks, and there was nothing she could say.

'Why don't you call it a day, and go home to your gorgeous young husband? Hell, Jessica, if I had him around, wild horses couldn't keep me here.'

'You know something? I think you're right.' It was the first real smile Jessica had produced all day. 'Are you heading home? I could use a ride.'

'Where's your baby?'

'The Morgan?' She tried to stall. She didn't want to lie, but . . . Astrid nodded, and Jessie felt a pain in her heart.

'I . . . it's in the shop.'

'No problem. I'll give you a ride.'

Ian watched Astrid drop her off from the window in his studio, and he looked puzzled. It was time to take a break anyway—he'd been working straight through since seven that morning. He opened the door for Jessie before she got out her key.

'What's with the car? Did you leave it at the boutique?'

'Yes . . . I . . .' She looked up and she could almost

feel the colour draining from her face. She had to tell him. 'Ian, I . . . I sold it.' She winced at the look on his face. Everything stopped.

'*You did what*?' It was worse than she had feared.

'I sold it. Darling, I had to. Everything else is tied up. And we needed almost seven thousand bucks in the next two weeks for Martin's fee, and the first half of Green's bill, and Green is going to hit us with another one in two weeks. There was nothing else I could do.' She reached out to touch him and he brushed her hand away.

'You could have asked me, at least! Asked me, said something—for God's sake, Jessica, don't you consult me on *anything* anymore? I gave you that car as a gift. It meant something to me!' He strode across the room and grabbed for the Scotch. He poured some into a glass while she watched.

'Don't you think it meant something to *me*?' Her voice was trembling, but he didn't hear, and she watched while he swallowed the half glass of Scotch neat. 'Darling, I'm so . . . I just couldn't see any other . . .' She fell silent, with tears in her eyes. She remembered so well the day he had driven it home for her. Now . . .

He swallowed the last of his drink and pulled on his jacket.

'Where are you going?'

'Out.' His face looked like grey marble.

'Ian, please, don't do anything crazy.' She was frightened at the look in his eyes, but he only stood there and shook his head.

'I don't have to do anything crazy. I already did.' The door slammed behind him a moment later.

He came back at midnight, silent and subdued, and Jessica didn't ask him where he'd been. She was afraid to: maybe Inspector Houghton would be paying them another visit. But she hated herself for the thought when she watched Ian take off his shoes. Two small hills of sand poured out of them, and she looked at his face. He looked better. They had always done that together—gone to the beach at night to talk things out, or think, or just walk quietly together. He had taken her there when Jake had died. To their beach. Always together. Now she was afraid even to reach out and touch him, but she wanted to, needed to. He looked at her silently and walked into the bathroom and closed the door. Jessie turned out the lights and wiped two tears from her face. She felt the funny gold lima bean at her throat and tried to make herself smile, but she couldn't. They were past laughing at lima beans now, past laughing at anything, and who knew—one day she might sell the lima bean too. She hated herself as she lay in the dark.

She heard the bathroom door open, then Ian's soft footsteps, and then she felt the bed dip on the far side. He sat there for what seemed like a long time, smoking a cigarette. He leaned against the headboard and stretched his legs. She knew all his movements without looking, and she lay very still, wanting him to think she was sleeping. She didn't know what to say to him.

'I have something for you, Jess.' His voice was gruff and low in the stillness of the room.

'Like a punch in the mouth?'

He laughed and put a hand on her hip as she lay on her side with her back to him.

'No, dummy. Turn around.' She shook her head like a child, and then peeked over her shoulder.

'You're not mad at me, Ian?'

'No, I'm mad at me. There was nothing else you could do. I know that. I just hate myself for getting us in this spot, and I'd rather have sold a lot of things than the Morgan.'

She nodded, still at a loss for words. 'I'm so sorry.'

'Me too.' He leaned over and kissed her gently on the mouth and then put something light and sandy in her hand. 'Here. I found it in the dark.' It was a perfect sand dollar, a milky white shell with a tiny fossil imprint at its heart.

'Oh, darling, it's beautiful.' She smiled up at him, holding it in the flattened palm of her hand.

'I love you.' And then with a slow, gentle smile he

pulled her into his arms and let his lips follow an exquisite path to her thighs.

The next two weeks spun past them crazily. Hours at the shop, long lunches at home, violent arguments about who wasn't watering the plants, and then passionate making up and making love and making out, and insomnia, and oversleeping, and forgetting to eat and then eating too much, and constant indigestion, and terror about the bills followed by spending huge amounts of money on a Gucci wallet for Ian or a suede skirt from another store for Jessie, when she could have gotten it at cost from her own, and baubles and junk and garbage, and all of it charged, of course, as though the day of reckoning would never come. Utter madness. None of it made any sense. Jessie felt for weeks as though she were ricocheting off walls, never to be stationary again. Ian had the impression he was drowning.

It was the day before the trial when everything finally stopped. Jessie had made arrangements at the shop to take a week off, two if things turned out that way. She left the boutique early and went for a long walk before going home to Ian. She found him sitting pensively in a chair, staring at the view. It was the first time she had seen him not working furiously on the new novel. That was all he seemed to do now, when he wasn't spending money, or silently and urgently taking her body. They talked less than they ever had. Even meals were either silent disasters or frantic and frenzied—never normal.

But that night they lit a fire together, and talked until dark. She felt as though she hadn't seen him in months. At last she was talking to Ian again, the man she loved, her husband, her lover, her friend. She had missed his friendship most of all in these endless lonely weeks. It was the first time they really hadn't been able to reach out to each other and help. Now they shared a quiet dinner, sitting on the floor in front of the fire. Their peacefulness made the trial seem less terrifying. And the reality of it had worn off in the weeks since Ian had been released from jail. Jail had been reality. Fighting her way upstream to bail had been reality. Leaving her mother's emerald ring had been reality. But what was the trial? Merely a formality. A verbal exchange between two paid performers, theirs and the State's, with a black-robed umpire looking on, and somewhere in the background a woman no one knew named Margaret Burton. A week, maybe two weeks, and then it would be over. That was the only reality.

She rolled over on her back on the rug in front of the fire and smiled up at him sleepily as he bent to kiss her. It was a long, haunting kiss that brought back the gentleness they had lost and made her body beg to respond, and in a few minutes they were hungrily making love. It was one of those rare nights when souls and bodies blended and ignited and burned on for hours. They said little, but they made love again and again. It was almost dawn when Ian deposited Jessica sleepily in their bed.

'I love you, Jessie. Get some sleep now. Tomorrow will be a long day.' He whispered the words, and she smiled at his voice as she drifted off to sleep. A long day? Oh . . . that's right . . . the fashion show . . . or was it that they were going back to the beach? . . . She couldn't remember . . . a picnic? Was that it?

'I love you too . . .' Her voice drifted off as she fell asleep at his side, her arms wrapped around him like a small child's. He stroked her arm gently as he lay beside her, smoking a cigarette, and then he looked down into her face, but he wasn't smiling. Nor was he sleepy. He loved Jessica more than ever, but there were too many other things crowding his mind.

He spent the rest of the night in a lonely vigil. Watching his wife, thinking his own thoughts, listening to her breathe and murmur, wondering what would come next.

The next morning he was going on trial for rape.

CHAPTER XV

The courtroom at City Hall was a far cry from the small room where the preliminary hearing had been held. This one looked like a courtroom in the movies. Gold leaf, wood panelling, long rows of chairs, the judge's bench set up high on a platform, and the American flag in plain view of all. The room was full of people, and a woman was calling names one by one. She stopped when she had twelve. They were selecting the jury.

Ian sat with Martin at the front of the room, at the desk assigned to the defence. A few feet away sat a different assistant district attorney, with Inspector Houghton at his side. Margaret Burton was nowhere in sight.

The twelve jurors took their seats, and the judge explained the nature of the trial. A few of the women looked surprised and cast glances at Ian, and one man shook his head. Martin made rapid notes and watched the prospective jurors closely. He had the right to excuse ten people from the jury, and the assistant D.A. could do the same. The faces looked innocuous, like those of people you'd see on a bus.

Martin had told Ian and Jessie earlier that morning about the nature of the jury he wanted. No 'old maids' who would be shocked at the accusation of rape, or who might identify with the victim; yet perhaps they might try to hang on to some staunch middle-class housewives who might condemn Burton for allowing Ian to pick her up. Young people might be in sympathy with Ian, yet they might resent the way the couple looked, too comfortable for their age. They were walking a delicate line.

Jessie watched the twelve men and women from her seat in the front row, searching their faces and that of the judge. But just as Martin stood up to question the first prospective juror, the judge called a recess for lunch.

It was a slow process; it was the end of the second day

before the jury had been picked. They had been interrogated by both attorneys as to their feelings about rape, had been questioned about their jobs and their mates, their habits and the number of children they had. Martin had explained that fathers of women Miss Burton's age would not be a good idea either; they'd feel too protective of the victim. One had to consider so many things, and some base was inevitably left uncovered. There were a couple of people on the jury even now who did not meet with Martin's full approval, but he had used up his challenges, and now they had to hope for the best. Martin had set up an easy bantering style with the jurors, and now and then someone had laughed at a foolish answer or a joke.

Finally the jury was set. Five men, three retired and two young, and seven women, five in their middle years and comfortably married, two young and single. That had been a stroke of good fortune. They hoped it would counterbalance two of the retired men Martin did not like. But on the whole, he was reasonably satisfied, and Ian and Jessie assumed he was right.

As they all left the courtroom at the end of the second day, Jessie felt as though she could have recited the jurors' life stories in her sleep, listed their occupations and those of their mates. She would have known their faces in a crowd of thousands, and would remember them for a lifetime if she never saw them again after that day.

Their first shock came on the third day. The quiet male assistant district attorney who had replaced the irritating female D.A. of the preliminary hearing did not appear in court. He had developed acute appendicitis during the night, it was reported to the court, and had been operated on early that morning for a perforated appendix. He was resting comfortably at Mt. Zion Hospital, which Jessica found to be small consolation. This news was reported to the judge by one of the sick man's colleagues, who happened to be trying a case in the adjoining courtroom. But His Honour was assured that a replacement had been chosen and would arrive at any moment. Jessie's and Ian's hearts sank. The woman from the preliminary hearing would be back on the case. It had seemed immeasurable good luck when she hadn't appeared at the opening of the trial, and now . . .

Martin bent to whisper something in Ian's ear as the judge called a short recess while they waited for the new assistant D.A. to arrive. Everyone stood up, the judge left the courtroom, and there was a stretching and shuffling toward the halls. It was still early, and even a cup of coffee from one of the machines in the hall would taste good. It was something to do. Jessica could feel depression weighing on her shoulders as she held her small Styrofoam cup of steaming, malevolent-looking coffee. All she could think of was that damned D.A. and how badly her presence might hurt their case. She glanced at Ian, but he said nothing. And Martin had vanished somewhere.

He had told them not to discuss the case in the hall during recesses or lunch, and suddenly it was difficult to find banalities with which to break the silence. So they kept silent, standing close together with the look of refugees waiting for a train to arrive, but not really understanding what was happening to them.

'More coffee?'

'Hm?' Her thoughts had been in limbo.

'Coffee. Do you want more coffee?' Ian tried it again. But she only shook her head with a vague attempt at a smile. 'Don't worry so much, Jess. It'll be okay.'

'I know.' Words. All words. With no meaning behind them. Nothing had any meaning anymore. Everything was confusing, impossible to understand. What were they doing there? Why were they standing around like awkward mourners at a funeral? Jessica crushed out a cigarette on the marble floor and looked up at the ceiling. It was ornate and beautiful and she hated it. It was too fancy. Too elaborate. It reminded her of where she was. City Hall. The trial. She lit another cigarette.

'You just put one out, Jess.' His voice was soft and sad. He knew what was happening too.

'Huh?' She squinted at him through the flame from her lighter.

'Nothing. Shall we go back?'

'Sure. Why not?' She tried a flip smile as she tossed the empty Styrofoam cup into a large metal ashtray filled with sand.

They walked back into the courtroom side by side, but not touching. Ian walked slowly toward the desk that set him and Martin apart from everyone else. And Jessica followed him with her eyes, watching him, watching Martin rapidly scratch out notes on a long yellow legal pad. The perfect lawyer, the image caught in a pool of sunlight splashed bravely across the inlaid marble floor. She stared at the light for a minute, thinking of nothing, only wishing herself somewhere else, and then absentmindedly she looked across at the desk reserved for the assistant D.A.

There she sat. Matilda Howard-Spencer, tall, lean; everything about her seemed sharp. She had a narrow head with blunt-cut short blonde hair, and long thin agile hands that seemed ready to point accusing fingers. She wore a sober grey suit and a pale grey silk shirt, and her eyes almost matched her suit. Slate grey, and just as hard. Long, skinny legs, and the only piece of jewellery she wore was a thin gold band. She was married to Judge Spencer, whose name she had incorporated into hers, and she was the holy terror of the D.A.'s office. Her best cases were rapes. Neither Ian nor Jessie knew any of that, but Martin did, and he had wanted to cry as he'd watched her walk into the courtroom. She had the delicacy and charm of a hatchet delivered bull's-eye to the balls. He had tried another case against her once, and he hadn't won. Nobody had. His client had committed suicide nine days into the trial. He probably would have anyway, but still . . . Matilda, darling Matilda. And all Ian and Jessie knew was what they saw and what they felt.

Ian saw a woman who made him nervous as she seemed to stalk within an invisible cage around her desk. Jessie saw a woman carved in ice, and sensed something that filled her with fear. Now it wasn't a game. It was a full-scale war. Just the way the woman looked at Ian told her that. She glared across at him once, and then through him several times, as though he were not a person to acknowledge, and considerably less than a man. She spoke to Houghton in a rapid flow of words, and he nodded several times, then got up and walked away. It was very clear who was in command. Jessica cursed the man with the appendix. This woman was one piece of luck they didn't need.

'All rise . . .' The judge was back in his seat, and tension filled the air. He showed obvious pleasure at the new addition to the scene, and acknowledged her presence with a respectful greeting. Terrific.

Matilda Howard-Spencer made a few quick, friendly remarks to the jury, all of which they seemed to respond to. She could inspire confidence as well as fear. Her voice and manner exuded authority, and belied her age: she must be no older than forty-two or -three. She was someone you could count on, someone who would take care of business, take care of you, see that things worked. This was a woman who could fight a war, lead an army, and still manage to see that the children took Latin as well as algebra. But she had no children. She had been married for less than two years. The law was her lover. Her husband was only her friend, and he was a man well into his sixties.

The sparring began with one of the least interesting of witnesses. The medical examiner took the stand and said nothing damaging to Ian, nothing helpful to Margaret Burton. He testified only that he had examined her, that there had been intercourse, but that nothing more than that could be ascertained. Despite Matilda Howard-Spencer's best urging, he stuck to his assertion that there was no evidence that force had been used. Martin's objections to her near-badgering were rapidly quelled, but the testimony was too colourless to make much difference. It all seemed very boring to Jessica, and after an hour she settled her attention on the middle red nylon stripe in the flag. It was something to stare at as she tried to float away from where she was . . . those words droning on endlessly . . . 'infamous crime against nature' . . . sodomy . . . rape . . . intercourse . . . rectum . . . vagina . . .

sperm . . . it was like a child's guide to fantasy. All those terrible words you looked up in the dictionary when you were fourteen, and were titillated by. Now she had a chance to try each one on for size. Vagina. The prosecutor seemed fond of that one. And rape. She said it with a capital letter 'R'.

The day ended at last, and they went home as silently as they had throughout the week. It was exhausting just being there, keeping up the front for those watchers in the jury box, for anyone who might be paying attention. If you frowned, the jury might think you were mad—mad at Ian—or upset. Upset? No, darling, of course not! If you smiled, it meant you took the proceedings too lightly. If you wore the wrong thing, you looked rich. Something too cheerful, and you looked flip. Sexy in court? At a rape trial? God forbid. Vagina? Where? No, of course I don't have one. It wasn't even frightening anymore, just exhausting. And that damned woman was relentless, squeezing every last thought and word out of the witnesses. And Martin was such a fucking gentleman. But what did it matter anymore? If they could just stay awake and keep turning up in court, soon it would be over. Soon . . . but it seemed as though it had just begun. There were lifetimes to go. They hardly said a word over dinner that night, and Jessica was fast asleep in her bathrobe before Ian came out of the shower. It was just as well; he was too tired to say anything. And what was there to say?

She stretched sleepily in the car the next morning and smiled tiredly at the early morning light on the buildings.

'What are you smiling at, Jess?'

'A crazy thought. I was just thinking that this is like when we used to go to work together in New York.' She looked thoughtful, but he didn't smile.

'Not exactly.'

'No. Do we have time to stop for a quick cup of coffee on the way?' They hadn't had time for breakfast, and it was already late.

'We'd better just settle for coffee out of the machine up there, Jess. I don't want to be late. They can hold me in contempt for that, and pull my bail.' Jesus. And all for a cup of coffee.

'Okay, love.' She touched his shoulder gently and lit a fresh cigarette. The only place she didn't smoke now was in court.

She slipped her hand inside his arm as they walked up the steps of City Hall, and everything seemed bright and shiny and new. It was that kind of morning, no matter what horrors were happening to their life. It almost seemed as though God didn't know. He went right on with the sunlight and pretty days.

They reached the hall outside the courtroom with three minutes to spare, and Jessica hurried for the coffee machine.

'Want some?' He started to answer no, but then nodded yes. How much worse could his heartburn get, and what did it matter? He took the cup from her hand; it was so shaky she almost spilled the coffee.

'Baby, it's going to take a year to put us back together after this.'

'You mean my adorable quivers?' He smiled back into her face.

'Have you seen mine?' He held out a hand and they both laughed.

'Occupational hazard, I guess.'

'For a rapist?' She had tried to sound flip, but he didn't.

'Okay, Ian, knock it off.' It ended the brief conversation between them, and Jessica noticed a flurry of activity near an unmarked door. There were people coming and going. Four men, a woman, the sound of voices, as though someone of importance were arriving.

The activity caught Jessie's attention, but it was Ian who looked strange, his head cocked to one side, listening intently. She wanted to ask him what was happening, but she wasn't sure she should. He seemed so totally absorbed by the sounds and the voices. Then there was the quick slam of a door, and a woman in a plain white wool dress rounded the corner. Jessica gasped. It was Margaret Burton.

Ian's mouth opened and then closed, but none of them

moved. Jessica stood, transfixed, feeling shaken and cold, her eyes driving into Margaret Burton, who had come to a rapid halt, taken one short step backward, and then stopped with an expression of astonishment on her face as the three of them stood there. It seemed as though the entire building had fallen silent, and they were the only three people left in the world. Nothing moved . . . except Margaret Burton's face. Slowly, ever so slowly, like a wax mask melting in the sun, her face moulded into an incredible smile. It was a rictus of victory, for only Ian to see. Jessica watched her, horrified, and then, as though her body moved of its own accord, she lurched wildly forward and swung at the Burton woman with the handbag held clenched in her hand.

'Why? Why, dammit, why?' It was a piercing wail of pain from Jessica's heart. The woman fell back a step, looking startled, as though waked from a dream, while at the same moment Ian leaped forward to grab Jessie. Something terrible could have happened. She had murder in her eyes. And that cry of 'Why?' was echoed again and again through the halls as Margaret Burton fled, her heels tapping a haunting staccato in the marble corridor as Jessie sobbed in Ian's arms.

A fleet of men rapidly came running, then turned away as they saw only Ian and Jessie standing there. There was no brawl to dispel, nothing more than a husband and wife fighting, and a wife having herself a good cry. But Martin had heard the sounds too, and for some reason, as he had been about to enter the court, something had told him to follow the sounds. And then seeing Margaret Burton hurry into a door near the court, he knew that something had happened. He found Jessie trembling on a bench, with Ian trying to soothe her.

'Is she all right?'

Ian looked grim in response and didn't answer.

'What happened?'

'Nothing. She . . . we just . . . had an unexpected encounter with the illustrious Miss Burton.'

'Did she do anything to Jessie?' Martin prayed that she had. It would be the best thing that had happened to their case.

'She smiled.' Jessie stopped sobbing long enough to explain.

'She smiled?' Martin was puzzled.

'Yes. Like someone who has just killed someone else, and is glad.'

'Now, Jess . . .' Ian tried to pacify her, but he knew she was right. That was exactly how Margaret Burton had looked, but they were the only ones who had seen it.

'You know damn well that's what she looked like.' She tried to explain it to Martin, but he made no comment.

'Are you all right now?' She nodded slowly and took a deep breath.

'I'm okay.'

'Good. Because we should get into court. We don't want to be late.'

Jessica rose unsteadily, with both men watching her worriedly. She took another deep breath and closed her eyes. What a hideous morning.

'Jessie . . .'

'No. Now just let me alone, and I'll be fine.' She had known what Ian was going to say. He wanted her to go home.

As they walked into court, she felt a few heads turn, and wondered who had heard her shrieks as the Burton woman had fled down the hall. It rapidly became clear who had. They were less than three feet into the courtroom before Inspector Houghton was standing belligerently in front of them, with an angry look on his face that was directed at Jessie.

'If you ever do that again, I'll have you arrested, and his bail pulled so fast both your heads will swim.' Ian looked agonised and Jessica gaped as Martin stepped in front of them.

'Do what, exactly, Inspector?'

'Threaten Miss Burton.'

'Jessica, did you threaten Miss Burton?' Martin looked at her as a father would, asking his five-year-old if she had poured Mommy's perfume down the toilet.

'No. I . . . I screamed . . .'

'What did you scream?'

'I don't know.'

'She said "why?" That's all she said,' Ian filled in for her.

'That doesn't sound like a threat to me, Inspector. Does it to you? As a matter of fact, I heard Mrs. Clarke shouting that word all the way down the hall, which was what drew me to the scene.'

'I consider that a threat.' I consider you an asshole. Jessie was dying to say it.

'Where I come from, Inspector, "why" is a question, not a threat. Unless our asking that kind of question threatens you.' And then, without another word, Houghton turned on his heel and returned to the chair next to Matilda Howard-Spencer. But he was looking none too pleased, and neither was Ian. Jessie could feel him shaking next to her.

'I'm going to kill that sonofabitch before this is over.' But the look on Martin's face stopped both of them. It was terrifying.

'No, dammit, you're going to sit here and look like Mr. and Mrs. America if it kills *you*. And right now. Is that clear? Both of you? Jessica, that means you too. Smile, beautiful, smile. Bullshit. Better than that. And take her arm, Ian. Jesus, all we need is for the jury to think there's trouble. There isn't. Yet. Just remember that.' And with that, he walked toward the desk at the front of the room with a look of solemnity but not of concern. He smiled in the direction of the prosecutor, and took in the room with a benevolent air. Jessie and Ian didn't do quite as well, though they tried. And they still had the Burton woman's testimony to live through. But remarkably, after that demonic smile, hearing her talk wasn't as bad as they had feared.

She told the now-familiar tale as she sat primly on the witness stand. The white dress looked terribly pure, overwhelmingly ladylike. She sat so demurely that her legs might have been soldered together just before she'd come into court, and Jessica noticed that her hair was now tinted more brown than red. If she was wearing makeup, you couldn't see it, and if she had a bosom, she had done remarkable things to make it disappear. She seemed to have no figure at all.

'Ms. Burton, would you care to tell us what happened?' The assistant district attorney was wearing an extremely sombre black dress, a perfect contrast to the witness's white one. It was like something out of a 'B' movie.

The recitation that followed sounded very familiar indeed. At the end of her client's story, the prosecutor asked, 'Had anything like this ever happened to you before?'

The witness hung her head and barely seemed able to whisper. 'No.' It was a gentle sound, like a leaf falling to earth, and Jessie felt her nails dig into her palms. It was the first time in her life she had ever hated anyone that much. And sitting there, watching her, having to listen to her, made her want to kill the woman.

'How did you feel after he left you there in that sleazy hotel?' Oh, Jesus.

'Like I wanted to kill myself. I thought about it for a while. That was why it took me so long to call the police.' What a performance! It almost required a standing ovation and a chorus of bravos. But it was far from amusing. Jessie knew Margaret Burton was winning over the jury with her demure little airs.

What could Martin do now? If he tore her to shreds, the jury would hate him. Cross-examining her was going to be like roller skating through a mine field.

After more than an hour of testimony, Matilda Howard-Spencer had finished her questioning, and it was Martin's turn to begin. Jessica felt her stomach rise and then rapidly fall. She wanted to hold on to Ian. She couldn't stand it anymore. But she had to. And she wondered what he was feeling as he sat isolated from the world. The accused. The rapist. Jessica shuddered.

'Ms. Burton, why did you smile at Mr. Clarke this morning outside the court?' Martin's first question shocked everyone in the courtroom, even Jessie. The jury looked stunned, while Houghton smoulded and whispered something to the prosecutor.

'Smile? . . . I . . . why . . . I didn't . . . I didn't smile at him!' She was blushing and looked absolutely furious, nothing like the virgin of a moment before.

'Then what did you do?'

'I . . . nothing, dammit . . . I . . . I mean . . . oh, I don't know what I did . . .' Here came the virgin again, and helplessness to boot. 'I was just so shocked to see him there, and his wife called me a name. She . . .'

'Did she? What did she call you?' Martin looked vastly amused, and Jessie wondered if he really was. It was hard to tell with him; she was learning that more each day. 'Go on, Miss Burton, don't be shy. Tell us what she called you. But do remember that you are under oath.' He smiled at her and assumed an attitude of waiting.

'I don't remember what she called me.'

'You don't? Well, if it was such a traumatic encounter, wouldn't you remember what she'd called you?'

'Objection, Your Honour!' Matilda Howard-Spencer was on her feet and looking annoyed. Very.

'Sustained.'

'All right. But just one minor point . . . isn't it true that you leered at Mr. Clarke, almost as though . . .'

'*Objection!*' The D.A.'s voice could have shattered concrete, as Martin smiled angelically. He had got his point across.

'Sustained.'

'Sorry, Your Honour.' But it was a good beginning. And the rest of the story droned on after that. How she had been debased, abused, used, humiliated, violated. The words were getting to be almost laughable. 'What exactly did you expect from Mr. Clarke?'

'What do you mean?' The witness looked haughty, but confused.

'Well, did you think he'd propose marriage in that hotel room, or whip an engagement ring out of his pocket, or . . . well, what did you expect?'

'I don't know. I . . . he . . . I thought he just wanted to have a drink. He was a little drunk anyway.'

'Did you find him attractive?'

'Of course not.'

'Then why did you want to have a drink with him?'

'Because . . . oh, I don't know. Because I thought he was a gentleman.' She looked delighted with her response, as though that said it all.

'Aha. That was it, eh? A gentleman. Would a gentleman take you to a hotel on Market Street?'

'No.'

'Did Mr. Clarke take you to a hotel on Market Street . . . or did you take him?' She flushed furiously, and then hid her face in her hands, muttering something no one could hear, until the judge admonished her to speak up.

'I didn't take him anywhere.'

'But you went with him. Even though you did not find him attractive. Did you particularly want to have that drink with him?'

'No.'

'Then what did you want to do?' Ouch. The question almost made Jessie smile. Beautiful.

'I wanted . . . I wanted . . . to be friends.'

'Friends?' Martin looked even more amused. She was making a fool of herself.

'Not, not friends. Oh, I don't know. I wanted to go back to work.'

'Then why would you agree to go and have a drink with him?'

'I don't know.'

'Were you horny?'

'Objection!'

'Rephrase your question, Mr. Schwartz.'

'How long had it been since you'd had intercourse, Miss Burton?'

'Do I have to answer that, Your Honour?' She looked pleadingly at the judge, but he nodded assent.

'Yes. You do.'

'I don't know.'

'Give us an idea.' Martin was insistent.

'I don't know.' Her voice was shrinking.

'Roughly. A long time? Not so long? A month . . . two months . . . a week? A few days?'

'No.'

'No? What do you mean by no?' Martin was beginning to look annoyed.

'I mean no, not a few days.'

'Then how long? Answer the question.'

'A while.' The judge glared at her, and Martin started moving closer. 'All right, a long time,' she said finally. 'Maybe a year.'

'Maybe longer?'

'Maybe.'

'Was it with anyone special the last time?'

'I . . . I don't remember . . . I . . . yes!' She almost shouted the last word.

'Someone who hurt you in some way, Miss Burton? Someone who didn't love you as much as he should have, someone who . . .' His voice was so soft it would have lulled a baby to sleep, and then the assistant district attorney jumped to her feet and broke the spell.

'Objection!'

It took two more hours to finish Martin's questioning, and Jessica felt as though she were going to melt into a small invisible blur by the time it was over. She couldn't even begin to imagine what Margaret Burton felt like as she was led, crying, from the stand. She was assisted by Inspector Houghton while Matilda Howard-Spencer rearranged her papers. Jessica had the impression that the austere prosecutor was interested in the case, not the victim.

The judge called a recess and dismissed them until Monday. For a moment they all stood numbly in the courtroom; it was only lunchtime, but Jessie wanted to climb into bed and sleep for a year. She had never been so tired in her life. Spent. And Ian looked five years older than he had that morning.

When they emerged from the courtroom with Martin behind them, Margaret Burton was nowhere to be seen. She had been escorted out through the judge's chambers, and Martin guessed that she would be taken out some more discreet exit, to avoid another encounter like the one that morning. He had a feeling that Houghton didn't quite trust the woman either, and didn't want any more trouble than he already had.

As they walked out into the sunshine, Jessie felt as though she hadn't seen it for years. Friday. It was Friday. The end of an interminable week, and now two whole days to themselves. Two and a half days. And all she wanted was to go home and forget this rococo hell-hole where their lives seemed to be coming to an end at the hands of a madwoman. It was like a Greek play, really . . . the jury could play the chorus.

'What are you thinking?' Ian was still worried about her after the morning's outburst. Now more than ever. The testimony had been grim.

'I don't know. I'm not sure I can think anymore. I was just drifting.'

'Well, let's drift on home. Shall we?' He guided her quietly toward the car, and opened the door for her, and she felt two hundred years old as she slid onto the seat of the Volvo. But it was familiar, it was home. She needed that right now more than anything. She wanted to scrub the whole morning out of her soul.

'What do you think, love?' She looked at him through a haze of cigarette smoke as he drove slowly home.

'What do you mean?' He tried to evade her question.

'I mean, how do you think it's going? Did Martin say anything?'

'Not much. He plays it pretty close to the vest.'

She nodded again. He hadn't said much as they'd left except that he wanted to see them in his office on Saturday. 'But I guess everything's going okay.' Sure it was. It had to be.

'It looks okay to me too.' Okay? Christ, it looked horrible. But it was supposed to. Wasn't it?

'I like Martin's style.'

'So do I.'

They both still thought they would win, but now they were beginning to realize the price they'd have to pay. Not in money, not in cars, but in flesh, guts, and souls.

CHAPTER XVI

On Saturday morning, Ian went down to Martin's office to discuss his testimony on the stand the following week. Jessica stayed home with a migraine. As a favour, Martin came to see her at the house that evening, to discuss her own testimony.

And on Sunday afternoon, Astrid called, as the pair sat zombielike in chairs, watching old movies on television.

'Hello, children. How about a spaghetti dinner at my place tonight?' For once Jessie was short with her friend.

'I'm sorry, Astrid, we just can't.'

'Oh, you two. Busy, busy, busy. I've tried to reach you all week, and you haven't been in the shop.' Shit.

'I know. I had some work to do here, and I'm helping Ian . . . edit his book.'

'That sounds like fun.'

'Yeah. Sort of.' But her voice didn't carry the lie well. 'I'll give you a call sometime next week. But thanks for the invitation.' They blew kisses and hung up, and Jessica marvelled at the fact that no one knew what was happening. It seemed remarkable that the newspapers hadn't picked it up, but she had finally realized that what was happening to them was in no way extraordinary. There were a dozen cases like it every day. It was new to them, but not to the news business. And there were far juicier cases than theirs to pick from—except, of course, for the Pacific Heights angle, and Jessie's exclusive boutique. It would destroy her business if it came out. But there didn't seem to be any danger of that. No members of the press had appeared thus far, and there had been no interest shown at all. It was something to be grateful for. And she was. And Martin had promised that if some stray reporter did happen through, he'd call the paper and ask for their discretion. He felt sure that they'd co-operate with him. They had before.

Jessie felt bad about having cut Astrid short. They hadn't

seen her in a while, and they hadn't seen their other friends in two months now. It would have been hard to face anyone. It was getting harder even to face Astrid. And it would have been impossible to confront the girls in the shop this week. Jessie had no intention of going near the place. She was afraid they'd read too much in her face. For the same reasons, Ian had been staying away from everyone he knew since the arrest. And he was content to lose himself in his book. The characters he'd invented kept him company.

And meanwhile, the bills continued to mount. Zina dropped off Jessie's mail every day during the trial, and most of it was bills, including Harvey Green's second bill, for another nine hundred dollars. And once again for nothing. It had been 'in case' money—in case Margaret Burton had done something she shouldn't have, in case something had turned up, in case . . . but nothing had. He had managed to come up with absolutely nothing. Until Sunday night, right after Jessie talked to Astrid.

The phone rang, and it was Martin. He and Green wanted to come right over. She woke Ian, and they were waiting, tensely, when the two men arrived. They were dying to know what Green had found out.

What he had was a photograph. Of Margaret Burton's husband from the rapidly annulled marriage of almost twenty years before. The photograph could have been of Ian. The man in the picture was tall, blond, blue-eyed with laughter in his face. He was standing next to an MG; it was of a much earlier vintage than the Morgan, but there was still a great deal of resemblance between the cars as well as the men. If you squinted, even a little, it looked like Ian and the Morgan. The man's hair was shorter than Ian's, his face was a little longer, the car was black instead of red . . . the details were off, but not by much. It was a shock just looking at the photograph. It told the entire story. Now they knew the why. And Martin's first suspicion had been right. It must have been revenge.

The four of them sat in the living room in total silence. Green had got the photograph from a cousin of Miss Burton's, a last-minute lead he'd decided to follow, just on a hunch. A damn good hunch, as it had turned out.

Schwartz heaved a sigh of what sounded like relief and leaned back in his chair. 'Well, now we know. The cousin will testify?' But Green shook his head.

'Says she'll take the Fifth, or lie. She doesn't want to get involved. She said that Burton would kill her. You know, this woman, the cousin I mean, almost sounds as though she's afraid of the Burton woman. Said she's the most vindictive person she's ever known. You gonna subpoena her?'

'Not if she's going to take the Fifth on us. Did she tell you why the Burton woman annulled the marriage?' Martin was pensively chewing on a pencil as he asked the questions, while Ian and Jessica listened silently. Ian still held the photograph in his hand, and it made him exceedingly nervous. The likeness was startling.

'Peggy Burton didn't annul the marriage. The husband did.'

Martin raised his eyebrows quickly. 'Oh?'

'The cousin thinks Margaret was pregnant—just a guess,' Green went on. 'She had just graduated from high school and was working in this guy's father's office, a law firm. Hillman and Knowles, no less.' Ian looked up and Martin whistled. 'She married Knowles's son. A kid named Jed Knowles. He was only in law school at the time, and was spending the summer working in his father's office. He's the kid in the picture.' Green waved vaguely at the snapshot still resting in Ian's hand.

'Anyway, they got married in a big hurry, but very quietly, at the end of the summer. And the father made a real stink that nothing be made public, no announcement of the marriage, no nothing. The Burton girl's parents were both living in the Midwest, so she didn't have any family out here except the cousin, who isn't even sure if they ever lived together. They just got married, and the next thing she remembers is that Margaret was in the hospital for a couple of weeks. She thinks she might have had a complicated abortion, miscarriage, something. Knowles had the marriage annulled right after that, and Margaret was out of a husband, out of a job, and maybe out of a baby. She had kind of a nervous breakdown, it sounds like, and spent three months in a Catholic retreat house. I went back to check out the retreat house, but it was torn down twelve years ago, and the sisters of that order are now located in Kansas, Montreal, Boston, and Dublin. Not very likely we'd find any records on it, and if we did they'd be privileged anyway.'

'What about the Knowles boy? Did you check him out?'

'Yeah.' Green didn't look pleased. 'He married some debutante, with a big splash and a lot of noise, at the Thanksgiving of that year. Parties, showers, announcements in all the papers. The clippings at the *Chronicle* said that they'd been engaged for over a year, which was obviously why Papa Knowles didn't want any publicity when sonny boy married the Burton girl.'

'Did you talk to Knowles?'

Green nodded unhappily. 'He and his bride crashed in a two-engine plane seventeen months later. The father died of a heart attack this summer, and his mother is travelling in Europe, no one seems to know where.'

'Terrific.' Martin scowled and started to gnaw on his pencil again. 'Any brothers and sisters? Friends who might know what happened? Anyone?'

'Its a dead end, Martin. No brothers and sisters. And who'd remember now, among his friends? Jed Knowles has been dead for eighteen years. That's a hell of a long time.'

'Yeah. A long time to carry a grudge. Shit. We have it all wrapped up, and we don't have a fucking goddam thing. Nothing.'

'What do you mean, nothing?' It was the first time Ian had spoken since seeing the photograph. He had been listening closely to the other men's exchange. 'It sounds like we've got everything.'

'Yes.' Martin rubbed his eyes slowly with one hand and then opened them again. 'And nothing we can use in court. It's all guesswork. That's all it is. What we have here is undoubtedly the truth, and the full psychological explanation of why Margaret Burton has accused you of rape. You look just like some rich man's son who got her pregnant, married her, probably made her have an abortion, and then ditched her and married his high society girlfriend a few weeks later. Miss Burton met the handsome prince and then he shat on her. Back to Cinderella again. And she's been out to get him for twenty years. Which is probably why she hasn't tried to hit you two for money. She doesn't want money. She wants revenge. She probably got a little money out of it the first time. Money is too easy for some people.' Jessica rolled her eyes at the remark and Ian gestured to her to keep still.

'The point is, she'd rather see you go to prison than hit you for bucks. In her mind, you're just another Jed Knowles, and you're going to take it for him. You look like him to a frightening degree, your car looks like his, you probably even sound like him, for all we know. And she probably spotted you at Enrico's months ago. You're a regular. She may well have set you up from beginning to end. But the problem is, that we can't prove that in court.' He turned back to Green. 'You're sure the cousin won't testify willingly?'

'Positive.' Green was curt and emphatic. Martin shook his head.

'Wonderful. And that, Ian, is why we can't prove a goddam thing in court. Because a hostile witness who takes the Fifth Amendment would ruin you faster than never having her on the stand at all. And besides, even if she took the stand, we couldn't prove any of this. All we could prove is that Burton married Knowles, and shortly thereafter Knowles had the marriage annulled. The rest is pure conjecture, hearsay, guesswork. That doesn't hold up in court, Ian, not without solid proof. The prosecution would have the whole theory thrown out of court in ten minutes. You and I now know what probably happened, but we could never prove that to the jury, not without someone to testify that she was pregnant when Knowles married her, that she did have an abortion, that she did have a nervous breakdown, that someone heard her swear to take revenge. And how're you going to prove all that, even if the cousin did take the stand? What we have here, I'm afraid, is the truth, and no way to prove it.'

Jessica felt tears burning her eyes as she listened, and

Ian was paler than she'd ever seen him. He looked almost grey.

'So what do we do now?'

'We give it a try, and we pray. I'll call Burton for redirect and see how much she'll admit to. And how much they'll let us get away with. But it won't be much, Ian. Don't count on anything.'

Green left a few moments later with a quiet handshake in the hall for Martin, and a shake of the head: 'I'm sorry.' Martin nodded, and left a few moments later.

The trial continued on Monday, and Martin recalled Margaret Burton to the stand. Had she been married to Jed Knowles? Yes. For how long? Two and a half months. Ten weeks? Yes, Ten weeks. Was it true that she had to marry him because she was pregnant? Absolutely not. Did she have a nervous breakdown . . . objection! . . . overruled! . . . did she have a nervous breakdown after the marriage was annulled? No. Never. Didn't the defendant bear a striking resemblance to Mr. Knowles? No. Not that she had noticed. Had Mr. Knowles remarried almost immediately after . . . objection! Sustained, with an admonition to the jury to disregard the previous line of questioning. The judge warned Martin about asking irrelevant questions and badgering the witness, and Jessica noticed that Margaret Burton was silent and pale but totally poised. Almost too much so. She found herself praying that the woman would lose control, would disintegrate on the stand and scream and shriek and destroy herself by admitting that she had wanted to destroy Ian because he looked like Jed Knowles. But Margaret Burton did none of those things. She was excused from the stand. And Jessica never saw her again.

Late that afternoon Martin asked Ian to drum up two friends to attest to his character and morals. Like Jessie's testimony it was going to be considered biased, but character witnesses never hurt. Ian agreed to ask a couple of people, but there was a look of despair in his eyes that it killed Jessica to watch. As though Margaret Burton had already won. She had simply slipped away. Dropped her bomb and left, leaving them with a photograph as explanation.

Ian hated having to explain to anyone what was happening, and in recent years he had not been as close to his friends as he once had. His writing seemed to devour more and more of his time, his energy, his devotion. He wanted to finish another book, to sell it, to 'make it', before he went back to hanging around bars with old buddies; he needed to do something, be something, build something first. He was tired of explaining about rejections, and agents, and rewrites. So he stopped explaining. He stopped seeing them. And the rest of the time he spent with Jessie. She had a way of making herself an exclusive. She didn't like sharing the time he could spare from the studio.

That night, he called a writer he knew and a classmate from college, a stockbroker who had also moved to the West. They were stunned about the charges, sympathetic, and anxious to help. Neither of them was overly fond of Jessie, but they felt bad for both of them. The writer felt that Jessie wanted too much of Ian, that she was too clinging and didn't leave him enough space to write in. The college friend had always thought Jessie too headstrong. She wasn't their kind of woman.

But the two men made pleasant, clean-cut appearances on the stand. The writer, wearing tweeds, testified that he had recently won an award and published three stories in *The New Yorker* and a hardcover novel. He was respectable, as writers went. And he spoke well on the stand. The college friend made an equally pleasing impression in a different vein. Solid, upper-middle-class, respectable family man, 'known Ian for years,' hip hip, tut tut, rah rah. They both did what they could, which wasn't much.

On Tuesday afternoon the judge dismissed them all early, and Ian and Jessie came home to relax.

'How are you holding up, babe? I can't say either of us looks like much lately.' He smiled ruefully and opened the icebox. 'Want a beer?'

'Make it a case.' She kicked off her shoes and stretched. 'Jesus, I'm sick of that shit. It just goes on and on and on and . . . and I feel like I haven't sat down and talked to you for a year.' She took the beer from him and went to lie down on the couch. 'Besides which, I'm running out of polite clothes to wear.' She was wearing an ugly brown tweed suit that she had had since her college days in the East.

'Fuck it. Go in wearing a bikini tomorrow. By now the jury deserves something to look at.'

'You know, I thought the trial would be a lot more dramatic. It's funny that it isn't.'

'The case isn't all that dramatic. Her word against mine as to who screwed whom and why, where, and for what. By now, I don't even feel uncomfortable with you there, listening to the testimony.' Now that Margaret Burton was no longer in court.

'It doesn't bother me much either, except I want to laugh every time someone says "an infamous crime against nature". It seems so overdone.' They laughed easily for the first time in a long time. As they relaxed in the familiar charm of their living room, the trial seemed like a bad joke. Somebody else's bad joke.

'Want to go to a movie, Jessie?'

'You know something? I'd love to.' The tension was beginning to drain away. They had decided that they had it made, even without solid proof that Margaret Burton was a freak looking for revenge on a man who had been dead for almost twenty years. So what? Ian was innocent. In the end, it was as simple as that. 'Want to take Astrid with us, darling?'

'Sure. Why not?' He smiled and leaned over to kiss her. 'But don't call her for another half hour.' Jessie returned the smile and ran a finger slowly up his arm.

Astrid was delighted with the invitation and the three went to a movie that had them in tears, they all laughed so hard. It was just what Jessie and Ian needed.

'I was beginning to think I'd never see you two again. It's been weeks! What have you been up to? Still working on the book?' They nodded in unison, changed the subject, and went out for coffee.

It was a pleasant evening that did them all good. And Astrid felt better now that she had seen them. Ian looked haggard and Jessica looked tired, but they looked happy again. Maybe whatever problem had been bothering them had been worked out.

Astrid reported having been in the boutique almost every day, and the fashion show had been a smash. Katsuko had done a great job. Astrid had even bought four or five things from the show, which Jessie told her was silly.

'That's ridiculous. Don't buy anymore when I'm not there. I'll give you a discount when I'm in. Wholesale at least. And on some things I can sell to you at cost.'

'That's crazy, Jessica. Why should you sell things any cheaper to me? You might as well share the wealth!' She threw her arms wide in a flash of jewellery and the three of them laughed.

They drove her home in the Volvo, and when she asked about the Morgan, Jessica claimed that the engine had needed too much work. They all agreed that it was a shame.

'What a fabulous evening!' Jessica slid into bed with a smile, and Ian yawned, nodding happily. 'I'm glad we went out.'

'So am I.'

She rubbed his back for him and they chatted about nothing in particular; it was the kind of talk they had always shared late at night. Casual mentions of the movie, thoughts about Astrid, Jessie noticed a small bruise on his leg and asked him how he'd got it, he told her never to cut her hair. Night talk. As though nothing untoward had ever happened to them. For once they even got some sleep, which was remarkable since Ian was to take the stand the next day.

CHAPTER XVII

Ian's testimony under direct examination lasted two hours. The jury looked a little more interested than they had in the previous days, but not much. And it was only during the last half hour that they actually seemed to wake up. It was Matilda Howard-Spencer's turn to question him. She seemed to pace in front of Ian, as though thinking of something else, while all eyes in the courtroom stayed on her, particularly Ian's. And at last she stopped, directly in front of him, crossed her arms, and tilted her head to one side.

'You're from the East?' The question surprised him, as did the friendly look on her face.

'Yes. New York.'

'Where did you go to college?'

'Yale.'

'Good school.' She smiled at him, and he returned the smile. 'I tried to get into their law school, but I'm afraid I didn't quite make it.' She had gone to Stanford instead, but Ian couldn't know that, and was suddenly baffled as to whether he was supposed to offer sympathy, silence, or a smile. 'Did you do any graduate work?' She didn't call him Ian, and she didn't call him Mr. Clarke. She talked to him as though she knew him, or honestly wanted to. An interested dinner partner at a pleasant soirée.

'Yes. I got my master's.'

'Where did you do that?' She tilted her head again with an expression of interest. This was not at all the line of questioning Martin had prepared him for. This was lots easier to deal with.

'I went to Columbia. School of journalism.'

'And then?'

'I went into advertising.'

'With whom?' He named a big firm in New York.

'Well, we certainly all know who they are.' She smiled at him again, and looked pensively out the window.

'Did you go out with anybody special in college?' Aha, here it came, but she still sounded gently inquiring.

'A few people.'

'Like who?'

'Just girls.'

'From neighbouring schools? Who? How about some names?' This was ridiculous. Ian couldn't see the reason for it.

'Viveca Harreford. Maddie Whelan. Fifi Estabrook.' She wouldn't know them. Why ask?

'Estabrook? As in Estabrook and Lloyd? They're the biggest stockbrokers on Wall Street, aren't they?' She actually looked pleased for him, as though he had done something wonderful.

'I wouldn't know.' Her remark had made him uncomfortable. Of course they were the Estabrooks of Estabrook and Lloyd, but that wasn't why he'd gone out with Fifi, for Chrissake.

'And it seems to me that Maddie Whelan has kind of a familiar ring too. Something tells me she was somebody important. Let's see, Whelan . . . oh, I know, the department store in Phoenix, isn't it?' Ian was actually blushing, but Matilda Howard-Spencer was still smiling angelically, seeming to enjoy the social pleasantries.

'I can't remember.'

'Sure you can. Anyone else?'

'Not that I can recall.' This was a ridiculous line of questioning, and he couldn't see where she was going, except making him look like a fool. Was it really as simple as that?

'All right. When did you first meet your wife?'

'About eight years ago. In New York.'

'And she has a lot of money, doesn't she?' The prosecutor's tone was almost embarrassed, as if she'd asked an indiscreet question.

'Objection!' Martin was livid; he knew exactly where she was going, whether Ian did or not. But Ian was beginning to; he had been led right into her trap.

'Sustained. Rephrase the question.'

'Sorry, Your Honour. All right, then, I understand that your wife has a wonderfully successful boutique here in San Francisco. Did she have one in New York too?'

'No. When I met her, she was the fashion co-ordinator and stylist at the ad agency where I worked.'

'She did that for fun?' Now there was an edge to her tone.

'No. For money.' Ian was getting annoyed.

'But she didn't have to work, did she?'

'I never asked.'

'And she doesn't have to work now, does she?'

'I don't . . .' He looked to Martin for help, but there was none forthcoming.

'Answer the question. Does she have to work now, or is her income sufficient to support her, and you, in a very luxurious style?'

'Not luxurious, no.' Christ. Jessie and Martin cringed simultaneously. What an answer. But the questions were coming at him like gumballs from a machine, and there was no time to dodge them.

'But her income is adequate to support you both?'

'Yes.' He was very pale now. And very angry.

'Do you work?'

'Yes.' But he said it too softly, and she smiled.

'I'm sorry, I didn't hear your answer. Do you work?'

'Yes!'

'At a job?'

'No. At home. But it's work. I'm a writer.' Poor, poor Ian. Jessie wanted to run up and hold him. Why did he have to go through all that? The bitch.

'Do you sell much of what you write?'

'Enough.'

'Enough for what? Enough to support yourself on?'

'Not at the moment.' There was no hiding from her.

'Does that make you angry?' The question was almost a caress. The woman was a viper.

'No, it doesn't make me angry. It's just one of the facts of life, for the moment. Jessica understands.'

'But you do cheat on her. Does she understand that?'

'Objection!'

'Overruled!'

'Does she understand that?'

'I don't cheat on her.'

'Come, come. You yourself claim that you willingly went to bed with Ms. Burton. Is that a normal occurrence in your life?'

'No.'

'This was the first time?'

His eyes were glued to his knees. 'I can't remember.'

'You're under oath; answer the question.' Her voice slithered like a cobra threatening to strike.

'No.'

'What?'

'No. This was not the first time.'

'Do you cheat on your wife often?'

'No.'

'How often?'

'I don't know.'

'And what kind of woman do you use—your own kind, or other kinds, "lesser" women, lower-class women, whores, poor girls, whatever?'

'Objection!'

'Overruled!'

'I don't "use" anyone.'

'I see. Would you cheat on your wife with Fifi Estabrook, or is she a nice girl?'

'I haven't seen her in years. Ten, eleven years. I wasn't married when I went out with her.'

'I mean, would you cheat on your wife with someone *like* her, or do you just sleep with "cheap" women, women you aren't liable to run across in your own social circle? It could be embarrassing, after all. It might be a lot simpler just to keep your playing as far from home as possible.'

'I do.' Oh, God. No, Ian . . . no . . . Martin was staring at the wall, trying to let nothing show on his face, and Jessie had sensed that disaster was near.

'I see. You do sleep with "cheap" women, to keep it as far as possible from home? Did you consider Ms. Burton a "cheap" woman?'

'No.' But he had, and his 'no' was a weak one.
'She wasn't of your social set, though, was she?'
'I don't know.'
'Was she?' The words closed in on him now.
'No.'
'Did you think she'd call the police?'
'No.' And then as an afterthought, he looked up, panic-stricken, and added 'She had no reason to'. But it was too late. The damage was done.
She excused Ian from the stand with the proviso that she might want to recall him later. But she had all but killed him as it was.
Ian left the stand quietly and sat down heavily next to Martin. And five minutes later, the judge called a recess for lunch.
They left the courtroom slowly, with Ian shaking his head and looking sombre until the threesome reached the street.
'I really blew it.' Jessie had never seen him look worse.
'You couldn't help it. That's how she works. The woman is lethal.' Martin heaved a sigh and gave them a small, wintry smile. 'But the jury sees that too. And the jury's not all that lily pure either.' There was no point making Ian feel even worse, but Martin was worried. The cheating didn't bother him nearly as much as the class conflict. 'I'm going to put Jessica on the stand this afternoon. At least this way, it'll be over with.'
'Yeah, she can massacre us both on the same day.' Ian looked tired and beaten, and Jessica looked tense.
'Don't be an ass.'
'You consider yourself a match for her?' Ian looked sarcastic and bitter.
'Why not?'
'I'll tell you why not. Because if you pit yourself against her, Ian'll lose,' Martin was quick to interject. 'You have to be the gentlest, sweetest, calmest wife in the world. You come on like a hellion, and she'll break you in two right on the stand. We went over everything this weekend. You know what you have to do.' Jessica nodded sombrely, and

Ian sighed. Martin had gone over everything with him too, but that damn woman hadn't asked any of the right questions. And God only knew what she'd ask Jessie. 'All right?'

'All right.' Jessica smiled softly, and they dropped Martin off near City Hall. He had to go back to his office, and they had decided to go home to unwind. Jessica wanted a little time to take care of Ian. He needed it after the morning, and it kept her mind off what she'd have to say that afternoon.

When they got home, she made him lie down on the couch, took off his shoes, loosened his tie, and ran a soft hand through his hair. He lay there for a few minutes, just looking at her.

'Jess . . .' He didn't even know how to say it, but she knew.

'None of that. Just lie there and relax. I'll go make some lunch.' For once he didn't argue; he was too tired to do anything more than just lie there.

When she came back with a covered bowl of steaming soup and a plate piled high with sandwiches, he was asleep. He had the exhausted look of tragedy. The pale rumpled look one got when someone has died, when a child is terribly ill, when one's business has failed. Those times when schedules were disrupted, and one was suddenly at home, in seldom-worn clothes, looking terribly tired and afraid. She stood looking down at him for a moment and felt a wave of pity for him rush up inside her. Why did she feel so protective of him? Why did she feel as though he couldn't cope with it all, but she could? Why wasn't she angry? Why didn't she look like that now? She had when he was in jail, but he was here now, she could touch him and hold him and take care of him. The rest wasn't real. It was awful, but it wouldn't last. It would hurt, and it would rock him and humiliate him and do all sorts of grim things, but it wouldn't kill him. And it wouldn't take him away. As she sat quietly next to him and lifted his hand onto her lap, she knew that nothing would ever take him away from her. No Margaret Burton, no district attorney, no court, not even a jail. Margaret Burton would fade, Matilda Howard-Spencer would go on to some other case, as would Martin and the judge, and it would all be over. It was just a question of keeping themselves afloat until the storm passed. And she needed Ian too desperately to let anything, even her own feelings, jeopardize what they had. She wouldn't let herself get angry. She couldn't afford to.

There was the briefest flash of bitterness as she looked out over the bay and thought of her father. He wouldn't have done something like this, and he wouldn't have let her mother go through it, either. He'd have protected his wife more than Ian was protecting her. But that was her father. And this was Ian. Comparisons served no purpose now. She had Ian. It was as simple as that. She demanded a lot of him, so she had to give a lot too. She was willing. And right now it was her turn to give.

Looking down at him, as he slept there on her grey skirt, he looked like a very tired little boy. She smoothed his hair off his forehead and took a deep breath, thinking of that afternoon. It was her turn now. And she wasn't going to lose. She had decided that after the disastrous morning. The case was going to be won. And that was that. It was insane that it had gone this far. But it was not going much further. Jessie had had enough.

Ian woke shortly before two and looked up in surprise.

'Did I fall asleep?'

'No. I hit you on the head with my shoe and you fainted.'

He smiled at her and yawned into her skirt. 'You smell delicious. Did you know that every single item of clothing you own smells of your perfume?'

'Want some soup?' She was smiling at the compliment. He'd gotten them into one hell of a mess, but one thing was certain, and that was how much she loved him. Not just needed him, loved him. How could she be angry? How dare she ask for his left arm when fate had already taken his right? They had suffered enough. Now it was time to finish it.

'Christ, you look determined. What've you been up to?'

'I haven't been up to a thing. Do you want soup?' She

eyed him alluringly as she held a Limoges cup in one hand and her mother's best soup ladle in the other.

'My, so fancy.' He sat up and kissed her and looked at the tray. 'You know something, Jessica, you're the most remarkable woman I know. And the best.' She wanted to tease him and ask if she was better than Fifi Estabrook, but she didn't dare. She suspected that the wounds of the morning were still raw.

'For you, milord, nothing but the best.' She carefully poured the asparagus soup into the cup and added two neat little roast-beef sandwiches to the plate. There was a fresh salad too.

'You're the only woman I know who can make a sandwich lunch look like a dinner party.'

'I just love you.' She put her arms around his neck and nibbled his ear, and then stretched and stood up.

'Aren't you going to eat?'

'I already did.' She was lying, but she couldn't have eaten a thing before going on the stand in less than an hour. She looked at her watch and headed for the bedroom. 'I'll straighten out my face. We have to leave in ten minutes.' He waved happily from the midst of his lunch and she disappeared into the bedroom.

'Ready?' He walked into the bedroom five minutes later, tightening his tie and glancing at his ruffled hair in the mirror. 'Good lord, I look like I've been sleeping all day.'

'As a matter of fact, darling, you do.' And she was pleased. The brief hour of sleep had done him good. The time they'd spent at home had done them both good. Jessie felt stronger than she had in weeks. Margaret Burton wasn't going to touch them. How could she? Jessie had decided to ignore her, to rob her of her powers. And it was as though Ian sensed the rebirth in his wife.

'You know something? I feel better. I was really beat after this morning.' And he hated to think of what Jessie would have to go through that afternoon, but she seemed ready for it. 'You changed?'

'I thought this looked more appropriate.' It was a wonderfully ladylike dress, the kind she might wear to a tea. It was a soft grey silk with full feminine sleeves, and a belt of the same fabric. The whole line of the dress was gentle and easy, and without being fancy, it screamed 'class'. 'As long as they're going to bill us as being so upper-class, we might as well look decent. I'm so sick of those fucking tweed skirts, I'm going to burn them all on the front steps the day this is over.'

'You look gorgeous.'

'Too dressed up?'

'Perfect.'

'Good.' She slipped on quiet black kid pumps, clipped pearl earrings on her ears, picked up her bag, and headed for the closet to get out her black coat. Ian truly did think she looked gorgeous. He was so damn proud of her. Not just of how she looked, but of how she was taking this.

Martin was not quite as pleased, though, when they walked into the courtroom. He noticed Jessica's black coat and the glimpse of grey silk. It was just what he didn't want. Everything about her looked expensive. It was as though she had set out to prove everything Matilda Howard-Spencer had suggested. Jesus. Where were their heads? Crazy kids, they didn't realise what was happening. They had an unnerving assurance about them as they took their seats, as though they had arranged everything and there was nothing more to worry about. It was a bad time for them to make a show of strength, however subtle. And yet, maybe it was just as well that they felt a little more confident. They had both looked so beaten after the morning.

This new look of confidence underlined the bond between them. One was always aware of that, of them as a pair, not just Ian or Jessie, but both. It was frightening to think what would happen to them both if someone tried to sever that bond. If they lost.

Jessica looked remarkably calm as she walked up to the witness stand. The grey dress moved gracefully with her, the full sleeves gentling her impressive stature. She took the oath and looked at Ian for one tiny instant before turning her attention to Martin.

His questions built up a picture of a devoted couple

and of a wife who respected her husband too much to doubt that he was telling the truth. He was pleased with Jessica's quiet, dignified manner, and when he relinquished his witness to the prosecutor, he had to repress a smile. He would have liked to see these two women roll up their sleeves and stalk each other around the room. They were evenly matched. At least he hoped so.

With Jessica, Matilda Howard-Spencer was not going to waste time. 'Tell us, Mrs. Clarke, were you aware that your husband had cheated on you before this?'

'Indirectly.'

'What do you mean by that?' The attorney looked puzzled.

'I mean that I assumed that was a possibility, but that it was nothing serious.'

'I see. Just a little lighthearted fun?' She was back on that track again, but Jessie had seen it coming.

'No. Nothing like that. Ian isn't flip about anything. He's a sensitive man. But I travel quite a bit. And what happens, happens.'

'Does it happen to you as well?' Now the attorney's eyes were glittering again. Gotcha!

'No, it does not.'

'You're under oath, Mrs. Clarke.'

'I'm aware of that. The answer is no.'

She looked surprised. 'But you don't mind if your husband fools around?'

'Not necessarily. It depends on the circumstances.' Jessica looked every inch a lady, and Ian was incredibly proud of her.

'And these particular circumstances, Mrs. Clarke, how do you feel about them?'

'Confident.'

'Confident?' Jessica's interrogator looked taken aback, and Martin fidgeted. 'How can you be confident, and what about?'

'I'm confident that the truth about this matter will come out, and that my husband will be acquitted.' Martin watched the jury. They liked her. But they had to like Ian too. And more than that, they had to believe him.

'I admire your optimism. Are you footing the bill for the expense of this?'

'No, not really.' Ian almost cringed. She was lying under oath. 'My husband made a very wise investment after he sold his last book. He put the investment in my care, and we decided to sell it to cover the expense of the trial. So I can't say I'm footing the bill.' Bravo! The Morgan! And she was telling the truth! He wanted to jump up and hug her.

'Would you say that you have a good marriage?'

'Yes.'

'Very good?'

'Extremely good.' Jessica smiled.

'But your husband does sleep with other women?'

'Presumably.'

'Did he tell you about Margaret Burton?'

'No.'

'Did he tell you about any of his women?'

'No. And I don't think there were very many.'

'Did you encourage him to sleep around?'

'No.'

'But as long as they were little nobodies, you didn't care, is that it?'

'Objection!'

'Sustained. Leading the witness.'

'Sorry, Your Honour.' She turned back to Jessica. 'Has your husband ever been violent with you?'

'No.'

'Never?'

'No.'

'Does he drink a great deal?'

'No.'

'Does he have problems about his manhood, because you pay the bills?' What a question!

'No.'

'Do you love him very much?'

'Yes.'

'Do you protect him?'

'What do you mean?'

'I mean, do you shield him from unpleasantness?'

'Of course, I'd do anything I had to to shield him from unpleasantness. I'm his wife.'

Matilda Howard-Spencer's face settled into a satisfied smile. 'Including lie in court to protect him?'

'No!'

'The witness is excused.'

The assistant district attorney turned on her heel and went back to her seat as Jessica sat gaping on the witness stand. That damned woman had done it again.

CHAPTER XVIII

Everyone was back in their seats the next morning for the two attorney's summations to the jury. Ian and Jessica were pleased by Martin's comments and his style in addressing the jury, and they felt that he created a real wave of sympathy for the defence. Everything was in control. Then Matilda Howard-Spencer stood up, and the assistant district attorney was demonic. She painted a portrait of a wronged, distraught, heartbroken, brutally abused woman—hard-working, clean-living Peggy Burton. She also made a strong case that men like Ian Clarke shouldn't be allowed to dally where they wished, use whom they wanted, rape whom they chose, only to toss the women away and go home to the wives who supported them, who would 'do anything to protect them', as Jessie herself had said. Martin objected and was sustained. He explained later that it was rare to have to object to a closing argument, but that this woman breathed fire at the mere mention of Ian's name. And Jessie was still steaming when the court adjourned for lunch.

'Did you hear what that bitch said?' Her voice was loud and strident and Martin and Ian quelled her rapidly with a look.

'Keep your voice down, Jess,' Ian pleaded. It wouldn't pay to antagonize anyone now, least of all the jury, who were filtering past them on their way out to lunch. He had seen two of them look at Jess as she'd started to talk.

'I don't give a damn. That woman . . .'

'Shut up.' And then he put an arm around her and gave her a squeeze. 'Bigmouth. But I love you anyway.' She sighed loudly and then smiled.

'Damn, that aggravated me.'

'Okay, me too. Now let's forget about this crap for a while, and go get some lunch. Deal? No talk about the case?'

'Okay.' But she said it grudgingly as they walked down the hall.

'No "okay", I want a solemn promise. I refuse to have my lunch wrecked by this. Just make believe we're on the jury and can't discuss it.'

'You really think they stick to that?' He shrugged indifferently and pulled a lock of his wife's hair.

'I don't care what they do. Just tell me if I have that promise from you. No talking about the case. Right?'

'Right. I promise. You nag, you.'

'That's me. Your basic nagging husband.' He seemed very nervous as they ran down the stairs to the street, yet in surprisingly good spirits.

They went home for lunch and Jessie glanced at the mail while Ian rifled through *Publishers Weekly* and then went on to read the paper over the sandwiches she had made.

'You're terrific company today.' She was munching a turkey sandwich and flicked at the centre of his paper with a grin.

'Huh?'

'I said your fly is open.'

'What?' He looked down and then made a face. 'Oh, for Chrissake.'

'Well, talk to me, dammit, I'm lonely.'

'I read the paper for five minutes and you get lonely?'

'Yup. Want some wine with lunch?'

'No, I'll pass. Do we have any Cokes?'

'I'll go check.' She went to look, and he was reading

the paper again when she came back with the cold can of Coca-Cola. 'Now listen, you . . .'

'Shh . . .' He waved at her impatiently and went on reading. There was something about his face, about the look in his eyes as he read. He looked shocked.

'What is it?' He ignored her, finished the article, and finally looked up with an expression of defeat.

'Read that.' He pointed to the first four columns on page two, and Jessie's heart turned over as she read the headline: RAPE—IT'S TIME TO GET TOUGH. The article reported on a criminal justice committee meeting held the day before to discuss current punishment of rapists. There was talk in the article of stiffer sentences, no probation, suggestions for making it easier and less humiliating to report rape. It made anyone accused of rape sound as though he should be hanged without further ado. Jessie put down the paper and stared at Ian. It was bad luck to have that in the paper on the day the jury would be going out to deliberate.

'Do you think it'll have any effect, Ian? The judge told them not to be influenced by . . .'

'Oh, bullshit, Jessica. If I say something to you and someone else tells you to unhear it, will you have heard it or not? Will you remember it or not? They're only human, for Chrissake. Of course they're influenced by what they hear. So are you, so am I, so's the judge.' He ran a hand through his hair and pushed his lunch away. Jessica folded the paper and threw it onto the counter.

'Okay, so maybe they read the paper today, maybe not. But there isn't a damn thing we can do about it. So why not just let it pass, darling? Just forget about it. Can we try to do that? You're the one who made me promise not to discuss the case, remember?' She smiled gently at him. His eyes looked like sapphires, dark and bright and troubled.

'Yes, but Jessie . . . for God's . . . all right. You're right. I'm sorry.' But it was a tense meal after that, and neither of them finished their sandwiches.

They were silent on the drive down to City Hall, and Jessica heard her heels echo on the marble floors as they walked in. Her heart seemed to be pounding with equal force and in tune to the echo, like a death knell.

The judge addressed the jury for less than half an hour, and they filed out silently to be locked into a room across the hall while a bailiff stood guard outside.

'Now what, gentlemen?' Martin and Ian had joined Jessie at her seat.

'Now we wait. The judge will call a recess if they haven't come to a decision by five. Then they'll come back in the morning.'

'And that's it?' Jessie looked surprised.

'Yes, that's it.' How strange. It was all over. Almost. All that droning and boredom mixed with tension and sudden drama. And then it's over. The two teams have done their debating, the judge makes a little speech to the jury, they go lock themselves in a room, talk to each other, pick a verdict, everyone goes home, and the trial is over. It was weird somehow. Like a game. Or a dance. All terribly organized and ritualistic. A tribal rite. The thought made her want to laugh, but Ian and Martin were looking so serious. She smiled up at her husband, and their attorney looked at her with worried eyes. She really didn't understand. And he wasn't sure Ian did either. Maybe it was just as well.

'What do you think, Martin?' Ian turned to him with the question, but Martin had the feeling that he was asking more for Jessie's benefit than his own.

'I don't know. Did you see this morning's papers?' Ian's face sobered further.

'Yes. At lunch. That doesn't help, does it?'

The lawyer shook his head.

'Well, at least we put on a good show.'

'It would have been a better show if Green could have come up with something solid about Burton and Jed Knowles. I just know that that was the crux of this.' Martin shook his head angrily, and Ian patted his shoulder.

'Will she be coming back for the verdict?' Jessie was curious.

'No. She won't be back in court.'

'Bitch.' It was a small, low word, from the pit of her gut.

'Jessie!' Ian was quick to silence her, but she wouldn't be silenced.

'Well? She fucks up our life, blasts us practically into bankruptcy, not to mention what she's done to our nerves, and then she just walks off into the sunset. What do you expect me to feel toward her? Gratitude?'

'No, but there's no point . . .'

'Why not?' Jessie was getting loud again, and Ian knew how nervous she was. 'Martin, can't we sue her after we win the case?'

'Yes, I suppose so, but what would you get out of it? She doesn't have anything.'

'Then we'll sue the state.' She hadn't thought of that before.

'Look, why don't you two go for a walk down the hall?' He gave Ian a pointed look and Ian nodded. 'It may be a while before the jury comes in, probably will be. Just stay close; don't leave the building.' Jessie nodded and stood up, reaching for Ian's hand. Martin left them and went back to the desk. It was terrifying the way Jessica would not accept the possibility that they might lose.

'I wish we could go for a drink.' She walked slowly into the hall and leaned against the wall while Ian lit their cigarettes. Her legs were shaking and she wondered how long she could keep up the front of Madam Cool. She wanted to sink to the floor and clutch Ian's knees in desperation. It had to go all right. Had to . . . had to . . . she wanted to pound on the door to the jury room . . . to . . .

'It'll all be over soon, Jess. Just hang in there.'

'Yeah.' She smiled a half-smile and linked her arm in his as they started to walk down the corridor.

They were silent for a long time, and Jessie let her mind travel as it chose, wandering and darting, floating between thoughts as she smoked, and walked, and held on to Ian. It took almost an hour, but her brain finally stopped whirling, probably from exhaustion. She felt lonely and tired and sad, but she no longer felt as if she were going at the wrong speed. It was something, anyway.

She decided to call the boutique, just to see how things were going. It was an odd time to call, but she suddenly wanted to touch base with something familiar, to know that the world hadn't simply shrunk to one endless corridor in which she and Ian were condemned to walk their lives away in terrified silence. She missed the bustle of the boutique. The trivia. The faces.

The girls told her what was happening and she felt better. It was like going to the movies with Astrid. Normalcy. It diminished the proportions of what was happening to them to something she could bear for a while longer.

By four o'clock Ian had relaxed too, and they were playing word games. At four-thirty they started trading old jokes.

'What's grey and has four legs and a trunk?'

'An elephant?' She was already giggling.

'No, dummy, a mouse going on vacation.' Ian grinned, pleased with his joke. They were like second-graders sent out to the hall.

'Okay, smartass. How can you tell if your pants have fallen down?' She came back at him quickly and he started to laugh, but then they saw Martin beckon them urgently from the end of the hall. The jokes were suddenly over. Ian stood up first and looked into Jessica's face. She felt pale as terror swept over her. Pale and hollow, as though her frame might break. It was happening now. No more games to make believe it would never happen . . . it was here. Oh God . . . no!

'Jessie, no panicking!' He could see the look on her face, and took her swiftly into his arms and held her as tightly as he could. 'I love you. That's all. I love you. Just know that, and that nothing will ever change that, and that you're fine, you're always fine. Got that?' She nodded, but her chin was trembling as he looked at her. 'You're fine. And I love you.'

'You're fine, and you love you . . . I mean me . . .' She laughed a watery laugh and he held her tight again.

'You're fine, silly. Not I'm fine.'

'You're not fine?' She was better now. She always was when he held her.

'Oh Jessie . . . I'll tell you one thing. I wish to hell my pants had never fallen down.' They both laughed and then he pulled away from her again. 'Everything's gonna be okay. Now let's go.'

'I love you, darling. I wish you knew how much I love you.' Tears blinded her as she walked along at his side, quickly, trying to tell him too much in too little time.

'You're here. That tells me everything. Now stop being so dramatic, and get the mascara off your face.' She giggled nervously again and ran her hands over her cheeks. There were black streaks on her palms when she stopped.

'I must look terrific.'

'Gorgeous.'

And then they were there. The door to the courtroom.

'Okay?' He looked at her long and hard as they stood facing each other. The bailiff watched them and then turned away.

'Okay.' She nodded quietly and they smiled into each other's eyes.

They walked into the courtroom and the jury was already seated; the judge was back at his bench. The defendant was asked to rise, and Jessica almost rose from her seat with him and had to remind herself not to. She kept silently repeating to herself. 'Okay . . . okay . . . okay . . .' Her fingers dug into the seat of her chair and she closed her eyes, waiting. It would be okay, it was just so horrible waiting. She thought it must be like having a bullet pulled out of your arm. It wouldn't kill you, but God it was so awful getting it out.

The foreman was asked to read off the verdict, and she held her breath, wishing she were standing next to Ian. This was it.

'How does the jury find the defendant on the charge of sodomy, an infamous crime against nature?' They were starting at the least of the charges, and working their way up . . . she waited.

'Guilty, Your Honour.' Her eyes flew open and she saw Ian flinch, as though the tip of a whip had struck his face. But he didn't turn around to look at her.

'And on the charge of forcible oral copulation?'

'Guilty. Your Honour.'

'And on the charge of forcible rape?'

'Guilty, Your Honour.'

Jessica sat there stunned. Ian hadn't moved.

Martin looked toward her, and she felt the tears begin to pour down her face as the jury was dismissed and left the room. Ian sat down now and she went toward him. His eyes were blank when she looked into his face. She couldn't think of anything to say, and two lone tears crept down his face toward his chin.

CHAPTER XIX

'I didn't do it, Jessie. I don't care about the rest, but you have to know that. I didn't rape her.'

'I know.' It was barely a whisper, and she clung to his hand as the assistant district attorney snappily asked that the defendant be taken into custody, pending sentencing.

It was all over in five minutes. They led him away, and Jessica stood alone in the courtroom, clinging to Martin. She was alone in the world, clinging to a man she hardly knew. Ian was gone now. She was gone. Everything was gone. It was as though someone had taken a hammer to her life and shattered it. And she couldn't tell what was mirror and what was glass, what was Ian and what was Jessie.

She couldn't move, she couldn't speak, she could hardly breathe, and Martin led her slowly and carefully from the courtroom. This great, tall, healthy-looking young woman had suddenly become a zombie. It was as though there were no insides left to Jessie, and her whole being was deflating. Her eyes stayed glued to the door Ian had passed through when they'd taken him away, as if by staring hard enough she could make him come back through that door. Martin had no idea how to handle her. He had never been left alone with a client in this kind of condition. He wondered if he should call his secretary, or his wife. The court was deserted now except for the bailiff who was waiting to lock up. The judge had looked at her regretfully when he'd left the bench, but Jessie hadn't noticed. She hadn't even seen Houghton leave, shortly after Ian. It was just as well. And all she could hear was the echo of the word that kept ringing through her head again and again and again. Guilty . . . guilty . . . guilty . . .

'Jessie, I'll take you home.' He led her gently by the arm and was grateful that she followed him. He wasn't entirely certain that she knew who he was or where they were going, but he was glad that she didn't fight him. And then she stopped and looked at him vaguely.

'No, I . . . I'll wait for Ian here. I . . . I want . . . need . . . I need Ian.' She stood beside the middle-aged attorney and cried like a child, her face hidden in her hands, her shoulders shaking. Martin Schwartz sat her down on a chair in the hall, handed her a handkerchief, and patted her shoulder. She was holding Ian's wallet and watch and car keys in her hand like treasures she had been bequeathed. Ian had left with empty pockets and dry eyes. In handcuffs.

'What . . . what . . . will they do . . . to him now?' She was stammering through her tears. 'Can . . . can . . . he come home?' Martin knew she was too close to hysterics now to be told anything even approaching the truth. He just patted her shoulder again and helped her to her feet.

'Let's just get you home first. And then I want to go down and see Ian.' He thought it would comfort her, but he had only excited her again.

'Me too. I want to see Ian too.'

'Not tonight, Jessica. We're going home.' It was the right tone to take. She got to her feet, took his arm, and followed him out of the building. Walking with her was like walking a mechanical rag doll.

'Martin?'

'Yes?' They were out in the fresh air now, and she took a deep breath as he turned to her.

'Can we app—appeal?' She was calmer again. She seemed to be floating in and out of rationality, but she knew what was happening.

'We'll talk about it.'

'Now. I want to talk about it now.' Standing on the steps

of City Hall, frantic and hysterical, at six o'clock at night. It was hard to believe that this broken woman was the confident, sophisticated Jessica Clarke.

'No, Jessica, not now. I want to talk to Ian first. And I want to get you home. Ian will be very upset if I don't get you home.' Oh, Jesus. And she was going to make it difficult every inch of the way. Just getting her to the car was taking forever.

'I want to see Ian.' She stood at the top of the steps like a pouting child, irrational again. 'I . . . I need Ian . . .' And the tears began to flow again. It made it easier to get her into the car. Until she remembered that she had to drive the Volvo home. It was Ian's.

'I'll have it brought to you tomorrow, Jessica. Just give me the garage stub.' She handed it to him, and he turned the ignition in the new chocolate brown Mercedes. He kept a close watch on her as he drove her home. She looked frighteningly vague and dishevelled, and he wondered if he should call her doctor for her when he got her home. He asked her about it and she objected vehemently. 'What about a friend? Is there someone you want me to call?' He hated to leave her alone, but she only shook her head, mute, with an odd look in her eyes. She was thinking of the jury . . . of Margaret Burton . . . of Inspector Houghton . . . she wanted to kill them all . . . they had stolen Ian . . .

'Jessica? *Jessica*?' She turned to look at him blankly. They were in front of the house on Vallejo.

'Oh.' She nodded silently again and opened the door carefully on her side. 'I . . . will you see Ian now?'

'Yes. Is there anything you want me to tell him?' She nodded quickly and tried to speak normally.

'Just that . . . that . . .' But she couldn't speak through her tears.

'I'll give him your love.' She nodded gratefully and looked into his eyes with an air of being almost herself again. The hysterical vagueness seemed to be fading. What he saw now was shock, and grief. 'Jessica, I'm . . . I'm terribly sorry.'

'I know.' She turned away then, closed the door, and walked slowly toward her house. She moved like a very old woman, and the long brown Mercedes pulled slowly away. It felt wrong to watch her. It seemed kinder to let her grieve in private. But he would never forget the way she looked, walking slowly up the brick walk, her head bent, her hair tangled, with Ian's things cradled in her hands. It was an unbearable sight.

She heard the car pull away and looked at their flower beds blankly as she approached the house. Was this the house where she had come for lunch with Ian that day? Was this the house where they lived? She looked up at it as though she had never seen it before, and stopped as though she couldn't walk any further. She lifted one foot slowly then and mounted the small step. But the other foot was too heavy to lift. She couldn't. She didn't want to. She couldn't go in that house. Not without Ian. Not alone . . . not . . . like this . . .

'Oh God, *no*!' She sank to her knees on the front step and sobbed with her head bowed and her hands full of what had been in Ian's pockets. A voice called her name and she didn't turn. It wasn't Ian. Why bother to answer . . . it wasn't Ian . . . he was gone now. Everyone was gone. She felt as though he had died in the courtroom—or maybe she had. She wasn't quite sure. The voice called her name again, and she felt as if she was sinking through the brick. The contents of her handbag lay strewn on the step, the knit of her skirt had snagged on the brick, and her hair covered her face like a pale widow's veil.

'Jessie! Jessica?'

She heard the rapid footsteps behind her, but couldn't turn around. She didn't have the strength. It was all over.

'Jessie . . . darling, what's wrong?'

It was Astrid. Jessica turned to look into her face, and the tears continued to flow.

'What happened? Tell me! Everything will be all right. Just take it easy.' She smoothed Jessie's hair like a child's, and wiped the tears from her face as they continued to come. 'Is it Ian? Tell me, darling, is it Ian?'

Jessie nodded with a distraught look of grief on her face, and Astrid felt her heart stop . . . oh no, not Ian . . . not like Tom. No!

'He was convicted of rape.' The words came out as though from someone else's mouth, and Astrid looked as if she'd been slapped. 'He's in jail.'

'Good lord, Jessica, no!' But it was true. She knew it as Jessica nodded and let her friend gently take her inside and put her to bed. The pills Astrid gave her put her out almost instantly. Astrid still carried them—ever since Tom.

It was three-thirty in the morning when Jessie woke up. The house was quiet. She could hear the clock tick. It was dark in the bedroom, but there were lights on in the living room. She listened for Ian's sounds—the typewriter, his chair squeaking back on the studio floor. She sat up in bed, listening, hearing nothing, and her head swam. Then she remembered the pills. And Astrid. And how it had all begun. She sat up in bed and reached for her cigarettes with a trembling hand. She was still wearing her sweater and stockings and slip. Her jacket and skirt were neatly draped over a chair. She couldn't remember getting into bed. All she could remember was the sound of Astrid's voice, cooing gently, saying things she didn't really understand as she drifted off to sleep. But there had been someone there . . . someone . . . now there was no one. She was alone.

She lay there smoking in the darkness of the bedroom, dry-eyed, faintly nauseated and still slowed from the pills, and suddenly she reached for the phone. She got the number from information and called.

'City Prison. Langdorf here.'

'I'd like to speak to Ian Clarke, please.'

'He work here!' The desk sergeant sounded surprised.

'No. He was taken into custody yesterday. After a trial.' She didn't volunteer the nature of the conviction. And she was surprised at the steadiness of her own voice. She didn't feel steady, but she knew that if she could make herself sound calm, they might give her what she wanted. All she had to do was sound terribly calm and put a little authority into her voice and . . .

'He'd be in the county jail, lady, not here. And you can't talk to him anyway.'

'I see. Do you have the number there?' She thought of telling them it was an emergency, but decided not to. She was afraid to lie to them. The desk sergeant at the city prison gave her the number of the county jail in the Hall of Justice, and she dialled quickly. But it didn't work. They told her that she could visit her husband the day after tomorrow, and he wasn't allowed to get phone calls. Then they hung up on her.

She shrugged one shoulder and flicked on a lamp. It was cold in the room. Jessie pulled a bathrobe over her sweater and slip and padded out to the living room in stocking feet. She stood in the middle of the room and looked around. The room was faintly messy, but not very, just enough to remind her . . . impressions in the softness of the couch, a mark where the back of a head had pressed into a cushion, the book he'd been reading last weekend . . . his loafers under the chair . . . his . . . she felt a sob rise and stick in her throat and she turned and walked into the kitchen for something to drink . . . tea . . . coffee . . . Coke . . . something . . . her mouth was dry and her head felt fuzzy, but everything else was so clear. She found the plates from lunch in the sink, and the newspaper on the counter where she had thrown it, the article on rape folded out. It was as though he had just been in the room, as though he had taken a walk around the block, as though . . . she sat down at the kitchen table, dropped her head, and cried.

The studio was as bad. Worse. Dark and empty and lonely. It looked as though it expected his presence but had been stood up. It needed him to come alive. Ian was the room's living soul. And hers. Jessie's soul. She needed him more than his studio did. She found herself moving from one foot to the other, like a disturbed child, standing in doorways, smoothing her hand over his books, or his shirts, holding his loafers close to her and jumping when a shadow cast an odd light. She was alone. In the house, in the night, in the world. With no one to help her, or take care of her, or give a damn about her, or . . . she opened her mouth to scream, but no sound came. She simply sank slowly to the floor, with the loafers in her arms, and waited. But no one came. She was alone.

CHAPTER XX

It was nine-thirty in the morning and she was sitting in the bathtub trying to fight a wave of hysteria when the doorbell rang. It was all right. All right. Everything was going to be all right. She'd stay in the bath for a little while and then she'd have a cup of tea, and some breakfast, and get dressed, and go to the boutique. Or maybe she'd stay in bed all day. Or . . . but it was all right. First the hot bath, and then . . . but she couldn't call Ian. She couldn't talk to him. She needed to talk to him. She took another deep breath and then listened. It sounded like the doorbell, or maybe that was just the running water playing games with her ears. but it wasn't. The bell went on ringing. But she didn't have to answer it. All she had to do was keep breathing and stay calm, and let the warm water relax her. Ian had shown her how to stay calm like that, and not get hysterical, when . . . when her mother . . . and Jake . . . but the doorbell. She jumped out of the tub suddenly, grabbed a towel, and ran for the door. What if it was Ian? She had his keys. What if . . . she ran to the front door, dripping water along the way, a half smile on her mouth, her eyes suddenly bright and large, the towel covering her torso inadequately. She pulled the door open without remembering to ask who was there, and then jumped back, startled. Too surprised to close the door again. She simply stood there, fear pounding in her heart.

'Good morning. I wouldn't make a habit of opening the door like that if I were you.' She looked down quickly and tightened the towel. The caller was Inspector Houghton.

'I . . . how do you. What can I do for you?' She pulled herself to her full height and stood regally in the doorway in spite of the towel.

'Nothing. I just thought I'd see how you are.' He wore the ironic look of victory in his eyes, the look that she had missed the day before. It made her want to scratch his eyes out.

'I'm fine.' You filthy bastard. 'Was there anything else?'

'Got any coffee ready, Mrs. Clarke?' From him the formalities were almost abusive.

'As a matter of fact, no, Inspector Houghton, I don't. And I have to get to work shortly. If you have business to discuss with me, I suggest you go buy yourself a cup of coffee on Union Street, and see me in my office in an hour.'

'Feisty, aren't you? You must have had a nasty shock yesterday, though.'

She closed her eyes, fighting the wave of nausea that rose to her throat. The man was sadistic. But she couldn't faint now. Couldn't. She heard Ian's voice saying 'Okay?' with that special way of his, and she nodded imperceptibly and thought 'Okay'.

'Yes, it was a shock. Do you enjoy that, Inspector? Seeing other people unhappy, I mean.'

'I don't see it that way.' He pulled out a pack of cigarettes and offered her one. She shook her head. He was enjoying this, all right.

'I guess not. Miss Burton must have been pleased.'

'Very.' He smiled at her through the cigarette smoke and she had to fight herself not to slap him or flail at him. That took more control than not getting sick.

'And what happens to you now?' So that's what this was all about.

'What do you mean?'

'Any plans?'

'Yes, work. And seeing my husband tomorrow. And dinner with friends next week, and . . .'

He smiled again, but did not look amused.

'If he goes to prison, it could wreak havoc with your marriage, Mrs. Clarke.' His voice was almost gentle.

'Possibly. Almost anything can wreak havoc with a marriage, if you let it. Depends on how good your marriage is, and how hard you want to work at keeping it that way.'

'And how good is yours?'

'Excellent. And from the bottom of my heart, Inspector Houghton, I thank you for your concern. I'll be sure to mention it to both my husband and our attorney. I know Mr. Clarke will be deeply touched. You know, you're really a very sensitive man, Inspector—or is it just that you have a particular fondness for marriage counselling?'

His eyes blazed back into hers, but it was too late; he had walked right into it. He had come to her house, rung the bell, and made his own mistakes that morning.

'You know, as a matter of fact, I think I might even call your superior to tell him what a marvellously thoughtful man you are. Imagine caring about how my marriage is.'

He slipped the cigarette pack back into his pocket and his smile was long since gone.

'All right, I get the point.'

'Do you? My, how quick you are, Inspector.'

'Bitch.' He said it through clenched teeth.

'I beg your pardon?'

'I said "bitch" and you can tell *that* to my superior too. But if I were you, baby, I wouldn't bother to call. You've got enough problems, and you ain't gonna see your old man around here for a long time. You'd better get used to it, sister. You and that little literary punk of yours are through. So when you get tired of sitting here by yourself in the dark, start looking around. There's better out there than what you got stuck with.'

'Oh, really? And I suppose you're a prime example?' She was trembling with fury now and her voice was rising to match his.

'Pick who you want, but you'll be out looking. I give you two months to be down at Jerry's with the rest of them.'

'Get out of here, Inspector. And if you ever set foot near this house again, with or without a search warrant, I'll call the judge, the mayor, and the fire department. Or I may not call a goddam living soul. I may just take aim at you out of my window.'

'Have a gun, do you?' He raised an eyebrow with interest.

'Not yet, but I will. Apparently I need one.'

He opened his mouth to say something and she took one graceful step backward and slammed the door in his face. Tactically, it was a poor move, but it made her feel better.

For a moment. When she walked back into the house, she threw up in the kitchen. It took her two hours to stop shaking.

Astrid arrived at eleven. She had flowers with her, and a roast chicken she'd bought for Jessie to pick on, and a bag full of fruit. And a small vial of yellow pills. But after twenty minutes of persistently ringing the doorbell there was still no answer; Astrid knew Jessie was there because she had called the boutique to make sure. Finally she began to worry seriously and knocked on the kitchen windows with her rings. Jessie peered cautiously between the curtains and then jumped half a foot when she saw Astrid. She had thought it was Houghton again.

'Good Lord, child, I thought something had happened. Why didn't you answer the door? Worried about press?'

'No, there's no problem with that. It's . . . oh . . . I don't know.' And then there were tears in her eyes again and she was standing there looking like an overgrown child and telling Astrid about the visit from Houghton. 'I just can't take it. He's so . . . so evil, and so happy about what happened. And he said that our . . . our marriage . . .' She was crying too hard to go on and Astrid made her sit down.

'Why don't you come and stay with me for a little while, Jessica? You could have the guest room and get away from here for a few days.'

'No!' Jessie sprang to her feet and started pacing the room, touching chairs as she sped past, or picking something up and then putting it down again. It was a series of odd little staccato gestures, but Astrid recognised them. She had reacted the same way when Tom had died.

'No. Thank you, Astrid, but I want to be here. With . . . with . . .' She faltered, not quite sure of what she wanted to say.

'With Ian's things. I know. But maybe that's not such a good idea. And is it worth the price of being heckled by people like that policeman? And what if there are others who show up the same way? Do you want to have to deal with that?'

'I won't open the door.'

'You can't live like that, Jessica. Ian won't want you to.'

'Yes, he will. Honest. Really . . . I . . . oh, God, Astrid, I'm going crazy, I can't . . . I don't know how without Ian.'

'But you're not without Ian. You'll see him. I still don't understand what happened, but maybe you can work it out. He's not gone, Jessica. He's not dead, for God's sake. Stop acting like he is.'

'But he's not here.' Her voice had a pitiful sound. 'I need him here. I'll go crazy without him, I'll . . . I'll . . .'

'No, you won't. Not unless you *want* to go crazy, or make yourself do so. Take yourself in hand, Jessica, and sit down. Right now. Come on, sit down.' Jessica had been popping in and out of chairs like a jack-in-the-box for the past five minutes. Her voice was rising to a desperate pitch. 'Have you had breakfast?' Jessica shook her head and started to say that she didn't want any, but Astrid held up her hand and vanished into the kitchen. She emerged five minutes later with toast, jelly, the fresh fruit she had brought, and a cup of steaming tea. 'Would you rather have coffee?' Jessie shook her head and closed her eyes for a moment.

'I just don't believe this is happening, Astrid.'

'Don't think about it yet. You can't make sense of it, so don't try. When can you see Ian?' Jessie's eyes opened and she sighed at the question.

'Tomorrow.'

'All right. Then all you have to do is try and stay calm till tomorrow. You can do that, can't you?'

Jessica nodded, but she wasn't quite sure. That meant a day, and a night, and a morning. And the night would be the worst. Full of ghosts and voices and echoes and terrors. She had twenty-four hours to survive until she saw Ian.

But there was one thing she did want to do. Now. Before she saw Ian. And that was to talk to Martin about an appeal. He was in his office when she called, and he sounded subdued.

'Are you all right, Jessica?'

'I'm okay. How's Ian?' Her voice caught on the words, and at the other end Martin frowned. He was remembering how she had looked the night before when he'd dropped her off.

'He's holding up. He was awfully shocked, though.'

'I can imagine.' She said it softly with a distracted smile. Shocked. They both were. 'Martin, I called because I wanted to ask you something now, right away, before I see Ian tomorrow.'

'What?'

'I want to know what we can do about an appeal, how we do it, do you do it, all of that.' And how the hell do we pay for it? That was another thing.

'Well, we can talk about that after the sentencing, Jessica. If he gets probation, then there isn't much point in pressing for an appeal, except as a matter of record, to clear Ian of the felony. He might want to do that. But I think you should wait till after the sentencing to make a decision. There's a limited time in which to file an appeal, but you'll still have plenty of time then.'

'How soon is the sentencing?'

'Four weeks from tomorrow.'

'But why wait till after that?'

'Because, Jessie, you don't know what's going to happen. If they send him home on probation, Ian may not want to spend his last dime, or yours, on an appeal. It's not as if he's in a delicate position professionally where it can hurt him to have that on his record. All right, it can hurt him,' he reconsidered, 'but not that badly in his profession. And if he's free, what do you care?'

'What do you mean, *if* he's free?' Jessie was feeling confused again.

'All right, the alternative is, if they don't give him probation, they'll send him to prison. In that case, you may well want to appeal. But all an appeal is going to do for you, Jessica, is get you a new trial. You'll have to go through the whole ordeal again. There isn't a shred of evidence we didn't submit. Nothing would change. So you'd be going through it all again, maybe to no avail. I think right now our push should be for probation. And we can worry about an appeal after we see what happens with that. All right?'

Jessica reluctantly agreed, and hung up. What did he mean, 'if' they set Ian free? What was the 'if'?

CHAPTER XXI

'Okay?'

'Okay.' She smiled and instinctively her hand went to the gold lima bean at her throat, and played with it for a moment as she looked at him. She had survived the twenty-four hours, and Houghton had not returned. 'I love you, Ian.'

'Darling, I love you too. Are you really all right?' He looked so worried about her.

'I'm fine. What about you?'

His eyes told their own tale. He was in county jail this time, and he was wearing the filthy overalls they had given him. They had stuffed his clothes in a shopping bag and returned them to Martin. He had sent them back to Jessie the evening before, along with the Volvo. After that she had taken the two pills Astrid had left her.

'Martin says they might give you probation.' But they both remembered the article they had read the day of the trial. It had been in favour of abolishing probation on rape cases. The public mood was not lenient just now.

'We'll see, Jessie, but don't count on it. We'll give it a try.' He smiled and Jessie fought back tears. What would happen if he didn't get probation? She hadn't even begun to face that yet. Later. Another 'later', like the trial, and the verdict. 'Have you been behaving yourself? No panic, no freakies?' He knew her too well.

'I've been fine. And Astrid's been taking care of me like a child.' She didn't tell him about Houghton. Or the night of semicraziness that she had had to fill with pills just to survive. She had crawled through that night as if it were a mine field.

'Is she here with you now?' He looked around but didn't see her.

'Yes, but she waited downstairs. She was afraid you'd feel awkward. And she figured we'd want to talk.'

'Tell her I love her. And I'm glad you're not here alone. Jessie, I've been worried sick over you. Promise me you won't do anything crazy. Please. Promise.' His eyes pleaded with her.

'I promise. Honest, darling. I'm okay.' But she didn't look it. They both looked like hell. Ravaged, shocked, exhausted, and in Ian's case two days' growth of beard didn't help.

For half an hour they exchanged the disjointed banalities of people still in shock. Jessie stayed busy trying not to cry, and she managed not to until she rejoined Astrid downstairs. They were tears of anger and pain.

'They have him up there in a goddam cage like an animal!' And that damn woman was probably in her office, doing her job, living her life. She had got her revenge and now she could be happy. While Ian rotted in jail, and Jessie went crazy alone at night.

Astrid took her home, cooked her dinner, and waited until she was half asleep. It was an easier night for Jessie, mostly because she was too exhausted to torture herself thinking, to wander. She simply slept. And Astrid was back early the next morning with fresh strawberries, a copy of *The New York Times* and a brand new *Women's Wear Daily* as though that still mattered.

'Lady, what would I do without you?'

'Sleep later, probably. But I was up so I thought I'd come over.' Jessie shook her head and hugged her friend as she poured two cups of tea. It was going to be a long haul, and Astrid was a godsend. It would be another twenty-seven days until the sentencing. And God only knew what would happen after that.

Jessie had the shop to think of too, but she wasn't ready to face that yet. She managed it with increasingly rare phone calls and a great deal of faith in Katsuko. Astrid took her along to her own appointment with the hairdresser, more to keep an eye on her than anything else. Jessie could only see Ian twice a week, and there was a frightening aimlessness about her in the meantime. She'd start to say things and then forget them, take objects out of her handbag and then forget why she'd brought them out; she would listen to Astrid talk and look right through her as though she couldn't see or hear her. She wasn't making a great deal of sense. She looked the way she felt, like a lost child far from home hanging desperately to a new mother. Astrid. But without Ian nothing made any sense. Least of all living. And with no contact, it was hard to remind herself that he still existed. Astrid was just trying to keep her afloat until the next time she could see him.

There had been a small article on the back page of the paper the day after the verdict. But no one had called, only the two friends who had appeared for Ian in court. They were shocked by the news. Astrid took the calls and Jessica dropped them each a note. She didn't want to talk to anyone now.

On Monday she went back to work, and Zina and Katsuko were subdued. Kat had spotted the article, but hadn't mentioned it on the phone; she had wanted to wait until she could say something to Jessie in person. And she had known from the sound of her voice on the phone that Jessie didn't want them to know. It was a painful moment when she and Astrid walked into the shop. She read the knowledge at once in their faces, and Zina instantly had tears in her eyes. Jessie hugged them both.

Now the two girls knew why Houghton had come to the shop, why Jessie had been so frantic, why the Morgan was gone. They finally understood.

'Jessie, is there anything we can do?' Katsuko spoke for both of them.

'Only one thing. Don't talk about it after this. There's nothing I can say right now. Talking doesn't help.'

'How's Ian?'

'He's surviving. That's about the best you can say.'

'Do you have any idea what'll happen?' She shook her head and sat down quietly in her usual chair.

'Nope. No idea at all. Does that answer everybody's questions?' She looked at the two women's faces, and she already felt tired.

'Do you need any help at home, Jessie?' Zina had finally spoken up. 'It must be lonely. And I don't live very far.'

'Thanks, love. I'll let you know.' She gave the girl a

squeeze as she headed toward her office with Astrid at her heels. The last thing she wanted was to spend evenings with Zina commiserating. It would be worse than the terrors of being alone. She turned at the door to her office with a serious look on her face. 'One thing, though. I'm not going to be around much for the next few weeks. I have things to do for Ian. People to see about the sentencing, and just a hell of a lot on my mind. I'll be here whenever I can, but you two count on carrying the ball for me. Like you've been doing. Okay?' Katsuko saluted and Jessie smiled. 'Couple of nuts. It's nice to be back.'

'What if I pitch in and help?' Astrid was looking at her with interest as she sat down at her desk.

'To tell you the truth, I need you more everywhere but the shop. Kat has this place under control. The real problem is me. Mornings, evenings, late nights . . . you know.' Astrid did know. She had seen Jessie's face at eight-thirty in the morning, and had heard her voice at two. It told a perfect tale of what the nights were like. The terror that daylight would never come again. That Ian would never come home. That the world would swallow her up and never spit her out. That Houghton would break down the door and rape her. Real fears and unreal fears, demons of her own making and men who weren't worthy of the name —all tangled together in her mind.

'Any idea what time you'll be through work? I'll pick you up. We can have dinner at my place tonight, if you feel up to it.'

'You're too good to me.' And it was amazing, considering how short a time they'd known each other. But Astrid knew what it was like. She had a healthy respect for what Jessica was going through.

Most of Jessica's efforts went toward Ian's sentencing. Twice she saw the probation officer detailed to the case, and she hounded Martin night and day. What was he doing? What did he have in mind? Had he spoken to the probation officer? What were the man's impressions? Should Martin talk to the man's superiors? She even went to speak to the judge one day at lunchtime. He was sympathetic, but didn't want to be pressured about the sentencing. Jessie had the distinct impression that had she been a little less ladylike the judge might have been a little less kind in his reception. As it was, he was not overly welcoming. She also collected letters from a number of discreet friends, testifying to Ian's good character. She even got a letter from his agent, hoping to show that Ian had to be free to complete the new book, and that going to prison would destroy his career.

Thanksgiving came and went like any other day. Or at least Jessica tried to ensure that it did. She treated it like any day when she wasn't working. She wouldn't allow herself to think of past Thanksgivings. She refused to let it be festive in any way. That would have been too much for her. She spent it with Astrid, and Ian spent it in jail. There was no visiting at the county jail on Thanksgiving Day. He ate stale chicken sandwiches and read a letter from Jessie. She ate steak with Astrid, who went out of her way to ignore the holiday this year, sacrificing a long weekend at the ranch with her mother. But the sacrifice was well worth it. She was worried about Jessie, who always seemed to move about in a haze now, stopping and starting, jangled, at one extreme or the other: fuzzy and full of pills, or wild from too much coffee.

And she worked night and day. Figuring out what to do for the sentencing, and suddenly pouring her energy back into Lady J, as she hadn't in years. She worked on Saturdays again. At home she did anything, everything—cleaned the basement, straightened out the garage, redid her closets, tidied the studio—anything, trying not to think. And maybe, maybe, if she did everything perfectly, maybe at the end of the month, he'd come home. Maybe they'd give him probation, maybe . . . she moved like a whirling dervish, but she had to; the pounding of her mind was deafening her. And constantly there was fear. She never escaped it. Sheer, raw, endless terror. Beyond human proportions. But she wasn't human anymore. She barely ate, she hardly slept. She wouldn't allow herself to feel. She didn't dare to be human. Humans fell apart. And that was what scared her most. Falling apart. Like Humpty-Dumpty. And all the king's horses and all the king's men . . . that was what she was afraid of. Ian knew it, but he couldn't stop her now. He couldn't touch her, hold her, feel her, make her feel. He couldn't do anything except watch her through the window and talk to her on the phone at the jail as she played nervously with the cord and snapped her earring absentmindedly.

And he continued to look steadily worse—unshaven, unwashed, ill fed, and with dark circles under his eyes that seemed to get darker each time she saw him.

'Don't you sleep in here?' There was a raw edge to her voice now. It was higher, shriller, scareder. He pitied her, but he couldn't help her now. They both knew it, and he wondered how long it would take her to hate him for it. For failing her. He was terrified that a day would come when he couldn't keep the boogey man from the door for her, and then she would turn on him. Jessie expected a lot. Because she needed so much.

'I sleep now and then.' He tried to smile. Tried not to think. 'What about you? Looks like a lot of makeup under your eyes, my love. Am I right?'

'Are you ever wrong?' She smiled back and shrugged, snapping the earring again. She had lost twelve pounds, but she was sleeping a little better. She just didn't look it. But the new red pills helped. They were better than the yellow ones, or even the little blue ones Astrid had let her graduate to after that. They were the same kind, only stronger. The red ones were something else. She didn't discuss it with Ian. He would have been difficult about it. And she was careful. But the pills were the best part of her day. The two bright moments with Ian were the only livable parts of her week, and in between she had to get through the days. The pills did that for her. And Astrid doled them out one by one, refusing to leave the bottle with her.

Ian would have been frantic if he had known. She had promised him solemnly, after Jake had died—no more pills. He had stood at her side all night while they'd pumped her stomach, and afterward she had promised. She thought about that sometimes when she took the pills. But she had to. She really had to. Or she'd die anyway. One way or another. She worried about things like jumping out a window, without wanting to. About little demons seizing her and making her do things she didn't want to. She couldn't talk to customers in the shop anymore. She stayed in the back office because she was afraid of what she'd say. She was no longer in control. Of anything. Jessica was not in her own driver's seat. No one was.

The four weeks between the verdict and the sentencing ground by like a permanent nightmare, but the sentencing finally came. The plea for probation was heard by the judge, and this time Jessie stood beside Ian as they waited. It was less frightening now, though, and she kept touching his hand, his face. It was the first time in a month that she had touched him. He smelled terrible and his nails were long. They had given him an electric razor at the jail and it had torn his face apart. But it was Ian. It was, at last the touch of the familiar in a world that had become totally unfamiliar to her. Now she could stand next to him. Be his. She almost forgot the seriousness of the sentencing. But the courtroom formalities brought her back. The bailiff, the court reporter, the flag. It was the same courtroom, the same judge. And it was all very real now.

Ian was not granted probation. The judge felt that the charges were too serious. And Martin explained later that with the political climate what it was, the judge could hardly have done otherwise. Ian was given a sentence of four years to life in state prison, and he would have to serve at least a fourth of his minimum sentence: one year.

The bailiff led him away, and this time Jessie did not cry.

CHAPTER XXII

Three days later, Ian was moved from county jail to state prison. He went, like all male prisoners in Northern California, to the California Medical Facility in Vacaville for 'evaluation'.

Jessica drove there two days later with Astrid, in the black Jaguar, and with two yellow pills under her belt. Astrid said these were the last she would give her, but she always said that. Jessica knew she felt sorry for her.

Except for the gun tower peering over the main gate and the metal detector that searched them for weapons, the prison at Vacaville looked innocuous. Inside, a gift shop sold ugly items made in the prison, and the front desk might have been the entrance to a hospital. Everything was chrome and glass and linoleum. But outside, it looked like a modern garage. For people.

They asked to see Ian, filled out various forms, and were invited to sit in the waiting room or wander in the lobby. Ten minutes later a guard appeared to unlock a door to an inner courtyard. He instructed them to pass through the courtyard and go through yet another door, which they would find unlocked.

The inmates in the courtyard wore blue jeans, T-shirts, and an assortment of shoes, everything from boots to sneakers, and Astrid raised an eyebrow at Jessica. It didn't look like a prison. Everyone was casually playing with the soda machines or talking to girlfriends. It looked like a high school at recess, with here and there the exception of a sober face or a watery-eyed mother.

What she saw gave Jessie some hope. She could visit Ian somewhere in the courtyard, could touch him again, laugh, hold hands. It was madness to be regressing to that after seven years of marriage, but it would be an improvement over the doggie-in-the-window visits at the county jail.

As it turned out, there was no improvement. Ian was months away from visits in the courtyard, if he stayed in that institution at all. There was always Folsom or San Quentin to worry about now. Anything was possible. And for the time being they were faced once again with more visits through a glass window, talking over a phone. Jessica felt a surging desire to smash the receiver through the window as she tried to smile into his face. She longed for the touch of his face, the feel of his arms, the smell of his hair. And instead all she had in her hands was a blue plastic phone. Next to her there was a pink one, and further down a yellow. Someone with a sense of humour had installed pastel-coloured princess-style phones all the way down the line. Like a nursery, with a glass window. And you could talk to the darling babies on the phone. What she needed was her husband, not a phone pal.

But he looked better—thinner, but at least clean. He had even shaved in the hope of a visit. They fell into some of their old jokes, and Astrid shared the phone with Jessica now and then. It was all so strange, sitting there, making conversation with a wall of glass between the two women and Ian. The strain told in his eyes, and the humour they inflicted on each other always had a bitter edge.

'This is quite a harem. For a rapist.' He grinned nervously at his own bad joke.

'Maybe they'll think you're a pimp.' Their laughter sounded like tinsel rustling.

The reality was that he was there. For at least a year. Jessie wondered how long she could take it. But maybe she didn't have to. Maybe neither of them did. She wanted to talk to him about an appeal.

'Did you talk to Martin about it?'

'Yes. And there won't be an appeal.' He answered her solemnly, but with certainty in his voice.

'*What*?' Jessie's voice was suddenly shrill.

'You heard me. I know what I'm doing, Jess. Nothing would change next time around. Martin feels the same way. For another five or ten thousand bucks, we'd sink ourselves further into debt, and when the second trial rolled around, we'd have nothing different to say. The suspicions we have about her husband are inadmissible on the flimsy evidence we have. All we've got is an old photograph and a lot of fancy ideas. No one will testify. There's nothing to hang our hats on except blind hope. We did that once, but we didn't have any choice. We're not going through that again. A new trial would come out the same goddam way, and it'll just make these people mad. Martin thinks I'm better off living through this, just being a nice guy, and they'll probably give me an early parole. Anyway, I've made my decision, and I'm right.'

'Who says you're right, dammit, and why didn't anyone ask me?'

'Because we're talking about my time in here, not yours. It's my decision.'

'But it affects my life too.' Her eyes filled with tears. She wanted an appeal, another chance, something, anything. She couldn't accept just waiting around until he got paroled. There was talk of changing the California laws to bring in a determinate sentence, but who had time to wait for that? And even then, Martin had once said that Ian might have to do a couple of years. Two years? Jesus. How would she survive? She could barely speak as she held the phone in her hand.

'Jessie, trust me. It has to be this way. There's no point.'

'We could sell something. The house. Anything.'

'And we might lose again. Then what? Let's just grit our teeth and get through this. Please, Jessie—please, please try. I can't do anything for you right now except love you. You've got to be strong. And it won't be for long. It probably won't be more than a year.' He tried to sound cheerful about it, for her sake.

'What if it's more than a year?'

'We'll worry about it then.' The tears spilled down her face in answer. How could they have decided this without talking to her? And why weren't they willing to try again? Maybe they could win . . . maybe . . . she looked up to see Ian exchanging a look with Astrid and shaking his head. 'Baby, you have to pull yourself together.'

'What for?'

'For me.'

'I'm okay.'

He shook his head and looked at her. 'I wish to hell you were.' Thank God she had Astrid.

They talked on for a while, about the other men there, about some tests they'd put him through, about his hopes of being kept there rather than sent on to another prison. Vacaville at least seemed civilised, and he expected that he could work on his book after he'd been there for a while and had calmed down. Jessie told herself that it made her feel better to know that he was still interested in the book. At least he was still alive mentally, spiritually. But she found that she didn't really care. What about her? After the outburst over the appeal, she felt even lonelier. She tried to pump life into her smile, but it hurt so much not to be able to reach out to him or be held in his arms.

He watched her face for a long moment and wished only that he could touch her. Even he didn't have enough words anymore, and too often they fell silent.

'How's the shop?'

'Okay. Great, really. Business is booming.' But it was a lie. Business was far from booming. It was the worst it had been in all the years since she'd opened Lady J. But what could she tell him, what was there to say without voicing agonising recriminations, and accusations, and cries of outrage and despair? What was left? There was always the truth that business was lousy and he should have been home working to help pay the bills . . . the truth that he shouldn't be in prison . . . the truth that he looked terrible and his haircut made him look old and tired . . . the truth that she even worried now that he'd become a homosexual in jail—or worse, that someone would kill him . . . the truth that she didn't know how to pay the bills anymore and was afraid that she couldn't survive the nights alone . . . the truth that she wanted to die . . . the truth that he never should have balled

Margaret Burton . . . the truth that he was a sonofabitch and she was beginning to hate him because he wasn't there anymore . . . he was gone. But she couldn't tell him the truth. There was too much of it now, and she knew it would kill him.

He was talking again; she had to look up and focus her attention.

'Jess, I want you to do something for me when you get home today. Get the book Xeroxed, put the copy in the bank, and send me the original. I'm getting special permission to work on it, and by the time the manuscript gets here, I'll have the paperwork squared away at this end. Don't forget, though. Try and get it out to me today.' There was summer in his eyes again as he spoke, but Astrid wondered at the look on Jessica's face. Jessie was stunned. He had just been sentenced to prison and he was worried about his book?

The visit was called to a close after little more than an hour. There was a frantic flurry of good-byes on the phone, cheery farewells from Astrid, a few last verbal hugs from Ian, and a moment of panic that Jessie thought would close her throat. She couldn't even kiss him good-bye. But what if she needed to hold him? Didn't they understand that all she had in the world was Ian? What if . . .

She watched him walk away slowly, reluctant to leave, but a big boyish smile hung on his face, while she tried to smile too. But she was running on an empty tank now, and secretly she was glad the visit was over. It cost her more each time she saw him now. It was even harder here than it had been in county jail. She wanted to throw a fist through the glass, to scream, to . . . anything, but she gave him a last smile, and numbly followed Astrid back to the car.

'Do you have any more of those magical little pills, fairy godmother?'

'No, I don't. I didn't bring them.' Astrid said nothing more, but touched her arm gently and gave her a hug before unlocking the car. There was nothing more she could say. And she left Jessie the dignity of not seeing her tears as they drove home in silence, the radio purring softly between them.

'Want me to drop you off at home, so you can relax for a while?' She smiled as they came to a stop on Broadway where the freeway poured them back into the city traffic. Two blocks later they drove past Enrico's.

'Nope. And that's where it all began.'

'What?' Astrid hadn't noticed, and she turned to see Jessie staring at the tables clustered on the sidewalk under the heaters. It was cold now, but a few hardy souls still sat outside.

'Enrico's. That's where he met her. I wonder what she's doing now.' There was a haunted look on Jessica's face, and she spoke almost dreamily.

'Jessie, don't think of that.'

'Why not?'

'Because there's no point now. It's over. Now you have to look ahead to the other end. You just have to trot on through the tunnel, and before you know it . . .'

'Oh, bullshit! You make it sound like a fairy tale, for Chrissake. Just what do you think it feels like to look at your husband through a glass window, not to be able to touch him, or . . . oh, God. I'm sorry. I just can't stand it, Astrid. I can't accept it, I don't want this happening to my life, I don't want to be alone. I need him.' She ended softly, with tears thick in her throat.

'And you still have him. In all the ways that matter. Okay, so he's behind a window, but he won't be there forever. What do you suppose it felt like when I looked down at Tom in that stinking box? He would never talk to me again, hold me again, need me again, love me again. Ever, Jessie. Ever. With you and Ian, it's only an intermission. The only thing you don't have is his presence in the house every night. You have all the rest.'

But that was what she needed. His presence. What 'rest' was there? She couldn't remember anymore. Was there a 'rest'? Had there ever been?

'And you've got to stop taking those pills, Jessie.' Astrid's tone brought her back again. They were a few blocks from her house now.

'Why? They don't do any harm. They just . . . they just help, that's all.'

'They won't in a while. They'll just depress you more, if they aren't doing that already. And if you don't watch out you'll get so dependent on them that you'll have a real problem. I did, and it was a bitch to get rid of. I spent weeks down at Mother's ranch trying to "kick", as it were. Do yourself a big favour—give 'em up now.' Jessie brushed off the suggestion and pulled a comb out of her bag.

'Yeah. Maybe I'll just go straight to the shop.'

'Why don't you at least go home for five minutes to unwind first? How would that be?' Lousy. Painful.

'Okay. If you'll come in for coffee.' She didn't want to be alone there. 'I have to pick up Ian's book and get it Xeroxed for him. He wants to start working again.' Astrid noticed the strained tone in her voice. Could she be jealous? It seemed almost impossible. But these days, anything was possible with Jessie.

'At least they'll let him work on the book.'

'Apparently.' Jessie shrugged as Astrid pulled into the driveway.

'It'll do him good.'

Jessie shrugged again and got out.

There was a look of slight disorder in the front hall, of jackets and coats tried on and discarded before her visit to Ian that morning. Astrid noticed Ian's coats crammed to one side of the closet and the now predominantly female clutter here and there. He had only been gone for five weeks, yet it was beginning to look like a woman's house. She wondered if Jessie had noticed the change.

'Coffee or tea?'

'Coffee, thanks.' Astrid smiled and settled into a chair to look at the view. 'Want any help?' Jessica shook her head and Astrid tried to relax. It was difficult to be with Jessica now. There was obviously so much pain, and so little one could do to help. Except be there. 'What are you doing for Christmas?'

Jessica appeared with two flowered cups and laughed hollowly. 'Who knows? Maybe I'll hang myself this year instead of a stocking.'

'Jessica, that's not funny.'

'Is anything anymore?'

Astrid sighed deeply and set down the cup Jessie had given her.

'Jessie, you have to stop feeling so sorry for yourself. Somehow, somewhere, you're going to have to find something to hang on to. For your own sake, not just for his. The shop, a group of people, me, a church, whatever it is you need, but you just have to grab on to something. You can't live like this. Not only will your marriage not survive, but, much worse, *you* won't.' That was what had been frightening Ian: Astrid knew that. Once or twice he had looked at her, and she had understood.

'This isn't forever, you know. You'll get back what you had before. It isn't over.'

'Isn't it? How do you know that? I don't even know that. I don't even know at this point what the hell we had, or if it's worth wanting back.' She was shocked at her own words but she couldn't stop herself now. She gripped her shaking hands together. 'What did we have? Me supporting Ian, and him hating me for it, so much that he had to go out and screw a bunch of other women to feel like a man. Pretty portrait of a marriage, isn't it, Astrid? Just what every little girl dreams of.'

'Is that how you feel about it now?' Astrid watched the hurt on Jessica's face and her heart went out to her. 'From what I've seen, there's a lot more to your marriage than that.' They had looked so young and so happy when she'd met them, but she realised now that there was a lot she didn't know. There had to be. She met Jessica's eyes now and ached for her. Jessica had a lot to find out in the next months.

'I don't know, Astrid. I feel as though I did everything wrong before, and I want to make it right now. But it's too late. He's gone. And I don't care what you say, it feels in my gut like he's never coming home again. I play games with myself, I listen for his footsteps, I wander around his studio—and then we go up and see him there, like an ape in a cage. Astrid, he's my husband, and they have him locked up like an animal!' Tears and confusion flooded her eyes.

'Is that what really bothers you, Jessie?'

She looked irate at the question. 'Of course it is! What do you think?'

'I think that bothers you, but I think other things bother you just as much. I think you're afraid everything will change. He'll change. He wants his book now, and that frightens you.'

'It does not frighten me. It annoys me.' At least that was honest. She had admitted it.

'Why does it annoy you?'

'Because I sit here by myself, going crazy, dealing with reality, and what does he want to do? Doodle around on his book, like nothing ever happened. And . . . oh . . . I don't know, Astrid, it's so complicated. I don't understand anything anymore. It's all making me crazy. I can't take it. I *just can't take it.*'

'You can take it, and so can Ian. You've already gone through the worst part. The trial must have been hell.' Jessie nodded soberly.

'Yeah, but this is worse. This goes on forever.'

'Of course not. And Jessie, you can take a lot more than you think. So can Ian.' As she said the words, she hoped she was right.

'How can you be so sure? Remember how he looked today, Astrid? How long do you think he can take all that? He's spoiled, spoiled rotten, and used to a comfortable life with civilised people. Now he's in there. We don't see what it's really like, but what do you think will happen when some guy pulls a knife on him, or some jerk wants to make love to him? Then what? Are you really sure he can handle it, Astrid?' Her voice was rising to an hysterical pitch. 'And you know what the real joke of this whole mess is? That he's in there because of me. Not because of Margaret Burton. Because of me. Because I castrated him so completely that he needed her to prove something. I did it. I might as well have put the handcuffs on him myself.'

The tragedy of it was that Astrid knew she believed that. She went to her and tried to put her arms around her as Jessica sobbed.

'Jessica, no . . . no, baby. You know . . .'

'I know. It's true! I know it. And he knows it. And the fucking woman even knew it. You should have seen how she looked at me in court. God knows what he told her. But I looked at her with hatred, and she looked at me with . . . pity. Dammit, Astrid, please give me some of those pills.' She looked up at Astrid with a ravaged face, but her friend shook her head.

'I can't.'

'Why not? I need them.'

'You need to think right now. Clearly. Not in a fogged state. What you just told me is totally crazy, and a lot of what you're thinking is probably pretty crazy. You might as well get it all straightened out in your head now, and have done with it. Pills won't help.'

'They'll get me through it.' She was begging now.

'No they won't. You've lost all perspective about what happened, and they'll only make it worse. And I can tell you one thing for sure. If you don't straighten out your thinking now, it will only get worse, and you won't have a marriage left when Ian comes out. You'll eventually wind up hating him, maybe even as much as you hate yourself right now, if that's possible. You owe yourself some serious thinking, Jessica.'

'So you're going to see that I get it, is that it?' Jessica's voice was bitter now.

'No, I can't do that. I can't force you to think. But I won't give you anything to cloud your thinking anymore either. I can't do that, Jessica. I just can't.' Jessica felt an almost irresistible urge to stand up and hit her, and then she knew that she must be going crazy. Wanting to hit Astrid was very crazy. But also very real. She wanted those goddam pills.

'You'll have to face it sooner or later anyway.' And then suddenly there were tears in Jessie's eyes again.

'But what if I go crazy? I mean really crazy?'

'Why should you?'

'Because I can't handle it. I just can't handle it.'

Astrid felt out of her depth and wondered how her mother had stood her when she had been in similar shape after Tom's death. It gave her an idea.

'Jessie, why don't you come down to the ranch with me at Christmas? Mother would love it, and it would do you good.'

Jessica shook her head even before Astrid had finished her sentence.

'I can't.'

'Why not?'

'I have to spend Christmas with Ian.' She looked mournful at the thought.

'You don't "have" to.'

'All right, I want to.' Christmas without Ian? No way.

'Even with the window between you?' Jessica nodded. 'Why, for God's sake? As a penance to absolve you of the guilt you're heaping on your own head? Jessica, don't be ridiculous. Ian would probably love to know that you're doing something pleasant, like going down to the ranch.' Jessica didn't answer, and after a pause, Astrid said what she had really been thinking. 'Or would you rather torture him by letting him see how much you can suffer on Christmas?'

Jessica's eyes flew wide open again on that one.

'Jesus, you make it sound like I'm trying to punch him.'

'Maybe you are. I think you just can't decide right now who you hate more—him or yourself. And I think you've both had enough punishment, Ian at the hands of the State, and you at your own. Can't you start to be good to yourself now, Jessica? And maybe then you'll be able to be good to him.' There was more truth in Astrid's words than Jessie was ready for.

'You *can* take care of you, Jessie. And Ian will take care of you, even at a distance. Your friends will help.

But most of all, you have to see that you're much more capable than you know.'

'How do you know?'

'I know. You're scared and you have a right to be. But if you'd just calm down a little, and take stock of yourself, *kindly*, you'd be a lot less scared. But you're going to have to stop running to do that.'

'And stop taking pills?'

Astrid nodded, and Jessie remained silent. She wasn't ready to do that yet. She knew it without even trying.

But she did try. Astrid left without giving her any, and Jessica went to the bank with Ian's manuscript—with trembling hands and trembling knees, but without taking another pill. From there she went to the post office, and from there on to the shop. She lasted at Lady J for less than an hour, and then she came home to pace. She spent the night huddled in a chair in the living room, nauseated, trembling, wide-eyed, and wearing a sweater of Ian's. It still had the smell of his cologne on it, and she could feel him with her. She could sense him watching her as she sat in front of the fireplace. She kept seeing faces in the fire—Ian's, her mother's, Jake's, her father's. They came to her late in the night. And then she thought she heard strange sounds in the garage. She wanted to scream but couldn't. She wanted pills but didn't have any. She never went to bed that night, and at seven in the morning she called the doctor. He gave her everything she wanted.

CHAPTER XXIII

At Christmas, Astrid spent three weeks at the ranch with her mother. Jessica was swamped at the boutique. She was falling into a routine now with her visits to Ian. She drove up two weekday mornings and on Sundays. She was putting four hundred miles a week on his car, and the Volvo wasn't going to take the wear much longer.

She almost wondered if she and the car would die together, simply keel over at the side of the road and die. In the Volvo's case it would be from old age; in Jessie's, from strain and exhaustion. That and too many pills. But she functioned well with them now. Most people still couldn't tell. And Ian hadn't yet confronted her about them. She assumed that he simply didn't want to see what was happening. It was fine with her.

She couldn't send him a Christmas present this year. He was allowed to receive only money, so she sent him a cheque. And forgot to buy Christmas presents for the two girls in the shop. All she thought about was putting gas in the car, surviving the visits with Ian on the opposite side of the glass window, and getting her prescriptions refilled. Nothing else seemed to matter. And whatever energy she had left she spent figuring out the bills. She was making some headway with them, and she would wake up in the morning figuring out how to cover this, if she borrowed from that, if she didn't pay that until . . . she was hoping that Christmas profits would put her back in the black. But Lady J was having its own problems. Something was off, and she couldn't bring herself to care as much as she'd used to. Lady J was only a vehicle now, not a joy. It was a means of paying bills, and a place to go in the daytime. She could hide in the little office in the back of the shop and juggle those bills. She rarely came out to see customers now. After a few minutes, the now familiar rising wave of panic would seize her throat and she'd have to excuse herself . . . a yellow pill . . . a blue one . . . a quick sip of Scotch . . . something . . . anything to kill the panic. It was easier just to sit in the back and let the girls handle the customers. She was too busy anyway. With the bills. And with trying not to think. It took a lot of effort not to think, especially late at night or early in the morning. Suddenly, for the first time in years, she had perfect recall of her mother's voice, her father's laughter. She had forgotten them for so long, and now they were back. They said things . . . about each other . . . about her . . . about Ian . . . and they were right. They wanted her to think.

Jake even said something once. But she didn't want to think. It wasn't time yet. She didn't have to . . . didn't want to . . . couldn't . . . they couldn't make her . . . they . . .

Christmas did not fall on a visiting day, so she couldn't spend it with Ian after all. She spent it alone, with three red pills and two yellow ones. She didn't wake up until four the next afternoon, and then she could go back to the shop. She wanted to mark some things down for a sale. They had lost money at Christmas and she had to make it up. A good fat sale would really do it. She would send out little cards to their best customers. It would bring them in droves—she hoped.

She worked on the books straight through New Year's, and finally remembered to give Zina and Kat cheques instead of the Christmas presents she had overlooked. Jessie had gotten three presents, and a poem from Ian. Astrid had given her a simple and lovely gold bracelet, and Zina and Kat had given her small, thoughtful things. A homemade potpourri in a pretty French jar from Zina, and a small line drawing in a silver frame from Katsuko. And she had read the poem from Ian over and over on Christmas Eve. It was quickly dog-eared as it lay on her nightstand.

She had taken it with her to the office, and now carried it in her bag, to bring out and read during the day. She knew it by heart the day after she'd gotten it.

Katsuko and Zina wondered what she did in her office all the time now. She would emerge for coffee, or to look for something in the stockroom, but she rarely spoke to them, and never joked anymore. Gone were the days of cosy gossip and the easy camaraderie the three had shared. It was as though Jessie had vanished when Ian did. She would appear at the door of her small office at the end of the day, sometimes with a pencil stuck in her hair, a distracted look, a small packet of bills in one hand, and sometimes with eyes that were bloodshot and swollen. She was quicker to snap at people now, quicker to lose patience over trivial matters. And there was always that dead look in her eyes. The look that said she lay awake at night. The look that said she was more frightened than she wanted them to know. And the unmistakable glaze from the pills.

Only the days when she visited Ian were a little different. She was alive then. Something sparkled behind the wall she had built between herself and the rest of the world. Something different would happen in her eyes then, but she would share it with no one. Not even with Astrid, who was spending more and more time at the shop, and getting to know Zina and Katsuko. In a sense, Astrid had replaced Jessie. She had the kind of easy-going ways that Jessie had had before. She enjoyed the shop, the people, the clothes, the girls. She had time to talk and laugh. She had new ideas. She loved the place, and it showed. The girls had grown fond of her. She even came in on the days when Jessie was with Ian.

'You know, sometimes I think I sit here just so I know when she gets back. I worry about her making that drive.'

'So do we.' Katsuko shook her head.

'She told me the other day that she just does it on "automatic pilot".' Zina's words weren't much comfort. 'She says that sometimes she doesn't even remember where she is or what she's doing until she sees that sign.'

'Terrific.' Astrid took a sip of coffee and shook her head.

'Grim, isn't it? I wonder how long she'll hold up. She can't just keep plodding on like that. She has to go somewhere, see people, smile occasionally, sleep.' And sober up. Katsuko didn't say it, but they all thought it. 'She doesn't even look like the same woman anymore. I wonder how he's doing.'

'A little better than she is, actually. But I haven't seen him for a while. I think he's less afraid.'

'Is that what it is with her?' Zina looked stunned. 'I thought she was just exhausted.'

'That too. But it's fear.' Astrid sounded hesitant to discuss it.

'And pressure. Lady J has been giving her a rough time lately.'

'Oh? Looks busy enough.'

Katsuko shook her head, reluctant to say more. She had taken calls lately from people Jessie owed money to. For the first time the business was in trouble, and there was no money to fall back on. Jessie had bled every last cent of their spare money for Ian. So now Lady J was paying Ian's price too.

Jessie walked into the shop then, and the conversation came to a halt. She looked haggard and thin but there was something brighter in her eyes, that indefinable something that Ian poured back into her soul. Life.

'Well, ladies, how has life been treating you all today? Are you spending all your money here again, Astrid?' Jessie sat down and took a sip of someone's cold coffee. The small yellow pill she slipped into her mouth at the same time was barely noticeable. But Astrid noticed.

'Nope. Not spending a dime today. Just dropped by for some coffee and company. How's Ian?'

'Fine, I guess. Full of the book. How was business today?' She didn't seem to want to talk about Ian. She rarely spoke of anything important to her anymore. Even to Astrid.

'It was pretty quiet today.' Katsuko filled her in on business while Zina watched the slight trembling of Jessie's hand.

'Terrific. A dead business, and a dead car. The Volvo just breathed its last.' She sounded unconcerned, as though it really didn't matter because she had twelve other cars at home.

'On your way home?'

'Naturally. I hitched a ride with two kids in Berkeley. In a 1952 Studebaker truck. It was pink with green trim and they called it the Watermelon. It drove like one too.' She tried to make light of it while the three women watched her.

'So where's the car?'

'At a service station in Berkeley. The owner offered me seventy-five bucks for it, and agreed to drop the towing charge.'

'Did you sell it?' Even Katsuko looked stunned.

'Nope. I can't. It's Ian's. But I guess I will. That car

has had it.' And so have I. She didn't say it, but they all heard it in her voice. 'Easy come, easy go. I'll pick up something cheap for my trips up to Ian.' But with what? Where would the money come from for that?

'I'll drive you.' Astrid's voice was quiet and strangely calm. Jessica looked up at her and nodded. There was no point in protesting. She needed help and she knew it, and not just with the drive.

Astrid drove Jessica up to see Ian three times a week from then on. It saved Jessie the trouble of waiting to take the two yellow pills when she got there. This way she could take two in the morning, and another two after she saw him. Sometimes she even threw in a green-and-black one. Every little bit helped.

And Astrid could no longer talk to her. There was no use even trying. All she could do was stand by and be there when the roof finally came down. If it did, when it did, wherever and however. Jessica was heading for a stone wall as fast as she could. Nothing less was going to stop her. And Ian couldn't reach her either. Astrid saw that clearly now. He couldn't face what was happening to Jessie, because he couldn't help. If he couldn't help, he wouldn't see. And each time Jessie appeared, looking more tortured, more exhausted, more brittle, more rooted in pain and draped in bravado, it would only hurt Ian more. He would feel greater guilt, greater indebtedness, greater pain of his own. Their eyes rarely met now. They simply talked. He about the book, she about the boutique. Never about the past or the future or the realities of the present. They never spoke of feelings, but only threw out 'I love you' at regular intervals, like punctuation. It was grisly to watch, and Astrid hated the visits. She wanted to shake them both, to speak out, to stop what she was seeing. Instead they just went on dying quietly on opposite sides of the glass wall, in their own private hells, Ian with his guilt and Jessica with hers, and each of them with their blindness about themselves and about each other. While Astrid watched, mute and horrified.

If only they could have held each other, then they might

have been real. But they couldn't, and they weren't. Astrid knew that as she watched them. She could see it in Jessie's eyes now. There was constant pain, but there was also the look of a child who does not understand. Her husband was gone, but what was a husband, and where had he gone? The pills had allowed her to submerge herself in a sea of vagueness, and she rarely came to the surface anymore. She was very close to drowning, and Astrid wasn't entirely sure if Ian hadn't already drowned. Astrid could have done without the visits. But they were all locked into their roles now. Husband, wife, and friend.

January bled into February and then limped into March. The boutique had a two-week sale that brought scarcely any business. Everyone was busy or away or feeling poor. The last of their winter line hadn't done well at all; the economy was weak, and luxuries were going with it. Lady J was not a boutique to supply ordinary needs. It catered to a select clientele of the internationally chic. And her clients' husbands were telling them to lay off. The market was bad. They were no longer amused by a 'little' sweater and a 'nothing' skirt that cost them *in toto* close to two hundred dollars.

'Christ, what are we going to do with all this junk?' Jessie paced the floor, opening a fresh pack of cigarettes. She had seen Ian that morning. Once again through the window. Still through the window. Forever through the window. She had visions of finally getting to touch him again when they were both ninety-seven years old. She didn't even dream of his coming home anymore. Just of being able to touch him.

'We're going to have a real problem, Jessie, when the spring line comes in.' Katsuko looked around pensively.

'Yeah, the bastards. It was due in last week and it's late.' She swept into the stockroom to see what was there. She was annoyed much of the time now. The pain was showing itself differently. It wasn't enough now to hide: it was taking more to silence her inner voices.

'You know, I've been thinking.' Katsuko had followed her into the stockroom and was watching her.

'Was it painful?' Jessie looked up, smiled awkwardly, and then shrugged. 'Sorry. What were you thinking, Kat?' That sounded like the old Jessie. But it was rare now.

'About next fall's line. Are you going to New York one of these days?' On what? A broomstick?

'I don't know yet.'

'What'll we do for a fall line if you don't?' Katsuko was worried. There was almost no money for a new line, and there were still unpaid bills all over Jessie's desk.

'I don't know, Kat. I'll see.'

She walked into her office and slammed the door, her mouth in a small set line. Zina and Kat exchanged a glance. Zina answered the phone when it rang. It was for Jessie. From some record store. She buzzed Jessie's office and watched her pick up the phone. The light on the phone Zina had answered went out only a few moments later.

And in her office Jessie's hands were trembling as she toyed with a pencil on her desk. It had been another one of those calls. They were sure it was an oversight, undoubtedly she had forgotten to send them a cheque for the amount that was due . . . at least these had been polite. The doctor's office had called yesterday and he had threatened to sue. For fifty dollars? A doctor was going to sue her for fifty dollars? . . . And a dentist for ninety-eight . . . and there was still a liquor store bill for Ian's wine for a hundred and forty-five . . . and she owed the cleaner's twenty-six and the drugstore thirty-three and the phone bill was forty-one . . . and I. Magnin . . . and Ian's old tennis club . . . and new plants for the shop and the electricians' bill when the lights had gotten screwed up over Christmas . . . and a plumbing bill for the house . . . and on and on and on it went, and the Volvo was gone, and Lady J was going down the tubes, and Ian was in prison, and everything just kept getting worse instead of better. There was almost a satisfaction in it, like playing a game of 'how bad can things get?' And meanwhile Astrid was buying sweaters from her at cost, and 'amusing' gold bracelets at Shreve's, and having her hair done every three days at twenty-five bucks a crack. And now there was the fall line to think about. Three hundred bucks' worth of plane fare, and a hotel bill, not to mention the cost of what she bought. It would sink her further into debt, but she didn't have much choice. Without a fall line, she might as well close up Lady J on Labour Day. But it was getting to the point where she was afraid to walk into the bank to cash a cheque. She was always sure that she'd be stopped on the way out and ushered to the manager. How long would they put up with the overdrafts, the problems, the bullshit? And how long would she?

As she was trying to figure out how expensive the trip to New York would be, the intercom buzzed to let her know she had a call. She picked up the phone absent-mindedly, without finding out from Zina who it was.

'Hi, gorgeous, how's about some tennis?' The voice was jovial and already sounded sweaty.

'Who is this?' She suspected an obscene phone caller and was thinking of hanging up as the man on the other end took a large swallow of something, presumably beer.

'Barry. And how've ya been?'

'Barry who?' She recoiled from the phone as though from a snake. This was no one she knew.

'Barry York. You know. Yorktowne Bonding.'

'What?' She sat up as though someone had slapped her.

'I said . . .'

'I know what you said. And you're calling me to play tennis?'

'Yeah. You don't play?' He sounded surprised, like a small boy who's just been severely disappointed.

'Mr. York, do I understand you correctly? You want to play tennis with me?'

'Yeah. So?' He belched softly into the phone.

'Are you drunk?'

'Of course not. Are you?'

'No, I'm not. And I don't understand why you called me.' Her voice was straight out of the Arctic Circle, long-distance.

'Well, you're a good-looking woman, I was going to

play tennis, and I figured maybe you'd want to play. No big deal. You don't dig tennis, we can go have dinner somewhere.'

'Are you out of your mind? What in God's name makes you think I have any desire whatsoever to play tennis, play hopscotch, have dinner, or do anything else with you?'

'Well, listen to the red-hot mama. Sing it, sweetheart. What's to get so excited about?'

'I happen to be a married woman.' She was shouting and Zina and Kat could hear her tone from the other side of the door. They wondered who had called. Kat raised an eyebrow, and Zina went to help a client. Inside, the conversation continued.

'Yeah, so you happen to be a married woman. And your old man happens to be sitting on his ass in the joint. Which is too bad, but which leaves you out here with the rest of us human beings who like to play tennis, play hopscotch, eat dinner, and get laid.' Now she felt genuinely nauseated. She was remembering his thick black hair and the smell of him, and the ugly ring with the pink stone in it. It was incredible. That man, that hideous pig of a man, that absolute total stranger was calling her and talking about 'getting laid'. She sat there pale and trembling with tears starting to sting her eyelids again. It was funny. She knew that somewhere in all this it was funny. But it didn't make her want to laugh. It made her want to cry, want to go home, want to . . . this was what Ian had left her. The Barry Yorks of the world, and people calling about the cheques she had 'forgotten' to send and that she would continue to forget for at least another six or seven or nine or ten weeks or maybe even years. To the point that she was afraid to walk into the florist now for so much as a bunch of daisies, because she probably owed him money too. She owed everyone money. And now this animal on the phone wanted to get laid.

'I . . . Mr. . . . I'm . . .' She fought the tears out of her voice and swallowed hard.

'Whatsa matter, sweetheart, married women in Pacific Heights don't get horny, or you already got a boyfriend?'

Jessica sat looking at the phone, her chin trembling,

her hand shaking, tears streaming down her face, and her lower lip pouting as if she were a child whose best doll had just been smashed to bits. It had finally all hit her. This was what had happened to her life. She shook her head slowly, and gently hung up the phone.

CHAPTER XXIV

'See you later, ladies.' She picked up her bag, and started out of the shop. It was early April, and a beautiful warm Friday morning. Spring seemed to be everywhere.

'Where are you going, Jessie?' Zina and Kat looked up surprised.

'To see Ian. I have some other things to do tomorrow, so I thought I'd go up today.'

'Give him our love.' She smiled at the two girls and left the shop quietly. She had been very quiet again lately. Oddly so. The irritability seemed to be passing, ever since the call from Barry York. That had been three weeks ago. She had never told Ian. But the degradation showed in her face.

York, Houghton, people calling for bills, it didn't really matter. It was her own fault. She had done it all to herself. The great Jessica Clarke. The all-powerful, all-knowing, all-paying Mrs. Jessica Clarke, and her wonderful husband Mr. Jessica Clarke. She saw it all now. The sleepless nights were beginning to pay off. She couldn't run away from it anymore. She was beginning to think, to remember, to understand. She heard it now like old tapes played back in the dark of night. She had nothing else to do but remember . . . incidents, moments, trivia, voices. Not her mother's voice now. Not Jake's. But her own, and Ian's. 'Fables, darling? Do they sell?' As though that were the only thing that mattered. He had blurted out half a dozen reasons, explanations—as though he owed her any—and the fables had been beautiful. But it didn't matter, she had killed them before they'd been born. With one line. 'Do they sell?' Who cared if they sold? It was probably why he had bought her the Morgan with his publisher's advance. It was the loudest way he could think of to answer.

And other times.

'The opera, sweetheart? Why the opera? It's so expensive.'

'But we enjoy it. Don't you, Jessie? I thought you did.'

'Yeah, but—oh, what the hell. I'll take it out of the house money.'

'Oh, is that it?' There had been a long pause. 'I already bought the tickets, Jess. With "my" money.' But he had decided not to go in the end. He had decided to work at the last minute. He hadn't gone all that season.

Tiny moments, minute phrases that slashed into hearts with the blow of a machete, leaving scars on a life, on a marriage, on a man. Why? When she needed him so much? Or was that it? That she needed him, and she knew he didn't need her in the same way?

'But he needed me too.' Her voice sounded loud in the solitude of the car. She couldn't allow Astrid to chauffeur her three times a week, so she now rented a compact to go up and see him. Another expense she could ill afford. But as she drove along, she wondered. Why the barbs? The small digs over the years? To clip his wings so he never flew away? Because if he had flown away, she couldn't have survived. And the joke of it was that he had flown anyway. For one afternoon, and maybe a thousand afternoons before that, but for one afternoon that had cost them everything. He had needed a woman who didn't shoot off her mouth, didn't cut him down. Someone who didn't need him, didn't love him, didn't hurt him.

It was crazy, really. Whatever she had done, she had done out of the fear of losing him. And now look at where they were. She was so engrossed in her thoughts that she almost missed the turnoff, and she was still pensive as she waited for him to appear at the window.

Even after Ian arrived, she seemed to have her mind

more on the past than the present. And he seemed wrapped up in his own thoughts too. She looked up at him and tried to smile. She had a splitting headache and she was tired. She kept seeing her own reflection in the glass window that stood between them. It made her feel as if she were talking to herself.

'You're not very chatty today, Mr. Clarke. Anything wrong?'

'No, just thinking about the book, I guess. I'm getting to the point where it's hard to relate to much else. I'm all wrapped up in it.' He noticed an odd flash in her eyes as he finished speaking, and started to tell her about the book. She let him ramble on for a few minutes and then interrupted.

'You know something? You're amazing. I come all the way up here to find out how you are, and to talk to you about what's happening in my life. And you talk to me about the book.'

'What's wrong with that?' He looked puzzled as he watched her from the other side of the glass. 'You tell me about Lady J.'

'That's different, Ian. That's real, for Chrissake.' She was sounding shrill, and it irritated him.

'Well, the book is real to me.'

'So real that you can't even take an hour of your precious time to talk to me? Hell, you've been sitting there like a zombie for the last hour, telling me about the goddam book. And every time I start to tell you about me, you fade out.'

'That's not true, Jess.' He looked upset and reached for a cigarette. 'The book is just going really well and I wanted to tell you about it. I don't think I've ever hit such a good writing spell, that's all.' He knew he'd said the wrong thing as soon as the words were out of his mouth. The look on her face was incredible. 'Jessie, what the hell is wrong with you? You look like someone just shoved a hot poker up your ass.'

'Yeah, or slapped my face, maybe. Jesus Christ, you sit there and you tell me how brilliantly your writing is going, how you've never "hit such a good writing spell", like you're on some kind of fucking vacation in there. Do you know what's happening in *my* life?' She took a deep breath and he felt as if poison were pouring at him through the phone. She had lost control and she wasn't about to stop now.

'You really want to know what's happening to me while you're having such a "good writing spell"? Well, I'll tell you, darling. Lady J is going broke, people are calling me up day and night telling me to pay our bills and threatening to sue me. Your car fell apart, my nerves have had it, I have nightmares about Inspector Houghton every night, and the bailbondsman called me up for a date three weeks ago. He figured I needed to get laid. And maybe the sonofabitch is right, but not by him. I haven't so much as touched your hand in I don't know how many months, and I'm going goddam crazy. My whole stinking life is on the rocks, and you're having a good writing spell! And you know what else is terrific, *darling*—' she dripped venom in his ear, and others in the room watched as he sat there incredulous. She wasn't keeping any secrets from anyone.

'What's absolutely marvellous, Ian my love, is that I drove all the way up here today blaming myself for the nine-thousandth time for everything I've done wrong in our marriage, about the pressures I've put on you, about the rotten things I've said. Do you realise that by now I've replayed every lousy scene in our marriage, everything I've ever done wrong that made you even want to go to bed with a piece of shit like Margaret Burton? I've been blaming myself ever since it happened. I've even blamed myself for supporting your writing career, thinking that I stole your manhood. And while I'm crucifying myself, you know what you're doing? Having the best writing spell in your life. Well, you know what? You make me sick. While you sit up here in this glorified writers' colony they call a prison, my whole life is coming apart and you're not doing a goddam thing about it, sweetheart. Nothing. And I'll tell you something else, I'm sick to death of that puking window, of having to twist around like a pretzel just to see you and not a reflection of myself. I'm sick of getting sweaty hands and sweaty ears and a sweaty brain just talking to you on the goddam phone here . . . I'm sick to death of the whole goddam mess!' She was shouting so loudly that the whole room was watching now, but neither of them noticed. It had been building for months.

'And I suppose you think I enjoy it here?'

'Yes, I think you enjoy it here. A colony for gigolo writers.'

'That's right, sweetheart. That's what this is. And that's all I do here, is write. I never think about my wife, and how I got here, and why, and of that damn woman, or of the trial. I never have to shove my way out of getting laid by some guy with the hots for me.

'Listen, lady, if you think this is my idea of living, you can shove it right up your ass. But I'll tell you something else. If you think our marriage is my idea of living you can put that in the same place. I thought we had a marriage. I thought we had something. Well, guess what, Mrs. Clarke? We didn't have a fucking thing. Nothing. No kids, no honesty, and two half-assed careers. Two half-assed people, the way I see it now. And you've spent most of the last six years trying not to grow up and playing cripple after you lost your parents. Not only that, but making me feel guilty for God knows what, so I'd stick around and hold your hand. And I was dumb enough to swallow all that because I was stupid enough to love you and I wanted to have my writing career too. Well, the combo, such as it was, was a lousy one, Lady Bountiful. And you can have it. I happen to need a wife, not a banker or a neurotic child. Maybe that's why I'm happy right now, believe it or not, as stinking as this place happens to be. I'm writing and you're not supporting me. How's that for a shocker, baby? You're not picking up the tab and I don't owe you one thing except for the fact that you held my hand every inch of the way during the trial and you were marvellous. But I'm going to pay you back for the bills on that eventually. And if your idea now is to make me suffer as much as possible, to make me feel as guilty as possible over how fucked up you can get, how bad the bills are, and how fast my car can fall apart, then fuck you. I can't do anything about anything in here. All I can do is give a damn about you, be grateful you come to see me, and finish my fucking book. And if you don't dig seeing me, do me a big favour and don't come anymore. I can live without it.'

Jessica felt the all-too-familiar surge of panic clutch at her chest as she watched his face. But this time it was worse. They had never said things like this to each other. And she couldn't stop now. She could still feel the bile frothing up in her soul.

'Why don't you want me to come see you, darling? Did you find another sweetheart in here? Is that it, angel? Does the big he-man have another he-man to love?' Ian stood up and looked as if were going to hit her, right through the glass window, much to the fascination of the now silent crowd on both sides of the glass.

'Is that it, darling? Have you gone gay!'

'You make me sick.'

'Oh, that's right, I forgot. You don't like "infamous crimes against nature". Or do you?' She looked intolerably sweet as she raised her eyebrows, and her heart pounded violently in her chest. 'Maybe you did rape that woman after all.'

'Lady, if I weren't in here I'd put my fist right through your face.' He towered over her, with the veil of glass between them, the phones still in their hands, and slowly Jessica rose to face him. She knew that the moment had come and she couldn't believe it. She still couldn't stop.

'Put your fist through my face?' Their voices were soft now. He had spoken to her with the measured tone of a man who is almost finished, and she was speaking in the silvery whisper of a viper about to strike the last blow. 'Put your fist through my face?' She repeated the words again with a smile. 'But why now, darling? You never had the balls to before. Did you, love?'

He answered her in less than a whisper, and her heart almost stopped when she saw the look in his eyes.

'No, Jess, I didn't. But I don't have anything to lose now. I've already lost it. And that makes everything a lot easier.' He smiled a small, strange smile that chilled her, looked at her thoughtfully for a brief moment, put down the phone, and walked out. He never looked back once, and she felt her mouth open in astonishment. What had he just said? She wanted him to come back, so she could ask him again, so that . . . what did he mean, 'that makes everything a lot easier'? What did . . . the sonofabitch . . . he was walking out on her, he had no right to, he couldn't, he . . . and what had she done? What had she said? She sank into her seat as though she were in shock, and slowly the babble of voices around her returned to normal. Ian had long since disappeared through the far door, was no longer visible. She had been wrong. He did have the balls. And he had done just what she had always feared most. He had walked out on her.

The front bumper of the rented car brushed the hedges in front of the house as she pulled into the driveway. She put her head down on the wheel and felt the breath catch in her throat. There was a sob lodged there somewhere, but it was stuck, it wouldn't come out. The weight of her head set off the horn, and the sound felt like it was blowing off the top of her head. It felt good. She wouldn't take her head off the steering wheel. She just stayed there until two men passing by came rushing into the driveway on foot. They knocked on the window and she turned her face slowly to one side, looked at them, and laughed, a high-pitched hysterical giggle. The men looked at each other questioningly, opened the car door, and gently eased Jessie's body back on the seat. She looked from one to the other, laughed hysterically again, and then the laughter snagged on a sob. It wrenched itself from her throat and became a long, sad, lonely wail. She shook her head slowly and said one word over and over between sobs: 'Ian'.

'Lady, are you drunk?' The older man of the two looked hot and uncomfortable. He had thought she was hurt, or sick, with her head down on the steering wheel like that, and making such a racket with the horn. But here she was, drunk, or crazy, or stoned. He hadn't bargained on that. The younger man looked at her, shrugged his shoulders, and grinned.

Jessie shook her head slowly from side to side and said the only word she could focus on: 'Ian'.

'Sister, you stoned?' She didn't answer and the younger man shrugged again and grinned. 'Must be good stuff.'

'Ian.'

'Who's Ian? Your boyfriend?'

Another blind shake of the head.

The two men looked at each other again and closed the door of the car. At least the horn wasn't blaring anymore, and she wouldn't sober up for hours. They walked away, the younger one amused, the older one less so.

'You sure she's stoned? She looks kind of mixed up to me. I mean like mixed-up sick. Kinda crazy.'

'Stoned crazy.' The younger man laughed, slapped his belly, and put his arm around his friend just as Astrid drove by and noticed them walking out of the driveway, laughing and looking pleased with themselves. She stopped the car and frowned as a ripple of fear ran up her spine. They didn't look like police, but . . . they noticed her watching them and the younger man waved while the older one smiled. Astrid couldn't understand what was happening, but they slid into a red sedan and seemed to be taking their time. There was nothing furtive or rapid about their movements, and Astrid noticed Jessie in her rented car now. Everything was all right. Astrid honked. But Jessie didn't turn around. She honked again, and once more, and the two men broke into raucous laughter.

'Not you too, sister. The woman in that car is so loaded we had to peel her off the steering wheel just to get her off the horn.' They waved vaguely toward Jessie's driveway, started their car, and pulled out of the parking space as Astrid hopped out of her car and ran into the driveway.

Jessie was still sitting there, crying and sobbing and holding her single word in her mouth. 'Ian.' Astrid wasn't so sure she was stoned. A little maybe, but not as much as she looked. In shock maybe. Something had snapped.

'Jessica?' She slid an arm around her and spoke gently

as Jessie slumped slightly in the seat. 'Hi, Jessie, it's me, Astrid.' Jessica looked at her and nodded. The two men were gone now. Everyone was gone. Even Ian.

'Ian.' She said it more clearly now.

'What about Ian?'

'Ian.'

Astrid wiped her face gently with a handkerchief.

'Tell me about Ian.' Astrid's heart was pounding and she was trying to keep her mind clear and watch Jessica's eyes. She didn't think it was an overdose of pills. More like an overdose of trouble. Jessie had finally had enough.

'What about Ian, love? Tell me. Was he sick today?'

Jessica shook her head. At least he wasn't hurt. Astrid had thought of that first, with tales of prison horrors from the newspapers instantly coursing through her head. But Jessica had motioned no.

'Was something wrong?'

Jessica took a deep breath and nodded. She took another deep breath and leaned back against the seat a little.

'We . . . we had . . . a fight.' The words were barely intelligible, but Astrid nodded.

'What about?'

Jessica shrugged, looking confused again. 'Ian.'

'What did you fight about, Jessie?'

'I . . . I don't . . . know.'

'Do you remember?'

Jessica shrugged again and closed her eyes. 'About . . . everything . . . I think. We both . . . said . . . terrible things. Over.'

'Over what?' But she thought she knew.

'Over. All over.'

'What's all over, Jessie?' Her voice was so gentle, and the tears poured down Jessica's face with fresh force.

'Our marriage is . . . all . . . over . . .' She shook her head dumbly and closed her eyes again. 'Ian . . .'

'It's not all over, Jessie. Just take it easy, now. You two probably just had a lot to get off your chests. You've been through a lot of rough times together lately. A lot of shocks. It had to come out.' But Jessica shook her head.

'No, it's over. I . . . I was so awful to him. I've always . . . been awful to him. I . . .' But then she couldn't speak anymore.

'Why don't we go inside so you can lie down for a while.' Jessica shook her head and wouldn't move, and Astrid fought to get her attention. 'Jessie, listen to me for a minute. I want to take you somewhere.' The girl's eyes flew open in terror. 'Someplace very nice, you'll like it. We'll go together.'

'A hospital?'

Astrid smiled for the first time in five minutes. 'No, silly. My mother's ranch. I think it would do you a lot of good, and . . .'

Jessica shook her head stubbornly. 'No . . . I . . .'

'What? Why not?'

'Ian.'

'Nonsense. I'm going to take you down there, and you'll have a good rest. I think you've really had enough for a while. Don't you?'

Jessica nodded mutely with her eyes closed again.

'Jessie, did you take a lot of pills today?'

She started to shake her head and then stopped and shrugged.

'How many? Tell me.'

'I don't know . . . not sure.'

'Just give me a rough idea. Two? Four? Six? Ten?' She prayed it wouldn't be that many.

'Eight . . . I don't know . . . seven . . . nine . . .' Jesus.

'Are they in your bag?' Jessica nodded. And Astrid gently took her handbag from the seat. 'I'm going to take them, Jessie, okay?' Jessica smiled then for the first time and took a long deep breath. She almost looked like herself again.

'Do I . . . have a choice?' The two women laughed, one fuzzily and the other nervously, and Jessica let her friend help her inside. She wasn't so much stoned as wrung out. She let herself slide slowly into a chair in the living room and didn't even move as she listened to the sounds of Astrid bustling around the bedroom and bathroom. It was going to be so good to be away from it all, even from the sight of Ian behind the glass window. She knew then that she would never see him there again. She'd work the rest out later, but she already knew that. She heaved a deep sigh and went to sleep in the chair until Astrid woke her and led her out to the Jaguar.

Her bags had been packed, the house was locked up, and Jessie felt as though she were a small child again, well taken care of and greatly loved.

'What about the car?'

'The one you rented?' It still sat crookedly in the driveway. Jessica nodded. 'I'll have someone pick it up later. Don't worry about it.' Jessica didn't. It was part of the bliss of having money. Having 'someone pick it up later'. Anonymous faces and hands to do menial tasks. 'And I called the girls at the shop and told them you were going away with me. You can call them yourself tomorrow and give them instructions.'

'Who'll . . . who'll . . . you know, well, run it?' Everything was still jumbled in Jessica's head, and Astrid smiled and patted her cheek gently.

'I will. And I can hardly wait. What a treat, a vacation for you and a job for me.' Jessica smiled and looked more like herself again.

'And the fall line?'

Astrid raised an eyebrow in surprise as she started the car.

'You must be sobering up. I'll send Katsuko, with your permission. I'll take care of the finances of it, and you can pay me back later.' Jessica shook her head and looked back at her friend. The brief nap had sobered her.

'I can't pay you back later, Astrid. Lady J is fighting just to survive. That's one of the reasons nobody's gone to New York yet.'

'Would Lady J accept a loan from me?'

Jessica smiled. 'I don't know, but her mother might. Can I give it some thought?'

'Sure. After Katsuko gets back. I have news for you. You're not allowed to make any decisions for the next two weeks. None. Not even what you eat for breakfast. That's part of the ground rules of this little vacation of yours. I'll advance the money for the fall line, and we'll work it out later. I need a tax write-off anyway.'

'I . . . but . . .'

'Shut up.'

'You know something?' Jessie looked at her with a small smile and tired, swollen eyes. 'Maybe I will. I need the fall line or the shop will fold anyway. What the hell. Was Katsuko happy about going?'

'What do you think?' The two women smiled again and Astrid pulled up in front of her own house. 'Can you make it up my stairs?' Jessica nodded, and slowly followed Astrid into the house. 'I just need a few things; I'll only be gone overnight. I want to be at work tomorrow.' She glowed at the words. And fifteen minutes later they were back in the car and heading for the freeway. Jessie still felt as though a bomb had hit her life, now everything was moving too quickly.

The words with Ian came back to her as they drove along in silence. She had closed her eyes and Astrid thought she was sleeping. But she was wide awake. Too much so. And more awake than she had been in a long time. She needed another pill, and Astrid had flushed them all down the toilet, back at the house. All of them. The red ones, the blue ones, the yellow ones, the black-and-green ones. There was nothing left. Except her own head, pounding with Ian's words . . . and his face . . . and . . . why had they done that to each other? Why the venom, the hatred, the anger? It didn't make sense to her. Nothing did. Maybe they'd always hated each other. Maybe even the good times had been a lie. It was so hard to figure it all out now. And it was too late anyway. Looking for the answers was like searching for your grandmother's silver thimble in the rubble of your home after it had burned to the ground. Together, she and Ian had set fire to their marriage, and from opposite sides of a pane of glass had watched it burn, fanning the flames, refusing to leave until the last beam was gone.

CHAPTER XXV

Astrid touched her shoulder again and she woke up, frightened and confused about where she was. The pills had really worn off now and she felt jangled.

'Take it easy, Jessie. You're at the ranch. It's almost midnight, and everything's fine.' Jessica stretched and looked around. It was dark but stars shone overhead. There was a fresh smell in the air, and she could hear the whinny of horses somewhere in the distance. And just to their right was a large stone house with bright yellow shutters. The house was well lit and a door stood open.

Astrid had slipped inside for a moment with her mother before waking Jessie. Her mother was not shocked or even surprised. She had been through crises before, with Astrid, with friends, with family years before. Things happened to people, they were shaken for a while, but most of them survived. A few didn't, but most did. And the ranch was a good place to recover.

'Come on, sleepyhead, my mother has some hot chocolate and sandwiches waiting, and I don't know about you, but I'm starved.' Astrid stood next to the open car and Jessica ran a comb through her hair with a rueful grin.

'How's she fixed for pills?'

'She's not.' Astrid looked searchingly at Jessie. 'Is it bad?'

Jessica nodded and then shrugged.

'But I'll live. Hot chocolate, huh? How does that compare to Seconal?' Astrid made a face at her and got her suitcase out of the trunk.

'I went through the same thing after Tom. I arrived here and my mother threw everything out. All the pills. And I was a lot less good-natured about it than you were this afternoon.'

'I was just too stoned to react. You were lucky. And here, let me carry that.' She reached for the suitcase and

Astrid gave it up to her. 'Ian always says that an Amazon like me . . .' And then she stopped and let her voice trail off. Astrid watched the bowed head as she quietly walked toward the house. She was glad she had brought her, and only sorry she hadn't done it before. She wondered just how serious the fight with Ian had been. Something told her this was for real, but it was impossible to tell.

Their shoes crunched on the gravel walk that led to the house, and the smell of fresh grass and flowers was everywhere. Jessie noticed that the place looked cheerful even in the dark. There was an array of multicoloured flowers all around the stone building and in great profusion near the door. She smiled as she walked past them and up the single step.

'Watch your head!' Astrid called out as she almost hit it against the doorway, and the two women arrived in the front hall side by side. There was a small upright piano there, painted bright red, a long mirror, a number of bronze spittoons, and a wall of exotic and colourful hats. Just beyond were pine floors and hooked rugs, comfortable couches and a rocking chair by the fire. There were warm-looking oil paintings and a long wall of books. It was an odd combination of good modern, delightful Victorian, simply enjoyable, and pleasantly old, but it worked. Plants and an old Victrola painted red like the piano, some first-edition books, and a very handsome modern couch covered in a pale oatmeal fabric. Old lace granny curtains hung at the windows, and a large tiled stove stood in one corner. The room looked happy and warm, with a surprising element of chic.

'Good evening.'

Jessica turned at the sound of a voice and saw a tiny woman standing in the kitchen doorway. She had the same blonde-grey hair as her daughter and cornflower blue eyes that sparkled and laughed. The simple words 'good evening' sounded as though they amused her. She walked slowly toward Jessica and held out a hand. 'It is very nice indeed to have you here, my dear. I take it Astrid has warned you that I'm a querulous old woman and the ranch is dull as dishwater. But I'm delighted you've come down.' The light in her eyes danced like flame.

'I warned her of no such thing, Mother. I raved about the place, so you'd better be on your best behaviour.'

'Good God, how awful. Now I shall have to put away all my pornographic books and cancel the dancing boys, shall I? How distressing.' She clasped her hands as though greatly disturbed and then burst forth with a youthful giggle. She gestured comfortably toward the couch and the two women followed her to seats near the fire. The promised hot chocolate was waiting in a Limoges china service patterned with delicate flowers.

'That's pretty, Mother. Is it new?' Astrid poured herself a cup of hot chocolate and looked at the china.

'No, dear. It's very old—1880, I believe.' The two women exchanged a teasing glance. One could easily see that they were not only mother and daughter, but also friends. Jessica felt a pang of envy as she watched, but also the glow of reflected warmth.

'I meant, is it new to you?' Astrid took a sip of the warm chocolate.

'Oh, that's what you meant! Yes, as a matter of fact it is.'

'Wretch, and you knew I'd notice and you used it tonight just to show it off.' But she looked pleased at the implied compliment, and her mother laughed.

'You're absolutely right! Pretty, isn't it?'

'Very.' The two women's eyes danced happily, and Jessica smiled, taking in the scene. She was surprised at the youthful appearance of Astrid's mother. And at the elegance that had stayed with her despite the passing of years and life on the ranch. She was wearing well-cut grey gabardine slacks and a very handsome silk blouse that Jessie knew must have come from Paris. It was in very flattering blues that picked up the colour of her eyes. She wore it with pearls and several large and elegant gold rings, one with a rather large diamond set in it. She looked more New York or Connecticut than ranch. Jessie almost laughed aloud remembering the image Astrid had portrayed of her months before, in cowboy gear. That was hardly the picture Jessie was seeing.

'You came at the right time, Jessica. The countryside is so lush and lovely at this time of year. Soft and green and almost furry-looking. I bought the ranch at this time of year, and that's probably why I succumbed. Land is so seductive in the spring.'

Jessica laughed. 'I didn't exactly plan it this way, Mrs. Williams. But my husband went to prison and I turned into a junkie on sleeping pills and tranquillisers and you see, I tried very hard to have a nervous breakdown and we had this awful fight this morning and . . .' she laughed again and shook her head. 'I didn't plan it at all. And you're very kind to have me down here on such short notice.'

'No problem at all.' She smiled, but her eyes took in everything. She noticed that Jessica was eating nothing and only sipping at her hot chocolate. She was smoking her second cigarette in the moments since the two women had arrived. She suspected that Jessica had acquired the same problem Astrid had had after Tom's death. Pills. 'Just make yourself at home, my dear, and stay as long as you like.'

'I may stay forever.'

'Of course not. You'll be bored in a week.' The old woman's eyes twinkled again and Astrid laughed.

'You're not bored here, Mother.'

'Oh yes, I am, but then I go to Paris or New York or Los Angeles, or come up to visit you in that dreadful mausoleum of yours . . .'

'Mother!'

'It is and you know it. A very handsome mausoleum, but nonetheless . . . you know what I think. I told you last year that I thought you ought to sell it and get a new house. Something smaller and younger and more cheerful. I'm not even old enough to live there. I told Tom that when he was alive, and I can't imagine why I shouldn't tell you now.'

'Jessica has the sort of place you would adore.'

'Oh? A grass hut in Tahiti, no doubt.' All three women

laughed and Jessica made an attempt at eating a sandwich. Her stomach was doing somersaults, but she hoped that if she ate something her hands might cease trembling. She suspected that she was in for a rough couple of days, but at least the company would be good. She was already in love with Astrid's outspoken mother.

'She lives in that marvellous blue-and-white house in the next block from us. The one with all the flowers out front.'

'I do remember it more or less. Pretty, but a bit small, isn't it?'

'Very,' Jessica said between bites. The sandwich was cream cheese and ham with fresh watercress and paper-thin slices of tomato.

'I can't bear the city anymore myself. Except for a visit. But after a while, I'm glad to come home. The symphonies bore me, the people overdress, the restaurants are mediocre, the traffic is appalling. Here, I ride in the morning, walk in the woods, and life feels like an adventure every day. I'm too old for the city. Do you ride?' Her manner was so brisk that it was hard to believe she was past fifty-five; Jessica knew she was in fact seventy-two. She smiled at the question.

'I haven't ridden in years, but I'd like to.'

'Then you may. Do whatever you want, whenever you want. I make breakfast at seven, but you don't have to get up. Lunch is a free-lance proposition, and dinner's at eight. I don't like country hours. It's embarrassing to eat dinner at five or six. And I don't get hungry till later anyway. And by the way, my daughter introduced me as Mrs. Williams, but my name is Bethanie. I prefer it.' She was peppery as all hell, but the blue eyes were gentle and the mouth always looked close to laughter.

'That's a beautiful name.'

'It'll do. And now, ladies, I bid you good night. I want to ride early in the morning.' She smiled warmly at her guest, kissed her daughter on the top of her head, and walked briskly up the stairs to her bedroom, having assured Jessica that Astrid would give her a choice of rooms. There were three to choose from, and they were all quite ready for guests. People came to visit Bethanie often, Astrid explained. It was a rare week when no one stayed at the ranch. Friends from Europe included her in their elaborate itineraries, other friends flew out to the Coast from New York and rented cars to drive down to see her, and she had a few friends in Los Angeles. And of course Astrid.

'Astrid, this is simply fabulous.' Jessica was still a bit overwhelmed by it all. The house, the mother, the hospitality, the openness of it all, and the peppery warmth of her hostess. 'And your mother is remarkable.' Astrid smiled, pleased.

'I think Tom married me just so he wouldn't lose track of her. He adored her, and she him.' Astrid smiled again, pleased at the look on Jessica's face.

'I can see why he loved her. Ian would fall head over heels for her.' Her tone changed as she said it, and she seemed to drift off. It was a moment before her attention returned to Astrid.

'I think it'll do you good to be down here, Jessie.'

Jessica nodded slowly. 'It sounds corny, but I feel better already. A little shaky—' she held up a hand to show the trembling fingers, and grinned sheepishly—'but better nonetheless. It's such a relief not to have to go through another night alone in that house. You know, it's crazy. I'm a grown woman. I don't know why it gets to me so badly, but it's just awful, Astrid. I almost hope the damn place burns to the ground while I'm gone.'

'Don't say that.'

'I mean it. I've come to hate that house. As happy as I once was there, I think I detest it twice as much now. And the studio—it's like a reminder of all my worst failings.'

'Do you honestly feel that you've failed, Jessica?'

Jessica nodded slowly but firmly.

'Single-handedly?'

'Almost.'

'I hope you come to realise how absurd that is.'

'You know what hurts the worst? The fact that I thought we had a fantastic marriage. The best. And now . . . it all looks so different. He swallowed his resentments, I did things my way. He cheated on me and didn't tell me; I guessed but didn't want to *know*. It's all so jumbled. I'm going to need time to sort it out.'

'You can stay down here as long as you like. Mother will never get tired of you.'

'Maybe not, but I wouldn't want to abuse her hospitality. I think if I stay a week, I'll be not only lucky, but eternally grateful.' Astrid only smiled over her hot chocolate. People had a way of saying they'd stay for a few days or a week and of still being there five weeks later. Bethanie didn't mind, as long as they didn't get in her hair. She had her own schedule, her friends, her gardening, her books, her projects. She liked to go her own way and let other people go theirs, which was part of her charm and her great success as a hostess. She was exceedingly independent and she had a healthy respect for people's solitude, including her own.

Astrid showed Jessica the choice of available rooms, and Jessie settled on a small, cosy, pink room with an old-fashioned quilt on the bed and copper pots hanging over the fireplace. It had a high slanted ceiling, high enough so she wouldn't bump her head when she got out of bed. There was a lovely bay window with a window seat, and a rocking chair by the fireplace. Jessica heaved a deep sigh and sat on the bed.

'You know, Astrid, I may never go home.' It was said between a smile and a yawn.

'Good night, puss. Get some sleep. I'll see you at breakfast.' Jessica nodded and yawned again. She waved as Astrid closed the door, and then called a last sleepy 'Thanks.'

She would have to write to Ian in the morning, to tell him where she was. To tell him something. But she'd worry about that tomorrow. For the moment she was a world and a half away from all her problems. The boutique, Ian, bills, that unbearable window in Vacaville. None of it was real anymore. She was home now. That was how it felt, and she smiled at the thought as she lit the kindling and put a log on the fire before slipping into her nightgown. Ten minutes later she was asleep. For the first time in four months, without any pills.

There was a knock on Jessie's door moments after she had closed her eyes. But when she opened them, sunlight was streaming in between the white organdie curtains, and a fat calico cat yawned sleepily in a patch of sunlight on her bed. The clock said ten-fifteen.

'Jessie? Are you up?' Astrid poked her head in the door. She was carrying an enormous white wicker tray laden with goodies.

'Oh no! Breakfast in bed! Astrid, you'll spoil me forever!' The two women laughed and Jessie sat up in bed, her blonde hair falling over her shoulders in a tumult of loose curls. She looked like a young girl and surprisingly rested now.

'You're looking awfully healthy this morning, madam.'

'And hungry as hell. I slept like a log. Wow!' She was faced with waffles, bacon, two fried eggs and a steaming mug of hot coffee, all of it served on delicate flowered china. There was a vase in the corner of the tray with one yellow rose in it. 'I feel like it's my birthday or something.'

'So do I! I can hardly wait to get to the shop!' Astrid giggled and slid into the rocking chair while Jessie went to town on the breakfast. 'I should have let you sleep a while longer, but I wanted to get back to the city. And Mother decided you needed breakfast in bed on your first day.'

'I'm embarrassed. But not too embarrassed to eat all this.' She chuckled and dived into the waffles. 'I'm starving.'

'You should be. You didn't have any dinner.'

'What's your mother up to this morning?'

'God knows. She went riding at eight, came back to change, and just drove off a few minutes ago. She goes her own way, and doesn't invite questions.'

Jessica smiled and sat back in the bed with a mouthful of waffle. 'You know, I should feel guilty as hell, sitting here like this with Ian where he is, but for the first time in five months, I don't. I just feel good. Fabulous, as a matter of fact.' And relieved. It was such a relief not to *have* to do anything. Not to have to be at the shop, or on the way to see Ian, or opening bills, or taking phone calls. She was in another world now. She was free. 'I feel so super, Astrid.' She grinned, stretched, and yawned, with a splendid breakfast under her belt, and the sun streaming across her bed.

'Then just enjoy it. You needed something like this. I wanted to bring you down here over Christmas. Remember?' Jessica nodded regretfully, remembering what she had done instead. She had blotted out Christmas with a handful of pills.

'If I'd only known.'

She stroked the calico cat and it licked her finger as Astrid sat in the rocking chair, quietly rocking and watching her friend. With one good night of sleep she already looked better. But there was still a lot to resolve. She didn't envy Jessica the task ahead of her.

'Why don't you stay down for a couple of days, Astrid?'

Astrid let out a whoop and shook her head. 'And miss all the fun of running the boutique? You're crazy. You couldn't keep me down here if you tied me to a gatepost. This'll be the most fun I've had in years!'

'Astrid, you're nutty, but I love you. If it weren't for you, I couldn't sit around down here like a lady of leisure. So go have a good old time with Lady J. She's all yours!' And then Jessie looked wistful. 'I almost wish I really never had to go back.'

'Do you want to sell me Lady J?' Something in Astrid's voice made Jessica look up.

'Are you serious?'

'Very. Maybe even a partnership, if you don't want to sell out completely. But I've given it a lot of thought. I just never knew how to broach it to you.'

'Like you just did I guess. But I've never thought of it. It might be an idea. Let me mull it over. And see how you enjoy it while I'm gone. You may hate the place by next weekend.'

But Astrid could tell from the sound of her voice that Jessica had no intention of giving up Lady J. There was still that pride of ownership in her voice. Lady J was hers, no matter how out of sorts with it she was at the moment.

'Were you really serious about sending Katsuko to New York, by the way?' Jessie was still stunned by all that had happened in a mere twenty-four hours.

'I was. I told her to plan on leaving tomorrow. That way you can give her any instructions you want. We can square the finances of it later. Much later. So don't go adding that to your pile of worries. What about the fall line? Any thoughts, orders, requests, caveats, whatever?'

'None. I trust her implicitly. She has a better buying sense than I do, and she's been in retailing for long enough to know what she's doing. After the season we just had, I'm not sure I'm fit to buy for the place anymore.'

'Everyone can have an off season.'

'Yeah. All the way around.' Jessie smiled and Astrid looked back at her friend with warmth in her eyes.

'Well, I'd best be getting my fanny in gear. I have a long drive ahead. Any messages for the home front?'

'Yeah. One.' Jessica grinned, then threw back her head and laughed. 'Good-bye.'

'Jerk. Have a good time down here. This place put me back together once.'

'And you look damn good to me.' Jessie climbed lazily out of bed, stretched again, and gave Astrid a last hug. 'Have a safe trip and give the girls my love.'

She watched her leave and waved from the bedroom window. Jessie was alone in the house now except for the cat, which was parading slowly across the window-seat. There were country sounds from outside, and a delicious silence all around her in the airy, sun-filled house. She wandered barefoot down the long upstairs hall, peeking into rooms, opening books, pirouetting here and there, looking at paintings, chasing the cat, and then went downstairs to do more of the same. She was free! Free! For the first time in seven years, ten years, fifty years, forever, she was free. Of burdens, responsibilities, and terrors. The day before she had hit rock bottom. The last support of her decaying foundation had come tumbling, roaring down . . . and she hadn't fallen with it. Astrid had held her up, and taken her away.

But the best part of all was that she hadn't cracked. She would remember all her life that moment when two strangers had pulled her back from the steering wheel where she was pressing on the horn. She had decided to let herself go crazy then, just slide into a pool of oblivion, never to return to the land of the ugly and dying and evil, the land of the 'living'. But she hadn't gone crazy at all. She had hurt. More than she had ever hurt in her life. But she hadn't gone crazy. And here she was, wandering around a delightful house in the country, barefoot, in her nightgown, with a huge breakfast in her stomach and a smile on her face.

And the amazing thing was that she didn't need Ian. Without him, the roof hadn't fallen in. It was a new idea to Jessie, and she didn't quite know what to do with it yet. It changed everything.

CHAPTER XXVI

It was late in the afternoon of her first day on the ranch that Jessica decided to sit down and write to Ian. She wanted to let him know where she was. She still felt she had to check in. But it was hard to explain to him why she was there. Having kept up the front for so long, it was difficult to tell him just what kind of shape she'd been in behind the façade. She had blown it the day before, but now she had to sit down and tell him quietly. It turned every 'fine' she had ever told him into a lie. And most of them had been lies. She hadn't been willing to admit to herself how far from fine she was, and now she had to do both—admit it to herself and to him. She had no more accusations to level at him, but no explanations she wanted to give either.

Words didn't come easily. What could you say? I love you, darling, but I also hate you . . . I've always been afraid to lose you, but now I'm not sure anymore . . . get lost . . . she grinned at the thought, but then tried to get serious. Where to begin? And there were questions. So many questions. Suddenly she wondered how many other women there had been. And why. Because she was inadequate, or because he was hungry, or because he needed to prove something, or . . . why? Her parents had never asked each other questions, but they had been wrong, or at least, wrong for her. She had followed their example, but now she wanted answers, or thought she did. But she recognised the possibility that the answers she sought were her own. Did she love Ian? Or only need him? Did she need him, or only someone? And how do you ask seven years of questions in half a page of letter . . . do you respect me? Why? How can you? She wasn't sure if she loved or respected him or herself at this point.

She wanted to take the easy way out and simply tell him about Mrs. Williams and the ranch, but that seemed dishonest. And so it took her two hours to write the letter. It was one page long. She told him that yesterday had shown her she needed a rest. Astrid had come up with a marvellous suggestion, her mother's ranch.

> It is precisely the kind of place where I can finally relax, come to my senses, breathe again, and be myself. Myself being, these days, an odd combination of who I used to be, who I have been catapulted into being during the past six months, and who I am becoming. It all frightens me more than a little. But even that is changing somewhat, Ian. I am tired of always being so frightened. It must have been a great burden on you all this time, my constant fears. But I am growing now. Perhaps 'up'; I don't know yet. Keep at the book, you're right, and I'm sorry for yesterday. I will regret all our lives that we have borne all of this with such dignity and self-control. Perhaps if we had screamed, shrieked, kicked, yelled, and torn at our hair on the courtroom floor instead—perhaps we'd both be in bet-

ter shape now. It has to come out sooner or later. I'm working on that now. Right? Well, darling. I love you. J.

She hesitated lengthily with the letter in her hands, and then folded it carefully and put it into an envelope. There was much she had not said. She just didn't want to say it yet. And she carefully inscribed his name on the envelope. But not her own. She wondered if he would think the lack of a return address was an oversight. It wasn't.

Jessica joined Astrid's mother in the living room for an after-dinner drink.

'You have no idea how happy you've made Astrid, my dear. She needs something to do. Lately all she's done is spend money. That's not healthy. The constant acquisition of meaningless possessions, just to pass the time. She doesn't enjoy it, she just does it to fill a void. But your boutique will fill that void in a far better way.'

'I met her through the boutique, as a matter of fact. She just walked in one day, and we liked each other. And she's been so good to me. I hope she really enjoys the shop this week. I'm relieved to be away from it.'

'Astrid mentioned that you'd had a hard time of late.'

Jessie nodded, subdued.

'You'll grow from it in the end. But how disagreeable life can be while one grows!' She laughed over her Campari, and Jessie smiled. 'I've always had a passionate dislike for character-building situations. But in the end, they turn out to be worthwhile, I suppose.'

'I'm not sure I'd call my situation worthwhile. I suspect it's going to be the end of my marriage.' There was a look of overwhelming sorrow in Jessica's eyes, but she was almost certain that she knew her mind now. She simply hadn't wanted to admit it to herself before this.

'Is that what you want now, child? Freedom from your marriage?' She was sitting quietly by the fire, watching Jessica's face intently.

'No, not my freedom, really. I've never had problems about my "freedom". I love being married. But I think we've reached a time when we're simply destroying each other, and it will only get worse. In looking back now, I wonder if we didn't always destroy each other. But it's different now. I see it. And there's no excuse for letting it continue once you see.'

'I suppose you'll have to take the matter in hand, then. How does your husband feel about it?' Jessie paused for a moment.

'I don't know. He's . . . he's in prison right now.' She couldn't think of anyone else she would have told, and she didn't know that Astrid had already told her mother, only that Bethanie appeared to take the news in her stride. 'And we've had to visit each other under such strained conditions that it's been difficult to talk. It's even hard to think. You feel obliged to be so staunch and brave and noble, that you don't dare admit even to yourself, let alone each other, that you've just plain had it.'

'Have you "had it"?' She smiled gently, but Jessie did not return the smile as she nodded. 'It must be very hard for you, Jessica. Considering the guilt attached to leaving someone who's in a difficult situation.'

'I think that's why I haven't allowed myself to think. Not past a certain point. Because I didn't dare "betray" him, even in my thoughts. And because I wanted to think of myself as noble and long-suffering. And because I was . . . scared to. I was afraid that if I let go, I'd never find my way back again.'

'The funny thing is that one always does. We are all so much tougher than we think.'

'I guess I'm beginning to understand now. It's taken me a terribly long time. But yesterday everything fell apart. Ian and I had an all-out fight where we both went for the jugular with everything we said, and I just let myself go afterward. I almost tempted the fates to break me. And . . .' She raised her hands palm up with a philosophical shrug. 'Here I am. Still in one piece.'

'That surprises you?' The old woman was amused.

'Very much.'

'You've never been through crises before?'

'Yes. My parents died. And my brother was killed in

Vietnam. But . . . I had Ian. Ian buffered everything, Ian played ten thousand roles and wore a million different hats for me.'

'That's a lot to ask of anyone.'

'Not a lot. It's too much. Which is probably why he's in prison.'

'I see. You blame yourself?'

'In a way.'

'Jessica, why can't you let Ian have the right to his own mistakes? Whatever got him into prison, no matter how closely it relates to you—doesn't he have a right to own that mistake, whatever it was?'

'It was rape.'

'I see. And you committed the rape for him.' Jessica giggled nervously.

'No, of course not. I . . .'

'You what?'

'Well, I made him unhappy. Put a lot of pressure on him, paid the bills, robbed him of his manhood . . .'

'You did all that for him?' The older woman smiled and Jessica smiled too. 'Don't you suppose he could have said no?' Jessica thought about it and then nodded.

'Maybe he couldn't say no, though. Maybe he was afraid to.'

'Ah, but then it's not your responsibility, is it? Why must you wear so much guilt? Do you like it?' The younger woman shook her head and looked away.

'No. And the absurd thing is that he didn't commit the rape. I know that. But the key to the whole thing is why he was in a position even to be accused of rape. And I can't absolve myself.'

'Can you absolve the woman, whoever she was?'

'Of course, I . . .' And then Jessica looked up, stunned. She had forgiven Margaret Burton. Somewhere along the line, she had forgiven her. The war with Margaret Burton was over. It was one less weight on her heart. 'I'd never thought of that before, not lately.'

'I see. I'm intrigued to know how you robbed him of his manhood, by the way.'

'I supported him.'

'He didn't work?' There was no judgment in Bethanie's voice, only a question.

'He worked very hard. He's a writer.'

'Published?'

'Several times. A novel, a book of fables, several articles, poems.'

'Is he any good?'

'Very—he's just not very successful financially. Yet. But he will be.' The pride in her voice surprised her, but not Bethanie.

'Then how dreadful of you to encourage him. What a shocking thing to do.' Bethanie smiled as she sipped her Campari.

'No, I . . . it's just that I think he hates me for having "kept" him.'

'He probably does. But he probably loves you for it too. There are two sides to every medal, you know, Jessica. I'm sure he knows that too. But I'm still not quite clear about why you want to get out of the marriage.'

'I didn't say that. I just said that I thought the marriage would end.'

'All by itself? With no one to help it along? My dear, how extraordinary!' The two women laughed and then Bethanie waited. She was adept with her questions. Astrid had know she would be, and had purposely not warned Jessica. Bethanie made one think.

Jessica looked up after a long pause and found the core of Bethanie's eyes. She looked right into them. 'I think the marriage already has ended. All by itself. No one killed it. We just let it die. Neither of us was brave enough to kill it, or save it. We just used it for our own purposes, and then let it expire. Like a library card in a town you no longer live in.'

'Was it a good library?'

'Excellent. At the time.'

'Then don't throw the card away. You might want to go back, and you can have the card renewed.'

'I don't think I'd want to.'

'He makes you unhappy, then?'

'Worse. I'd destroy him.'

'Oh, for God's sake, child. How incredibly boring of you—you're being noble. Do stop thinking of him, and think of yourself. I'm sure that's all he's doing. At least I hope so.'

'But what if I'm not good for him and never was good for him, and . . . what if I hate the life I lead now, waiting for him?' Now they were getting to the root of it. 'What if I'm afraid that I only used him, and I'm not even sure if I love him anymore? Maybe I just need someone, and not specifically Ian.'

'Then you have some things to think out. Have you seen other men since he's been gone?'

'No, of course not.'

'Why not?' Jessica looked shocked and Bethanie laughed. 'Don't look at me like that, my dear. I may be ancient, but I'm not dead yet. I tell Astrid the same thing. I don't know what's wrong with your generation. You're all supposed to be so liberated, but you're all terribly prim and proper. It could just be that you need to be loved. You don't have to sell yourself on a street corner, but you might find a pleasant friend.'

'I don't think I could do that, and stay with Ian.'

'Then maybe you ought to leave him for a while, and see what you want. Perhaps he *is* a part of your past. The main thing is not to waste your present. I never have, and that's why I'm a happy old woman.'

'And not an "old" woman.'

Bethanie made a face at the compliment. 'Flattery won't do at all! I seem extremely old to me, each time I look in the mirror, but at least I've enjoyed myself on the way. And I'm not saying that I've been a libertine. I haven't. I'm merely saying that I didn't lock myself in a closet and then find myself hating someone for what I chose to do to myself. That's what you're doing right now. You're punishing your husband for something he can't help, and it sounds to me as though he's been punished enough, and unjustly at that. What you have to think about, and with great seriousness, is whether or not you can accept what happened. If you can, then perhaps it'll all work itself out. But if you're going to try to get restitution from him for the rest of your lives, then you might as well give up now. You can only make someone feel guilty for so long. A man won't take much of that, and the backlash from him will be rather nasty.'

'It already has been.' Jessica was thinking back to the argument in Vacaville as she looked dreamily into the fire.

'No man can take that for very long. Nor any woman. Who wants to feel guilty eternally? You make mistakes, you say you're sorry, you pay a price, and that's about it. You can't ask him to pay and pay and pay again. He'll end up hating you for it, Jessica. And maybe you're not just making him suffer for the present. Maybe you're just using this as an opportunity to collect an old debt. I may be wrong, but we all do that at times.'

Jessica nodded soberly. It was exactly what she had been doing. Making him pay for the past, for his weaknesses and her own. For her insecurities and uncertainty. She was thinking it out when Bethanie's voice gently prodded into her thoughts again.

'Maybe you should tell me to mind my own business.'

Jessica smiled and sat back in her chair again. 'No, I think you're probably right. I haven't been looking at any of this with much perspective. And you make a great deal of sense. More than I want to admit, but still . . .'

'You're a good sport to listen, child.' The two women smiled at each other again and the older woman rose to her feet and stretched delicately, her diamond rings sparkling in the firelight. She was wearing black slacks and a blue cashmere sweater the colour of her eyes, and as Jessica watched her, she found herself thinking again what a beauty the woman must have been in her youth. She was still remarkably pretty in a womanly way, with a gentle veil of femininity softening whatever she did or said. She was actually even lovelier than her daughter. Softer, warmer, prettier—or perhaps it was just that she was more alive.

'You know, if you'll forgive me, Jessica, I think I'll go up to bed. I want to ride early in the morning and I won't ask you to join me. I rise at such uncivilized hours.' Laughter danced in her eyes as she bent to kiss Jessica's forehead, and Jessie quickly lifted her arms to hug her.

'Mrs. Williams, I love you. And you're the first person who's made sense to me in a very long time.'

'In that case, my dear, do me the honour of not calling me "Mrs. Williams". I abhor it. Couldn't you possibly settle for "Bethanie", or "Aunt Beth" if you prefer? My friends' children still call me that, and some of Astrid's friends.'

'Aunt Beth. It sounds lovely.' And suddenly Jessica felt as though she had a new mother. Family. It had been so long since she'd had any, other than Ian. Aunt Beth. She smiled and felt a warm glow in her soul.

'Good night, dear. Sleep well. I'll see you in the morning.'

They exchanged another hug, and Jessica went upstairs half an hour later, still thinking about some of the things Bethanie had said. About punishing Ian ... it made her wonder. Just how angry at Ian was she? And why? Because he had cheated on her? Or because he was in prison now and no longer around to protect her? Because he had gotten "caught" sleeping with Margaret Burton? Would it have mattered as much if she hadn't been forced to confront it? Or was it other things? The books that didn't sell, the money that only she made, his passion for his writing? She just wasn't sure.

Breakfast was waiting for Jessica when she came down the next morning. A happy little note signed 'Aunt Beth' told her there were brioches being kept warm in the oven, crisp slices of bacon, and a beautiful bowl of fresh strawberries. The note suggested that they drive over the hills in the Jeep that afternoon.

They did, and they had a marvellous time. Aunt Beth told her stories about the 'ghastly' people who had lived at the ranch before and had left the main house in 'barbarous condition'.

'I daresay the man was a first cousin of Attila the Hun, and their children were simply frightful!'

Jessica hadn't laughed as easily or as simply in years, and as they tooled over the hills in the Jeep, it dawned on her how well she was doing without pills. No tranquillisers, no sleeping pills, nothing. She was surviving with Aunt Beth's company, a lot of sunshine, and much laughter. They cooked dinner together that night, burned the hollandaise for the asparagus, underdid the roast, and laughed together at each new mistake. It was more like having a roommate her own age than being the guest of a friend's mother.

'You know, my first husband always said I'd poison him one day if he wasn't careful. I was a terrible cook then—not that I'm much better now. I'm not at all sure these asparagus are cooked.' She crunched carefully on one of the stems, but seemed satisfied with what she found.

'Were you married twice?'

'No. Three times. My first husband died when I was in my early twenties, which was a great shame. He was a lovely boy. Died in a hunting accident two years after we were married. And then I had a rather enjoyable time for a while—' she sparkled a bit and then went on—'and married Astrid's father when I was thirty. I had Astrid when I was thirty-two. And her father died when she was fourteen. And my third husband was sweet, but dreadfully boring. I divorced him five years ago, and life has been far more interesting since.' She examined another asparagus stalk and ate it as Jessica laughed.

'Aunt Beth, you're a riot. What was the last one like!'

'Dead, mostly, except no one had told him yet. Old people can be so painfully dull. It was really quite embarrassing to divorce him. The poor man was dreadfully shocked. But he got over it. I visit him when I'm in New York. He's still just as boring, poor thing.' She smiled angelically and Jessica dissolved in another fit of laughter. Aunt Beth wasn't nearly as flighty as she liked to make herself sound, but she certainly hadn't led a dull life either.

'And now? No more husbands?' They were friends now. She could ask.

'At my age? Don't be ridiculous. Who would want an old woman? I'm perfectly content as I am, because I enjoyed my life when I was younger. There's nothing worse than an old woman pretending that she isn't. Or a young woman pretending she's old. You and Astrid do a fine job of that.'

'I didn't use to do it.'

'Neither did she, when Tom was alive. It's time she found

herself someone else and burned down that tomb of a mansion. I think it's appalling.'

'But it's so pretty, Aunt Beth. More than pretty.'

'Cemeteries are pretty too, but I wouldn't dream of living in one—until I had no other option. As long as one has the option, one ought to use it. But she's getting there. I think your shop might do her some good. Why don't you sell it to her?'

'And then what would *I* do?'

'Something different. How long have you had the shop?'

'Six years this summer.'

'That's long enough for anything. Why not try something else?' Long enough for a marriage, too?

'Ian wanted me to stay home and have a child. At least that's what he was saying recently. A few years ago he was perfectly happy with things as they were.'

'Maybe you've just found one of the answers you've been looking for.'

'Such as?' Jessica didn't understand.

'That a few years ago he was "perfectly happy with things as they were". How much has changed in those few years? Maybe you forgot to make changes Jessica. To grow.'

'We grew . . .' But how? She wasn't really sure they had.

'I take it you didn't want children.'

'No, it's not that I didn't want any, it's that it wasn't time yet. It was too soon and we were happy alone.'

'There's nothing wrong with not having children.' Aunt Beth looked at her very directly. A little too directly. 'Astrid has never wanted any either. Said it wasn't for her, and I think she was quite right. I don't think she's ever regretted it. Besides, Tom was really a bit past that when they married. Your husband is a young man, isn't he, Jessica?'

She nodded.

'And he wants children. Well, my dear, you can always stay on the pill and tell him you're trying, can't you?' The older woman's eyes hunted Jessie's. Jessica averted her gaze slightly and looked thoughtful.

'I wouldn't do that.'

'Oh, you wouldn't, would you? That's good.' And then Jessica's eyes snapped back to Aunt Beth's.

'But I've thought of it.'

'Of course you have. I'm sure a lot of women have. A lot of them have probably done more than thought of it. Sensible in some cases, I imagine. It seems a pity to have to be that dishonest. You know, I was never that sure I wanted children. And Astrid was a little bit of a surprise.' Aunt Beth almost blushed, but not quite. It was more a softening of her eyes as she looked backward in time and seemed to forget Jessica for a moment. 'But I really grew quite fond of her. She was very sweet when she was small. And simply horrid for a few years after that. But still sweet in an endearing sort of way. I actually enjoyed her very much.' She made Astrid sound more like an adventure than a person, and Jessica smiled, watching her face. 'She was very good to me when her father died. I thought the world had come to an end, except for Astrid.' Jessie almost envied her as she listened. She made it sound as though life were less lonely because of Astrid, instead of more so.

'I've always been, well, afraid, I guess. Afraid of having children, because I thought it would put an obstacle between me and Ian. I thought it would make me lonely.' Bethanie smiled and shook her head.

'No, Jessica. Not if your husband loves you. Then he'll only love you that much more because of the child. It's an additional bond between you, an extension of both of you, a blending of what you love most and hate most and need most and laugh at most, of the two of you. It's a very lovely thing. I can think of a good many reasons to fear having children, but that shouldn't be one of them. Can't you love more than one person?'

It was a good question, and Jessica decided to be honest.

'I don't think so, Aunt Beth. Not anymore. I haven't loved anyone but Ian in a long time. So I guess I can't imagine him loving someone besides me—even a child. I know it must sound selfish, but it's how I feel.'

'It doesn't sound selfish. It sounds frightened, but not really selfish.'

'Maybe one day I'll change my mind.'

'Why? Because you think you ought to? Or because you

want to? Or so you can punish your husband some more?' Aunt Beth didn't pull any punches. 'Take my advice, Jessica. Unless you really want a child, don't bother. They're a terrible nuisance, and even harder on the furniture than cats.' She said it with a straight face as she stroked the calico cat sitting on her lap. Jessica laughed in surprise at the remark. 'As pets go, I much prefer horses. You can leave them outside without feeling guilty.' She looked up with another of her saintly smiles, and Jessica grinned. 'Don't always take me seriously. And having children is really a matter of one's own choice. Whatever you do, don't be pressured by what other people think or say—except your husband. And my, my, aren't you lucky to have me stomping about where angels fear to tread?'

The two women laughed then and moved on to other subjects. But it amazed Jessica to realise the depth of the topics they discussed. She was finding herself revealing secrets and feelings to Aunt Beth that before she would have shared only with Ian. She seemed to be constantly showing Aunt Beth one piece or another of her soul, pulling it out to exhibit, dusting it off, questioning; but she was beginning to feel whole again.

The days were delightful and relaxing on the ranch, filled with fresh air and pleasant mornings spent on horseback in solitary canters over the hills or in idle walks. And the evenings flew by with Aunt Beth to laugh with. Jessica found herself taking naps in the afternoon, reading Jane Austen for the first time since high school, and making small idle sketches in a notebook. She had even made a few secret sketches that could be worked into an informal portrait of Aunt Beth. She was feeling shy about asking her new friend to sit for a portrait. But it was the first one she had wanted to paint since Ian's, years before. Aunt Beth's face would lend itself well to that sort of thing, and it would make a nice gift for Astrid—who appeared, much to Jessica's chagrin, two weeks later.

'You mean I have to come home now?' Astrid looked tired but happy, and Jessica had the sinking feeling she'd had as a child when her mother had arrived too early to fetch her home from a birthday party.

'Don't you dare come home, Jessica Clarke! I came down to see how Mother was doing.'

'We're having a great time.'

'Good. Then don't stop now. I'll be miserable when you come back to the city and take away my toy.' She filled Jessie in on Katsuko's trip to New York, and the spring line was doing better than Jessie had dared to hope. It seemed years since she had bought those pastels, years since she'd come home and Ian had been arrested, centuries since the trial. The shock of it all was finally beginning to fade. The scars barely showed. She had gained five pounds and looked rested. Astrid brought her a letter from Ian, which she didn't open until later.

> . . . I can't believe it, Jess. Can't believe I'd say those things to you. Maybe this disaster is finally taking its toll. Are you all right? Your silence is strange now, your absence stranger. And I find that I don't really know what I want: you to reappear, or for that damn window between us to disappear. I know how you hate it, darling. I hate it as much. But we can overcome it. And how is the vacation? Doing wonders, I'm sure. You've really earned it. I suppose that's why I'm not hearing from you. You're 'busy resting'. Just as well, probably. As usual, I'm all wrapped up in the book. It's going unbelievably well, and I'm hoping that . . .

The rest was all about the book. She tore the letter in half and threw it into the fire.

Aunt Beth quizzed her about the letter later, after Astrid had gone to bed. There was a kind of conspiracy between them now that excluded even Astrid.

'Oh, he says that he loves me and the book is going well, all in the same breath.' She tried to sound blithe and only succeeded in sounding a trifle less bitter.

'Aha! So you're jealous of his work!' Aunt Beth's eyes sparkled. Now she saw something she had not seen before, not clearly, anyway. It was all coming into focus.

'I am not jealous of his work. How ridiculous!'

'I quite agree. But why do you begrudge him his writing? What would happen, Jessica, if you no longer had to support him? You'd have no control over him then, would you? What if he actually did get successful? Then what would you do?'

'I'd be delighted for him.' But it didn't sound convincing, even to Jessica.

'Would you? Do you think you could handle it? Or are you much too jealous even to try?'

'How absurd.' She didn't like the sound of Beth's theory.

'Yes, it is absurd. But I don't think you know that yet, Jessica. The fact is that he either loves you or he doesn't. If he doesn't you couldn't keep him. And if he does, you probably can't lose him. And if you insist on supporting him forever, my dear, he'll wind up finding someone he can support, who lets him feel like a man. Someone who might even give him children. Mark my words.'

Jessica fell silent and they went up to bed. But Aunt Beth's words had hit home. Ian had said the same thing to her himself, in his own way. In Carmel, he had told her that things would have to change. Well, they were going to. But not in the way Ian had in mind.

CHAPTER XXVII

'Good morning, Aunt Beth . . . Astrid.' There was a look of determination on Jessica's face as she sat down to breakfast with them. That expression was new to her friends.

'Good heavens, child, what are you doing up at this hour?' She had rarely risen before ten since she'd been on the ranch, and Aunt Beth was surprised.

'Well.' She looked carefully at Astrid, knowing how disappointed she would be. 'I want to enjoy my last day. I've decided to go home with you tonight, Astrid.' Her friend's face fell at the words.

'Oh no, Jessie! Why?'

'Because I have things to do in town, and I've been lazy for long enough, love. Besides, If I don't go back now, I probably never will.' She tried to make her tone light as she helped herself to some cinnamon toast, but she knew that the words were a blow to Astrid. And she felt bad about leaving the ranch too. Only Aunt Beth looked unruffled by the news.

'Did you tell Mother before you told me, Jessie?' Astrid had noticed the look on her mother's face.

'She did not.' Aunt Beth was quick to answer. 'But I felt it coming last night. And Jessica, I think you're probably right to go back now. Don't look like that, Astrid, it will give you wrinkles. What did you think? That she'd never go back to her own shop? Don't be foolish. Are either of you going to ride with me this morning?' She buttered her toast matter-of-factly, and Astrid cleared the frown from her brow the way a child smoothes messages out of the sand. Her mother was right about Jessie going back, of course. But she had enjoyed Lady J even more than she had thought she would.

Jessie had been watching her face and now looked almost remorseful. 'I'm really sorry, love. I hate to do it to you.' The two younger women fell silent and Aunt Beth shook her head.

'How tedious you both are. I'm going riding. You're quite welcome to mope here. One feeling ridiculously guilty, the other feeling childishly deprived, and both of you making fools of yourselves. I'm surprised either of you has time for such nonsense.' Jessica and Astrid laughed then, and decided to ride with their more sensible elder.

It was a pleasant ride and an enjoyable day, and Jessie left Aunt Beth with regret. She vowed to come back as soon as she could, and struggled for the words to tell her how much the two weeks had meant.

'They restored me.'

'You restored yourself. Now don't waste it by going back to the city and doing something foolish.'

So she knew. It was astonishing. There was nothing you could hide from her.

'I won't approve if you do something stupid, child. And I'm not at all sure I like the look in your eye.'

'Now, Mother.' Astrid saw Jessie's discomfort, and

Bethanie did not pursue the matter after the interruption. She simply gave them a bag of apples, a tin of homemade cookies, and some sandwiches.

'That ought to keep you two well fed till you get home.' Her expression softened again and she put a gentle arm around Jessica's waist. 'Come back soon. I shall miss you, you know.' There was a soft hug about the waist, a warmth in the eyes, and Jessica bent her head to kiss her on the cheek.

'I'll be back soon.'

'Good. And Astrid, dear, drive safely.'

She waved at them from the doorway, until the sleek black Jaguar had turned a corner and sped out of sight.

'You know, I really hate to leave here. The last two weeks have been the best I've had in years.'

'I always feel like that when I leave.'

'How come you don't just move down here, Astrid? I would if she were my mother, and it's such beautiful country.' Jessie settled back in her seat for the long drive, musing over the two precious weeks, and the last few moments of conversation with Aunt Beth.

'Good Lord, Jessica, I'd die of boredom down here. Wouldn't you, after a while?'

Jessica shook her head slowly, a small, thoughtful frown between her eyes. 'No, I don't think I'd be bored. I never even thought of that.'

'Well, I have. In spite of my mother. There's nothing to do here except ride, read, take walks. I still need the insanity of the city.'

'I don't. I almost hate to go back.'

'Then you should have stayed.' For the tiniest moment, the spoiled child was back in Astrid's voice.

'I couldn't stay, Astrid. I have to get back. But I feel like a rat taking the shop back, if you can call it that. You really gave me the most marvellous vacation.' Astrid smiled back at Jessie's words.

'Don't feel bad. The two weeks were a lovely gift.' Astrid sighed gently and followed the serene country road. The sun had just set over the hills, and there was a smell of flowers in the air. In a distant field they could see horses in the twilight.

Jessie took a long look around the now familiar countryside, and sank back in her seat with a small private smile. She'd be back. She had to come back. She was leaving a piece of her soul here, and a new friend.

'You know something, Mrs. Bonner?'

Astrid grinned in response. 'What, Mrs. Clarke?'

'I adore your mother.'

'So do I.' The two women smiled, and Astrid stole a glance at Jessie. 'Was she good to you? Or did she give you a hard time? She can be very tough, and I was a little bit afraid she'd indulge herself with you. Did she?'

'Not really. Honest, but not tough. And never mean. Just straightforward. Sometimes painfully so. But she was generally right. And she made me think a lot. She saved my life. Hell, I'm not even a junkie anymore!' Jessica laughed and bit into one of the apples. 'Want an apple?'

'No, thanks. And I'm glad it worked out. How did Ian sound in the letter I brought you, by the way? I meant to ask, and I forgot.' Jessica's face set at the question, but Astrid had her eyes on the road and didn't see.

'That's why I'm going back.'

'Something wrong?' Astrid stole a quick look at Jessica.

'No. He's fine.' But her voice was strangely cold.

'You're going back to see him, Jessie?' Astrid was a trifle confused.

'No. To see Martin.'

'Martin? Ian's lawyer? Then something is wrong!'

'No, not . . . not like that.' And then she turned her face away and watched the hills drift past the window. 'I'm going back to get a divorce.'

'You're what?' She slowed down the car and turned to face Jessie, stunned. 'Jessica, no! You don't want that! Do you?'

Jessica nodded, holding the apple core in her trembling hand. 'Yes. I do.' They did not speak for the next hundred miles. Astrid couldn't think of anything to say.

Martin was free to see her when Jessie called him the next morning. She went right down to his office and was shown down the painfully familiar corridor. It seemed that she was never there for anything except the high points of drama in her life.

As usual, he was sitting at his desk with his glasses pushed up on his head and the standard frown on his face. She hadn't seen him since December.

'Well, Jessica, how have you been?' He looked her over as he stood up and held out his hand. It still gave her a sinking feeling to see him. In his own way, he was as painful a reminder to her as Inspector Houghton was. He was part of an era. But the era was finally coming to a close.

'I've been fine, thank you.'

'You look very well.' So much so it surprised him. 'Have a seat. And tell me, what brings you here? I had a letter from Ian last week. He sounds like he's weathering it.' A flash of something passed through Martin's eyes. Regret? Sorrow? Guilt? Or maybe Jessie only wished it. Why hadn't he been able to keep Ian free? Why hadn't he talked him into an appeal and then won? If he had, she wouldn't be in his office now. Or maybe she would.

'Yes, I think he's surviving.'

'He mentioned that he thinks he might be selling his book. Said he was waiting to hear more from his agent.'

'Oh.' That was news. 'I hope he does sell it. That would do a lot for him.' Especially now. But that was all Ian wanted anyway. Another book, and this time a big one, a hot seller. He wouldn't need her if he had a book. Wouldn't even miss her.

'So? You still haven't told me what brings you here.' The amenities were now officially over. Jessica took a small breath and looked him in the eyes.

'What brings me here, Martin, is a divorce.' But nothing registered on his face.

'A divorce?'

'Yes. I want to divorce Ian.' Something inside her trembled at the words, turned over and gasped, and tried to clutch at the old familiar branch. But she wouldn't let it. It didn't matter if she fell into a bottomless pit now; she had to do this. And she knew now that she would survive the bottomless pit. She had already been there.

'Jessica, are you tired of waiting for him? Or is there someone else?' The questions seemed indiscreet, but perhaps he had to know.

'No. Neither, really. Well, maybe a little tired of waiting. But only because I don't think we'll have a marriage left when he gets out. So what is there to wait for?'

'Did you have a marriage before?' He had always wondered, had never been quite sure. It had looked as if they had a strong bond and a firm commitment, but you never knew from the outside.

Jessica nodded at his question, and then looked away, her hands clenched in her lap.

'I thought we had a marriage. But . . . I told myself a lot of fairy tales then.'

'Such as?' She wondered why they had to get into all of this now.

'Such as I thought we were happy. That was a lie, among other lies. Ian was never really happy with me. Too many things got in the way. My shop, his work, other things. He'd never have gone off with that woman if he'd been happy.'

'Do you really believe that?'

'I don't know. I didn't at first. But now I begin to see what I didn't give him. Self-respect, for starters. And my time . . . my faith, maybe. I mean real faith that he could make a big success of another book.'

'You didn't respect him?'

'I'm not absolutely sure. I needed him, but I don't know if I respected him. And I never wanted him to know how much I needed him. I always wanted him to think he was the one who needed me. Pretty, isn't it?'

'No. But it's not unusual either. So why the divorce? Why not just clean up the picture and stick to what you've got? It's still better than most, and you're lucky—you see the mistakes; most don't. Does Ian see it as clearly as you do?'

'I have no idea.'

'You haven't spoken to him about this?' He looked shocked as she shook her head. 'He doesn't know you want a divorce?' She shook her head again and then looked up at him squarely.

'No, he doesn't. And . . . Martin, this is just the way I want it. It's too late to "clean up the picture". I've given it a lot of thought, and I know this is the right way. We have no children, and, well . . . this is as good a time as any.'

He nodded, chewing on the stem of his glasses.

'I can understand your thinking, Jessica, and you're a young woman. It may prove to be quite a burden to be married to a man who was sent to prison for rape. Maybe you should be free now to start another life.'

'I think so.' But why did it feel like such a betrayal of Ian? Such a rotten thing to do . . . but she had to. Had to. She wanted this for herself. She had decided. But she kept hearing Aunt Beth's words, just before she'd left the ranch the night before: 'I won't approve if you do something stupid.' But this wasn't stupid. It was right. But what was Ian going to say? . . . And why should she care now? Except that she did. She did, dammit.

'Would it affect your decision in any way if he sold this new book, Jessica?' She thought about it for a moment and then shook her head.

'No, it wouldn't. Because nothing would change. He'd come home, bitter about the time he's spent in prison, and even more bitter against me, because I'd just be supporting him all over again eventually, and nothing would have changed. Book advances don't last long, unless the book is a success.'

'You don't think he's capable of writing a success?' The tone of Martin's voice filled her with shame, and she lowered her eyes again.

'I didn't mean that. And that's not the point anyway. Everything would still be the same. I'd still have the shop, the bank account . . . no, Martin. This is what I want. I'm absolutely sure.'

'Well, Jessica, you're old enough to make your own decisions. When are you going to tell Ian?'

'I thought I'd write to him tonight. And—' she hesitated, but she had to ask him—'I was hoping you'd go up to see him.'

'To break the news?' Martin looked very tired as he asked. She nodded slowly. 'Frankly, Jessica, I don't normally handle domestic affairs. Marital law, as you know, is not my speciality.' And this was going to be a mess. But Ian was his client. And his client's wife was sitting opposite him, looking at him as though it were his fault that she was getting the divorce, as though he had cost her her marriage. And why the hell did he always feel guilty if things didn't work out just right?

'Oh well, I suppose I could handle this for you. Will it be a complicated sort of affair?'

'No. Terribly simple. The shop is mine. The house belongs to both of us, and I'll sell it if he wants, and put his share of the money in an account for him. That's all there is. I get custody of the plants, and he gets his file cabinets in his studio. End of a marriage.' The only thing she had left out was the furniture, and neither of them cared, except for the few pieces that were her parents', which were obviously hers. So simple. So miserably simple after seven years.

'You make it sound very quick and easy.' But he was dubious, and sad for them both.

'Maybe quick, but no, not very easy. Will you go up and see him soon?'

'By the end of the week. Will you be going up to see him yourself?' She shook her head carefully. She had seen Ian for the last time . . . on that godawful day when he had gotten up and walked away and she had watched him from behind a window, holding a dead phone in her hands. Her eyes filled with tears at the memory, and Martin Schwartz looked away. He hated this kind of thing. It seemed so wasteful.

Jessica looked up at Martin, holding back the tears. Her voice was barely a whisper. 'No, Martin, I won't see him anymore.'

He told her that she would be divorced in six months.

In September. A year after he had been arrested, a year after the end of their marriage had begun.

There was a letter from Ian waiting when she stopped by the house for her mail on her way to the boutique. It was only a brief note. And a poem. She read it with wide, sad eyes, and then tore it carefully in half and threw it away. But it had stuck in her mind somehow. Like a satin thorn. It was the last letter from Ian she opened. The poem decided her.

You are the explosive celebration
of my sunbursts
every morning,
You are the whisper
in my late
late nights,
You are the symphony in my sunsets,
You are the splendour and the glory
of the dawning
of my life.

The dawning of his life was past, with her, at least. But she felt as though she had singlehandedly killed the sunrise. Cancelled it. Sent it away. Made it cry. Broken something sacred. Him, and herself, and the thing that was both of them. The thing she now believed had never been at all. But she knew she had to do what she was doing.

CHAPTER XXVIII

The boutique was in beautiful shape. There were new displays all over the main room, and the window looked like a vision of spring. Astrid had done it herself. And the pastels and creams and delicate shades Jessie had bought in New York more than six months before looked good on display. There were two new plants in her office, with bright yellow flowers in full bloom, and there was a neat, crisp air to the shop that she had almost forgotten. She had been gone for only two weeks, but Lady J had been reborn, just as she had been. It looked the way it had when Jessie had first opened it, in the days when she'd been madly in love with it and had put her heart and soul into its birth. Now it showed the signs of Astrid's fresh enthusiasm and love. She hadn't changed anything radically, she had just pulled it together. Even Katsuko and Zina looked happier.

'How was the vacation?' Katsuko looked up, delighted to see her, but she didn't need to ask. Jessie looked like Jessie again, only better.

'It was exactly what I needed. And look at this place! It looks like you painted it or something. So cheerful and pretty.'

'That's just the new line. It looks pretty damn good.'

'How's it selling?'

'Like hotcakes. And wait till you see what I picked up for fall. Everything's orange or red. Lots of black, and some marvellous silver knits for the opera.' The browns of the winter before were already forgotten. Next year it would be red. Bright, busy, alive, maybe that was a good sign for her new life . . . new life. Jesus. She didn't want to think about it yet. And there would be so many people to tell . . . to explain to . . . to . . .

Jessica settled down in her office, looked around with pleasure, and enjoyed the feeling of having come home. It softened the burden of the morning, the meeting with Martin. She tried to keep it out of her mind. She would write to Ian tonight. For the last time. She didn't want to get into a long exchange of letters with him. He was too good at it. The letters would be . . . too much. They could work everything out through their lawyer. The less they said to each other, even by letter, the better. She had made up her mind. It was done now, and it was for the best. Now she had to look ahead and steel herself not to look back at the years with Ian. They were over now. A part of her past, like out-of-date fashions. Jessica and Ian were 'passé'.

'Jessie? Got a minute?' Zina's curly head poked in the door, and Jessie looked up and smiled. She felt older, quieter, but no longer tired. And she felt strong. For the first time in months, the nights alone did not terrify her. The house was no longer haunted. Her life was no longer infested by ghosts. Her first night back in the house had actually been peaceful. Finally.

She forced her attention back to Zina, still hovering in the doorway. 'Sure, Zina. I've got lots of time.' The slower pace of the country was still with her. She didn't feel harried yet, and she loved it.

'You're lookin' good.' Zina sat in the chair next to Jessie's desk and looked slightly uncomfortable. She asked a few questions about Jessie's vacation, and seemed to hesitate each time there was a pause. Finally, Jessie had had enough.

'Okay, lady, what's on your mind?'

'I don't know what to say, Jessie, but . . .' She looked up and suddenly Jessie sensed it. The hard months had taken their toll on everyone, not only on her. And she was almost surprised that neither of them had done it before. They probably hadn't because they were too loyal. She took a long breath and looked into Zina's eyes.

'You're quitting?'

Zina nodded. 'I'm getting married.' She said it almost apologetically.

'You are?' Jessie hadn't even known that Zina had a boyfriend. She hadn't had one the last time they'd talked . . . but when had that been? Last month? Two months ago? More like six. Since then she'd been too busy with her own problems to inquire or to care.

'I'm getting married in three weeks.'

'Zina, that's lovely news! What are you looking so sorry about, dummy?' Jessie smiled broadly and Zina looked overwhelmingly relieved.

'I just feel bad about leaving you. We're moving to Memphis.'

Jessica laughed. It sounded like a horrible fate, but she knew Zina didn't think so, and now that the news was out, Zina looked ecstatic.

'I met him at a Christmas Eve party, and oh . . . Jessie! He's the most beautiful man, in all possible ways! And I love him! And we're going to have lots of babies!' She grinned contentedly and Jessica jumped up and gave her a hug. 'And look at my ring!' She was pure Southern belle as she flashed the tiniest of diamonds.

'Were you wearing that before I went on vacation?' Jessica was beginning to wonder just how much she'd been missing.

'No. He gave it to me last week. But I didn't want to write and tell you, so I waited till you got back.' And Astrid had forbidden all potentially disturbing communications to Jessie. Like news of the creditors who kept calling about the bills she still hadn't paid. 'It's such a pretty little ring, isn't it?'

'It's gorgeous. And you're crazy, but I love you, and I'm so happy for you!' And then a flash of pain struck through to her core. Zina was getting married, she was getting divorced. You come, you go, you start, you end, you try, you lose, and maybe later you get another try, a fresh start, and this time win. Maybe. Or maybe it didn't really matter. She hoped Zina would win on the first try.

'I feel so bad giving you such short notice, Jess. But we just decided. Honest.' She almost hung her head, but the smile was too big to hide.

'Stop apologising, for heaven's sake! I'm just glad I came home. Where's the wedding?'

'In New Orleans, or my mother would kill me. I'm flying home in two weeks, and she's already going crazy over the wedding. We didn't give her much notice either. She called me four times last night, and you should have heard Daddy!' They both giggled, and Jessica started to think.

'Do you need a dress?'

'I'm going to wear my great-grandmother's.'

'But you need a trousseau. Right? And a going-away dress, and . . .'

'Oh, Jessie, yes, but . . . no . . . I can't let you do that . . .'

'Mind your own business, or I'll fire you!' She waggled a finger at Zina and they both started to laugh again. Jessie flung open her office door and marched Zina into the main room of the shop and stopped in front of a startled Katsuko.

'Kat, we have a new customer. VIP. This is Miss Nelson, and she needs a trousseau.' Katsuko looked up in astonishment, then understood and joined in their giggles and smiles. She was relieved that it had gone well. She had been worried for Zina. For the last couple of months it had been frightening to tangle with Jessie. But she was all right now. They could all tell. And now she was bubbling on about Zina's trousseau.

'It's going to be perfect with all the spring colours. Kat, give her anything she wants at ten percent under cost, and I'll give her her going-away suit as a wedding present. And as a matter of fact . . . don't I know just the one!' A gleam had come into her eyes, and she walked into the stockroom and came out with a creamy beige silk suit from Paris. It had a mid-calf skirt and a jacket that would subtly conceal Zina's oversized chest. She pulled out a mint green silk blouse to go with it, and Zina practically drooled.

'With dressy beige sandals, and a hat . . . Zina, you're going to look unbelievable!' Even Katsuko's eyes glowed at the outfit Jessie held up in her hand. Zina looked shocked.

'Jessie, no! You can't! Not that one!' She spoke in a whisper. The suit sold for over four hundred dollars.

'Yes, that one.' Her voice was gentle now. 'Unless there's another one you like better.' Zina shook her head solemnly and Jessica gave her a warm hug, and with a smile and a last wink at Zina she walked back into her office. It had been a startling morning, and now she had another startling idea.

She reached Astrid at the hairdresser.

'Is something wrong?' Maybe Jessie had hated the window display, or didn't like what she'd done with the stock. She was worried as she stood there dripping hair-setting lotion on her new suede Gucci shoes.

'No, silly, nothing's wrong. Want a job?'

'Are you kidding?'

'No. Zina just quit. She's getting married. And I may be crazy, because with you in the shop there'd be three of us capable of running this joint, but if you don't mind being the overqualified low man on the totem pole for a while, the job's all yours.'

'Jessie! I'll take it!' She grinned broadly and forgot about what she was doing to her shoes.

'Then you're hired. Want to go to lunch?'

'I'll be right over. No, I can't, dammit, my hair is still wet . . . oh . . . shit.' They both laughed and Astrid's smile seemed to broaden by the minute. 'I'll be there in an hour. And Jessie . . . thanks. I love you.' They both hung up with happy smiles and Jessica was glad she had called.

The four of them closed the doors to Lady J promptly at five instead of at five-thirty, and Jessica brought out a bottle of champagne she had ordered that afternoon. Zina had decided to leave a week earlier than planned now that Jessie had Astrid to take her place. They finished the bottle in half an hour, and Astrid drove Jessica home.

'Want to come home with me for a drink? I still haven't celebrated my new job.'

Jessie smiled, but shook her head. She was beginning to feel the effects of the day . . . which had begun with seeing Martin about the divorce. It was odd how she kept forgetting that. The morning seemed light years behind her. She wished the divorce were already behind her too.

'No thanks, love. Not tonight.'

'Afraid to fraternise with the help?' Jessie laughed at the thought.

'No, silly, I'm pooped and I'm already half crocked from the champagne, and . . . I've got a letter to write.' Astrid's face sobered as she listened.

'To Ian?' Jessica nodded gravely, the laughter totally gone from her eyes now.

'Yes. To Ian.'

Astrid patted her hand and Jessie slid quietly out of

the car with a wave. She unlocked the door and stood in the sunlit front hall for a moment. It was so quiet. So unbearably quiet. Not frightening anymore. Only empty. Who would take care of her now? It was odd to realise that no one knew what time she came home or went out, or where she was. No one knew and no one cared. Well, there was Astrid, but no one to report to, explain to, rush home for, do errands for, wake up for, set the alarm for, buy food for . . . an overwhelming sensation of emptiness engulfed her. Tears slid down her face as she looked around the house that had once been their home. It was a shell now. A hall of memories. Someplace to come back to at night after work. Like everything else, it had suddenly been catapulted into the past. It was all moving so quickly. People were going and changing and moving away, new people were taking their places . . . Zina getting married . . . Astrid in the shop . . . Ian gone . . . and in six months she'd be divorced. Jessica sat down on the chair in the front hall, her coat still on, her handbag slung on her shoulder, as she tasted the word aloud. Divorced.

It was almost midnight before she licked the stamp on the letter. She felt a hundred years old. She had forced Ian out of her life, and she would stand by her decision. But now she had no one except herself.

CHAPTER XXIX

'Well, look at you! What are you up to tonight?'

Astrid looked embarrassed as she buttoned the mink coat. It was May, but still chilly at night, and the fur coat looked good on her.

Jessie had just locked the doors to the shop. The arrangement was working out well. She, Katsuko, and Astrid got along like sisters. They made a powerful team, almost too much so, but they liked it, and the boutique was doing much better. Calls from creditors were getting rare. You could see the relief in Jessica's face.

'All right, nosey-body—' Astrid looked at Jessica watching her with amusement—'I happen to have a date.' She said it like a sixteen-year-old, with a faint blush on her cheeks, and Jessica burst out laughing.

'And you already look guilty as hell. Who's the guy?'

'Some idiot I met through a friend.' She looked almost pained.

'How old is he?' Jessie was suspicious of Astrid's passion for men over sixty. She was still looking for Tom.

'He's forty-five.' With a virginal expression, she finished buttoning the coat.

'At least he's a decent age. For a change.'

'Thank you, Aunt Jessie.' The two women laughed and Jessica pulled a comb out of her handbag.

'As a matter of fact, I have a date too.' She looked up with a small smile.

'Oh? With whom?' The tables were turned now, and Astrid looked as though she enjoyed it. But Jessie had been going out a good deal in the past weeks. With young men, with old ones, with a photographer, a banker, even with a law student once. But never with writers. And she never talked about Ian anymore. The subject was forbidden and mention of Ian met with silence or black looks.

'I'm going out with a friend of a friend from New York. He's just in San Francisco for a week. But what the hell, why not? He sounded decent on the phone. A little bit of a Mr. New York Smoothie, but at least he seemed halfway intelligent. He had a nice quick sense of humour on the phone. I just hope he behaves himself.' Jessica sighed softly as she put her comb back in her bag. Her hair hung well past her shoulders in a sheet of satiny blonde.

'*You* should worry about how he behaves? Big as you are, you can always beat him up.'

'I gave that up when I was nine.'

'How come?'

'I met a kid who was bigger than I was, and it hurt.' She grinned and propped her feet up on the desk.

'Want a ride home, Jessie?'

'No thanks, love. He's picking me up here. I thought I'd show him the action at Jerry's.' Astrid nodded, but Jerry's wasn't her style. It was a local 'in' bar, full of secretaries and ad men looking to get laid. It made her feel lonely. She was having dinner at L'Etoile. That was much more her style. It would have been Jessie's style too, if she'd let it. But she was still seeking her own level. A new level. Any level. Jessie knew Jerry's wasn't for her, but the action gave her something to watch as she listened to the hustles being carried on at the bar.

'See you tomorrow.'

Jessie waved good night, and Astrid passed a young man on the steps. He was slightly taller than Jessie and had dark bushy hair. He was wearing a grey turtleneck sweater and jeans. Nice-looking, but too 'fuzzy', Astrid decided, as she smiled and walked past. She wondered how Jessie stood them; they all looked the same, no matter what colour their hair, or how they dressed, they looked hungry and horny and bored. Astrid was suddenly glad she was no longer thirty. Thirty-year-old men had so far to go. With a sigh, she slipped into the Jaguar and turned on the ignition. She wondered how Ian was doing. She had wanted to write to him for a month, but she hadn't dared. Jessica might have considered it treason. Astrid saw the letters torn in half before they were opened when she emptied the wastebasket in the office they now shared. Jessie could be unyielding when she decided to be. And she had decided to be. The door to the shop opened and Astrid saw the young man go inside.

'Hi, Mario. I'm Jessie.' She assumed he was the young man she was waiting for, and offered him her hand. He ignored it with a casual smile.

'I take it you work here.' No greeting, no introduction, no handshake, no hello. He was just looking the place over. And her with it. Okay, sweetheart, if that's how it is.

'Yes. I work here.' She decided not to tell him she owned it.

'Yeah. I think I just passed your boss on the stairs. An old chick in a fur coat. Ready to go?' Jessie was already bristling. Astrid was not an 'old chick', and she was her friend.

He seemed bored with the action at Jerry's, but he had four glasses of red wine anyway. He explained that he was a playwright, or was trying to be, and he tutored English, maths, and Italian on the side. He had grown up in New York, in a tough neighbourhood on the West Side. At least that's how he put it. But Jessie wondered. He looked more like middle-class West Side than tough anything. Or maybe even the suburbs. And now he had grown up to be unwashed, unfriendly, and rude. It made her wonder about the friends who'd given him her name. People she knew through business, but still . . . how could they send her this?

'Well, how's New York? I haven't been back in a while.'

'Yeah? How long?'

'Almost eight months.'

'It's still there. I went to a great cocaine party last week in St. Mark's Place. How's the action out here?'

'Cocaine? I wouldn't know.' She sipped her wine.

'Not your thing?' He continued to look bored while working hard at looking cynical. Big-city kid in the provinces. Jessie was wishing he would drop dead on the spot. Or disappear, at least.

'You don't dig cocaine?' He pursued the point.

'No. But this is a nice city. It's a good place to live.'

'It looks dull as shit.' She looked up and smiled brightly, hoping to disappoint him. Mario the playwright was turning out to be an A-1 pain in the ass.

'Well, Mario, it's not as exciting as West Side New York, but we do have our fun spots.'

'I hear it's an intellectual wasteland.' So are you, darling.

'Depends on who you talk to. There are some writers out here. Good ones. Very good ones.' She was thinking of Ian and wanted to cram him down this jerk's throat. Ian was quality. Ian was charming. Ian was brilliant. Ian was beautiful. What was she doing out with this pig? This boor? This . . .

'Yeah? Like who?'

'What?' Her mind had wandered away from Mario to Ian.

'You said there are some good writers out here. And I said like who. You mean science-fiction writers?' He said it with utter distaste and that cynical smile that made Jessica want to plant the wineglass in his teeth.

'No, not just science-fiction writers. I mean like fiction, straight fiction, nonfiction.' She started reeling off names, and realised that they were all friends of Ian's. Mario listened, but offered no comment. Jessica was fuming.

'You know what knocks me out?' No. But tell me quick, I'll find one.

'What?'

'That a bright woman like you sells dresses in some shop. I don't know, I figured you were doing something creative.'

'Like writing?'

'Writing, painting, sculpture, something meaningful. What kind of existence is that, selling dresses for old broads in fur coats?'

'Well, you know how it is. One does what one can.' Jessie tried to keep her lip from curling as she smiled. 'What sort of play are you writing?'

'New theatre. An all-female cast, in the nude. There's a really great scene taking shape now for the second act. A homosexual love scene after a woman gives birth.'

'Sounds like fun.' Her tone went over his head. 'Hungry yet?' And she still had dinner to look forward to with him. She was considering pleading a violent attack of bubonic plague. Anything to get away from him. But she'd live through it. She'd been through it before. More often than she wanted to admit.

'Yeah. I could dig a good meal.' She made several suggestions and he settled on Mexican, because good Mexican food was rare in New York. At least he had that much sense. She took him to a small restaurant on Lombard Street. The company stank, but at least the food was good.

After dinner she yawned loudly several times and hoped he'd take the hint, but he didn't. He wanted to see some 'night life', if there was any. There was, but she wasn't going for it. Not tonight and not with him. She suggested a coffeehouse on Union Street, close to home. She'd have a quick cappuccino and ditch him. She needed the coffee anyway. She had drunk three or four glasses of wine at dinner. But Mario had had at least twice that, after his earlier consumption at Jerry's. He was beginning to slur his words.

They settled down in the coffeehouse, he with an Irish coffee and she with a frothy cappuccino, and he eyed her squintingly over the top of his glass.

'You're not a bad-looking chick.' He made it sound like a chemical analysis. Your blood type is O positive.

'Thank you.'

'Where do you live, anyway?'

'Just up a hill or two from here.' She drank the sweet milk foam on the top of her coffee and busied herself looking evasive. One thing she was not planning to share with Mario was her address. She'd had more than enough already.

'Big hills?'

'Medium. Why?'

''Cause I don't want to walk any big motherfucking hills, sister, that's why. I'm piss-eyed tired. And just a wee bit drunk.' He made a pinch with his fingers and smiled leeringly. It almost made Jessie sick to look at him.

'No problem, Mario. We can take a cab and I'll be happy to drop you off wherever you're staying.'

'What do you mean "wherever I'm staying"?' There was a small spark of anger in his eyes, smouldering in confusion.

'You're a smart boy. What did it sound like?'

'It sounded for a minute there like you were being a prissy pain in the ass. I assume that I'm staying with you.' For a moment she wanted to tell him she was married, but she wouldn't solve it that way. Besides, then how could she explain going out to dinner with him?

'Mario—' she smiled sweetly at him—'you assumed wrong. We don't do things that way out in the provinces. Or I don't, anyway.'

'What's that supposed to mean?' He sat slumped in his chair now, with a disagreeable expression on his face.

'It means thank you for a lovely evening.' She started buttoning her jacket and stood up with a wistful look in her eyes. But he leaned across the table and grabbed her arm. His grip on her wrist was surprisingly painful.

'Listen, bitch, we had dinner, didn't we? I mean what the fuck do you think . . .' There was a look on his face that she never wanted to see again, and suddenly the earlier conversation with Astrid flashed into her mind . . . 'If he misbehaves, you can hit him' . . . and she wrenched her arm free, and something in the set of her face told him not to press the point.

'I don't know what you think, mister. But I know what I think. And I think you'll be extremely sorry if you touch me again. Good night.' She was gone before he could react again, and it was the waiters who bore the brunt of his anger as he swept his arm across the table, knocking the cups and glasses to the floor. It took two waiters to convince him that what he wanted was some air.

Jessica was almost home by then. As she walked quietly up the last hill to the house, the night air was soft on her face, and she felt surprisingly peaceful. It had been a rotten evening, but she was rid of him. And she would never have to see him again. Men like that made her flesh crawl, but at least she knew how to handle them. And herself. At first, such evenings had terrified her. But she had dated all types by now—all the creeps in creepdom. The good ones were either married or off hiding somewhere. And what was left were all the same. They drank too much, they laughed too hard or not at all, they were pompous or neurotic or borderline gay, they were into drugs or group sex, or wanted to talk about how they hadn't had an erection in four years because of what their ex-wives had done to them. She was beginning to wonder if she wouldn't be happier staying home by herself. The libertine life wasn't much fun.

'How was last night?' Jessie asked Astrid first, as she came into the shop the next morning. She was hoping to quell Astrid's questions that way. She had no desire to talk about Mario.

'It was a nice evening, actually. I sort of liked it.' She looked happy and relaxed and almost surprised. Unlike Jessie, she didn't really expect to have a good time on a date. It made her easier to please.

'How was your evening? I think I passed your young man on the steps on my way out.'

'I think you did too. Damn shame you didn't trip him up on your way.'

'That bad, huh?' Astrid looked sympathetic, which hurt more.

'Actually, considerably worse. He was the pits.' In Astrid's opinion, he had looked it. 'Well, back to the drawing board.'

Jessie managed a thin smile as she sifted quickly through the mail, sorting out the letters from the bills. She paused only for a moment to look at a long plain white envelope before tearing it in half and dropping the pieces in the wastebasket. Another letter from Ian. It hurt Astrid every time she saw Jessie do that. It seemed so unkind, such a waste. She wondered if Ian knew, or suspected, that Jessie wasn't reading his letters. She wondered what he was saying in the letters.

'Don't look like that, Astrid.' Jessica's voice broke into her thoughts.

'Like what?'

'Like I tear your heart out every time I throw out his letters.' She had continued sorting the mail, looking almost indifferent. But not quite. Astrid saw her hands tremble just a trifle.

'But why do you do that?'

'Because we have nothing to say to each other anymore. I don't want to hear it, read it, or open any doors.

It would be misleading. I don't want to get suckered into any kind of dialogue with him.'

'But shouldn't you give him a chance to say what he thinks? This way seems so unfair.' Astrid's eyes were almost pleading, and Jessica looked back at the mail as she answered.

'It doesn't matter. I don't give a damn what he says. I've made up my mind. He could only make things harder now. He couldn't change anything.'

'You're that sure you want the divorce?'

Jessica looked up before she answered and fixed Astrid's eyes with her own. 'Yes. I'm that sure.' In spite of the Marios, in spite of the loneliness and the emptiness, she was still sure divorce was the right thing. But that didn't mean it didn't hurt.

Two customers walked into the shop at that moment and spared Jessica any further discussion. Katsuko was out, and Astrid had to offer to help. Jessica walked into her office and gently closed the door. Astrid knew what that meant. The subject was closed. It always was.

It was a busy day after that, a busy week, a busy month. The shop was in fine shape now, and people were buying for summer.

They had occasional postcards from Zina, who was already pregnant, and Katsuko had decided to grow her hair long again. Life had returned to trivial details: who was going to Europe, what the new hemline would be, whether or not to paint the front of the shop, planting new geraniums in Katsuko's tiny garden apartment. Jessie never ceased to feel gratitude for the trivia. The orchestration in her life had been so sombre for so long; now it was Mozart and Vivaldi again. Simple and easy and light. And having made the decision to get the divorce, there were no big decisions left.

It was almost as if the horror story had never happened. Her mother's emerald ring was safely back in the bank. The ownership on the house and the shop were free and clear again. The shop was back on its feet. But there had been changes. A lot more than she wanted to admit. And she had changed. She was more independent, less frightened, more mature. Life was moving along.

They were all having coffee in the boutique one morning when Jessie got to her feet and started going through some of the racks.

'Planning to knock five or ten inches off your height?' Astrid smiled as she watched Jessie go through the size eights.

'Oh, shut up.' She looked over her shoulder with a grin, and then knit her brow. 'Kat, what size does Zina usually wear?'

'Oh, Jesus. That's a tough one. A size four on the hips, and about a fourteen up top.'

'Terrific. So in a smock shape, what size would you say?'

'An eight.'

'That's what I was looking at.' She cast a victorious glance at Astrid. 'I thought maybe we should send her a present. That kid she married doesn't have much money, and she's going to be hard to fit now that she's pregnant. What do you think of these?' She pulled out three tent-shaped dresses from the spring line, in ice cream colours and easy shapes.

'Super!' Kat instantly approved, and Astrid looked touched.

'What a sweet thing to do.'

Jessie looked almost embarrassed as she smiled and handed them to Katsuko.

'Ahh . . . bullshit.' All three of them laughed and Jessie sat back down to her coffee. 'Send those out to her today, okay, Kat? Do you suppose we ought to send her something for the baby?' She didn't know why, but she wanted to celebrate Zina's baby. As though he, or she, were someone special.

'Not yet. It isn't due for months. Besides, that's bad luck.' Astrid looked slightly uncomfortable. 'What's with all the interest in maternity goodies?'

'I've decided that if I'm never going to be a mother, I might as well enjoy being an aunt. Besides, I figured that if I started buttering her up early, she might make me godmother.' Astrid laughed, and Katsuko carefully folded the dresses into a box full of yellow tissue paper. She glanced quickly at Jessie, but Jessie got up and walked away. She felt lonely suddenly. Lonely for a child for the first time in her life. And why now? She decided that it was just because she was ready to love somebody again.

'She's going to adore them, Jessie. And who says you're never going to be a mother?' Katsuko was intrigued. It was the first time Jessie had talked openly about children. Katsuko had always suspected that Jessie must have come to some decision about children, but it was rare for her to open up about anything personal. She was not one of those women who discussed her sex life and her dearest dreams in the office. But Jessie seemed to be in an unusually chatty mood. And she didn't have Ian to confide in anymore. She often seemed hungry for someone to talk to these days. She sat down once more before she replied.

'*I* say I'm never going to be a mother. I mean, Jesus, have you seen what's out there these days? If I've been seeing any kind of standard sampling, I wouldn't think of propagating the breed. They ought to be considering how to stamp it out!' The other two women laughed and Jessie finished her coffee. 'Halfwits, no wits, nitwits, and dimwits. Not to mention the ones who've blitzed out their brains on acid, the sonsofbitches cheating on their wives, and the ones with no sense of humour. You expect me to marry one of those darlings and have a kid, maybe?' And then her face grew serious. 'Besides, I'm too old.'

'Don't be ridiculous.' Astrid spoke up first.

'I'm not. I'm being honest. By the time I got around to having a child, I'd be thirty-four, thirty-five maybe. That's too old. You should do it at Zina's age. How old is she? Twenty-six? Twenty-seven?' Katsuko nodded pensively and then asked Jessie a question that hit hard.

'Jessie . . . are you sorry now that you didn't have children with Ian?' There was a long pause before she answered, and Astrid was afraid she'd lose her temper, or her cool, but she didn't.

'I don't know. Maybe I am. Maybe I can only say that because I've never been within miles of a kid. But it seems sad—worse than sad, wasted, empty—to live so many years with a man and have nothing. Some books, some plants, a few pieces of furniture, a burnt-out car. But nothing real, nothing lasting, nothing that says "We were", even if we aren't anymore, that says "I loved you", even if I don't love you anymore.' There were tears in her eyes as she shrugged gently and stood up. She avoided their eyes and looked busy as she headed back to her little office. 'Anyway, so it goes. Back to work, ladies. And don't forget to send the dresses to Zina right away, Kat.' They didn't see her again until lunchtime, and neither Astrid nor Katsuko dared comment on the conversation.

But they were all basically happy. Jessie was restless and sick of the men she was going out with, but she wasn't unhappy. There were no traumas, no crises in her life anymore. And Astrid was still seeing the same man she had been seeing earlier that spring. And enjoying it more than she wanted to admit. He took her to the theatre a lot, collected the work of unknown young sculptors, and had a small house in Mendocino that Astrid finally admitted she'd been to. She was spending weekends there, which was why Jessie never heard from her anymore between Friday and Monday.

Jessica was busy too; she was working Saturdays at Lady J, and there were always new men. The trouble was that there were never 'old' men, men she had known long enough to feel comfortable with. It was always a birthday party, never old galoshes. She got bored with the constant explanations. Yes, I ski. Yes, I play tennis. No, I don't like to hike. Yes, I drive a car. No, I'm not allergic to shellfish. I prefer hard mattresses, wear a size eight narrow shoe, a size ten dress, am five feet ten and a half, like rings, love earrings, hate rubies, love emeralds . . . all of the above, none of the above. It was like constantly applying for a new job.

She was having trouble sleeping again, but she had stayed away from pills ever since her stay at the ranch. She knew they weren't the solution, and someday . . . someday . . . someone would come along, and she'd want him to stay. Maybe. Or maybe not. She had even considered the possibility that no one would come along again. No one she could love. It was a horrible thought, but she did admit it as a possibility. It was what had made her suddenly and almost cruelly regret never having had children. She had always thought she had the option. Now her options were gone.

But maybe it didn't matter if she never had children, or loved another man, or . . . maybe it didn't matter at all. She wondered if she had already fulfilled her destiny. Seven years with Ian, an explosion at the end, a boutique, and a few friends. Maybe that was it. There was a sameness to her life now, a blandness and lack of purpose that made her wonder. All she had to do was get up, go to work, stay at the shop all day, close it at five-thirty, go home and change, go out to dinner, say good night, go to bed. And the next day it would all start all over again. She was tired, but she wasn't depressed. She wasn't happy, but at least she wasn't frightened or lonely. She wasn't anything. She was numb.

Ian had sent a message, via Martin, not to sell the house; he'd buy her half eventually if he had to, but he didn't want the house to go. So she went on living there, but now it was just a house. She kept it tidy, it suited her needs, it was comfortable, and it was familiar. But she had put all of Ian's things in the studio and locked it. And the house had lost half its personality when she'd done that. It was just a house now. Lady J was just a shop. She was just another soon-to-be divorcee on the market.

'Morning, madam. Want a date?' Astrid was carrying lily of the valley as she walked into the shop, and she dropped a clump of it next to Jessie's coffee cup.

'Jesus, don't you look happy for this time of the morning.' Jessica attempted a smile and winced, regretting the last half bottle of white wine the night before. But it pleased even Jessie to see Astrid like that, wearing her hair down much of the time now, and with a happy light in her eyes.

'Okay, Miss Sunshine. What kind of date?' She tried

another smile and meant it. It was impossible not to smile at Astrid.

'A date with a man.' She looked almost girlish.

'I should hope so. You mean a blind date?'

'No, I don't think he's blind, Jessica. He's only thirty-nine.' The two women laughed and Jessica shrugged.

'Okay, why not? What's he like?'

'Very sweet, and a little bit "not too tall".' Astrid looked cautiously at Jess. 'Does that matter?'

'Will I have to stoop over to talk to him?'

Astrid giggled and shook her head. 'No. And he's really very nice. He's divorced.'

'Isn't everyone?' It constantly amazed Jessie to realise how many marriages failed. She hadn't been that aware of it before she'd filed for divorce herself. It had always seemed that everyone she knew was married. And now everyone she knew was divorced.

They had dinner as a foursome that Thursday night, and Astrid's beau was delightful. He was elegant, amusing, and good-looking. In fact, he was the first man Jessie had met in a long time who actually appealed to her. He had the same kind of graceful looks as Ian, but with silver hair and a well-trimmed narrow rim of beard. He had travelled extensively, was knowledgeable in art and music, was very funny as he told of some of his exploits, and he was wonderful with Astrid. Jessica wholeheartedly approved, but what pleased her most about the evening was seeing Astrid's happiness. She had really found the perfect man for her.

Jessie's date for the evening was pleasant, kind, and unbearably boring. Divorced with three children, he worked in the trust department of a bank. He was also five feet seven, and Jessie had worn heels. She stood almost a head taller than he. But when Astrid suggested dancing, Jessie didn't have the heart to argue. At least this one didn't wrestle her at the door. He shook her hand, told her he'd call her while she made a mental note not to hold her breath waiting, and he went home alone. She was sure that by the next morning she wouldn't even remember his name. Why bother?

She took off her clothes and went to bed, but it was two hours later when she finally fell asleep. She felt as if she had just closed her eyes when the phone rang the next morning. It was Martin Schwartz.

'Jessie?'

'No. Veronica Lake.' Her voice was husky and she was still half asleep.

'I'm sorry, I woke you.'

'That's okay, I have to get to work anyway.'

'I have something for you.'

'My divorce?' She sat up in bed and reached for her cigarettes. She wasn't sure she was prepared for that kind of news.

'No. That won't be for another four months. I have something else. A cheque.'

'What in hell for?' It was all very confusing.

'Ten thousand dollars.'

'Jesus. But why? And from whom?'

'From your husband's publisher, Jessica. He sold the book.'

'Oh.' She exhaled carefully and frowned. 'Well, put it in his account, Martin. It's not mine, for Chrissake.'

'Yes, it is. He endorsed it to you.'

'Well, unendorse it, dammit. I don't want it.' Her hands were shaking now, and so was her voice.

'He says it's to reimburse you for my trial fee, and Green's fee, and a number of other things.'

'That's ridiculous. Just tell him I don't want it. I paid those bills, and he doesn't owe me anything.'

'Jessica . . . he signed it over to you.'

'I don't give a damn. Cross it out. Tear it up. Do whatever you want with it, but *I don't want it*!' Her voice was rising nervously.

'Can't you do it for him? It seems to mean so much to him. I think it's a question of integrity with him. He really seems to feel that he owes this to you.'

'Well, he's wrong.'

'Maybe I'm wrong.' Martin could feel a thin film of sweat veiling his brow. 'Maybe he just wants to give it to you as a gift.'

'Maybe so. But whatever the case, Martin, I will not accept the cheque.' Martin's voice had been pleading and she shook her head vehemently as she stubbed out her cigarette. 'Look. It's simple. He doesn't owe me anything. I don't want anything. I won't accept anything. I'm glad he sold the book, and I think that's just wonderful for him. Now he should keep the money and leave me alone. He's going to need money when he gets out anyway. Now that's it, Martin. I don't want it. Period. Okay?'

'Okay.' He sounded defeated and they hung up. At her end, she was trembling; at his he sat looking out at the view, wondering how to tell Ian. His eyes had been so alive when he'd talked about paying Jessie back. And now Martin had to tell him this.

Jessie's day was off to a bad start. She burned her coffee, and her shower ran cold. She stubbed her foot on the bed, and the newspaper boy forgot to leave her the morning paper. She looked fierce by the time she got to the shop. Astrid looked at her sheepishly.

'All right, all right. I know. You hated him.'

'Hated who?' Jessica looked suddenly blank.

'The guy we introduced you to at dinner last night. I never realised he was that dull.'

'Well, he is, but that's not what I'm mad about, so forget it.' And then she looked up and saw Astrid's face, hurt and confused, like a child's. 'Oh, hell, Astrid, I'm sorry. I'm just in a stinking lousy mood. Everything has already gone wrong today. Schwartz called this morning.'

'What about?' Astrid's face instantly turned worried.

'Ian sold his book.'

'What's wrong with that?' The worry turned to confusion again.

'Nothing. Except he's trying to give me the money, and I don't want it, and it's a pain in the ass, that's all.' She poured herself a cup of coffee and sat down. But Astrid's face was grave now.

'Now you know how he used to feel. Taking your money.'

'What does that mean?'

'Just what it sounded like. Sometimes it's easier to give than it is to take.'

'You sound like your mother.'

'I could do worse.'

Jessie nodded and walked into her office. She stayed there until lunchtime.

Astrid knocked on the closed door at twelve-thirty. A smile was struggling to escape her serious face . . . wait till Jessie saw it! She forced her features back into an expression of official business and looked almost sombre when Jessie opened the door.

'What's up?'

'We have a problem, Jessica.'

'Can't you take care of it? I'm just checking the invoices.'

'I'm sorry, Jessica, but I simply can't handle this.'

'Terrific.' Jessie threw her pen on the desk behind her and walked into the main room. Astrid watched her nervously. She had signed for it. Maybe Jessie would kill her, but she didn't care. She owed that much to Ian.

Jessie looked around. There was no one in the shop but Katsuko, busy on the phone. 'So? Who's here? What's the problem?' She was beginning to look extremely annoyed.

'It's a delivery, Jessie. Outside. They made a big fuss about not unloading inside. Said something about not having to do anything more than make sidewalk deliveries, muttered about the waybill, and drove off.'

'Damn them! We hassled that out with them last month, and I told them that if . . .' She yanked open the door and stalked outside, her eyes blazing, checking the sidewalk for their delivery. And then she saw it. Parked in the driveway where Astrid's Jaguar had been a little while earlier.

It was a sleek little racing green Morgan with black trim and red leather seats. The top was down. It was a beauty, and in even better condition than her old Morgan had been. Jessica looked stunned for a moment, and then looked at Astrid and started to cry. She knew it was from Ian.

CHAPTER XXX

With Astrid badgering her day and night, she decided to keep it. 'As a favour to him.' She wouldn't admit how much she loved it, and she still wouldn't open his letters.

In June she decided to take a five-day vacation and go down to visit Aunt Beth at the ranch.

'Hell, Astrid, I've earned it. It'll do me good.' She was vaguely embarrassed about going but she wasn't sure why.

'Don't make excuses to me. I'm taking three weeks off in July.' Astrid was flying to Europe with her beau, but she was loath to discuss it. She kept her affairs very private, even from Jessie. Jessie wondered if maybe she was afraid things would fall through.

Jessica left early on a Wednesday afternoon in the Morgan, in high spirits, her hair flying out behind her. Aunt Beth had been delighted to hear she was coming.

'Well, well, you have a new car, I see. Very pretty.' She had heard Jessica drive up on the gravel, and had come out to meet her. The sun was setting over the hills.

'It was a present from Ian. He sold his book.'

'Very handsome present. And how are you, dear?' She hugged Jessica fondly, and the younger woman bent to kiss her cheek. Their hands found each other and held tightly. They were equally pleased to see each other.

'I couldn't be better, Aunt Beth. And you look wonderful!'

'Older by the hour. And meaner too, I've been told.' They chuckled happily and walked into the house arm in arm.

The house looked the same as it had two months before, and Jessica let a sigh escape her as she looked around.

'I feel like I'm home.' She looked at Aunt Beth from across the room, and found her own face being carefully searched by the other woman's piercing blue eyes.

'How have you really been, Jessica? Astrid says very little, and your letters tell me even less. I've wondered how things worked out. Cup of tea?' Jessica nodded and Aunt Beth poured her a cup of Earl Grey.

'I've been fine. I filed for a divorce when I went back, but I told you that in my first letter.'

Aunt Beth nodded expressionlessly, waiting for more. 'Do you regret it?'

Jessica hesitated for only a split second before answering and then shook her head. 'No, I don't. But I regret the past a great deal of the time, more than I like to admit. I seem to find myself hashing it over, reliving it, thinking back to "if only" this and "if only" that. It seems so pointless.' She looked sad as she set down the cup of tea and looked up at Aunt Beth.

'It is pointless, my dear. And there is nothing more painful than looking back at happy times that no longer are. Or just simply old times. Do you hear from him?'

'Yes, in a way.' Jessica tried to look vague.

'What does that mean?'

'It means he writes to me and I tear his letters up and throw them away.' Aunt Beth raised an eyebrow.

'Before or after you read them?'

'Before. I don't open them.' She felt foolish and averted her eyes from the old woman's.

'Are you afraid of his letters, Jessica?'

To Aunt Beth she could tell the truth. She nodded slowly.

'Yes. I'm afraid of recriminations and pleas and poems and words that are perfectly designed to sound the way he knows I want to hear them. It's too late for that. It's over. Done with. I did the right thing, and I won't hash it over with him. I've seen other people do that, and there's no point. He'd only make me feel guilty.'

'You do that to yourself. But you know, you make me wonder. If he weren't in prison, would you still be pressing for this divorce?'

'I don't know. Maybe eventually it would have come to this anyway.'

'But aren't you rather taking advantage of his situation, Jessica? If he were free, he could force you to discuss it with him. Now all he can do is write, and you won't give him the courtesy of reading his letters. I'm not sure if that's rude, or cowardly, or simply unkind.' They were harsh words, but her eyes said she meant them. 'And I also don't understand about the car. You said he gave you the new car. You accepted that . . . but not his letters?' Jessica flinched at the inference.

'That's Astrid's fault. She said that I owed it to him to keep it. He wanted to pay me back the money I put out for the trial, and I wouldn't accept the cheque from our attorney. So Ian had him buy me the car. And I assume he kept the rest of the money.'

'And you didn't thank him for the car?' She sounded every bit a mother. What? No thank-you note to your hostess? Jessica almost laughed.

'No, I didn't.'

'I see. And what now?'

'Nothing. The divorce will be final in three months. And that'll be that.'

'And you'll never see him again?' Aunt Beth looked doubtful, but Jessica shook her head firmly. 'I think you'll regret it, Jessica. One needs to say good-bye. If you don't, in a satisfactory way, you never quite get all the splinters out of your soul. It might trouble you more like this. You can't really wash seven years out of your life without saying good-bye. Or can you? Well, you seem to have made up your mind, in any event.' She sat watching Jessica's bent head as the younger woman played with the calico cat. 'You have made up your mind, haven't you?' She was determined to get at the truth, if only for Jessie's sake.

'I . . . yes, well . . . oh, damn. I don't know, Aunt Beth. Sometimes I just don't know. I've made up my mind, and I'll go through with it, but now and then, I . . . oh, I suppose it's just regret.'

'Maybe not, child. Maybe it's doubt. Maybe you don't really want to divorce him.'

'I do . . . but . . . but I miss him so awfully. I miss the way we know each other. He's the only person in the whole world who really knows me. And I know him just as well. I miss that. And I miss what we used to dream, what I thought we once were, what I wanted him to be. Maybe I didn't even know him, though. Maybe I only think I did. Maybe he cheated on me all the time. Maybe that woman was his girlfriend, and she accused him of rape because she was mad about something else. Maybe he hated me for paying the bills, or maybe that's why he stayed married to me. I just don't know anything anymore. Except that I miss him. But it could just be that what I'm missing never even existed.'

'Why don't you ask him? Don't you think he'd tell you the truth now? Or is it that you're afraid he might indeed tell you the truth?'

'Maybe that. Maybe the truth is something I'd never want to hear.'

'So you'll keep tearing up letters and make sure you never do. And what'll you do when he gets out? Move to another town and change your name?' Jessica laughed at the preposterous suggestion.

'Maybe by then he won't want to talk to me either.' But she didn't sound as though she believed it.

'Don't count on it. But more important, Jessica, do you realize what you're saying? You're saying that the man probably never loved you, that there was nothing about you he loved except your ability to pay his bills. Isn't that it?'

'Maybe.' But her eyes grew sullen. She had had enough of the painful probing. 'What difference does it make now?'

'All the difference in the world. It means the difference between knowing you were loved, and thinking you were used. And what if he did use you, if he loved you too? Didn't you use him too, Jessica? Most people who love each other do, and not necessarily in a bad way. It's part of the arrangement, to fulfil each other's needs—financial, emotional, whatever.'

'I never thought of it that way. And the funny thing is

that I always thought I was using him. Ian's not afraid to be alone. I always was. I felt so lost without my family after they all died. I had no one except Ian. I could make all the decisions in the world, do anything I wanted, be proud of myself . . . as long as I had Ian. He kept me propped up so I could go on fooling the world, and myself, that I was such tough stuff. I used him for that, but I never thought he knew it.' She looked almost ashamed to admit it.

'And what if he did know it? So what? It's no sin to have weaknesses, or to use the strength of the person you love. As long as you don't use it unkindly. And what about now? Are you stronger?'

'Stronger than I thought.'

'And happy?' That was the crux of it.

She hesitated and then shook her head. 'No. I'm not. My life is so . . . so empty, Aunt Beth. So dead. Sometimes I feel as if I have nothing to live for. For what? For myself? To get dressed up every morning and changed at six o'clock at night? To go out with some idiot stranger with bad breath and no soul? To water my plants? What am I living for? A boutique I don't give a damn about anymore? . . . What?' Aunt Beth waved a hand and she stopped.

'I can't bear it, Jessica. You sound just the way Astrid used to. And it's all nonsense. You have everything to live for, with or without young men with bad breath. But at your age, above all you have *yourself* to live for. You have it all ahead of you. You have youth. And look at me, I still find things to live for, many things, and not just begrudgingly. I thoroughly enjoy my life, even at my age.'

'Then I envy you. I wake up in the morning and I honestly wonder why sometimes. The rest of the time I just keep moving like a robot. But what in hell do I have?'

'You have what you are.'

'And what's that? A thirty-one-year-old divorced woman who owns a boutique, half a house, several plants, and a sports car. I have no children, no husband, no family, no one who loves me and no one to love. Jesus, why bother?' There were hot tears filling her eyes as she continued.

'Then find someone to love, Jessica. Haven't you tried?

Other than the soulless ones with bad breath.' Aunt Beth's eyes twinkled and Jessica laughed tearfully and then shrugged.

'You should see what's around. They're awful.' The tears started to creep down her cheeks now. 'They're really just awful. And ... no one knows me.' She closed her eyes tightly on the last words, and bent her head.

'That's what Astrid used to say, Jessica, and now look at her.' Aunt Beth walked around the back of Jessica's chair and gently stroked her hair. 'She's flapping around like a schoolgirl, pretending to be "discreet", and having a marvellous time. She's about as discreet as the sunrise. But I'm glad for her. She's finally happy. She's found someone, and so will you, my dear. It takes time.'

'How much time?' Jessie felt twelve years old again, asking the impossible of an all-knowing parent.

'That's up to you.'

'But *how*? *How*?' Jessie turned in her seat to look up at Aunt Beth. 'They're all so awful. Young men who think they're terrific and want to go to bed with you and every woman on the street, who want to leave their track shoes on the dining-room table, and their drug stash in your house. They make you feel like a parking meter. They put a dime in and come around later ... maybe ... if they remember where they parked you. They make me feel like a nameless nothing. And the older men aren't much better; they're all out proving they're macho and pretending to love women's lib because it's expected ... but Ian never was ... oh, hell. It all bores me to tears. Everything does. The people I know bore me, and the people I don't know bore me. And ...' She knew she was whining, but she didn't sound bored as much as she sounded frantic.

'Jessie, darling, *you* bore *me*. With garbage like that. All right, you need a change. Let's agree on that much. Then why not leave San Francisco for a while? Have you thought of that?' Jessie nodded sorrowfully, and Aunt Beth gave her the look she reserved only for very spoiled children. 'Are you thinking of going back to New York?'

'No ... I don't know. That would be worse. Maybe the mountains or the beach, or the country. Something like that. Aunt Beth, I'm so tired of people.' She sat back with a sigh, dried her face, and stretched her legs. Aunt Beth was looking annoyed.

'Oh, shut up. Do you know what your problem is, Jessica? You're spoiled rotten. You had a husband who adored you and made you feel like a woman, and a very loved woman at that, and you had a boutique you enjoyed, and a home that you both shared and seemed to have enjoyed too. Well, by your own choice, you no longer have the husband, and you've squeezed all you can from that shop, and maybe the house has served its usefulness too. So get rid of it. All of it. And start afresh. I did when I got my divorce, and I was sixty-seven. Jessica, if I can do it, so can you. I came out from the East, bought this ranch, met new people, and I've had a wonderful time since. And if in five years it begins to bore me, then I'll close up shop, sell, and do something else, if I'm still alive. But if I *am* alive, then I'll *be* alive. Not living here half dead and no longer interested in what I'm doing. So, what are you going to do now? It's time you did *something*!' The old woman's eyes blazed.

'I've been thinking of getting rid of the shop, but I can't sell the house. It's half Ian's.'

'Then why not rent it?'

It was a thought. The idea had never occurred to her before. And she was a little bit shocked at what she had just said. Sell the shop? When had she thought of that? Or had she been thinking of it all along? The words had just slipped out.

'I'll have to think it all out.'

'This is a good place to do it, Jessica. I'm glad you came down.'

'So am I. I'd be lost without you.' She went to her side and gave her a hug. Aunt Beth was becoming a mainstay to her.

'Are you hungry yet?'

'I'm getting that way.'

'Good. We can burn dinner together.'

They made hamburgers and artichokes with hollandaise sauce, a favourite of Aunt Beth's, and this time they neither burned nor curdled the sauce. It was a delightful meal and they sat up until almost midnight, speaking of easier subjects than those they had covered before dinner.

Jessica stretched out on the bed in her now familiar pink room and watched the fire glow and flicker as the old calico cat settled down next to her. It was good to be back. It really did feel like home. This was one place she was not tired of.

Aunt Beth was out riding when Jessie arose the next morning, and there was a note in the kitchen explaining which horse she could ride if she chose to. She had learned the terrain well enough the time before to handle a ride in the hills on her own now.

Shortly after eleven, she set off on a pleasant chestnut mare. She wore a wide-brimmed straw hat and had tucked a book and an apple into a small saddlebag. She felt like being alone for a while, and this was a perfect way to do it. After a half hour's ride, she found a small stream and tied the horse to the limb of a tree. The mare didn't seem to object, and Jessie took off her boots and went wading. She laughed as she sang songs to herself and unbuttoned her cuffs to roll up her sleeves. She felt freer than she had in as long as she could remember. It was then that she saw the man watching her.

She looked up with a start and he smiled an apology. It was frightening to suddenly see someone in what she thought was her own private wilderness, but he was tall and very well dressed in a fawn-coloured riding habit. He spoke gently, and with a British accent.

'I'm sorry. I meant to say something earlier, but you looked so happy, I hated to spoil your fun.' She was suddenly glad she hadn't taken off her shirt, which she had been considering.

'Am I trespassing?' She stood barefoot in the stream, one sleeve rolled up, and her hair loosely tied in a knot on top of her head. To him, she looked like a vision. A golden-haired Greek goddess in modern riding dress. One didn't see many women like that—not here in the 'provinces'. Lost on a hillside, barefoot in a stream. It was like a scene in an eighteenth-century painting, and it made him want to walk down and touch her. Kiss her perhaps. The thought made him smile again as she watched him.

'No, I fear I'm the trespasser. I came out for a ride this morning, and I'm not very familiar with the territory, property boundaries and the like. I daresay I'm intruding.' The accent was pure public-school English. Eton, perhaps. The alleged 'intruder' was every inch a gentleman. And as she looked at him, it struck her how much he resembled Ian. He was taller, a little broader, but the face . . . the eyes . . . the tilt of the head . . . his hair was very blonde, blonder than Jessie's. But still there was something of Ian about him, enough to haunt her. She looked away from him and sat down to put on her boots, carefully rolling her sleeves down first. While the unknown man continued to watch her with a small smile.

'You needn't leave because of me. I have to get home now in any case. But tell me, do you live here?' She shook her head slowly, unpinned her hair, and looked up at him. He was very good-looking.

'No, I'm a houseguest.'

'Really? So am I.' He mentioned the name of the people he was staying with, but she didn't recall having heard Aunt Beth mention them. 'Will you be down here long?'

'A few days. Then I'll have to get back.'

'To?' He was very inquisitive. Almost annoyingly so, except that he was so damned good-looking.

'San Francisco. I live there.' She had avoided the next question, and now it was her turn. Why not? 'And you?' The idea of questioning him amused her.

'I live in Los Angeles. But I'll be moving to San Francisco within the month, actually.' She almost giggled as she listened to him. He sounded like all the imitations she'd ever heard of stuffy Englishmen. He was *sooo* British, standing there on a hilltop in his impeccable riding habit and flicking a riding crop across his palm. He was really quite something.

'Did I say something funny?'

'No, sir.' With a half smile, she started up the hill toward him. Her horse was tied quite close to where he stood.

'My firm is transferring me to San Francisco. I came out

from London three years ago, and I've had enough of L.A.'

'You'll like San Francisco; it's a wonderful town.' It was a totally mad conversation between two strangers in the middle of nowhere; they were behaving as though they were on Fifth Avenue, or Union Street, or the Faubourg St. Honoré. She burst into laughter as she found herself standing next to him.

'I seem to have a way of amusing you without intending to.'

She smiled again and shrugged gently. 'Lots of things do that.'

'I see.' He held out a hand to her then and looked rather solemn, but the smile still danced in his eyes. 'How do you do? I'm Geoffrey Bates.'

'Hello. I'm Jessica Clarke.' Standing under the tree, they shook hands and she smiled at him again. At close range, he didn't look quite so much like Ian. But he was very pretty in his own right, Mr. Geoffrey Bates from London. And he was thinking how much he liked the way she looked when she smiled. And she seemed as though she did that a lot.

He hesitated for a moment before asking her the next question, but he finally gave in. He wanted to know.

'Where are you staying, by the way?' By the way? It made Jessica smile again and then laugh.

'With the mother of a friend.' She was vague, and he smiled as he raised an eyebrow.

'And you won't tell me who? I promise not to disgrace you and appear uninvited to dinner.'

She laughed back and felt silly, but the Englishman's face had grown serious. He had just realized that she might well be travelling with a man. That would be awkward. He had looked at her left hand almost instantly and been relieved to see it bare of rings, especially plain gold ones. But he hadn't looked closely enough to see the little worn ridge or the slightly paler strip where she had worn her wedding band for seven years before removing it a few months before.

'I'm staying with Mrs. Bethanie Williams.'

'I believe I've heard someone mention her name.' He looked enormously relieved. 'Leg up?' She was standing next to her horse as he asked, and she turned to him with a look of amusement.

'Hardly. But should I say yes?' She thought she saw him blush as she swung easily into the saddle. It was a foolish question to ask someone as tall as she was, but then she noticed his height. He was at least four or five inches taller than Ian . . . six five? Six six? Not even Ian was that tall . . . 'not even' . . . why did she still think of him that way? As though he were the ultimate man. The paragon of perfection to which all other men would always be compared, in her mind.

'May I call you at Mrs. Williams'?' Jessica nodded, cautious again. This was certainly an unusual way to meet a man, and she really had no idea who or what he was.

'I won't be here for very long.'

'Then I'll have to call you soon, won't I?' Persistent bastard, aren't you? She smiled again, wondering. But he didn't look like a bastard. He looked like a nice man. Somewhere in his mid-thirties, with gentle grey eyes and soft silky hair. And the clothes he wore looked expensive. He was also wearing a small gold ring on the smallest finger of his right hand; she thought she could see a crest etched into the gold, but she didn't want to stare. Everything about him looked formal and elegant. With his jodhpurs we was wearing polished black boots and a soft blue shirt with a stock. His fawn-coloured tweed jacket hung from a branch and he looked a bit odd in the rugged setting, but at the same time incredibly beautiful. Better and better as she watched him. Which was precisely how he felt about her, although Jessica had begun to wonder how dishevelled her hair looked.

'Nice to meet you.' She prepared to ride off with a smile and a wave.

'You didn't answer my question.' He held her horse's bridle as he watched Jessica's eyes. She knew what he meant. And she liked his style.

'Yes. You can call me.' He stepped back in silence and, with a dazzling smile, swept her a bow. She liked that about him too. His smile. And she laughed to herself as she rode off towards the ranch.

CHAPTER XXXI

'Have a nice ride, dear?'

'Very. And I met a very strange man.'

'Really? Who?' Aunt Beth looked intrigued. Strange men were few and far between around the ranch, except an odd foreman here and there.

'He's someone's houseguest, and terribly British. But he's also very nice-looking.'

Aunt Beth smiled at the look on her face. 'Well, well. A tall, dark, handsome stranger on my ranch? Good heavens! Where is he? And how old?'

Jessica giggled. 'I saw him first. And besides, he's not dark. He's blonde, and a lot taller than I am.'

'Then he's yours, my dear. I never did like tall men.'

'I adore them.'

Aunt Beth looked over the top of her reading glasses with careful solemnity. 'You haven't much choice.' They both laughed again and enjoyed a blazing sunset over the hills.

It was another peaceful evening, and Jessica was up at seven the next day. She had a craving to wander, but this time not on the chestnut mare. She made herself a cup of coffee—for once up before Aunt Beth was—and took off as quietly as she could in the Morgan. She had never driven much around there, and she had been itching to explore.

The sun was high in the sky when she found it. And it was in very sad shape. But it was a beauty. It looked as though someone had lost it in the tall grass and then tired of looking for it, decades before. And now there it sat, alone and unloved, with a FOR RENT sign listing badly to one side just beyond the front steps. It was a small but perfectly proportioned Victorian house. She tried the front door, but it was locked. And Jessica found herself sitting on the front steps fanning her face with her large-brimmed straw hat, smiling. She wasn't sure why, but she felt good. And incredibly happy.

She drove home at fifty on the dusty country road and strode into the house with a grin. Aunt Beth was checking her mail and looked up, surprised.

'Well, where have you been? You left awfully early.' There was mischief in the old woman's blue eyes, and delighted suspicion.

'Wait till you hear what I've found!'

'Another man on my land? And this time a Frenchman! I knew it. Dear girl, you're having delusions from the sun.' Aunt Beth clucked sympathetically and Jessica burst into laughter and tossed her hat high in the air.

'No, not a man! Aunt Beth, it's a house! An incredible, beautiful, marvellous, Victorian house! And I'm madly in love with it.'

'Oh God, Jessie, not the one I think it is? The old Wheeling house out on the North Road?' She knew exactly which one.

'I haven't the vaguest idea, I just know that I love it.'

'And you've bought it, and your decorator is due in from New York first thing tomorrow morning.' Aunt Beth refused to be serious.

'No. I mean it. It's lovely. Did you ever stand back and look at it? I did, for an hour this morning, and I sat on the front steps for almost as long. What's it like inside? It was locked, dammit. I even tried all the windows.'

'God only knows what it looks like inside. No one's lived in it for almost fifteen years. Actually, it used to be very lovely, but it hasn't much land, so no one will buy it. You could probably get more land with it now, though, because the Parkers behind there just decided that they want to sell off a very nice parcel. Almost forty acres, if I remember correctly. But as far as I know, the Wheeling place just sits there empty. Year after year. The realty people showed it to me when I came down to buy the ranch, but I had no interest in the place. Too much house, too little land, and I wanted something more modern. Why on earth would you want a Victorian house out in the middle of nowhere?'

'But Aunt Beth, it's so beautiful!' Jessica looked young and romantic as she smiled at her friend.

'Ah, the illusions of youth. Maybe you have to be young

and in love to want a house like that. I wanted something more practical-looking. But I can see why you liked it.' She was noticing the brightness in her young friend's green eyes. 'Jessica, what exactly do you have in mind?' Her voice was quiet and serious now.

'I don't know yet. But I'm thinking. About a lot of different things. Maybe they're all crazy ideas, but something's brewing.' Jessica looked decidedly pleased with herself. It had been a marvellous morning, and something wonderful had happened in her head or her heart, she wasn't sure which, but she felt alive and excited and brand new again. It was crazy, really. A Bible passage that she had once learned in Sunday school had come to mind as she sat looking at the house. 'Behold, old things are passed away. All things are become new.' She had kept thinking of that, and she knew it was true. All the old things were drifting out of her life . . . even the horror of the trial . . . even Ian . . .

'Well, Jessie, let me know what you come up with when everything's "brewed". Or before that, if I can help.'

'Not just yet. But maybe later.' Aunt Beth nodded and went back to her mail and Jessie headed up the stairs, humming to herself. And then she stopped and looked back at Aunt Beth. 'How would I go about seeing the inside of that house?'

'Call the realtors. They'll be thrilled. I don't suppose they get to show the place more than once every five years. Just look them up in the book. Hoover County Realty. Terribly original name.' Aunt Beth was beginning to wonder . . . but she couldn't take Jessie seriously. This must be a passing fancy, a mood. But it would keep Jessie amused. Just thinking of something other than her own boredom would do her good. One thing was certain—she hadn't looked bored when she'd come in. Not that morning. And certainly not the evening before.

Geoffrey Bates telephoned that afternoon while Jessie was out, and he called again around five, just when she got back. He politely inquired if he could 'come around' for a drink, or bring her over to meet the people where he was staying. Jessie opted to have him for drinks at Aunt Beth's. And she was in high spirits.

He was terribly charming, very amusing, very proper, and quite taken with Aunt Beth, which pleased Jessie. But he was even more taken with Jessie, which pleased Beth. He looked even more splendid than Jessie had warned, in a blazer and ivory gabardine slacks, a Wedgewood blue shirt, and a navy ascot at his neck. Terribly elegant, but also very appealing. And they made a spectacular couple, both tall and blonde, with a natural grace. They would have turned heads anywhere, just as they looked sitting easily in the living room at the ranch.

'I rode the hills in search of you today, Jessica, and all in vain. Where were you hiding?'

'In a house with a bathtub four feet deep and a kitchen straight out of a museum.'

'Playing Goldilocks, I presume. Did the three bears come home before you left, and how was the porridge?'

'Delightful.' She laughed at him and blushed slightly when he reached for her hand. But he held it for only a second.

'I thought you were an apparition yesterday on the hills. You looked like a goddess.'

'Aunt Beth accused me of delusions from the sun.'

'Yes, but she didn't think she'd seen a god, at least.' Aunt Beth cut him down to size just to see how he'd take it, but he took it well. He was very gracious, and left them shortly before dinner, having invited them both to join him at his hosts' for lunch the next day. Aunt Beth excused herself on the grounds that she would have business to attend to on the ranch, but Jessica accepted with pleasure. He drove off in a chocolate brown Porsche, and Jessica looked up with a girlish gleam in her eyes.

'Well, what do you think?'

'Too tall by far.' Aunt Beth tried to look stern, but instantly failed as her face broke into a grin. 'But otherwise, I heartily approve. He's perfectly lovely, Jessica! Simply lovely.' Aunt Beth sounded almost as excited as Jessie herself felt. She was trying to fight it, but with difficulty.

'He is nice, isn't he?' She looked dreamy for a moment and then pirouetted on one foot. 'But he's not as nice as my house.'

'Jessica, you confuse me! I'm too old for such games! What house? And how dare you compare a man like that to a house?'

'Easily, because I'm mean. And I'm talking about *my* house. The one I rented today, for the whole summer!'

Aunt Beth's face grew serious at the news. 'You rented the Wheeling house for the summer, Jessica?'

'Yes. And if I like it, I'll stay longer. Aunt Beth, I'm happy down here, and you were right, it is time for a change.'

'Yes, child. But to something like this? This is a life for an old woman, not for you. You can't lock yourself up in the country. Who will you talk to? What will you do?'

'I'll talk to you, and I'll start to paint again. I haven't done that in years, and I love it. I might even paint you.'

'Jessica, Jessica! Always so flighty! You worry me at times. Last time you leapt to your feet and ran home to get a divorce, and now what are you doing? Please, dear, think this over with care.'

'I have, and I am, and I will. I only rented it for the summer. And we'll see after that. It's not a permanent move. I'll try it. The only permanent decision I've come to is to sell the shop.'

'Good God, you have been busy. Are you sure about all this?' Aunt Beth was more than slightly taken aback. She'd suggested selling the shop, but she hadn't thought Jessica would take her seriously. What had she done?'

'I'm absolutely sure. I'm going to sell Lady J to Astrid, or offer it to her, anyway, when I go back.'

'And she'll buy it. You can be sure of that, Jessica. I can't say I'm sorry. I think it would be good for her. But won't you be sorry? The boutique seems to mean a lot to you, dear.'

'It did, but it's a part of the past now. A part I have to get rid of. I don't think I'll regret it.'

'I hope not.' There was a change in the air again; they both sensed it. But for the first time in a long time, Jessie felt alive, and not in the least bored.

'Is the house livable?'

'More or less, with a good scrub. A very good scrub.'

'What will you do about furniture?'

'Live in a sleeping bag.' She didn't look at all perturbed.

'Don't be ridiculous. I have some spare furniture out in the shed, and more in the attic. Help yourself. At least you'll be comfortable.'

'And happy.'

'Jessie ... I hope so. And please try not to do anything major too quickly. Take your time. Think. Weigh your decisions.'

'Is that what you do?'

Aunt Beth couldn't stifle her mirth at the question. 'No. But it's the sort of advice old women are supposed to give young girls. I always rush in and do what I want, and mend fences later. And to tell you the truth, I'll love having you down here for the summer.' The older woman smiled gently and Jessica grew pensive.

'And what if I stay after the summer?'

'Oh, I'll close my doors to you and shoot at you from the kitchen windows. What do you suppose I'd do? Be delighted, of course. But I won't encourage you to move down here for my sake. I don't even do that to Astrid.' But she didn't really think Jessie would move down; by the end of the summer she'd be tired of the lack of excitement ... and the Englishman who was moving to San Francisco looked very promising.

He came to take Jessie to lunch the next day, and she returned to Aunt Beth's in high spirits. She had liked his friends, and they had been delighted at the prospect of her moving down for the summer, and had extended an invitation to drop in on them anytime she liked. They were a couple in their fifties who invited friends up often from L.A. Geoffrey was among them ...

'I see I'm going to be spending a lot of time here this summer.' he'd said.

'Oh?'

'Yes, and it's a damn long drive down from San Francisco. You could have picked someplace closer for your summer haunt, Jessica.' She had not yet mentioned to him that she was thinking of moving down for good. She'd laughed up into his eyes as he'd handed her out of his car at Aunt Beth's. 'Speaking of which, Miss Clarke, when are you going back to the city?'

'Tomorrow.' But the 'Miss' Clarke had unnerved her ... Miss? It had sounded so strange. So ... so empty.

'I'm going back to L.A. tomorrow too. But as a matter of fact—' he'd looked down at her almost slyly, and definitely pleased with himself—'I'm planning to be in San Francisco on Wednesday. How about dinner?'

'I'd love it.'

'So would I.' He'd looked surprisingly serious as they'd walked towards the house, and he'd quietly slipped his hand around hers.

CHAPTER XXXII

Astrid was stunned by Jessica's offer, but she leapt at the idea. She had wanted to buy the boutique since the first time she'd seen it.

'But are you sure?'

'Positive. Take it. I'll give you an idea of what the inventory's worth, talk to my attorney, and we'll come up with a price.' She spoke to Philip Wald and two days later they set a price. Astrid didn't hesitate.

She asked her own attorneys to have the papers drawn up. Lady J would become hers for the sum of eighty-five thousand dollars. Both she and Jessie were pleased with the price. The only twinge Jessica felt was at the mention of Astrid's changing the name of the boutique to Lady A. At least it would sound almost the same to their clients. But it wouldn't be the same anymore. It would be Astrid's. The end of an era had finally come.

They were sitting in the back office discussing plans for the sale when Katsuko appeared in the doorway with a smile on her face.

'There's someone here to see you, Jessie. Someone very pretty to look at, I might add.'

'Oh?' She poked her head out of the door and saw

Geoffrey. 'Oh! Hello.' She beckoned him into the office, and introduced him to Astrid, explaining that Mrs. Williams was her mother.

'You know my mother?' Astrid was surprised. Her mother didn't know anyone like Geoffrey.

'I had the pleasure of meeting her this weekend, at the ranch.' Astrid's eyebrows shot up as she cast a look of surprise at Jessica, and Geoffrey added quickly, 'I was down there visiting friends.' And suddenly Astrid's face said that she understood why Jessica was planning to spend the summer down there, in her creaking rented Victorian house. Astrid almost wondered if that was why she was selling the shop. But she felt as though she had missed a piece of the story somehow. Had Jessica been keeping secrets? She looked over to see Geoffrey looking at Jessica warmly. And Astrid restrained the questions on the tip of her lips. How? When? What next? Did he . . . was he . . . would he . . . He broke into her thoughts with another blistering smile.

'May I invite you two lovely ladies to lunch?' He even managed gently to encompass Katsuko with a look of regret; he knew someone would have to stay home, to mind the store. His manners were impeccable. And Astrid liked that. She was almost tempted into lunch, out of curiosity, but she didn't want to do that to Jessie. But Jessica was quick to shake her head about lunch.

'Don't even tempt us, Geoffrey. We were just discussing some business matters, about the sale of the shop, and . . .'

'Oh, for heaven's sake, Jessica!' Astrid broke in on Jessie's conscientious protests. 'Don't be silly—we can talk business later. I have some errands to do anyway. I have to go downtown—' she looked sorrowfully at Geoffrey—'but you two go ahead and have a nice lunch. I'll meet you back here around two or two-thirty.'

'Make it two-thirty, Mrs. Bonner.' Geoffrey was quick to step in. And Jessica sat back and watched. She liked the way he dealt with things. He was used to wielding power and it showed. It made her feel safe, but not threatened. Now that she didn't need to be taken care of, his attentions were a luxury, not a life-giving plasma. She was enjoying the difference, and found herself wondering what it would have been like with Ian, had her needs not been so desperate, had she been more sure of herself. But she brushed the thought from her mind.

They had lunch nearby, in a garden restaurant on Union Street, and it was a very pleasant meal. He had a passion for horses, and flew his own plane, was planning a trip to Africa the following winter, and had gone to Cambridge, after Eton. And it was clear that he was very taken with Jessie. And every time he smiled that magnificent smile of his, she melted.

'I must say, Jessica, you look very different up here, in town.'

'It's amazing what a difference it makes when I comb my hair.' They both smiled at the memory of their first meeting. 'I even wear shoes around here.'

'Do you? How refreshing. Let me take a look.' He teasingly swept aside the tablecloth to glance at her feet, and saw a very handsome pair of cinnamon suede Gucci shoes. They were almost exactly the colour of the suede skirt she had on with a salmon silk blouse. The salmon shade was Ian's favourite colour, and she had had to force herself to put it on this morning. So what if it was Ian's favourite? That was no reason to give it up. She hadn't worn the blouse in months, as though by not doing so she were somehow renouncing him. Now it seemed foolish.

'I approve of your shoes. And by the way, that's a very handsome blouse.' She blushed at the compliment, mostly because it reminded her of Ian. There was something about Geoffrey . . .

'What were you just thinking?' He had glimpsed a shadow passing rapidly across her eyes.

'Nothing.'

'Shame on you, telling lies. Something serious crossed your mind. Something sad?" It had looked that way.

'Of course not.' She was embarrassed that he had seen so much. Too much. He was very observant.

'Have you never been married, Jessie? It seemed remarkable to have the good fortune to find a woman like you, free and unattached. Or am I making assumptions?' But he had wanted to know ever since he'd met her.

'You're making the right assumptions. I'm free and unattached. And yes, I was married.' His timing was amazing, as thought he had read her mind.

'Any children?' He raised an eyebrow with a curious air.

'No. None.'

'Good.'

'Good?' It was an odd thing to say. 'You don't like children, Geoffrey?'

'Very much. Other people's.' He smiled without embarrassment. 'In fact, I'm a perfectly marvellous uncle. But I'd make a perfectly terrible father.'

'What makes you say that?'

'I move about too much. I'm too selfish. When I love a woman, I detest sharing her in any major way, and if you're going to be a proper mother, you've got to spread yourself pretty thin between husband and offspring. Perhaps I'm too much a child myself, but I want to enjoy long romantic evenings, unexpected trips to Paris, skiing in Switzerland without three little runny-noses crying in the car . . . I can give you a thousand dreadful, horribly selfish reasons. But all of them honest. Does that shock you?' He didn't apologise for what he was saying, but he was willing to accept that she might not approve. He had long since stopped making excuses. In fact, he had seen to it that there was no longer a possibility of a 'slip'. He had made up his mind, and now there was no question of it.

'No, it doesn't shock me. I've always felt that way myself. In fact, exactly that way.'

'But?'

'What do you mean?'

'There was a "but" in your voice.' He said it very softly, and she smiled. 'Was there? I'm not sure. I used to have very definite ideas on the subject. But I don't know . . . I've changed a lot.'

'Changing is natural if you've gotten divorced. But suddenly you find you want children? I should think you'd want permanent freedom.'

'Not necessarily. And I haven't made any grandiose policy changes about children either. I've just started asking myself a lot of questions.'

'Actually, Jessie—' he held her hand gently as he said it —'I rather think you'd be happier without children. You seem very much like me. Determined, free; you enjoy what you do; I somehow can't imagine you chucking all that for a little squally person in diapers.' She grinned at the thought.

'God.'

'Quite.' They laughed for a moment, and took a sip of their wine as the second batch of lunch customers began to arrive. They had already been sitting there for almost two hours. It was odd to be talking to him about children all of a sudden. She got the feeling that the subject was important to him, and he wanted to get it out of the way early. And he certainly shared all the views she'd held dear for a decade.

Jessica stretched her legs and finished her wine, wondering if she should get back to the shop, and then suddenly thinking that she must be keeping him from appointments too. But the time together was so pleasant, it was hard to bring it to an end.

'I'm going to Paris on business next week, Jessica. Is there anything I can bring you?'

'What a lovely thought. Paris.' Her eyes danced at the idea. Paris.

'Let's see ... you could bring me ... the Louvre ... Sacré-Coeur . . . the Café Flore . . . the Brasserie Lipp . . . the Champs Elysées ... oh, and the entire Faubourg St. Honoré.' She giggled at the thought of it.

'That's what I like. A woman who knows what she wants. As a matter of fact, how about coming with me?'

'Are you kidding?'

'I certainly am not. I'll only be gone for three or four days. You could get away for that long, couldn't you?' Yes, but with a total stranger? God only knew who he was.

'I've been meaning to go to New York for the shop, but now I don't need to, and ... Paris ... ?' She didn't know what to say. After all those jerks who had crawled all over her, here was a perfectly heavenly man, and he wanted to take her to Paris.

'We don't ...' He looked awkward but sweet. 'We don't

have to share the same room. If you'd be more comfortable . . .'

'Geoffrey! You're an angel. And stop it, or I'll wind up doing it and neglecting all the things I ought to do here. I'm very touched that you'd ask, but I really can't.'

'Well, let's wait and see. You might change your mind.'

Wow. Geoffrey was really quite amazing. Paris? She almost wanted to say yes, but . . . why not? Why the hell not? Paris? . . . God, it would be gorgeous, but . . . dammit, why did she feel as if she'd be cheating on Ian? What difference did it make now? She was free. He wouldn't even know. She never saw him anymore anyway. But . . . somehow . . . he was there . . . with a look of pain in his eyes, as though he didn't want her to go. She tried to shake his face from her mind, and smiled at Geoffrey.

'Thank you for the offer.'

'I do wish you'd come. See what I mean about enjoying impromptu trips? I love that sort of thing! Not much fun if you have to drag along a nanny and four brats, or leave them at home and feel guilty. Being an uncle is really much simpler. Have you any nieces or nephews?' She shook her head quietly. 'Brothers or sisters?'

'No. I had a brother, but he died in the war.'

Geoffrey looked puzzled for a moment. 'The second one, or Korea? In either case, he must have been quite a bit older.'

'No. Vietnam.'

'Of course. How stupid of me. How awful. Were you very close?' His pressure on her hand grew a trifle stronger, as though to support her. His thoughtfulness pleased her a great deal.

'Yes. We were very close. It did awful things to me when he died.' It was the first time she had ever been able to say that. The last few months had freed her in more ways than she knew.

'I'm sorry.'

She nodded and smiled. 'And how many brothers and sisters do you have?'

'Two sisters, and a very stuffy brother. My sisters are quite mad. But very amusing.'

'Do you still spend much time in Europe?'

'Quite a bit. A few days here, a few days there. I enjoy it very much that way. By the way, Jessica, shouldn't I be taking you back to the shop for your meeting with Astrid?'

'Christ. I forgot all about it. You're right!' She looked at her watch regretfully, and smiled at him again. It had been a lovely few hours.

'I've been keeping you from your appointments too, I suspect.'

'Yes, I . . .' But laughter took the place of seriousness and he looked at her with a mischievous smile. 'No, I didn't have a single appointment. I came up here entirely to see you.' He sat back in his chair and laughed at himself, as though very pleased.

'You did?' Jessica looked astonished.

'I most certainly did. I hope you don't mind.'

'No. I'm just surprised.' Very surprised, and a little taken aback. What did that mean? He had come up to see her . . . and the suggestion of the trip to Paris . . . dammit. Was he going to be like everyone else and expect to exchange a meal for her body?

'Oh, the look on your face, Jessica!'

'What look?' There was laughter and embarrassment in her voice. What if he really had known what she'd been thinking? He seemed to do that a lot.

'Would you like to know what look?'

'Okay. See if you can guess.' She might as well brazen it out.

'Well, if I tell you that I have a room at the Huntington, will you feel any better?'

'Oh! You!' She swatted him with her napkin. 'I was not . . . !'

'You were too!'

'I was too!'

They both laughed, and he slipped a large bill onto the waiter's plate and got up to help Jessica into her jacket.

'I apologise for my thoughts.' Jessica hung her head with a grin.

'You certainly ought to.' But he gave her a friendly

hug on their way out and they laughed and teased all the way back to the shop. Astrid was waiting for them with a relaxed smile when they got in. It pleased her to see Jessie happy again, and with a man.

'I'll leave you now to your meetings and your business and your whatever-it-is-you-do. And Jessica, what time shall I fetch you?'

'From here?' She looked surprised. It was strange to be taken care of again, escorted and assisted, picked up and brought back. She had missed it for so long, and now she didn't quite know how to handle it again. It was like coming back to shoes after months of bare feet.

'Would you rather I meet you after work?'

'Either way.' She looked at him happily, and for a moment neither of them spoke. She had been about to offer him her car, but she couldn't quite do that. Not . . . not the Morgan. She felt rotten for not offering it, but she couldn't.

'Why don't I give you time to go home and relax? May I pick you up there?' Since he already knew that she was a little bit skittish, they both laughed, but she nodded.

'That'll be fine.'

'Say at seven? Dinner at eight.'

'Super.' And then suddenly she had a thought. He was almost at the door of the shop, and she quickly walked toward him. 'You don't know San Francisco very well, do you?'

'Not very. But I expect I can find my way around.' He looked amused at her concern.

'How would you like a tour at the end of the day?'

'With you?'

'Of course.'

'That's a splendid idea.'

'Great. Where will you be around five?'

'Anywhere you say.'

'All right. I'll pick you up outside the St. Francis Hotel at five. Okay?'

'Very much so.'

He gave her a quick salute and ran quickly down the steps of the shop as Jessica turned back to Astrid.

Somehow she had a hard time keeping her mind on what they were saying as they discussed the sale of Lady J.

'Right, Jessie?'

'Huh?' Astrid was grinning at her when she looked up. 'Oh, shit.'

'Don't tell me you're falling in love.'

'Nothing like it. But he's a very nice man. Isn't he?' She wanted Astrid's approval.

'He looks like it, Jessie.'

Jessica looked up at her friend and giggled like a schoolgirl. It seemed hours before they had their business settled, although both women were pleased with the results. Jessica got up jubilantly from her desk, pirouetted on one heel of the pretty Gucci shoes, and looked at her watch.

'And now, I have to go.' She picked up her bag, blew Astrid a kiss, and paused happily at the door for a moment. 'In fifteen minutes I have to pick up Ian.' With a rapid wave she was out the door and down the steps—without ever realising what she had said. Astrid shook her head and wondered if she'd ever get over him. More than that, she wondered how Ian was doing. She missed him. And thinking of him threw a damper on her excitement about Jessie's new friend.

Jessie was already backing out of the drive and on her way to meet Geoffrey.

CHAPTER XXXIII

'Am I late?' She looked worried as she pulled up in front of the St. Francis. She had run into unexpected traffic on the way downtown. But he looked happy and relaxed, like a man who is looking forward to seeing someone, not like a man who has been kept waiting.

'Oh, I've been here for hours.'

'Liar.'

'Heavens! What an outrageous thing to call a man!' But he looked delighted to see her, and allowed himself to lean over and give her a peck on the cheek. She liked the friendliness of it. The hugs before passion ever became an issue. The little touches of the hand, the quick kiss on the cheek. It made things less awesome that way. They were becoming friends. She was falling in like.

'Where are you taking me?'

'Everywhere.' She eyed him with pleasure as she drove up to Nob Hill.

'What a promise. Well, I know where we are now, anyway. That's my hotel.' She ignored him, and he grinned.

'This is Nob Hill.' And she pointed out Grace Cathedral, the Pacific Union Club, and three of the city's poshest hotels. From there they swooped down California Street to the Embarcadero, the Ferry Building, and a quick view of the docks. Up toward Ghirardelli Square and the Cannery, where she pointed out the honeycomb of boutiques right after they passed Fisherman's Wharf (where she had stopped and bought him a well-filled cup of fresh shrimp and a huge hunk of sourdough bread).

'What a tour. My dear, I'm overwhelmed.' And she was having a marvellous time as well.

From there, they went on to watch the old men playing boccie on the rim of the bay, and then up to the yacht basin and the St. Francis Yacht Club. This was followed by a sedate tour past blocks and blocks and blocks of elaborate mansions. After which they took refuge in Golden Gate Park. And her timing was perfect. It was just nearing sunset, and the light on the flowers and lawns was gold and pink and very lovely. It was Jessica's favourite time of day.

They walked past endless flower beds, and along curved walks, past little waterfalls, and around a small lake, until at last they reached the Japanese tea garden.

'Jessica, you give an extraordinarily good tour.'

'At your service, sir.' She swept him a formal curtsy,

and he put a quick arm around her shoulders. It had been a beautiful day and she was beginning to feel as though she really knew him.

She liked his reactions, his way of thinking, his sense of humour, and the gentle way he seemed to care about how she felt. And he seemed so much like her. He had the same kind of free and easy ways, the same craving for independence. He seemed to like his work, and he certainly didn't appear to be suffering financially. He really seemed the perfect companion. For a while, anyway. And he was nice to her. She had learned to be grateful for that, without leaning on him too heavily.

'What do you like to do more than anything in this world, Jessica?' They were sipping green tea and munching little Japanese cookies in the tea garden.

'More than anything else? Paint, I guess.'

'Really?' He seemed surprised. 'Are you good? Stupid question, but one always feels compelled to ask that, useless though it is. People who are any good insist that they're awful. And of course the bad ones tell you they're the best.'

'Now what do I say?' They both laughed and she shared the last cookie with him. 'I don't know if I'm any good or not, but I love it.'

'What sort of things do you paint?'

'It depends. People. Landscapes. Whatever. I work in watercolour or oils.'

'You'll have to show me sometime.' But he sounded indulgent and not as though he took her very seriously. He had a kind of placating, fatherly way about him sometimes, which made her feel like a little girl. It was odd that now that she had gotten used to being a grown-up, someone had appeared who would have let her go on being a child. But she wasn't sure she still wanted to be one.

When the tea garden closed, they walked slowly back to the car, and Geoffrey seemed to see it for the first time.

'You know, Jessica, it's really a beauty. These are almost collectors' items now. Where did you get it?'

'I'm not sure one should admit that sort of thing, but it was a gift.' She looked proud as she said it.

'Good lord, and a handsome one.' She nodded in silence and he cast her a glance without asking the question. But whoever had given her the car, he knew it was someone important in her life, and most likely her husband. Jessica was not the sort of woman to accept large gifts from just anyone. He already knew that much about her. She was a woman of breeding, and considerable style.

'Have you ever flown? I mean flown a plane yourself.' She laughed at the idea and shook her head. 'Want to try?'

'Are you serious?'

'Why not? We'll go up in my plane sometime. It's not hard flying at all. You could learn in no time.'

'What a funny idea.'

He was full of funny ideas, but she liked them. And she liked him.

They shared a wonderful evening. The food at L'Etoile was superb, the piano in the bar was gentle, and Geoffrey was delightful to be with. They shared a chateaubriand with truffles and béarnaise, white asparagus, hearts of palm with endive salad in a delicate mustard dressing, and a bottle of Mouton-Rothschild wine, 1952, 'a very good year,' he assured her in his clipped English way, but warmed by a smile produced just for her. He always managed to create an atmosphere of intimacy without making her feel uncomfortable.

And after dinner they danced at Alexis'. It was a far cry from the evening she'd spent there with the blind date Astrid had provided. Geoffrey danced beautifully. It was a thoroughly different evening from any she had spent in years. There was luxury and romance and excitement. She hated to go home and see it end. They both did.

They drove to her house in silence, and he kissed her gently at the door. It was the first time he had really kissed her, and it didn't send rockets off in her head, but it pulled threads all the way up her thighs. Geoffrey was a totally magnetic man. He pulled away from her slowly, with the tiniest of smiles tugging at one side of his mouth. 'You're an exquisite woman, Jessica.'

'Would you like to come in for a drink?' She wasn't sure if she wanted him to, and the way she said it told him so. She almost hoped he'd refuse. She didn't want to . . . not yet. But he was so appealing, and it had been such a long time.

'Are you sure you're not too tired? It's awfully late, young lady.' He looked so gentle, so thoughtful, so much like . . . like Geoffrey. She forced her thoughts back to the present and smiled into his eyes.

'I'm not too tired.' But she stiffened a little and he sensed it. He smiled at her back as she opened the door with her key. She had nothing to fear from him. He wanted much more than she could give in a night. He wasn't going to rush her. He already knew what he wanted, and what he wanted was for keeps.

She opened the door and turned on some lights, and he lit the candles as she poured cognac into two handsome snifters.

'Is cognac all right?'

'Perfect. And so is the view. This is quite a house.' But he wasn't surprised. He had expected something like this. 'And what a beautiful woman you are . . . taste . . . style . . . elegance . . . beauty . . . intelligence . . . a woman of a thousand virtues.'

'And a fat head, if you don't stop soon.' She handed him the snifter of cognac and sat down in her favourite chair. 'It's a nice view from here.'

'It is. I'll be looking for something like this in a few weeks.'

'Will you?' She couldn't resist a burst of laughter. 'Or did you make up that story about moving to San Francisco too?'

He smiled boyishly. 'No, that was true. Are houses like this hard to find?'

'You mean you want to buy?' She had assumed that he would rent.

'That depends.' He looked into her eyes and then into his cognac while she watched him.

'Maybe I'll rent you this place for the summer.' She was teasing, and he raised an eyebrow.

'Are you serious?'

'No.' Her eyes grew sad as she looked into the candle and spoke. 'You wouldn't be happy here, Geoffrey.' And she didn't want him in 'their' house. It would have made her uncomfortable.

'Are *you* happy here, Jessica?'

'I don't think of it that way.' She looked back into his eyes, and he was surprised at the pain he saw lurking there. It made her seem suddenly years older. 'To me, it's just a house now. A roof, a clump of rooms, an address. The rest is gone.'

'Then you should move out. Maybe we'll find a . . . I'll find . . . a larger place. Would you consider selling this?'

'No, just renting. It's not mine to sell.'

'I see.' He took another sip of his cognac and then smiled at her again. 'I should be going soon, Jessica, or you'll be terribly tired tomorrow. Are you busy for breakfast?'

'Not usually.' She laughed at the thought.

'Good. Then why don't we have breakfast somewhere amusing before I fly back to L.A. I can pick you up in a cab.' She loved the idea of breakfast with him. She would have preferred to cook it for him and sit naked at the kitchen table with him, or juggle strawberries and fresh cream on a tray in bed. But she almost wondered if one did that sort of thing with Geoffrey. He looked as if he might wear a dressing gown and silk pyjamas. But there was a definite sensuality about him too.

'What do you eat for breakfast?' It was a crazy question, but she wanted to know. It suddenly mattered to her. Everything did.

'What do I eat?' He seemed amused. 'Generally something light. Poached eggs, rye toast, tea.'

'That's all? Not even bacon? No waffles? No French toast? No papaya? Just poached eggs and rye toast? Yerghk.' He roared with laughter at her reaction and began to enjoy the game.

'And what do you eat for breakfast that's so much more exotic, my love?'

'Peanut butter and apricot jam on English muffins. Or cream cheese and guava jelly on bagels. Orange juice, bacon, omelettes, apple butter, banana fritters . . .' She let her imagination run wild.

'Every day?'

'Absolutely.' She tried to look solemn but had a hard time.

'I don't believe you.'

'Well, you're right . . . about most of it. But the peanut butter and cream cheese part was true. Do you like peanut butter?'

'Hardly. It tastes like wet cement.'

'Have you eaten a lot of that?' She looked across at him with interest.

'What?'

'Wet cement.'

'Certainly. Marvellous on thin wheat toast. Now, are you serious about joining me for breakfast tomorrow? I'm sure we can get you some peanut butter on croissants. Will that do?'

'Perfect.' She was starting to be Jessie now, and it amused him. He liked everything about her. She kicked off her shoes and curled her legs up in her chair. 'Geoffrey—' she tried to sound solemn—'do you read comic books?'

'Constantly. Particularly Superman.'

'What? No Batman comic books?'

'Oh yes, of course, but Superman has always been my favourite.' He stopped playing for a minute then and looked into his glass. 'Jessica . . . I like you. I like you very much.' He surprised her with the directness of his words, and she was touched by the way he said them. His style was an odd mixture of formality and warmth. She hadn't thought the combination was possible, but apparently it was.

'I like you too.'

They sat across from each other and he made no move

to approach her. He didn't want to rush her. She was a woman you got close to gradually, after much thought.

'You haven't said much about it, nothing in fact, but I somehow have the feeling that you've suffered a lot. A very great deal, even.'

'What makes you think that?'

'The things you don't say. The times you back off. The wall you run behind now and then. I won't hurt you, Jessica. I promise I'll try very hard not to.'

She didn't say anything, but only looked at him and wondered how often promises turned to lies. But she wanted him to prove her wrong, and he wanted to try.

CHAPTER XXXIV

'Well, how was your evening?' Astrid was already at the shop when Jessie got there the next day. Jessie wasn't getting in as early anymore. She didn't have to. Or want to.

'Delightful.' She beamed, even more enchanted with their breakfast at the Top of the Mark that morning, but she didn't feel like telling Astrid about it. 'Very, very nice.' She looked cryptic and pleased with herself.

'I'd say he's "very, very nice" too.'

'Now, Mother. Don't push.' The two women laughed, and Astrid held up a hand innocently in protest.

'Who needs to push? He sells himself all by himself. Are you in love with him, Jessie?' Astrid looked serious and so did Jessica.

'Honestly? No. But I like him. He's the nicest man I've met in a long time.'

'Then maybe the rest will come later. Give him a chance.' Jessica nodded and looked at the mail that was hers. She didn't like sharing the shop anymore. It was different now. And it was like prolonging the end. She wanted to say good-bye to Lady J and get out of town.

This was just like one more divorce. And there was another letter from Ian with the rest of her mail. She took it and set it apart from the rest. Astrid noticed, but she didn't say anything. This was the first time Jessie hadn't torn up one of his letters. She saw Astrid's look and shrugged as she poured herself a fresh cup of coffee.

'You know, I keep thinking that maybe I should drop him a note and thank him for the car. Seems like the least I could do. Your mother and I talked about it last weekend.'

'What did she say?'

'Nothing much.' Which only meant that Jessie wasn't telling.

In the end, she threw out the letter he had sent her.

They met with the lawyers for the next two afternoons, and everything was settled. On Saturday morning, Jessie went to three real-estate agents and listed the house as a summer rental. But she wanted careful screening of the tenants; she was leaving all her furniture there. And Ian's studio would be locked. She felt she owed him that.

It was almost midnight on Sunday when she sat down to write him a note about the car. In the end, she jotted down five or six lines, telling him how pleased she had been, how lovely it was, and that he hadn't had to do that. She wanted to cancel the debt between them. He didn't owe her anything. But it took her almost four hours to compose the short note.

Five days later the house had been rented from the fifteenth of July till the first of September, and she was almost ready to leave town. She hoped to be gone in a week. Geoffrey wanted to come up and see her again, and even invited her down to L.A. for a weekend, but she was too busy. She had found leads to two houses and an apartment for him, but she was tied up with her own affairs. There didn't seem to be room for Geoffrey just then, and she wanted him to stay away until she had closed the house, given up the shop, put away the past. She wanted to come to him 'clean' and new, if he would just give her the time. She had to do it that way. Be alone to sever the last cords by herself. It was harder this way, but he didn't belong in her life yet. She would see him in the country once she was settled.

She seldom went to the shop now, except to answer questions for Astrid. But now Astrid knew fairly well how everything worked, and Katsuko was a great help. She was staying on at Lady J. And Jessie just didn't want to be there anymore. Workmen were busy changing the sign, and cards were being sent to all their customers announcing the small change in the name. It still hurt, but Jessica told herself that all changes did, perhaps especially those for the better. She wouldn't regret it once she left town. But then what would she do? Yes, paint . . . but for how long? She wasn't ready to become another Grandma Moses. But something would turn up . . . something better. Geoffrey? Maybe he was the answer.

Jessica stopped in at the shop for the last time on a Friday afternoon. She was leaving two days later, on Sunday. She had put away all the small treasures she didn't want to share with her new tenants. And photographs of Ian. She had unearthed so much as she'd packed. Everything hurt now. It seemed as though every moment were filled with painful reminders of the past.

She slid the car into the driveway behind Astrid's car and walked quietly into the shop. It already looked different. Astrid had added a few things, and a lovely painting in what was now her office. It was all Astrid's now. And the money from the sale was all Jessie's. It was funny how little that meant to her now. Nine months before, seven months, six . . . she would have begged for one-tenth of that money . . . and now . . . it didn't matter. The bills were paid, Ian was gone, and what did she need? Nothing. She didn't know what to do with the money, and she didn't really care. It hadn't dawned on her yet that she had made a great deal of money selling the shop. Later she would be pleased, but not yet. And she still felt as though she had sold her only child. To a good friend, but still . . . she had abandoned the only thing she had ever nurtured and helped to grow.

'Mail for you, madam.' Astrid handed it to her with

a smile. She looked happy these days, and even younger than she had when Jessie had met her. It was difficult to believe that she had just had a birthday and turned forty-three. And in July, Jessie would be thirty-two. Time was moving. Quickly.

'Thanks.' Jessie slid the letters into a pocket. She could look at them later. 'Well, I'm all packed and ready to go.'

'And already homesick.' Astrid had guessed. She took her out to lunch and they drank too much white wine, but Jessie felt better. It helped. She went home in a much better mood.

She opened the windows and sat in a patch of sunlight on the floor, looking around the living room she had sat in so often with Ian. She could see him sprawled out on the couch, listening to her talk about the shop, or telling her about something brilliant he'd said in a new chapter. That was what was missing—that excitement of sharing the things they loved doing. Of laughing and being two kids on a warm sunny day, or a cold winter afternoon while he lit the fire. A man like Geoffrey would spoil her, and take her to the best restaurants and hotels all over the world, but he wouldn't take a splinter out of her heel, or scratch her back just right where it itched . . . he wouldn't burp over a beer watching a horror movie in bed, or look like a boy when he woke up in the morning. He would look very handsome, and smell of the cologne he had worn to dinner that time . . . and he hadn't been there when Jake had died . . . or her parents . . . but Ian had. You couldn't replace that. Maybe you shouldn't even try.

She wondered as she stared out at the bay, and remembered the letters Astrid had handed her before lunch. She went back to them now, digging into her jacket pocket . . . she hoped . . . she didn't . . . and she did . . . and there was . . . a letter from Ian. Her eyes swept quickly across the lines. He had gotten her note about the car.

> . . . I write these to myself now, wondering only for a moment if you read them. And then suddenly, a few quick nervous lines from you, but you kept the car.

That's all that mattered. I wanted you to have that more than you can know, Jess. Thanks for keeping it.

I assume that you don't open my letters . . . I know you. Rip, snap, gone.

She smiled at the image. And he was, of course, right.

But I seem to need to write them anyway, like whistling in the dark, or talking to myself. Who do you talk to now, Jessie? Who holds your hand? Who makes you laugh? Or holds you when you cry? You look such a mess when you cry, and God, how I miss that. I imagine you now, driving the new Morgan, and that note the other day . . . it sounded like something you'd write to your grandmother's best friend. 'Thank you, dear Mr. Clarke, for the perfectly lovely car. I needed one just that colour to go with my best skirt and my favourite gloves and hat.' Darling, I love you. I only hope that you'll be happier now. With whomever, whenever. You have a right to that. And I know you must need someone. Or do you have a right to that? My heart aches so at the thought, yet I can't see myself stamping my feet and raising hell. How could I possibly say anything after all this? Nothing except good luck . . . and I love you.

It does make me sad that now that the book has sold, and I have sat back and taken a look at my life, you're not here to enjoy the changes. I've grown up here. It's a tough school to learn in, but I've learned a lot about you, and myself. It isn't enough just to make money, Jessie. And I don't give a damn who pays the bills. I want to pay them, but I don't think I'd get an ulcer anymore every time you signed a cheque. Life is so much fuller and simpler than that, or it can be. In an odd way, my life is full now, yet so empty without you. Darling, impossible Jessie, I still love you. Go away, leave my mind, let me go in peace, or come back. Oh God, how I wish you'd do that. But you won't. I understand. I'm not angry. I only wonder if it would have been different if I hadn't walked out that day, leaving you there with the phone in your hand. I still see your face on that day . . . but no, it's not all because of that one stinking day. We're both paying for old, old sins now—because I still believe that we are both suffering this loss. Or are you free of it now? Maybe you don't care anymore. I can't tell you the empty feeling that gives me, but that's what will happen in time, I suppose. Neither of us will give a damn. Not something I look forward to. A lot of good years 'from dust to dust'. Gone. And I still see you and see you and see you. I touch your hair and smile into your eyes. Perhaps you can feel that now—my smile into your eyes as you go your own way. Go in peace, Jessie dearest, and watch out for lizards and ants. They won't bite you, I promise, but the neighbours might call the cops when you scream. Just keep the hair spray handy, and take it easy on yourself. Always, Ian.

She laughed through her tears as she read it . . . lizards and ants. The two things she had always feared most. Other than loneliness. But she had lived with that now, so maybe she could even get used to lizards and ants . . . but to life without Ian? That would be so much harder. She hadn't realised how much she had missed the sound of his voice until she read the letter. It was there. His words, his tone, his laughter, his hand rumpling her hair as he talked. The look he gave her that made her feel safe.

Without thinking, she got to her feet and went to the desk. There was still some paper there. She reached for a pen and wrote to him, telling him that she had sold the shop, and about the house near Aunt Bethanie's ranch. She described the house down to its tiniest detail as he had taught her to do when she had thought she wanted to write. She didn't have a knack for it, but she had learned how to write careful descriptions so that her reader could see all that she did. She wanted him to see the fading Victorian in all its possible splendour, now nestled in weeds. She was going to clean it up and make it pretty. That would keep her busy for a while. She gave him the address and mentioned that she had rented the house, but to a pleasant couple without children or pets. They'd keep it in good shape, and she was sure to tell him that the studio was locked. His file cabinets were safe. And she would try to stay safe from lizards and ants. It all flowed into the letter. It was like writing to a long-lost best friend. He had always been that. She put a stamp on the envelope and walked out to the mailbox on the corner, slipped it in, and then noticed Astrid driving home. She waved, and Astrid drove into the block and stopped at the corner.

'What are you up to tonight, Jessie? Want to have dinner?'

'You mean you're not busy for a change, Mrs. Bonner? I'm stunned.' Jessica laughed, feeling happier than she had in ages. She was actually looking forward to leaving. For the past weeks, she had almost wondered if she'd done the wrong thing. It was all so brutal, so final. But now she knew that she'd been right, and she was glad. She felt relieved, and as though she had just touched base with her soul. Ian still lived there. In her soul. Even now. Jessica tried to pry her thoughts from Ian as she smiled at Astrid.

'No smartass, I'm not busy. And I have a wild craving for spaghetti. How's the packing going?'

'All done. And spaghetti sounds great.'

They dined in the noise and chaos of Vanessi's, and moved on to a sidewalk café, for cappuccino after that. They watched the tourists beginning to appear, the first wave of summer, and the air was surprisingly warm.

'Well, love, how do you feel? Scared, miserable, or glad?'

'About leaving? All three. It's a little bit like leaving home forever . . .' Like leaving Ian—again. Packing up their private treasures and odds and ends had revived so many feelings. Feelings that were better left buried now. She would not unpack those boxes again, and she had separated her things from Ian's. It would be very easy now, if they ever sold the house. Their worldly goods were no longer in one heap.

'Well, that house of yours will keep you busy. Mother says it's a mess.'

'It is. But it won't be for long.' Jessica looked proud as

she said the words. She already loved the place. It was like a new friend.

'I'll try to get down to see it before we go away in July.'

'I'd love that.' Jessica smiled, feeling lighthearted and happy. A burden she couldn't quite identify had been lifted from her shoulders. She had felt its absence all evening. It was like no longer having a toothache or a cramp that she had lived with for months, not really aware of it yet subtly crippled by its presence.

'Jessica, you look happy now. You know, I felt terribly guilty for a while, for taking the shop away from you. I was afraid you'd hate me for it.' Astrid looked young and unsure as she looked into Jessie's face. But Jessica only smiled and shook her blonde mane.

'No. You don't need to worry about that.' She patted her friend's hand. 'You didn't take it away from me, Astrid. I sold it to you. I had to. To you, or to someone else, even if it hurt a little. And better to you. I'm glad it's yours now. I had outgrown it, I guess. I've changed a lot.'

Astrid nodded assent. 'I know you have. I hope it all works out.'

'Yeah, me too.' Her smile was almost rueful, and the two women finished their coffee. They were like two soldiers who have weathered the war together and now have nothing left to talk about except to make occasional guesses about the peace. Would it work? Jessie hoped so. Astrid wondered. They had both come a long way in the past months. And Astrid knew she had what she wanted now. Jessica wasn't yet quite as sure.

'Any news of Geoffrey this week, Jessie?'

'Yes. He called and said he'd come up to the country to see me next week.' He had been sensitive enough to know she needed to be left alone in the city.

'That'll do you good.'

Jessica nodded, but she didn't say more.

The doorbell rang at nine-fifteen the next morning. Her bags were packed and Jessica was washing the breakfast dishes for the last time, keeping one eye on the view. She wanted to remember it all, hang on for one last hour, and then leave. Quickly. She felt almost the way she had the morning she had left for college, old times packed away in mothballs and a new life ahead. She planned to come back, at least that was what she said, but would she? She wasn't really sure. She had the odd sensation that she was leaving for longer than a summer. Maybe forever.

The bell rang again and she dried her hands on her jeans and ran to the front door, throwing her hair back from her face, barefoot, her shirt buttoned but not quite far enough. She looked precisely the way she did when Ian loved her best. Pure Jessie.

'Who is it?' She stood beside the front door with a small smile on her face. She knew it was probably Astrid or Katsuko. One last good-bye. But this time she would laugh, not cry as they all had at the shop.

'It's Inspector Houghton.' Everything inside her turned to stone. With trembling hands, she unbolted the door and opened it. The party mood was suddenly gone, and for the first time in months, there was terror in her eyes again. It was amazing how quickly it could all come flooding back. Months of slowly rebuilding the foundations, and in as long as it took to ring a doorbell her life was a shambles again. Or that was how she felt.

'Yes?' Her eyes looked like greenish-grey slate and her face was set like a mask.

'Good morning. I ... uh ... this isn't an official call exactly. I ... I found your husband's pants in the property room the other day and I thought I'd drop them off and see how you were doing.'

'I see. Thank you.' He handed her a brown bag with an awkward smile. Jessie did not return the smile.

'Going on a trip?' His eyes glanced over the bags and boxes in the hall, and she looked over her shoulder and then quickly into his eyes. Bastard. What right did he have to be there now? Jessica nodded in answer to his question and looked down at her feet. It was a good time to end the war, to hold out a hand in peace, to go quietly. But she couldn't. He made her want to scream again, to pummel him, to scratch his face. She couldn't bear the sight of him. Terror and hatred swept over her like a tidal wave and she had the sudden urge to slither down the wall and crumple into a heap and cry. She felt as though she had been swept up in a hurricane and then cast aside by her own emotions. She looked up at him suddenly, with open pain in her eyes.

'Why did you come here today?' There was the look of a child who does not understand in her face, and he looked away and down at his hands.

'I thought you'd want your husband's ...' His voice trailed off and his face grew hard. Coming to see her had been a dumb thing to do, and now he was sure of it. But he had just had that feeling for days now. Of wanting to see her. 'Your husband's pants were just lying around the property room. I thought ...'

'Why? Why did you think? Is he liable to be coming home and needing them in the immediate future? Or aren't they wearing denims in prison anymore? I'm a little out of touch. I haven't been up there in a while.' She instantly regretted the words. His eyes showed interest and warmed again slightly.

'Oh?'

'I've been busy.' She looked away.

'Problems?' Vulture. And then she found his eyes again.

'Do you really give a damn?' She wouldn't let go of his eyes. She wanted to scratch them out.

'Maybe I do give a damn. Maybe ... I'm sorry. You know, I always felt sorry for you through the whole case. You seemed to believe in him so much. You were wrong, though. You know that now, don't you?' She hated the tone of his voice.

'No. I wasn't wrong.'

'The jury said you were.' He looked so smug, the bastard, so sure of 'the system'. So sure of everything, including Ian's guilt. She wanted to hit him. The urge was almost overpowering now.

'The jury didn't make me wrong, Inspector Houghton.' She held tightly to the brown bag he had given her and clenched her fists.

'Are you ... are you free now, Mrs. Clarke?'

'Does that mean, have I left my husband?' He nodded

and pulled a pack of cigarettes out of his coat pocket. 'Why?'

'Curious.' Horny.

'Is that why you came back here? Out of curiosity? To see if I'd left my husband? Would that make you happy?' She was boiling now. 'And why didn't you bring this to the shop?' She held out the brown bag with Ian's pants in it.

'I did. I was there yesterday. They told me that you don't work there anymore. True?' She nodded.

'I don't. So now what?' She looked him in the eye again and suddenly almost a year of fear vanished. He could try to do anything he wanted and she'd kill him. With pleasure. It was a relief to confront him. She looked at him again and six months of pain passed from her eyes to his. It was a naked vision he saw there, of a human being badly scarred, and he took a long drag on his cigarette and looked away.

'What time are you leaving on your trip? Have you got time for lunch?' Oh, Jesus. It was almost laughable, except that it still made her want to cry.

She shook her head slowly, looked down, and then slowly she looked up again as tears filled her eyes and slid down her cheeks. It was over now. The last of the anger and the horror and the terror and the pain slid slowly down her cheeks; the trial and the jury and the verdict and the arrest and Inspector Houghton all melted into silent tears, pouring slowly down her face. He couldn't bear to look at her. It was much worse than a slap in the face. He was sorry he had come. Very sorry.

She took a deep breath, but she did nothing about the tears. She needed them to wash all the filth away. 'I'm leaving this town to get away from a nightmare, Inspector. Not to celebrate it. Why would we possibly want to have lunch together? To talk about old times? To reminisce about the trial? To talk about my husband? To . . .' A sob caught in her throat and she leaned against the wall with her eyes closed, the paper bag still clutched in her hand. It was all rushing in on her again. He had brought it all back in a brown paper bag. She put a hand to her forehead, squeezed her eyes tightly shut, took a slow breath, and then opened her eyes again. He was gone. She heard the door of his car slam shut at that precise moment, and a moment later the green sedan pulled away. Inspector Houghton never looked back. She closed the front door slowly and sat down in the living room.

The trousers she pulled out of the bag had large holes carefully cut out of them at the crotch, where the police lab had tested the fabric for sperm. As she looked at them she remembered that first time she had seen Ian in jail, in the white pyjama bottoms. The pants were a great good-bye present.

But now she knew once again why she was leaving town. And she was glad. As long as she stayed it would all have stayed with her. In some form or other. She would always have wondered if Houghton might appear again. Sometime. Somewhere. Somehow. He was gone now. Forever. As was the nightmare. And the trial. All of it. Even Ian. But she had had to leave it all. There was no carving the good from the bad anymore. It was all bad, corrupt, venomous, cancerous. And suddenly she wasn't even angry at Ian anymore. Or at Inspector Houghton. She dried her face and looked around the room and realised something. It wasn't hers anymore. None of it was. Not the pants, not the problems, not the inspector, not even the bad memories. They no longer belonged to her. They belonged in the garbage with the trousers she held in her hand. She was leaving. She had left.

It was all behind her now. His papers in the studio. Her old check stubs filed in boxes in the basement. She was leaving all of that forever. What she was taking with her were the beautiful moments, the tender memories from long before, the portrait of Ian that she had painted when they were first married—she couldn't leave that with the new tenants—favourite books, cherished treasures. Only the good stuff. She had decided that was all she had room for anymore. To hell with Inspector Houghton. She was almost glad he had come. Now she knew she was free. Not wanting to be free, or trying to be free, or working at being free. But free.

CHAPTER XXXV

Leaving San Francisco was easier than she had thought it would be. She wouldn't let herself think. She just got on the highway and kept driving. No one had come to wave handkerchiefs or cry bitter tears and she was glad.

After Inspector Houghton's visit, she had had a cup of tea, finished the dishes, put on her shoes, checked the house and the windows one last time, and left.

The drive south was lovely, and she felt young and adventurous when she reached her decaying house on the old North Road. And she was touched when she went inside and saw what Aunt Beth had done. The house was spotlessly clean, and the sleeping bag she had left there earlier was unnecessary. There was a narrow bed in the bedroom with a bright patchwork quilt carefully folded at the foot. It was the one from her bedroom at Aunt Beth's. A young girl's Victorian desk stood in a corner, and two lamps made the room bright. The kitchen was stocked, and there were two rocking chairs and a large table in the living room, and a large easy chair by the fire. There were candles all around, and logs near the fire. She had everything she needed.

And dinner with Aunt Beth the next day was a jovial affair. She had spent the first night alone in the new house. She had wanted it that way, and had wandered from room to room like a child, not feeling lonely, only excited. It was like the beginning of an adventure. She felt reborn.

'Well, how do you like it? Are you ready to go home yet?' Aunt Beth chuckled with her over tea.

'Not on your life. I'm ready to stay here forever. And thanks to you, the house is as cosy as can be.'

'It'll take more than that to make it cosy, my dear.'

But what Jessica had sent in the two crates helped a bit. Photographs, planters, a little marble owl, a collection of treasured books, two bright paintings, and the portrait of

Ian. There were also blankets and brass candlesticks, and odds and ends that she loved. And she filled the house with plants and bright flowers. At the end of the week, she added to her old treasures with a few new ones she acquired at auction. Two low rough-hewn tables, and an oval hooked rug. She put them in the living room and stood back, looking pleased. It looked more like home every day. She had sent books in the trunks, and her painting things were set up in a corner, but she hadn't had time to paint anything yet. She was too busy with the house.

The foreman's son from Aunt Beth's spent the week-end pulling weeds and mowing the lawn, and they had even discovered a crumbling gazebo far out in the back. And now she wanted a swing. Two of them. One to hang from a tall tree near the gazebo, where she could swing high and watch the sunset on the hills, and another to sit in front of the house, the kind on which young couples sat and whispered 'I love you's' on warm summer nights, creaking slowly back and forth, sure that they were unique in the world.

The letter from Ian came on Saturday morning. She had been in her new house for six days.

And there you are, funny girl, with dust in your hair and a smudge on your nose, grinning with pride at the order you're making from chaos. I can see you now, barefoot and happy, with a cornstalk in your teeth. Or wearing your Guccis and hating it? What's it like? I can see the house perfectly now, though I can't imagine you happy in a sleeping bag on the floor. Don't tell me you've gotten that rugged! But it sounds lovely, Jessie, and it will do you good. Though I was shocked to hear about the shop. Won't you miss it? Sounds like a hell of a good price, though. What'll you do with that pile of bucks? At this end, I'm hearing news about the making of a movie from the book. Don't hold your breath; I'm not. Those things never happen. They just get talked about. Though on the other hand, I never thought you'd sell the shop. How does that feel? Painful, I'll bet, but maybe a relief? Time to do other things. Travel, paint, clean up that palace you've saddled yourself with for the summer—or longer? I heard something in the tone of your last letter. It sounds like love for the house, and the country around it, and Aunt Beth. She must be a remarkable woman. And how are the ants and the lizards so far? Staying away? Or all wearing your best hair spray and loving it?

She chuckled as she read; once she had tried to kill a lizard in their hotel room in Florida with her hair spray. They had asphyxiated themselves out of the room, but the lizard had loved it.

She finished reading the letter and went to sit at the large table Aunt Beth had provided. She wanted to tell him about the things Aunt Beth had put in the house, and the goodies she'd found at auction. It didn't seem fair to let him think she was sleeping on the floor.

The correspondence got under way as simply as that, and without the determination of their halt in communication. She didn't think about it, she just wrote to him to give him the news. It was harmless, and she was pleased for him about the movie. Maybe this time it would happen. She hoped so, for him.

She was surprised at the length of her response. It covered six tightly written pages, and it was almost dark when she sealed the envelope and put on the stamp. She cooked dinner on the old stove, went to bed early, and got up very early the next morning. She drove into town, mailed the letter, and stopped at Aunt Beth's for a cup of coffee. But Aunt Beth was out riding.

The afternoon was quiet and pretty. Jessie did some sketches while sitting dangling her feet on her front porch. She felt like Huck Finn's older sister, in overalls and a red T-shirt and bare feet. The sun was bright on her face and it was a beautiful day, and her hair looked like spun gold looped up in loose curls at the top of her head.

'Good afternoon, mademoiselle.' Jessica jumped, the sketch pad flying from her hands. She had thought there was no one anywhere near the house. But when she looked up, she laughed. It was Geoffrey.

'My God, you scared me to death!' But she hopped

lightly from the porch as he picked up her pad and looked at it with surprise.

'Great Scott, you *can* draw! But much more interesting than that, you're exquisite and I adore you!' He folded her into a great warm hug, and she smiled up at him from her bare feet in the tall grass around the house. They hadn't quite gotten up all the weeds yet. 'Jessica, you look perfectly beautiful!'

'Like this?' She laughed at him, but she was slow to leave his embrace. She was just beginning to realise how much she'd missed him.

'Yes, I adore you like that. The first time I saw you, you were barefoot and had your hair looped up like that. I told you, you looked just like a Greek goddess.'

'Heavens!'

'Well, aren't you going to give me the grand tour, after you've kept me at arm's length all this time?'

'Of course, of course!' She laughed delightedly, and pointed majestically toward the house. 'Won't you come in?'

'In a moment.' But first he drew her into his arms for a long tender kiss. 'Now I'm ready to see the house.' She laughed at him, and then stopped and took a long look at him.

'No, you're not.'

'I'm not?' He looked confused. 'Why not?'

'First take off your tie.'

'Now?'

'Absolutely.'

'Before we go inside?' She nodded insistently, and, smiling at her, he took off the navy blue tie dotted with white, which she correctly guessed was from Dior.

'It's a lovely tie, but you don't need it here. And I promise, I won't tell a soul you took it off.'

'Promise?'

'Solemnly.' She held up a hand and he kissed it. The feeling in the centre of her palm was delicious.

'Oh, that was nice.'

'You're a tease. All right, then, will this do?' She looked him over again but shook her head. 'What?'

'Take your jacket off.'

'You're impossible.' But he slipped out of it, dropped it over his arm, and swept her a bow. 'Satisfied, milady?'

'Quite.' She imitated his accent and he laughed as, at last, he followed her inside.

She took him around room by room, holding her breath a little, afraid he might hate it. And she wanted him to love it. It was important to her. The house meant so much to her. It was symbolic of so much in her that had changed. And it was still a little bare, but she liked it that way. She had room to grow in, and to collect new things. She felt freer here than she had in San Francisco. Here, it was all new and fresh.

'Well, what do you think?'

'Not exactly overdecorated, is it?' She smiled as he chuckled, but she wanted him to like it, not make fun of it. 'All right, Jessica, don't look so sensitive. It's lovely, and it ought to be great fun for a summer.' But what about for a life? She hadn't said anything to him yet about staying there, but she wasn't quite sure yet either, so there was no point. And it didn't really matter. If he fell in love with her, he could fly down to see her in his plane. It would give her the weeks alone to paint and walk and think and spend time with Aunt Beth, and the weekends with him.

'What on earth are you thinking about?' She jumped as he broke into her thoughts. 'You had the most outrageous little smile on your face.'

'Did I?' But she couldn't tell him what she had in mind. It had to grow slowly, she couldn't sketch it all out for him ahead of time.

'You did, and I love your little house. It's sweet.' But he made it sound silly, and she was disappointed. He meant well, but he just didn't understand.

'Would you like a cup of tea?' It was a hot day, but he seemed to like hot tea whatever the weather. That or Scotch. Or martinis. She already knew.

'Love some. And then, Jessica my love, I have a surprise for you.'

'Do you? I love surprises! Give it to me now.' She

looked like a little kid again as she plonked down on the couch and waited.

'Not now. But I thought we'd do something special tonight.'

'Like what?' She wanted to do something special too, and it showed in her smile, but he let it pass.

'I want to take you down to Los Angeles; there's a party at the consulate. I thought you might rather enjoy it.'

'In Los Angeles?' But why Los Angeles? She wanted to stay in the country.

'It's going to be quite a nice party. Of course, if you'd rather not . . .' But the way he said it didn't leave her much choice.

'No, no . . . I'd love to . . . but I just thought . . .'

'Well, what would we do here? I thought it would be much nicer to run down to the city for a bit. And I want to introduce you to some of my friends.' He said it so nicely that she felt badly about her reluctance. It was just that she had wanted to share a quiet evening with him in the new house. But there would be other times. Lots of them.

'All right. It sounds terrific.' She was going to get into the spirit of it. 'What sort of party is it?'

'White tie. Late dinner. And there ought to be quite a lot of important people there.'

'*White* tie? But that means tails!'

'As a rule, yes!'

'But Geoffrey, what in hell can I wear? I don't have anything here. Just a lot of country stuff.'

'I thought that might be the case.'

'So what'll I do?' She looked horrified. White tie? Christ. She hadn't even seen white tie since all those ridiculous deb balls her mother had made her go to fifteen years ago. And she had nothing even remotely possible to wear. Everything dressy was still in San Francisco.

'Jessica, if you won't be too cross at me, I took the liberty of . . .' He looked more nervous than she had ever seen him. He knew she had exquisite taste and he was terrified of what he had done. 'I hope you won't be angry, but I just thought that under the circumstances . . . admittedly, I . . .'

'What on earth is going on?' She was half amused, half frightened.

'I bought you a dress.'

'You did what?' She was dumbfounded.

'I know, it was a ridiculous thing to do, but I just assumed that you probably didn't have anything here and . . .' But she was laughing at him. She wasn't angry. 'You're not cross?'

'How could I be cross? No one's ever done that for me before.' Certainly not a man she barely knew. What an amazing man he was turning out to be! 'That was a lovely thing to do.' She hugged him and laughed again. 'Can I see it?'

'Of course.' He bolted toward the door and returned five minutes later, as he had parked a little distance away. He had wanted to surprise her when he arrived, and the Porsche didn't lend itself well to surprises. But he was back with an enormous box in his arms, and a large bag that seemed to hold several smaller boxes.

'What on earth did you do?'

'I went shopping.' He looked pleased with himself now. He dumped all of it on the couch and stood back with a breathless look of pleasure.

Jessica slowly pulled open the large box and gasped. The fabric was the most delicate she'd ever seen. It was a silk crepe, the lightest imaginable. It seemed to float through her fingers, and it was a warm ivory, which would set off her dark tan to perfection. When she took the dress out of the box, it seemed to clasp at one shoulder and leave the other bare. And when she saw the label it explained the design and the fabric. Geoffrey had bought her a couture dress, which must have cost him at least two thousand dollars.

'My God, Geoffrey!' She was speechless.

'You hate it.'

'Are you kidding? It's magnificent. But how could you buy me that?'

'Do you like it, dammit?' He couldn't make head or tail out of what she was saying, and it made him nervous, waiting to find out.

'Of course I like it. I love it. But I can't accept it. That's a terribly expensive dress.'

'So? You need it for tonight.' She laughed at the logic.

'Not exactly. That's like wearing a new car.' And a Rolls, yet.

'If you like it, I want you to wear it. Will it fit?' She considered not even trying it, but she was dying to know how it looked, how it felt. Just for a moment.

'I'll try it. But I won't keep it. Absolutely not.'

'Nonsense.'

But she went to try it on, and when she came back she was smiling. And the vision he saw made him smile too.

'Good heavens, you're beautiful, Jessica. I've never seen anyone look like that in a dress.' It looked as though it had been made for her. 'Wait, you have to try it with these.' He dived into the bag of goodies and came out with a shoebox. Little ivory satin strands of sandals on delicate heels. Again, a perfect fit. Geoffrey certainly knew how to shop. A little silver and white beaded bag. All put together, it was dazzling. And they were equally overwhelmed. He with looking at her, and she to be wearing it all. She was used to good clothes, but these were extravagantly beautiful. And outrageously expensive.

'Well, it's settled, then.' He looked decisive, and pleased. 'Where's my tea?'

'You don't expect me to serve tea in this, do you?'

'No. Take it off.'

'Yes, love, and I'm going to keep it off. It's so pretty, but I just can't.'

'You can and you will, and I won't discuss it. That's all.'

'Geoffrey, I . . .'

'Quiet.' He silenced her with a kiss, and she had the feeling that the entire matter had been taken out of her hands. When he wanted to be, he was very forceful. 'Now get me my tea.'

'You're impossible.' She took off the dress and got him the tea, but in the end he won. At six o'clock she got out of the tub, did her makeup and her hair, and slipped into the dress. She felt faintly as though she were prostituting herself. A two-thousand-dollar dress was no small gift. Somehow he made it seem like a scarf or a hankie, but this was no hankie. As she slipped the dress over her head, she practically drooled.

And so did he when he saw her twenty minutes later in her new bedroom doorway. The house certainly wasn't used to this sort of grandiose coming and going in its halls. Geoffrey had gone to his friends' house to change, and had come back looking impeccable in white tie and tails. His shirt front was perfectly starched. Nothing on him appeared to move. He looked like someone in a 1932 movie. And Jessica smiled when she saw him.

'You look beautiful, sir.'

'Madam, you have no idea how extraordinary you look.'

'I must say, this all feels pretty super. But I feel like Cinderella. Are you sure I won't turn into a pumpkin at midnight?' She was still more than a little embarrassed by the extravagance of it all, but for some reason she had let herself be swept away on the tide of his insistence. And she had to admit, it was fun.

'Are you ready to go, darling?' The 'darling' was new, but she didn't mind it. She could get used to it. She supposed that she could get used to a lot of things if she tried.

'Yes, sir.' She looked down at her bare hands then and wished she had both jewellery and gloves. At any event as formal as this one obviously was going to be, it seemed as though long white kid opera gloves were in order, and jewellery . . . jewellery . . . she thought of something as they started to leave. 'Wait a second, Geoffrey.' She had brought it with her, and she had totally forgotten it. She had hidden it, for safety's sake. But it would be perfect.

'Something wrong?'

'No, no.' She smiled mysteriously and ran back into the bedroom, where she bent down carefully to look for a tiny package tied in the underside of the bed. It had been the only place she could think of. But she had wanted to bring it with her. She didn't know why, but she had wanted to. She quickly took the box from its hiding place and then opened it, pulling the soft suede jewel case out of the box, and then spilling the gem into her hand. It was more beautiful than ever, and for a moment her heart stopped as she saw it. It brought back so many painful memories, but so many nice ones as well. She could remember seeing it on her mother's hand . . . and then taking it out for Ian . . . putting it back when the trial was all over. It was her mother's emerald ring. She had never brought herself to wear it, just as a piece of jewellery, a thing, a bauble. But tonight was a night to wear it, as a thing of beauty and pride, as something special that had been given to her. Tonight it signified a new beginning to her life. It was perfect. And tears came to her eyes as she slipped it on. She felt her mother approve.

'Jessica, what are you doing? We've got quite a drive to L.A.—do hurry up.'

She smiled to herself as she slipped it on her hand. It was exactly what she needed. She also had on a pair of pearl earrings that Ian had given her years ago. They were the only jewellery she had brought, except for the ring, which she really hadn't planned to wear. She caught a last glimpse in the mirror, and smiled to herself as she rushed out to join Geoffrey. 'Coming!'

'Everything all right?'

'Wonderful.'

'Ready?'

'Yes, sir.'

'Oh, and by the way, I forgot to give you these.'

'These' were two more boxes, a long thin flat one and a small cube.

'More? Geoffrey, you're crazy! What are you doing?' It was like Christmas. And why was he doing this? She didn't even want presents, but he looked so hurt when she baulked that she started to open the packages. No man had ever done this to her before.

As she began with the long thin box, Geoffrey suddenly exclaimed.

'Jessica, how lovely. What an extraordinarily fine piece of jewellery.' He was admiring her mother's ring, and with a trembling hand, she held it up for him to see. 'It means a great deal to you, doesn't it?' She nodded, and then, after a pause, his voice softened. 'Was it your engagement ring for when you were married?'

'No.' She looked at him solemnly. 'It was my mother's.'

'Was? . . . Is she . . .' So that was why she never spoke of her family. She had told him about the brother, but she had never mentioned her parents. Now he understood.

'Yes, she and my father died only a few months apart. It's a long time ago now, I suppose, though it doesn't really feel like it. But I've never . . . I've never worn the ring, like tonight.'

'I'm honoured that you'd wear it with me.' He pulled her face gently toward him with the tip of one finger, and kissed her ever so carefully. It made her whole body tingle. And then he stood back and smiled. 'Go on. Finish opening your things.' She had forgotten the boxes, and she went back to them now.

The long thin box yielded the gloves she had thought of as she was dressing. It was as though he read her mind. Again.

'You think of everything!' They made her laugh, but she was delighted as she slid one into place. 'How did you know all my sizes?'

'A lady should never ask a question like that, Jessica. It implies I have too much knowledge of women.'

'Aha!' The idea amused her. And she went on to the next box. This one was small enough to fit into the palm of her hand. Geoffrey was watching her with interest as she tore off the paper and got to the small navy blue leather box. It had a snap holding it closed and she flicked it open and gasped. 'Jesus. Geoffrey! No!' He couldn't tell if she was angry or pleased, but he quietly took the box from her and took them out, holding the diamond teardrops to her ears.

'They're just what you need. Put them on.' It was a

quiet order, but Jessica took one step backward and looked at him.

'Geoffrey, I can't. I really can't.' Diamonds? She hardly knew him. And the earrings were not terribly small. They were heavenly, but not at all something she could accept. 'Geoffrey, I'm sorry.'

'Don't be silly. Just try them for tonight. If you don't like them, you can give them back.'

'But imagine if I lost one.'

'Jessica, they're yours.' But silently she shook her head and stood firm.

'Please.' He looked so woebegone that she felt sorry for him, but she couldn't take diamonds from this man . . . she had already accepted the outfit she was wearing, which was far too expensive a gift as it was. But diamonds? Who in heaven's name was he? No matter who, she knew who *she* was, and what she could and could not do. This she could not. No. But he was looking at her so sadly that she finally wavered for an instant. 'Just try them on.'

'All right, Geoffrey, but I won't wear them tonight and I won't keep them. You save them. And maybe someday . . .' She tried to make him feel better about them as she reached up to take off one of her own earrings, and then she remembered that she was wearing Ian's pearls.

The pearls were much less grandiose than the diamonds, but she loved them. She tried on one of Geoffrey's sparkling teardrops and it looked dazzling on her left ear . . . but on the right ear sat the pretty little pearl from the man who had loved her . . . from Ian . . .

'You don't like them.' He sounded crushed.

'I love them. But not for right now.'

'You looked just now as though something had made you terribly sad.'

'Don't be ridiculous.' She smiled, and handed him back the earring, and then leaned up to kiss him chastely on the cheek. 'No man has ever been as good to me, Geoffrey. I don't quite know what to do with it all.'

'Sit back and enjoy it. Now. We're off.' He didn't press

the point about the earrings, and they left them carefully hidden in her desk drawer. She felt relieved not to be wearing them. Geoffrey had been right. Taking off Ian's pearls would have made her sad. She wasn't quite ready to yet. It would come in time. She still clung to some of their souvenirs. Like his portrait, which now hung over the fireplace.

The party was like something in a multimillion-dollar movie. Gallons of champagne, platoons of liveried butlers, and armies of black-uniformed maids. Every two feet of inlaid marble floor space seemed to be covered by the looming shadow of an immense crystal chandelier. And pillars and columns and Aubusson rugs and Louis XV furniture, and a fortune in diamonds and emeralds and sapphires, and hundreds of minks. It was the kind of party you read about but couldn't even faintly imagine going to. And there she was, with Geoffrey. Almost everyone there was either British or famous or both. And Geoffrey seemed to know everyone. Movie stars whom Jessie had only read of in the papers ran up to greet him, promised to call him, or left lipstick on his cheeks. Ambassadors cornered him over the pâté, or urged Jessie to dance. Businessmen and diplomats, socialites and politicians, movie stars and celebrities of dubious fame. Everyone was there. It was the kind of party people worked years to get invited to. And there she was, with Geoffrey, who turned out to be not "Mr.", but "Sir".

'Why didn't you tell me?'

'Why? It's silly. Don't you think so?'

'No. And it's part of your name.'

'So now you know. Does it matter?' He looked amused, and she shook her head. 'All right, then. Now how about dancing with me, Lady Jessica?'

'Yes, sir. Your Majesty. Your Grace. Your Lordship.'

'Oh, shut up.'

The party went on until two and they stayed till the end. It was almost four when they got back to the little Victorian house tucked into the hills.

'Now I know I'm Cinderella.'

'But did you have fun?'

'I had a fabulous evening.' She had felt a tiny bit as though he had put her on display, like a pretty new doll, but he had introduced her to everyone, and how could she complain? How many dates give you two-thousand-dollar evening dresses and diamond earrings? What an evening. She looked down at her mother's ring again as they got out of the car. She was glad she had worn it. Not just because it was an emerald, but because it had been her mother's.

'You looked radiant tonight, Jessica. I was so proud of you.'

'It was just the dress.'

'Bullshit.'

'What?' She gave a tired little crow of laughter and looked at him with amusement. '*Sir* Geoffrey said "bullshit"? I didn't think you said things like that!'

'I do, and I say lots of things you don't know about, my dear.'

'That sounds intriguing.' They exchanged a glance of mutual interest in front of her house. 'I don't know whether to offer you brandy, coffee, tea, or aspirin. Which'll it be?'

'We can figure that out inside.' She glided up the steps with the grace of a butterfly in the magnificent white dress. Even at the end of the evening, she looked like a vision, and seemed scarcely tired. She pleased him enormously. In fact, he had decided not to wait a great deal longer. She was everything he wanted, and it was time for him. He had been waiting for Jessie for a long, long time. He knew that she wasn't quite ready, but she would be very quickly. He would help her sweep the cobwebs from her present. Now and then he saw old ghosts haunting her eyes, but it was time she left them. He needed her. And she had done beautifully at the party. Everyone said so.

'Do you go to things like that often?' She stifled a yawn as she slipped out of the sandals he had given her.

'Fairly. Did you really enjoy it?'

'What woman wouldn't, for heaven's sake? Geoffrey . . . excuse me, *Sir* Geoffrey—' she grinned—'that's like being queen for a day. And everyone in the whole world was there. I must say, I was very impressed.'

'So were they.'

'About what?'

'About you. You were the most beautiful woman there.' But she knew that wasn't true, and more than half the attention she'd got had been over the dress. He had equipped her well for her debut, even down to the virginal white dress. But some of the great beauties of the world had been at that party. She was hardly stiff competition. She just wasn't that kind of woman. Not the sort who drips diamonds ear to ear while dragging chinchilla behind her, in the latest Givenchy dress. Those women were in the big leagues.

'Thank you.' It seemed simpler not to argue. 'Tea?'

'Not really.' He was looking at her pensively, a little distracted.

'Would you like me to light a fire?' She felt like sitting with him and talking, as she'd used to do with . . . no! She couldn't let herself do that.

'Who's that?' He waved to the boyish face over the fireplace, and Jessica smiled. 'Your brother?'

'No. Someone else.'

'Mr. Clarke?' She nodded, sober-faced now. 'You still keep his portrait up?'

'I painted it.'

'That's not much of a reason. Do you still see him?' Somehow he had thought she didn't, though they had never discussed it.

'No. Not anymore.'

'That's for the best.' And then he did something that made Jessica's heart stop. Very quietly, without asking, without saying a word, he lifted the portrait from where it hung and set it gently down on the floor near her desk, facing the wall. 'I think this is a good time to put that away, darling, don't you?' But there was no question in his voice and for a moment she was too stunned to speak. She wanted it up. She liked it. She had brought it specially from San Francisco. Or was he right? Was there no place for that anymore? There shouldn't have been, and they both knew it.

'Don't you want tea?' She couldn't think of anything else to say, and her voice was only a croak.

'No.' With a gentle smile he shook his head and walked slowly toward her. He stopped in front of her and kissed her longingly. It stirred the very tip of her soul. She needed him now. He was stripping her of something she had needed to survive. And now she was beginning to need him. He couldn't take Ian from her, but he was going to, and she was letting him. They stood together, their mouths hungrily discovering each other, and ever so gently he unclasped the hook at the shoulder of her dress. As it gave, the dress fell loosely to her waist, and he lowered his mouth slowly to her breasts, as her whole body seemed to reach out to him—but something inside her said no.

'Geoffrey . . . Geoffrey . . .' He went on kissing her, and the dress fell slowly away from her. All that exquisite silk crepe lying heaped at her feet as carefully, relentlessly he undressed her. She fumbled at the hard white starched shirt front, and got nowhere. All she could reach of him was the bulge in his trousers, but even his zipper seemed to resist her. And in a moment she stood there, naked before him, and he was still fully dressed in white tie and tails.

'My God, Jessica, how beautiful you are, my love . . . beautiful, beautiful, elegant little bird . . .' He led her slowly into her bedroom, speaking loving words to her all the way, and she followed him, as though in a trance, until he laid her carefully on her bed and slowly slipped off his jacket as she waited. He seemed to purr at her, and she felt she was under his spell. He had the jacket off now, but the starched white front was still in place. It made him look like a surgeon, and as she turned her head on the pillow, something pinched her ear. She was still wearing her earrings, and she reached up to take them off and felt the pearls fall into her hand. The pearls . . . Ian's pearls . . . and here was this man undressing in front of her. He had undressed her. She was naked and he was going to be, and he had taken Ian's portrait off the wall . . .

'No!' She sat bolt upright on the bed and stared at him as though he had just thrown cold water in her face.

'Jessica?'

'No!'

He sat down next to her and folded her into his arms, but she fought free of them, still clutching the pearl earrings in her hand. 'Don't be afraid, darling. I'll be gentle, I promise.'

'No, no!' There were tears welling up in her throat now and she jumped past him, pulling at Aunt Beth's quilt at the foot of the bed and covering herself with it. What was wrong with her, though? For a moment she thought she was crazy. Only a few minutes before she had wanted him so desperately, or had thought she did. And now she knew that she didn't. She couldn't. Now she knew everything.

'Jessica, what in hell is going on?' She was cowering near the window, with tears running down on her face.

'I can't go to bed with you. I'm sorry . . . I . . .'

'But what happened? A moment ago . . .' For once, he looked totally baffled. This had never happened to him. Not like this.

'I know. I'm sorry. It must seem crazy, it's just that . . .'

'That what, dammit?' He stood in front of her, and he was looking very unnerved by the experience. His jacket lay strangely on the floor, as though it had been thrown there. 'What happened to you?'

'I just can't.'

'But, darling, I love you.' He walked to her again and tried to put his arms around her, but she wouldn't let him.

'You don't love me.' It was something she could sense, not something she could explain. And more importantly, she didn't love him. She wanted to love him. She knew she *should* love him. She knew that he was the kind of man women are supposed to love, and beg to marry. But she didn't, and she couldn't, and she knew she never would.

'What do you mean I don't love you? Goddammit, Jessica, I want to marry you. What sort of game do you think I've been playing? You're not the sort of woman one makes a mistress of. Do you think I'd have taken you to that party tonight if I weren't serious? Don't be absurd.'

'But you don't know me.' It was a plaintive wail from the corner.

'I know enough.'

'No, you don't. You don't know anything.'

'Breeding shows.' Oh, Jesus.

'But what about my soul? What I think, what I feel, what I am, what I need?'

'We'll learn that about each other.'

'Afterward?' She looked horrified.

'Some people do it that way.'

'But I don't.'

'You don't know what the devil you do. And if you have a brain at all, you'll marry a man who tells you what to do and when to do it. You'll be much happier that way.'

'No, that's just it. I used to want that, Geoffrey, but I don't anymore. I want to give as well as take, I want to be the grown-up as well as the child. I don't want to be pushed around and shown off and dressed up. That's what you did tonight. I know you meant well, but I was nothing more than a Barbie doll, and that's all I ever would be. No! How could you!'

'I'm sorry if I offended you.' He stooped down and picked up his jacket. He was beginning to wonder about her; it was almost as though she were a bit mad.

But suddenly she didn't feel mad at all. She felt good, and she knew she was doing the right thing. Maybe no one else would think so, but she knew it.

'You don't even want children.' It was a ridiculous accusation to be making at five o'clock in the morning, standing wrapped in a quilt, talking to a man in white tie and tails.

'And you do want children?'

'Maybe.'

'Nonsense. The whole thing is nonsense, Jessica. But I'm not going to stand here and argue with you. You know where I stand. I love you and I want to marry you. When you come to your senses in the morning, give me a call.' He looked at her pointedly, shook his head, walked to the corner, kissed the top of her head, and patted her shoulder. 'Good night, darling. You'll feel better in the morning.'

She didn't say a word as he left, but when he was gone she packed all of his gifts into the large white box he had brought; in the morning she would send it all over to the house where he was staying. Maybe it was an insane thing to do, but she was so sure of it. She had never been so sure of anything in her life. She had put the pearl earrings down on her night table, and now she wasn't even sleepy. She stood happy and naked in her living room, drinking steaming black coffee, as the sun rose over the hills. The portrait was back on the wall.

CHAPTER XXXVI

'And how's your young man?' She and Aunt Beth were drinking iced tea after a long ride, and Jessica had been unusually quiet.

'What young man?' But she wasn't fooling anyone.

'I see. Are we going to play cat and mouse, or has he fallen out of the running?' Aunt Beth's eyes searched hers and Jessie ventured a smile. Cat and mouse, indeed.

'Your point. Fallen out of the running.'

'Any special reason?' For once she was surprised. 'I saw a rather spectacular photograph of you two, at some very posh party in L.A.'

'Where in hell did you see that?' Jessica was not pleased.

'My, my. He must have fallen into considerable disfavour! I saw the photograph in the L.A. paper. Something about a consulate party, wasn't it? Quite a number of illustrious people seemed to be hovering around you too.'

'I didn't notice.' Jessie sounded gloomy.

'I'm impressed.' And so was Jessie. But not pleasantly so. She was wondering who else had seen the picture. There was no point in being linked with Geoffrey now. Oh, well—like everything else, the gossip would die down eventually. And it was probably much harder on Geoffrey. He had to live with all those people. She didn't.

'Did he do something dastardly, or was he simply a bore, or should I mind my own business?'

'Of course not. No, I just couldn't, that's the only way to put it. I wanted to make myself love him. But I couldn't. He was perfect. He had everything. He did everything. He was everything. But . . . I . . . I can't explain it, Aunt Beth. I had the feeling he was going to try to make me into what he wanted.'

'That's a disagreeable feeling.'

'I kept feeling that he was checking me out, like a quarterhouse. I felt so . . . so lonely with him. Isn't that crazy? And there was no reason to.' She told her about the dress and the diamond earrings. 'I should have been thrilled. But I wasn't. It frightened me. It was too much . . . I don't know. We were such strangers.'

'Anyone will be a stranger at first.' Jessica nodded pensively and finished her iced tea. 'He seemed nice enough, but if that special ingredient isn't there, that special magic . . . there's really no point.' It made Jessica think back to that night.

'I'm afraid I didn't back off very elegantly. I went bananas.' She smiled at the memory, and the older woman laughed.

'Probably did him good. He was awfully proper.'

'He certainly was. And he was wearing white tie and tails while I freaked out and practically started throwing things. I sent back all his goodies the next day.'

'Did you hurl them through the window?' Beth looked

greatly amused, and almost hoped that she had. Men needed excitement.

'No.' She blushed for a moment. 'I had one of your ranch hands take them over.'

'So that's what they do with their afternoons.'

'I'm sorry.'

'Don't be. I'm sure whoever it was enjoyed the whole thing immensely.'

They sat quietly for a moment with their iced teas, and Jessica was frowning.

'You know what bothered me too?'

'I'm anxious to hear.'

'Stop teasing—I'm serious.' But she enjoyed the banter with her friend. 'He didn't want children.'

'Neither do you. What bothered you about that?'

'That's a good question, but something's been happening. I don't think the idea of children frightens me so much anymore. I keep thinking that . . . I don't know, I'm too old anyway, but I keep thinking that . . .' She knew she wasn't too old, but she wanted someone to tell her so.

'You want a baby?' Beth was stunned. 'Do you mean that?'

'I don't know.'

'Well, it's certainly not too late at your age. You're not even thirty-two yet. But I must say, I'm surprised.'

'Why?'

'Because your fear of it ran so deep. I didn't think you'd ever be sure enough of yourself to weather the competition. What if you had a beautiful daughter? Could you bear that? Think about it. That can be very painful for a mother.'

'And probably very rewarding. Doesn't that sound corny? I feel like an ass. It's been bothering me for a while, but I haven't had the courage to tell anyone. Everyone is so sure that I am what I am. Career woman, city slicker, child hater, now gay divorcee. Even when you stop being the same person, it seems as though no one will let you take the old labels off.'

'Then burn them. You certainly have, though. You got

rid of your husband, the shop, the city. There's not much left to change.' She said it ruefully, but with affection. 'And to hell with other people's labels. There's plenty we can't change, but if there are things you want to change and can, go ahead and enjoy it.'

'Imagine having a baby . . .' She sat there, smiling, enjoying the thought.

'You imagine it. I can't even remember it, and I'm not sure I'd want to. I never felt very romantic on the subject, but I love Astrid very much.'

'You know, it's as though I've lived several chapters of my life one way, and now I'm ready to move on. Not to throw the past out the window, but just to go on. Like a journey. We've been long enough in the same country; after a while you have to move on. I think that's what happened. I've just moved on to different places, different needs. I feel new again, Aunt Beth. The only sad thing is that I have no one to share it with.'

'You could have had Geoffrey. Just think what you missed!' But Aunt Beth didn't think she'd missed anything either. There hadn't been enough fire in the man, enough daring and wild dreams. He was travelling a well-charted course. If nothing else, it would have been very boring. She knew Jessie had done the right thing. She wondered only at the violence of Jessie's reaction. 'Something else has been bothering you lately too, hasn't it?'

'I'm not sure what you mean.'

'Yes, you are. Quite sure. You're not only quite sure of what I mean, but you're quite sure of the rest. In fact, I daresay that was the problem with Geoffrey, wasn't it? It had damned little to do with him after all.' Jessica was laughing, but she wouldn't say anything.

'You know me too well.'

'Yes, and you're finally beginning to know yourself too. And I'm glad. But now what are you going to do about it?'

'I was thinking of going away for a couple of days.'

'You don't want permission from me, do you?' Aunt Beth was laughing, and Jessica shook her head.

She began the drive at six the next morning as the sun peeked its nose over Aunt Beth's hill. She had a long way to go. Six hours, maybe seven, and she wanted to be there in time. She had worn a light shirt for the ride, and a skirt, which was cooler than pants. She had a Thermos full of iced coffee, a sandwich, a bag full of apples, and some nuts and cookies in a tin that the foreman's boy had brought her a few days before. She was fully equipped. And determined. And also afraid. They had exchanged letters two and three times a week for two months now. But letters were very different. It had been four months since she'd seen his face. Four months since he'd turned his back and walked out on her after they had both thrown rocks they should never have picked up. And so much had changed now. They were both cautious in their letters. Careful, afraid, and yet joyful. Bursts of fun would turn up on every page, silly remarks, casual references, foolishness, and then caution again, as though each was afraid to show too much to the other. They kept to safe subjects. Her house, and his book. There was still no news on the movie contract, but the book was due out in the fall. She was excited for him. As excited as he was about her house. He was careful always to call it "hers", and it was. For the moment.

They were separate people now, no longer woven together of a single cloth. They had been blasted apart by what had happened to them, by what they had done to each other, by what neither could any longer pretend. She wondered if there was a way to come back after something like that. Maybe not, but she had to know. Now, before they waited any longer. What if he expected never to see her again? He sounded as though he had almost accepted it. He never asked for a visit. But he was going to get one. She wanted to see him, to look into his face and see what was there, not just hear the echo of his voice in the letters.

She drove up to the familiar building at one-thirty that afternoon. They checked her through, searched her handbag, and she went inside and wrote her name on a form at the desk. She took a seat and waited an endless half hour, her eyes restlessly darting between the wall clock and the door. Her heart was pounding now. She was here. And she was terrified. Why had she come? What would she say? Maybe he didn't even want to see her, maybe that was why he hadn't mentioned her coming for a visit. It was madness to have come here . . . insanity . . . stupid . . .

'Visit for Clarke . . . visit for Ian Clarke.' The guard's voice droned his name and Jessica jumped from her seat, fighting to keep her pace normal as she walked toward the uniformed man who stood sentry at the door to the visiting area. It was a different door from the one she had passed through before, and as she looked beyond she realised that Ian was in a different section now. Maybe there would be no glass window between them.

The guard unlocked the door, checked her wrist for the stamp they'd impressed on the back of her hand at the main gate, and stood aside to let her through. The door led out to a lawn dotted with benches and framed with flower beds, and there were no apparent boundaries, only a long strip of healthy-looking lawn beyond. She crossed the threshold slowly and saw couples wandering down walks on either side of the lawn. And then she saw Ian, at the far end, standing there, watching her, stunned. It was like a scene in a movie, and her feet felt like lead.

She just stood there and so did he, until a broad smile began to take over his face. He looked like a tall, gangly boy, watching her and grinning, his eyes damp, but no more so than her own. It was crazy—half a block of lawn between them and neither of them moved . . . she had to . . . she had come here to see him, to talk to him, not just to stand there and gape at him with a smile on her face. She walked slowly along the walk, and he began to walk toward her too, the smile on his face spreading further, and then suddenly, finally, at last, she was in his arms. It was Ian. The Ian she knew. It smelled like Ian, it felt like Ian, her chin fit in the same place on his shoulder. She was home.

'What happened? You run out of hair spray, or did the lizards get to be too much for you?'

'Both. I came up so you could save me.' She was having a hard time fighting back tears, but so was he, and still their smiles were like bright sunshine in a summer shower.

'Jessie, you're crazy.' He held her tightly and she laughed.

'I think I must be.' She was clinging to him tightly. He felt so damn good. She put a hand on his head and felt the silk of his hair. She would have known it blindfolded in a room full of men. It was Ian. 'Jesus, you feel good.' She pulled away from him just to look at him. He looked fabulous. Skinny, a little tired, a little suntanned, and totally overwhelmed. Fabulous. He pulled her close again and nestled her head on his shoulder.

'Oh, baby, I couldn't believe it when you started writing. I'd given up hope.'

'I know. I'm a shit.' She felt bad suddenly for the long months of silence; now, looking right into his face, she could see how much they must have hurt him. But she had had to. 'I'm a super-shit.'

'Yeah, but such a beautiful super-shit. You look wonderful, Jessie. You've even gained a little weight.' He held her at arm's length again and looked her over. He didn't want to let go. He was afraid she'd vanish again. He wanted to hold on to her, to make sure she was real. And back. And his. But maybe . . . maybe she had only come back to visit . . . to say hello . . . or good-bye. His eyes suddenly showed the pain of what he was thinking, and Jessica wondered what was on his mind. But she didn't know what to say. Not yet.

'Country life is making me fat.'

'And happy, from the sound of your letters.' He pulled her close to him again, and then pinched her nose. 'Let's go sit down. My knees are shaking so bad, I can hardly stand up.' She laughed at him and wiped the tears from her cheeks.

'*You're* shaking! I was afraid you wouldn't see me!'

'And pass up the chance to make the other guys drool? Don't be ridiculous.' He noticed then that she was wearing the gold lima bean, and he quietly took her hand in his.

They found a bench to one side of the lawn and sat down, still holding hands. He had one arm around her, and her hand was trembling in his. And then the words began to rush out. She couldn't hold back anymore. The dam had finally given way.

'Ian, I love you. It's all so lousy without you.' It sounded so corny, but that was what she had come to tell him. She was sure of it now. She knew what she wanted. And now it was a question of want more than need. She still needed him, but differently. Now she knew how much she wanted him.

'Your life doesn't sound lousy, baby. It sounds good. The country, the house . . . but . . .' He looked at her with gratitude rushing over his face. '. . . I'm glad if it's lousy, even if it's only a little bit lousy. Oh Jess . . . I'm so glad.' He pulled her back into his arms.

'Do you still love me a little?' She was wearing her little-girl voice. It was so long since anyone had heard that, so long since he had. But what if he didn't want her anymore? Then what would she do? Go back to the Geoffreys of the world and the fuzzy-haired idiot playwrights from New York? And the emptiness of a house and a gazebo and a swing and a world made for Ian . . . but without him? What was there to go back to? Staring at his portrait? Thinking of his voice? Wearing the pearl earrings he'd given her?

'Hey, lady, you're drifting. What were you thinking?'

'About you.' She looked him square in the eyes. She needed to know. 'Ian, do you still love me?'

'More than I can ever tell you, babe. What do you think? Jessie, I love you more than I ever did. But you wanted the divorce, and it seemed fair. I couldn't ask you to live through all this.' He gestured vaguely to the prison behind him. It brought worry to her eyes.

'What about you? Are you surviving it?' She pulled away to look at him again. He looked a lot thinner. Healthy, but much thinner.

'I'm making it a lot better than I thought I would.

Ever since I finished the book. They're letting me teach in the school now, and I'm due . . .' He seemed to hesitate, looked at something over her head, and took a deep breath. 'I'm due for an early hearing in September. They might let me go. In fact, it's almost certain they will. Through some kind of miracle, they've knocked out the famous California indeterminate sentence since I've been here, and as a first-time offender my time could be pretty much up, if they're amenable. So it looks like I could be coming home pretty soon.'

'How soon could it be?'

'Maybe six weeks. Maybe three or four months. Six months at worst. But that's not the point, Jess. What about all the rest of it? What about us? My being in prison wasn't our only problem.'

'But so much has changed.' He knew it was true. He had heard it in her letters, knew it from what she'd done, and now he could see it in her face. She was more woman than she had ever been before. But something magical also told him that she was still his. Part of her was. Part of her belonged only to Jessie now, but he liked it that way. She had been that way long, long ago. But she was better now. Richer, fuller, stronger. She was whole. And if she still wanted him now, they would really have something. And he had grown a lot too.

'I think a lot has changed, Jess, but some of it hasn't and some of it won't. And maybe it's more than you want to mess with. You could do a lot better.' He looked at her, wondering about the photograph he'd seen in the paper. He had seen the same article Beth had. And if she could have Sir Geoffrey Whatnot, why the hell did she still want him?

'Ian, I like what I've got. If I've still got it. And I couldn't do better. I don't want to do better. You're everything I want.'

'I don't have any money.'

'So?'

'Look, I got a ten-thousand-dollar advance for the book, and half of that went for your new car. And the other five thousand won't go very far when I get out. You'll be stuck supporting me again. And baby, I have to write. I really know that. It's something I have to do, even if I have to wait table in some dive to support myself in the meantime. There's no way I'll give up writing, though, to be "respectable".' He looked rueful but firm. And Jessie looked impatient.

'Who gives a damn about "respectable"? I made a fortune selling the shop to Astrid. What the hell difference does it make now who earns what doing what, for what . . . so what, dummy? What do you think I'll do with that money now? Wear it? We could do such nice things with it.' She was thinking of the house. And other things.

'Like what?' He smiled at the sound of her voice and held her closer.

'All kinds of things. Buy the house in the country, fix it up a little. Go to Europe . . . have a baby . . .' She turned her face and smiled at him, nose to nose.

'What did you say?'

'You heard me.'

'I'm not so sure I did. Are you serious?'

'I think so.' She smiled mysteriously and kissed him.

'What brought that on?'

'A simple process, darling. I've grown up since I saw you last. And it's just something I've been thinking about lately. And I realised something else. I don't just want "a baby". I want *your* baby. Our baby. Ian . . . I just want you, with kids, without kids, with money, without . . . I don't know how else to tell you. I love you.' Two huge tears slid down her face and she looked at him so intensely that he wanted to hold her forever.

He threw his arms around her and held her to him with a huge smile on his face. 'You know what's going to happen, Jess? Any minute, some asshole with a flashlight is going to walk up to me, it's going to be two in the morning, and I'm going to wake up, holding my pillow. Because this can't be real. I've dreamed it too often. It's not happening. I want it to be, but . . . tell me it's for real.'

'It's for real . . . but you're breaking my left arm.'

'Sorry.' He pulled away from her for a moment and

they both laughed. 'Sweetheart, I love you. I don't even care if you want a baby anymore. I love you, in that ramshackle empty house you got yourself, or in a palace, or wherever. And aside from that, I happen to think you're nuts. I don't know what made you come back, but I'm so damn glad you did.'

'So am I.' She threw her arms around him again, nibbled his ear, and then bit him. 'I love you,' she whispered it in his ear, and he pinched her. It had been so long since he'd even touched her, held her, felt her. Even pinching and biting felt good. It was all such a luxury now. 'Christ, Ian, what's the matter with you?'

'What do you mean?' He looked suddenly worried.

'You didn't even yell when I pinched you. You always yell when I pinch you. Don't you love me anymore?' But her eyes were dancing as they hadn't in years. Maybe as they never had before, Ian thought.

'You came up here for me to yell at you?'

'Sure. And so I could yell at you. And hug you and kiss you, and beg you to get the hell out of here and come home, for Chrissake. So will you please, dammit? Will you!' Jesus. Twelve hours ago, she hadn't even been sure he still wanted her. But he did! Thank God he did!

'I will, I will. What's your hurry? What do you have, snakes in that place? Spiders? That's why you want me, right? The exterminator—I know your type.'

'Bullshit. No spiders, no snakes, but . . .' She grinned.

'Aha!'

'Ants. I walked into the kitchen the other night to make a peanut-butter sandwich, and I screamed so loud, I . . . what are you laughing at? Goddam you, what are you laughing at?' And then suddenly she was laughing too, and he had his arms around her and he was kissing her again, and they were both laughing through their tears. The war was over.

And eight weeks later, he was home.

ZOYA

Danielle Steel

One woman's odyssey through a century of turmoil . . .

St Petersburg: one famous night of violence in the October Revolution ends the lavish life of the Romanov court forever – shattering the dreams of young Countess Zoya Ossupov.

Paris: under the shadow of the Great War, émigrés struggle for survival as taxi drivers, seamstresses and ballet dancers. Zoya flees there in poverty . . . and leaves in glory.

America: a glittering world of flappers, fast cars and furs in the Roaring Twenties; a world of comfort and café society that would come crashing down without warning.

Zoya – a true heroine of our time – emerges triumphant from this panoramic web of history into the 80s to face challenges and triumphs.

0 7221 8315 1
GENERAL FICTION